C.J. CHERRYH

THE PALADIN

A Baen Books Original

Baen Publishing Enterprises
P.O. Box 1403
Riverdale, NY 10471
www.baen.com

ISBN: 0-671-31837-3

Cover art by Gary Ruddell

First printing, July 1988
Second printing, January 2002

Distributed by Simon & Schuster
1230 Avenue of the Americas
New York, NY 10020

Printed in the United States of America

CHIYADEN

KIANG

THE EDGE OF HEAVEN

P·ENG

YIUNGEI

AYENDEN

SHANGEI

ANGEN

HISEI R.

CHAIGHIN R.

PAN·YEI

KENJI

CHENG·DI

TENGU

ANOGI

FEIYAN

LUNGAN

YIJANG

KYUTANG

PAIGJI R.

MURA

HUA

HAINANG

CHOEDRI

BOTAI

SENGU

TEI R.

TAIYI

CHAIYEI

KEIDO

CHISEI R.

MUIGAN

DAI

MANDI

HOISHI

YGOTAI

YAN

HOI R.

MON

MENDANG

HOISAN

THE OUTER LANDS

THE GREAT RIVER

Prologue

They were haunted hills. The villagers of Mon said that, trying to warn the young traveler. They warned of vengeful ghosts who would lead a boy astray, demons which could appear as foxes and owls, and dragons which could take human form. Most persuasive in their estimation—the boy's quest was useless: the master took no students. Rich men's sons had come to beg to be Saukendar's disciples, and come down from Saukendar's mountain again, refusing to speak to the villagers or to linger there. Lords' messengers had come to see Master Saukendar to plead causes with him, and returned unhappy and unanswered. Monks had come to ask the swordmaster for his secrets, and left unenlightened, for the master turned all inquiries away. Twice each year a boy from the village would go up to the cabin on the mountain to bring the salt and the tea and the small things that the master needed and to take the master's request for rice and straw which they would leave at the appointed place. The village gave those things, with small gifts as well, fruit in season, a few good apples or pears, or fresh vegetables, because the fear of the master drove away the bandits. This was the only converse the master allowed himself with the world.

Emphatically, the master took no students . . . and certainly no students as ragged as this—so small and so starved and so evidently some yeoman farmer's son, no different than any of their own.

The traveler wore a quilted coat that had been blue once; black rough-spun breeches flapped ragged ends about his skinned knees; a red, healing scar ran from cheek to chin to neck and down beneath the grimy collar. He carried a badly made longbow for a walking-staff, and had a quiver of white-feathered arrows slung at his side, the kind of weapons a farmer might legally carry on the road against bandits and brigands.

There were troubles in the east. In a hoarse, low voice the traveler told them news from the heart of the Empire; told of farms burned in Hua province and Yijang; of livestock slaughtered; of whole families murdered, his own among them.

But all that was far away, the village assured the boy. It was safe here. The bandits who lived over the hills in Hoisan province stayed out of this valley safely within the borders of Hoishi, under the rule of good lord Reidi; and the beneficent gods and fear of the master kept the troubles far from the village of Mon.

"I have a place on my floor for a pallet," widower Gori said wistfully. Gori had all daughters, six of them. "I have a garden to keep. I could find a permanent place for an honest boy who'd work for his keep."

But the traveler—he could hardly have been sixteen—who squatted barefoot in the shade by the well and drank an offered cup of water, thanked the widower in a low voice and gave back the cup, then tied his reed hat under his chin, thrust his arms again through the woven-rush ropes that held the barrel-sized basket, struggled up with the unstrung bow for a staff and walked away, ant-like under his ungainly burden, virtually obscured by the hat, the towering basket. Only the legs showed beneath, ragged breeches, skinny calves, dust-caked.

The villagers shook their heads, especially Gori.

"He'll be back," Gori's neighbor said.

The road that had been broad and friendly and sunlit down in the valley, dwindled to a track and finally to a narrow slot among the rounded boulders and the tree-roots of the forest, and wound in steeper and steeper climbs into the hills.

The ragged young traveler hitched the pack up against the rake of branches and the angle of the trail and kept going, using the bowstaff for balance in the climb.

It would have been wiser, perhaps, to have slept in the hedgerows another night, and attempt the hill path by morning; but Taizu was beyond fear of ghosts and demons, and the only dragons Taizu thought worth fearing always walked in human form.

The sun sank below the hills now, throwing the path beneath the trees into deep shade. Not far, the villagers had said; but if that estimation was wrong, then Taizu reckoned the villagers were right in at least one thing, these woods were safe from bandits: the bandit was a fool, who would hunt on Saukendar's mountain.

And that was greater safety than Taizu had known in weeks.

So Taizu climbed in the forest shadow, struggling with the basket-pack in the clutch of branches, until the scent of smoke and horse came on the wind; until the shape of rustic buildings showed in the twilight: pen and pasture and a sun-edged shape of a man carrying water to a bay horse whose coat shone brilliant red in a sudden glimpse of sunset. There was a storm passing to the north, clouds like a slate-gray wall above the hills. Red light from the waning sun edged everything in fire; the horse, the edges of the buildings, the man.

Taizu did not breathe for a moment. Saukendar seemed less real in that moment than he had been all the weeks

since Hua province—less real and more godlike. But a
man who had renounced the world could not be reckoned like other men. Saukendar had turned his back on
the court, his great wealth and high station, and escaped the Regent and the Emperor who had betrayed
him. He had come here, beyond the limits of the
kingdom, to perfect his art and to perfect his soul in the
solitude of the mountains. Saukendar had come close as
any man to that perfection when he was in the world—
the old Emperor's right hand, the one honest man in a
court increasingly corrupt and full of wicked men.
Saukendar had defended the law and the old Emperor,
upheld the poor against the rich, and upheld the honest
lords against the flatterers while the old Emperor grew
weaker and died.

But Saukendar had not been able to stand against the
foolishness of the boy-heir Beijun, who had allied himself with lord Ghita of Angen province and accused his
father's appointed Regent lord Heisu of conspiracy and
adultery with his wife.

That was how lord Ghita of Angen came to stand
behind the throne, and how lord Heisu and the Em-
press Meiya both went under the axe, and how five
hundred men of the Imperial Guard had hunted
Saukendar to kill him; but Saukendar had killed twenty
of them on his way to the border, and, they said, no
few after, until he had gone into retirement in these
hills just outside Hoishi province and lord Ghita and his
men had understood it was far wiser to let him stay
there unmolested.

That was Saukendar. And if he had renounced the
world and decided to seek his own perfection, then
perhaps he had succeeded in that too and the gods cast
a special light about him.

But a second glance showed this man limped; and the
light went out when he passed the barn and when the
horse moved toward the rail fence: it was not lord
Saukendar himself, then—only some servant. Taizu felt
somewhat the fool: of course the weapons-master, the

Emperor's bodyguard and champion, would have had at least one menial to go with him, or he would have taken a servant from the village below . . . someone to cook his meals and tend the ordinary things. Saukendar had been a great lord, with lands and servants. Even as an ascetic he would not change that.

So Taizu walked out into the twilight, out into the open, disappointed, but braver in the failure of a miracle.

Chapter One

Shoka was well on his way back to the porch when the apparition came out of the forest, a huge lump moving on two thin legs, that proved only a basket and a skinny boy in a hat.

He had seen it first out of the tail of his eye; and mindful of bandits, he had poured the water for the old horse, patted it on the neck and walked casually toward the house where his bow was, carrying an empty bucket which itself could be a weapon, if there was nothing else to hand.

But he recognized the visitor now for solitary, likely another petitioner. He pretended not to notice him, for safety's sake, all the same—the bandits could use a child—and because, to his annoyance, the evening hour obliged him to some measure of hospitality, a cup of tea, a bowl of rice, a place to sleep—he reckoned that he might as well go up to the house in the first place. By the size of the legs that supported the monstrous basket, the waif was too young to turn away to walk the road again in the dark of night.

7

So he walked up onto the low porch of weathered boards, beneath the small thatched roof, in easy reach of the doorway and his weapons, just in case: then he set down the bucket, turned and looked straight at the boy, who brought his ungainly burden as far as the steps.

The boy slipped the woven ropes and set the basket down, then made a polite little bow. "I've come to see the master."

"You've found him," Shoka said; and saw, weary of seeing, the young face come up, the mouth open and the eyes widen in dismay. "I'm Saukendar. What do you want?"

The boy took off the oversized hat and stared at him—a gaunt and exhausted boy with a scar that made a man see that first and the desperation of the eyes second. That attraction to the scar embarrassed Shoka, who found himself both rude and careless; and by that, discovered himself snared in an attention to the whole face that he did not generally pay to his few visitors.

"I want justice," the boy said; and snared him twice over.

"Have I done you some wrong?" Shoka asked.

The boy shook his head; and looked close to tears for a second, his chin about to tremble. Then he clamped his jaw and leaned his whole weight against the bowstaff he used for a walking-stick—a child's bow, rough-hewn. "No, lord. I want you to teach me."

Shoka frowned and drew back then, angry at the approach and sorry for the boy, when for an instant he had felt a little pang of interest, the prospect of a problem that might engage him. "Another one. Didn't they tell you in the village? Or didn't you listen?"

"They said you were an honest man. People everywhere sing about you. They say if you were still in Chiyaden you'd kill lord Ghita and all of the lords around him. Maybe you don't want to come back to the world, master Saukendar, but you can teach me and I'll do it and you don't ever have to leave here. I'll work for my keep. I'll cut your wood and feed your horse—"

"And I tell you, you should have listened to the advice you got in the village. I have nothing further to do with Chiyaden. I'm not a teacher. I don't have any damn wisdom, I'm not a saint. I don't have anything to give you and I cut my own wood. You've had a long walk for nothing. Off my porch! Go back to the village! They'll take care of you!"

The youngster stared at him in dismay.

"Off!"

The boy backed up, turned in sudden retreat down the steps.

There was a cant to that movement, a little angle of a hip, a centering of balance that drew Shoka's eye and jarred with his assumptions. Yes. No. As the youngster turned a defiant face on him from a safer distance.

"Girl," Shoka said; and saw the little flicker of the eyes, alarm but not offense. He shook his head and folded his arms, thinking again about the bandits and their tricks. "I'm a weapons-master. I'd be blind if I couldn't tell *that*. Did you think you could fool me? What are you doing up here on the mountain? Who sent you? Who do you belong to?"

"My name is Taizu. From Hua province. I walked here to find you. They say you're the best there is, they say you could come back to Chiyaden and set everything right, only you've decided to stay here and have nothing to do with the world. But I will. I've got a reason to. I'll do the things you'd do if you came back."

He laughed. It was not a usual thing for him. "Tell me another fable, girl. What do you really want?"

"I want you to teach me the sword."

"You're not from Hua. You're from Hoisan. You're a spy for the bandits."

"No!"

"They think I wouldn't hurt children?"

"I'm sixteen. And I'm not a bandit. I didn't mean to fool you, just until you'd take me and I could show you I can learn. I have my own bow. I have a sword." She gestured at the basket. "I have my own clothes, my own blankets, I *made* my bow and my arrows."

Shoka came down to the bottom step, took the bow from her hand, gave the wretched thing a glance and shoved it back at her. "It does better as a walking-stick."

She frowned up at him. "Then show me how to make better."

"I'm not showing you anything. Where did you come from?"

"From Hua province."

"That's four weeks' walk, girl! Don't tell me that."

"I don't know how long it is." The voice was low and hoarse. The chin trembled slightly. "But I walked it."

"Alone."

"There's a lot of people on the roads into Yijang: they got burned out too. I walked with them; and then I walked with some that were going on to relatives in Botai—"

"Where are you from? Who's your lord?"

"Kyutang village, in Hua. We belonged to lord Kaijeng. He's dead now. The whole family. Everyone. Lord Gitu came over his border and burned Kaijeng castle and burned Kyutang and Jhi and all the villages and killed everything, even the pigs." The girl's chin trembled and steadied. "Lord Ghita won't do a thing. Everyone knows that. Lord Gitu can murder people and nobody will do anything about it. But I will. I promised that. And I'll do it."

"You'll get your head cut off. That's what you'll get, girl. Leave the fighting to your menfolk."

"There aren't any. There isn't anybody left."

Shoka looked at her, at the ragged coat, the scar, the burning eyes, and felt something stir inside him that he had felt for none of the other petitioners who had come to him, even the earnest and honest ones. He mistrusted that impulse. She might still be a bandit, come to find out if he was truly alone; or even to kill him in his sleep, if he was a fool. Maybe they thought he was that desperate for a woman. But her accent was genuine: it clipped and shorted ends of words in the pattern of the eastern reaches of Chiyaden, which could well be Hua province, and in that consideration she might be even a spy brought safely along the roads and sent up here on orders of lord Ghita himself. For a moment that seemed far more likely than bandits: but Ghita had not bothered with him in years and he saw no reason the Regent should begin now. Or she might in fact be a demon, which was also possible, but her feet were bare human feet and her thumbs were on the right way around; and he had been nine years in these hills without seeing any evidence of one. "Come in," he said, grudging the impulse that made him hospitable, and motioned toward the door. "I'll feed you, at least."

"Will you teach me?"

He scowled. "Teach you. I've turned away a score of young men, bright young men, serious and able students—and now I'm to take on a girl? What would I tell the ones I've turned down? That I'm a weapons-master for women? Gods. Come on inside. —You don't have to worry. I won't lay a hand on you. I've never yet assaulted children."

She stood fast.

"Damn." He came down the steps and she backed up again, snatching up her basket as she went. "Fool girl. A sword, for gods' sakes. Do you know if the magistrates found you with that you could lose your right hand, at the least."

"There's no law here."

"The law here is mine," he said. And as she backed further he waved a hand at her. "If you're going, then get out and don't stop on the road. If I find you skulking about here after, you'll find out what the law is on this mountain."

"I want you to teach me."

"I told you: I've turned down better boys than you. Get out."

"Not without what I came for."

"Dammit," he said, thinking of her hanging about—

gods knew with what intention. "If you steal anything around here, or if you lay a hand on my horse, I'll show you what that's worth with me."

Then, on the second, self-chastising thought that she was not the boy she looked to be, and that a girl alone had every reason to be wary of shut doors and a strange man at night, "Look here, if you don't want to go inside, I'll bring you a bowl and a cup of tea onto the porch. I'll give you that much hospitality. You can sleep out here and nothing will bother you. But you'll be out of here and down the road in the morning."

"I'll take the food," she said.

He brought tea and rice out onto the porch, and set it down on the far side of the steps. He took his own supper to the other end and sat down as the girl came up by the steps and took the bowl and the chopsticks. She sat down and began to eat without seeming to stop for breath. He had cooked twice and half again his ordinary supper, and given her a heaping bowl, which he saw diminishing with amazing speed. They sat on the porch, cross-legged, in the deep twilight. He ate his own without attention to manners, throwing looks her direction. She sat like a lump in the tattered coat, her bare head bowed over her dinner—black, thick hair bobbed off like a farmer-lad's, hands so thin the sinews stood up and made shadows when the fingers moved, eyes twice dark with the shadows around them when she looked up at him over the rim of the bowl.

"I could have cooked for us," she said with her mouth full. "See, you need some help up here. The rice is overcooked."

"It hasn't killed your appetite."

"Still could be better. Tomorrow I'll show you."

"And I'm telling you there's no bargain. You sleep on this porch tonight. In the morning I'll take you down to the village. I'll arrange for someone to take you in."

She shook her head; a slow, definite move.

He scowled at her, thinking of his solitude and his

peace of mind; and thinking of the nights. Sometimes
he damned the loneliness; but he had his ways: he got
up each morning and he tended his horse and his
garden; or he hunted or he mended whatever time and
the weather had broken, and took no thought for the
world at all. He refused to regret the court or Chiyaden
or the fine clothes or the praise of men who had done
nothing, when the need came, but save themselves.

Til this fool girl came talking about justice, disturbing
his peace and, staring at him with her dark, mad eyes,
making him think of other advantages of human company he had forsworn nine years ago, scrawny un-
washed waif that she was. He was already promising
her things he would never promise, to come down into
the village and deal with the people; but she had walked
a long and dangerous way on her foolish notion—a very
long way from Hua province, and she had been appeal-
ingly clever about it. No eye would expect the girl bent
under the peasant basket-pack, the oversized coat, the
reed hat.

The basket changed the balance center, changed the
walk, made the bearer neuter and neutral. It had fooled
even his eye until he saw her walk without it.

Clever, he thought—if she had in fact thought at all
about that part of it.

But even a *man* with a tatty basket could draw bandits and trouble somewhere along that road. Four weeks.
He could not reckon how she had gotten as far as she
had.

Except she was uncommonly lucky.

Or she *was* someone's spy, and she had had abundant
help getting this far.

"I know livestock," she said. "Have you got pigs?"

"No. I hunt."

"I can take care of the horse. And I know lots of ways
to cook rabbits."

"That's fine. Your new master down in the village
will like to know that. And they keep pigs."

"I want you to teach me."

"To do what?" he asked. "To be a fool? You couldn't even make it back again to Hua. You're lucky to have gotten this far."

"I'll make it. And I'll get my revenge. Nobody will stop me."

Hua province. Gitu. The names conjured images of the court and Ghita and his hangers-on. The old anger stirred in him, outrage for old insults; he shook it off like unwelcome rain and said around a mouthful of rice: "Carrying a sword. You're just *damned* lucky the magistrates didn't lay hands on you. Don't you know the law?"

"That's why it's in the basket."

"You'd lose your right hand, girl. Do you understand that?"

"That's after they catch me," she said. "No one caught me. No one caught you. You rode right out, with the soldiers all hunting you."

"I ran for my life, girl. That's the plain truth of it."

"You killed the men they sent after you."

"I was lucky. It was a bad day for them. A better one for me. But I'll limp for the rest of my life. I don't know any damn secrets. I'm not a teaching master. I just live up here in peace, thank you, and I don't need a cook and I don't need a pig-keeper."

"You'll change your mind."

"Listen to me, girl. I'm not going to change my mind on this, no more than on anything else in the last nine years. That's one of the privileges of living alone, you know. I do what I want; and what I want is my mountain, alone; and my quiet; and no damn chattering girl to complicate my life. You talk too much. You're going down into the village where there's someone to take care of you, get you a husband and a roof over your head."

"No."

"The road down there is the border of the Empire. If I have to go all the way to the village I'm violating the terms of my exile. But I'll take you as far as the bottom of the mountain. I'll take you right into the village."

"No."

"That's all I can do. Forget about Gitu. Forget about
Hua province. You're safe. You're out of reach of Gitu
and Ghita, and you'll do well to stay that way."

"All you have to do is teach me. Then you don't have
to worry about taking me anywhere, do you? I can go
anywhere; and they won't catch me."

"Fool," he said. And he thought, looking at her in
the soft twilight, that there might have been a hand-
someness about the girl before she was hurt: and more
than likely reckoning what could happen to a girl on the
roads and in a raid—hurt in more ways than that wound
down her cheek. . . .

She was old not to be married. She was very young
to be a widow. But that was entirely possible. That she
had been raped was altogether likely, somewhere along
her journey. He did not want to set off a flood of tears,
but as he thought about it, the more it was likely that
the girl, scarred and foreign and surely no virgin, would
find no husband in the village, that she would spend
her days as some family's nurse, someone's drudge or
some farmer's untitled concubine. He thought of the
damnable nuisance she posed to him; thought finally
with a sense of comfortable moral sacrifice he had not
felt in years, that there was a nunnery in Muigan, a few
days north, inside Hoishi province, and there was a
chance to do something charitable and maybe win a
little virtue in the gods' record-keeping, if the gods in
fact cared for anything lately. The little gold he had
would have been a small thing to him, in his days in
Chiyaden, but it was a great deal to border folk, in
these uncertain times; and if he could give the girl
dowry enough to buy her into Muigan nunnery, she
would not be so ungracious as to forget her benefactor:
she would make prayers for his well-being and his
father's. That way he could do his father a service,
discharging an obligation that had worried him, do himself one, if it mattered, and a girl with no prospects
would find a decent life and a respectable old age,

much more than she would ever find as a farm-wife in Hua province.

There was risk in that plan. Certainly he thought he should not entrust her or the money to some boy from the village. He had to go to Muigan himself and conspicuously violate his exile to do it. But probably the Regent would not notice it, or the Regent would hear the whole of the business and, understanding it for what it was, be sensible enough to let the matter lie and not stir up a long-settled problem. It had been a long time since someone had presented him a problem that had a clean, easy solution. He felt quite magnanimous then, congratulated himself on his good sense and his exemplary behavior, and gestured at her with the chopsticks. "I'll tell you what I'll do. You stay here and rest a day or two, then I'll take you a way through the mountains to Muigan up in Hoishi. There's a nunnery there—"

"No."

"Listen to me, little fool. I'll buy you in. I can do that much for you. You'll have a respectable dowry. What do you think of that?"

"I don't want any nuns and prayers. They did me no good. I want Gitu's head. I want his—"

"I'm offering you a respectable dowry. I'm offering you a safe place to live, with enough to eat, good clothes, security for your old age. Think about growing old. Think about living beyond this year, girl. Gitu's head! You're talking nonsense."

"I don't want to be a nun."

"Then take the money! Try to find a husband in the village. There's no way you can get back to Hua; you're lucky to have gotten this far alive."

"I want Gitu dead."

"*You'll* die, that's what's going to happen if you go back on that road."

"Not if you teach me."

He restrained his temper. He took a slow, slow sip of the cooling tea. "You want me to go. Is that it? You want me to go up to Hua and be a fool in your cause."

"No."

"Let me tell you something. Kill Gitu and there'll be another of his breed in his place before the seat cools. It's not one man. It's the whole damn court. It's the young fool on the throne. You think I wouldn't have stayed, if there'd been a chance to better things? There wasn't. That's why I'm here, on this mountain. Kill Gitu! You go to that nunnery, girl, and you spend a long life praying for your family: that's the most good you'll do them. *I* can't do anything, *I* have no intention of throwing my life away for a fool—you *or* the young Emperor. Listen. You're a brave girl. You've come a long way. I've no doubt you mean all of it. But I'd do you no favor by doing what you ask. If you were a boy, I'd say you're too small. But you're not a boy; and what you ask is out of the question. —Listen," he said, and held up a finger as she opened her mouth. "In the morning it'll be different. You sleep on it. You think about it. It's stupid to throw your life away. Nobody expects you to take on a man's job, and trying it, let me tell you, that makes you a fool. You don't have to die; and that's what it amounts to, because you haven't got a chance in hell of taking anyone with you. You take my offer, and go to Muigan. If you want to learn—the nuns can teach you."

"No."

"Dammit, you will. I'm being generous. You'd better recognize the fact."

"No."

He raked a hand through his trailing hair. "You're tired. You've been through an ordeal. Listen: this much I'll do. You can rest here as long as it takes you to come to your senses about this. I promise you, I won't lay a hand on you. You can sleep wherever you like. It's summer. The porch is pleasant enough, a damn sight more pleasant than the road. You don't have to do anything until you have your strength back. Then you'll know I'm right; and I'll take you to Muigan and make sure you're all right before I leave."

"No."

"You're deaf, girl! Your whole idea's preposterous. Enough about it. You're going." He put the tea-bowl into the empty rice-bowl and stood up, walked over and took hers, from which every grain had vanished.

She stared at him flatly as she gave them to him.

"I'll bring you out a mat and a blanket," he said. "You can have the porch to yourself. Or you can be sensible and come inside where it's a little warmer."

She said not a thing.

"The porch, then," he said; and shook his head as he walked inside.

He set the bowls on the table, went over and rolled up the topmost of his two sleeping mats; and took his topmost blanket with it. "Girl," he said, walking out onto the porch.

But she was gone, basket, bow, and all.

He flung the mat and the blanket down.

"Girl?"

She might have gone aside to the woods for a moment, for a call of nature.

But to have taken the basket with her—

"Girl?"

Damn.

She might worry about his intentions. Gods knew she had likely had reason.

She might have taken her basket of rags to the woods to make a bed for the night. Or gone to the stable. Either one was safe enough.

But her behavior worried him, not for her, but because there was a great deal more than strange about her; and because of the deep twilight, considering which most girls would not choose the woods for safety, or go off to a strange, dark stable, if they were too afraid of a gentleman to sleep on his porch. Dammit, she had proposed living here as his student: and she was afraid to share the porch with him.

He had an uneasiness himself now, about the girl, the hour, the peculiar look of her.

He was reluctant to call out again and betray that worry. He was ashamed to go back in to the house again and take up his sword from the peg by the door; but he was not a fool, either, to go down to the stable in the dark without it.

Jiro was down there, in the stable for the night, not loose in his pen where he could deal with an intruder. At least, Shoka thought, he would let the horse free, and the girl would be ill-advised to go into that pen or bother things in the stable after that.

There was no commotion down at the stable. No one, he was sure, could have come near Jiro without him sounding the alarm. But he thought again of bandits; of the chance of fire, if the girl was crazed enough; and Jiro was the only living creature he cared about. The thought of the girl or any possible accomplice doing harm to the horse was unbearable.

Damn, he thought, there was no chance the girl could come into the stable without noise. He was being a fool. The girl upset his evening and his sense of order in things and all of a sudden it seemed the whole world was unraveling, old instincts waking, old apprehensions coming back to haunt him.

He reached the ramshackle stable, walked along beside the wall in the almost-dark, hearing Jiro's quiet, ordinary moving on the other side of the wall and taking reassurance in the sound.

Then something hit the shed beside his head; and he dropped and rolled and scrambled, muscles acting while mind realized that what had dropped to the dust with him was a spent arrow with white, ragged fletchings and a forged bronze point.

He reached the dark of the stable door, rolled aside on his shoulders and tumbled into the interior, kneeling on the straw. Jiro's soft, worried snort reassured him he was the first and the only disturbance in the dark inside; and he trusted absolutely what was at his back. It was outside, the forest-edge, the near-dark all about: that was what he looked to.

"Girl!" he shouted out. "Damn you, your pallet's on the porch, the way I said; I did exactly what I said! Don't make me hurt you!"

"I'll come in," the girl's voice came back, far away from among the trees, "when you swear on your honor you'll teach me."

"Girl, I won't put up with this nonsense. You're asking to get hurt!"

Silence. Long silence, from the woods. He shifted his position on the straw, favoring the leg an assassin's knife had lamed, rested his shoulders against the rough post of the door and gazed toward the woods in the deepening dark.

He thought about fire again, the complete vulnerability of everything he owned up there in the cabin.

And Jiro, who was a target even those wretched arrows would not miss if he were outside in the pen.

At closer range—that ragged-feathered arrow could have killed.

He swore to himself, and clenched his hands and thought that at least he could break the mud and moss out of the gaps in the sapling logs that made the stable, and get a view of the house from the back wall. He could make holes like that all around, and keep an eye to things in the clearing so far as a moonless night let him.

The thought crossed his mind that the girl might indeed be working with the bandits; or she might be a demon under illusion.

But a madwoman loose in the dark with a bow and a crazed notion of revenge was worry enough to keep a man from his sleep.

Chapter Two

Shoka changed position in the nest of straw he had piled up by the stable wall, rubbed the cramp in his leg—it had been one side or the other all night long, sleep by fits and snatches, and the damned straw prickles coming through the open weave of his shirt and breeches. The ground was stable-soil and stank no matter how clean he kept the place; it was a damp and damned uncomfortable bed to spend the night in.

He had a bit of twine strung across the door-frame and tied to a bucket on the far side. He kept a watch out in various directions, not neglecting the far slope of the hill from the long bare slope of the pasture. He did not know how many he might be dealing with, or whether it was in truth only one mad girl; but he had not lived this long by taking matters lightly.

Nine years on the mountain had taught him to let go his suspicions, to let a leaf fall without suspecting some hand had disturbed it, let a fish jump in the brook without his body tensing, prepared for all the things his father's teaching had set in him, mind and muscle. Go easy, he had told himself year after year, breathe the wind, let the leaves fall and the seasons turn and put the old life away.

That was all the wisdom he had learned on the mountain, the simple art of sleeping sound at night with no traps rigged, the simple assumption it took to walk to the spring unarmed, to watch a fox's antics, to ride old Jiro bareback and doze on his back on the lower pasture, the both of them content in the sun and the summer and the smell of sun-warmed grass.

Now he sat in the dark with his sword across his lap, with straw coming through his clothes and the damp making his forty-year old joints ache: more, every nerve in his body was on edge and his stomach was uneasy with the old anxiousness, his brain working on every detail of the land and every noise in the dark.

Like old times.

Like everything he had tried for years to bury.

Damn the girl—who, by doing nothing, was doing everything right: others who had come against him, by doing *something*, had succeeded in *nothing*—and made themselves easy marks.

He waited, and traded views on the house and the clearing, the woods and the pasture. Nothing stirred and Jiro gave no alarms, only shifted quietly at his moves about the stable.

He most expected trouble in the hour just before dawn, and rubbed his eyes and kept scanning the shadows on all sides of the stable for small movements. What chilled his blood was the thought, with him through the night, that all the fool girl had to do, if she was intent on murder, was to fire the woods itself and take out on the trail. If she did that and did it the smart way, from several points about the clearing, it would be a narrow thing to get himself and Jiro down the root-tangled slot of a trail; if she did that, enemies would know the only road down and archers could wait in ambush.

He had been in worse situations, even granted they set the woods afire; but he had hard shift to remember any more embarrassing, trapped as he was by a sixteen-

year-old farm-girl. While the sun came up he fought
the urge to sleep, trying to think whether there was any
possibility he had overlooked, anything an enemy might
do; and what approaches bandit allies or Ghita's men
might have used and where they might set an ambush.

But at last, with the daylight enough to show the
green in the trees and dispel the shadows around the
stable, he got up, gave Jiro a bucket of grain and
dipped up stale water from the rain barrel outside, with
frequent glances toward the woods and the constant
feeling that there might be another arrow aimed at him.

Jiro wanted out of his stall, and kicked at the boards,
impatient at being penned up on a fine clear morning.

"I know," he said to the horse, and talked to him,
reasonably, patting his neck. "Patience. Patience."

None so easy, he thought to himself. He did not
think that the girl had left. He felt exposed the whole
while he walked up to the cabin, limping in the morning chill—walked, being a fool, because he had felt the
fool all night long and he was not going to run now,
reckoning by daylight that he knew the cast that bow
could make: it was dangerous, but it lacked just a little
of sufficient force at any range she could get from inside
the forest. If there was anyone with her, they had made
no move when they had had the best chance, in the
dark, so he reckoned by now that it was not a case of
bandits: waiting till daylight when they had had the
dark was certainly not their preference; and it would
not be the choice of Ghita's assassins, either.

No, likely it was one girl, who was out there being a
fool and who had given him a sore hip and an aching
shoulder this morning.

It was one girl who was perhaps crazed enough or
mad enough to take chances; but with that bow she had
to get closer.

Unless she had gotten into the cabin.

He walked up from the side of the porch, walked as
far as the door and spun suddenly around the side of
the door-frame and into the single room.

Empty. Nothing seemed disturbed. He leaned against

the wall and stood there taking account of things, whether anything was missing or in any way disturbed; and thought of poisons, and his foodstuffs on which he had once, years ago, kept protective seals; and he wondered what mischief a madwoman could bring in a basket that large.

Damn, no. He was attributing to a sixteen-year-old girl the things that a cannier enemy might do. He was fighting himself, that was the ghost he had conjured up last night. He was fighting Saukendar, not a peasant girl with a pitiable mad notion of getting her way out of him.

He stirred up the coals in the little cookpit, got a small fire going, between keeping an eye to the outside, and put a little rice and water in a pot. He had his breakfast sitting in the doorway where he could watch the whole clearing, particularly the stable, figuring that the smell of cooking-smoke and breakfast might bring the girl out into the open. He had a sincere hope that she might be more reasonable by daylight, when everything else was sane.

But she did not come.

He put away his bowl and thought then what he was to do, and where she might have spent the night and where she might be now. Watching from the edge of the woods, he thought, and for the first time in years he assembled his silk and steel armor from the oiled quilts where he kept it, put on the sleeves and his armor-robe and laced the body-armor about him.

It settled to his frame with the assertion of old, unwelcome patterns, a ridiculous precaution, he told himself. The girl who was probably hiding in the brush in clear sight of the cabin, would laugh when she saw him, dammit, but he had no wish to die at the hands of a madwoman, or by some stupid girl's blind luck.

He put on his sword; and walked outside, and sat down on the steps of the porch, dourly surveying his kingdom, the clear ground around about the cabin and the stable. For the first time since he had come to the mountain he found himself hampered and hemmed about by what someone else intended: he would have gone hunting; and he dared not leave the house and the stable unwatched; he would have gone out riding, but he would not expose Jiro to the girl's arrows. That left working the garden, in a stone-weight of armor; or sitting and mending his tack or doing leatherwork, the likelier.

No, damn it, there was no way that could go on for days and weeks. She might not have moved last night, but he was sure that she was out there; and no child was long on patience. If she failed to have her way by any easy course, she only would make some further provocation, and something more and something more until she found a way to move him: and that childish game might get someone seriously hurt.

So the thing to do, he thought, was to take up his own bow and his quiver and go off as if he was going hunting—let her guess what the game was—then simply sit and wait in concealment until she either tried to follow or tried the house.

There was a place in the brush just uphill that afforded a clear view of the house and the stable: and there was no sign when he had reached that little knoll, that the girl Taizu might have used it for a vantage. He crouched down in it, he put his bow beside him, he laid out an arrow in case he needed one—still remembering the possibility of bandits. Then he put his back against an accommodating tree trunk and settled in to wait.

The sun rose higher, passed zenith, and the air warmed, the bushes hummed with insects and rustled with the light breeze. He nodded without meaning to, jerked his head up and fought the overwhelming urge to sleep while the cicadas and the sun conspired to numb the mind.

He drowsed as he could, not truly asleep, but at least getting some rest, and watching, between nods of his head.

And by afternoon he was hungry, thirsty, bitten by ants and not a damned thing had stirred but the birds, the insects, and Jiro, who had begun to attack the boards of the stall in a fit of temper.

"Easy, easy," he said, soothing Jiro with his hands, and the old warhorse cow-kicked the slats again for sheer frustration, not mollified by the grain, the water, or the other attentions. A good currying helped, but Jiro had his ears laid back and kept reaching around to nip him, not hard, just Jiro's little way of saying he was damned mad.

Finally nothing would do but he should risk both their hides—put Jiro's halter on and climb up onto his bare back and ride him out into the pen and on into the pasture, back and forth, back and forth, all the while he kept thinking how large a target they both made; and he kept looking back over his shoulder toward the house and the stable whenever they were on the outward course—which he was sure the girl was watching, probably rolling in the bushes in laughter.

Everything was out of joint. Jiro was confused, and *he* was worrying every time he took his eyes off the clearing, the stable, or the cabin, and thinking at every turn of a half a score of ways a determined enemy could get at him.

Fighting himself again. It was the only standard he knew.

And she was pushing him, not having done a thing. Minimal force. *She* was doing everything right.

If she was even out there.

Dammit, fighting himself again, and again, and again.

He worked Jiro into a sweat and brought him back to his stall in a better humor than he had left it, dried him, brushed him, all the while watching the edge of the woods and thinking that the one place he could not watch was the back of the cabin, where the woods came much closer; and thinking that it was possible, given the rain-barrel and the woodpile he had been lax enough to have up against the cabin's back wall, to climb up to the roof and get in through the thatch—

If one were Saukendar . . .

He was afraid to work behind the house to move the things because if he was working there he could not see the other side: all an enemy needed was a free run at the stable, if she was willing to harm the horse. . . .

. . . to get him agitated enough to come running down there, straight into ambush. She needed only watch his activities and see what he guarded to figure out what was valuable to him, and how to get him to react without thinking.

Damn.

He cooked a plain supper, ate it sitting in the doorway of the cabin as the sun was going down. He wondered whether the girl had food in that basket, and how long she could hold out and whether she knew how to forage in these mountains.

But a peasant would know the berries and the roots, the edibles and the dyes. . . .

And the poisons . . .

The rice went a little strange on his tongue when he thought of that. He kept eating. There was nothing the matter with it. Nothing in the tea.

In Chiyaden lady Bhosai had died, they said, of poison on the bottom of a tea-bowl.

Damn, he was thinking back again, back to court, back to the whole damn mess.

Back to his father's teachings, the midnight exercises, the traps his father set for him—

—the things that had kept him alive when three others of the aging Emperor's friends had met with accidents. He had proved the case of lord Riga, but not the connection of the assassin with Ghita—

He should have killed Ghita when he had the chance. But then Ghita had been one of many, and the old Emperor had forbidden—

He set the rice-bowl aside and drank his tea, trying to push all the past away again, while the armor weighed heavy on his shoulders and bound about his ribs, and the sun sank toward twilight.

Change on the mountain was like that, dawn to dark to dawn, winter to spring to winter again—and one day was like another day, one storm like another storm, one leaf like another leaf, from unfolding to fall. Nine years of cycles that, taken together, might be one day, one year, one lifetime all reduced to small patterns. Changing, nothing changed. Once one became a part of the patterns, one's changes became those changes, perfect equilibrium, as perfect as a man ever became.

But it was all one day, all one year, no matter that the man got older, that he fell down someday and died on this mountain, and the grass grew up around his bones, and no one knew. . . .

Dammit, he had given over a night and most of a day to this interruption in his life. That was already too much to spend.

Once he had had a lot of days to spend, before the days had become one day, every day. He saw that now, and was amazed to realize that he had not acquired patience, he had merely lost his flexibility. He could watch an ant crawl across the porch without a sense of guilt for time wasted. But he could not abide this change in the pattern of his life. That was like an old man. It was very much like an old man, a hermit, a crazed, solitary old man of almost-forty.

That idea upset his stomach.

He spent the night in the stable again.

Like a crazy man.

He had his breakfast in the first light of a misty, dewy dawn, sitting in the doorway of his cabin, and thought about shouting out to the woods, to the girl— Come in, let's talk.

But that notion stuck in his throat.

Like two days of rice with no fish, no rabbit.

He had very little smoked meat and no preserved fruits: those came in fall, and he stored them for the lean times, the winter months. In summer he trusted to nature and his garden.

But if the situation dragged on—

Gods, there was no damned sense in his patience. He had, he decided, to hunt the girl down and tie her hand and foot if need be, and carry her to Muigan.

Let the nuns deal with her.

If she had been about the edges of the clearing she had inevitably left sign; and once he started hunting her, then she would panic and make mistakes.

If she was still out there at all.

If she was out there she had had a worse night than he had, that was sure. The night air could turn cold in the mountains even in late summer; and when the dew settled like this, with the passing of rain just to the north, it meant damp blankets and damper clothes: boughs dumped water down one's neck and soaked one's sleeves and breeches and shoes in a few moments of walking.

Good. He hoped for a nice few days of it, as long as the mist got no worse than it was—a light haze that still let one see the edges of the clearing. That was friendlier to him than it was to her.

So long as it got no worse.

He put up his rice bowl, stretched his shoulders against the weight of the shirt, and went back to the porch and around the side of the house, quickly, to get a few sticks from the woodpile.

More than a few, he thought. The more wood he could carry at one time, the fewer times he had to do this and take his eye off things. He gathered up a quick armful and headed back around the corner of the house and up onto the porch.

The unmistakable hiss of an arrow passed him at hip level.

He dropped the wood, dived for the doorway and

rolled inside, grabbing up his bow and quiver from where he had left then leaning against the doorframe.

"Dammit," he yelled at the darkening woods, "you're asking for it, girl! That's enough. You listen to me! I don't want to hurt you. I've been patient, gods know. I've offered you a dowry. I offered you all the gold I've got, because I didn't want to see you come to harm. I think that deserves at least a little courtesy, don't you think?"

Silence.

"Look here, girl, I won't force you to anything. If you don't want to go to Muigan, that's your choice. If you don't want to stay in the village, that's your choice too. You can go back to Hua, you can go wherever you like. I promise you I won't lay a hand on you. Just come in and talk like a civilized person and stop this nonsense!"

Silence.

"Dammit, you're asking for trouble, girl! I'm not going to be a sitting target for a lunatic."

Silence still.

Should I really have said that last, he wondered uneasily, in dealing with a madwoman?

He had a good idea at least where she had been standing when she had taken that shot, and finding the arrow, he had a better one: a triple-split tree and a small thicket on the other side of the house.

So he put on his leather breeches, which he generally used for hunting, but which were double-sewn with pieces of horn, particularly the front of the thighs, covering what the armor-coat did not. He left only the shin-guards, which were miserable for a long walk, and he took his canteen and his bow with him as he walked to the edge of the woods. It was the full light of dawn; but the dew was still on the leaves, and it was no difficult thing to see that she had been where he had thought—that, in fact, she had spent some little time there, and come and gone.

And gone again.

It had been a foolish time, he thought, for her to have taken that shot, when there was the dew to help him. She had made a mistake, a simple, beginner's mistake—a little overconfidence, a little desire to stir things up when they had been too quiet for her taste.

That thought cheered him immensely.

He smiled to himself as he saw the track plain as could be through the brush.

Fighting himself, indeed. No girl, even if she knew the land, was going to pass through the woods without a trail on a morning like this, and by the state of the dew on the leaves he could judge well enough how long ago she had passed.

The trail took him away from the house and deeper into the woods: he did not like that. She had enough time to double back if he did not move faster and, surer; and he ignored his aching leg and trotted along the clear spots. The rising sun was beginning to burn the mist away, the clouds were breaking; and the advantage a fugitive might have had in the hills was much less by daylight.

It was no difficult thing once he saw the tracks, to sort out the pattern she had been following—he could see other evidences, a regular trail worn on a slope, the plants broken down, stones dislodged—clear as a highway in the brush once he was onto it.

But it was not a place or a moment to be careless.

"Master Saukendar!" a voice drifted down to him, from out of the hills. "You don't have to track me. I'll come down. All you have to do is promise to teach me. You don't have to worry about me."

He was not fool enough to answer her.

Let her worry now, he thought, and quickened his pace along the trail she had left, not cutting across toward the voice, even though it came from across a ravine and off another hill in a place where he could guess very likely where she might go. If she were clever she might do that to find out where he was, or to lure him off the trail and then, hiding hers very well, make him waste time retracing to find the track again.

If she were skilled. Likely she was a very anxious girl just now; and there were trails around that hill: he had worn them and he knew them much better than she did. If he could find out which one she was on, then he could indeed take a short-cut.

"Master Saukendar!" Very high up the mountain and far away now. "Haven't I proved myself? That's all I'm after. That's all I was ever after. I never meant to hit you. I could have. I'm not a bad shot with the bow."

He kept going. He had an idea now that she knew where she was going. He found the same kind of trail, stones disturbed, plants flattened and some of the stems browned: not only this morning, her passage in this direction.

Why?

"Master Saukendar?"

He did not answer. She was leading him off from home, he thought; then she would take the trail downhill and try to double back to the cabin ahead of him.

But there was a way across and up to that trail she was on now.

He took the downhill slope off the side of the trail, going from tree to tree to stop himself gathering too much momentum. The climb up the other side was a quick scramble up among the pines, because her trail descended to that point.

Only one way down her side of the hill, unless she went down the slope or doubled back again; and if she did that, there was still another place he could catch her.

But there, dammit, she did head down the other slope, further up the bend of the two hills: he heard the crashing in the brush; and then thought: no. Not.

He simply sat down where he was, figuring he could take the down-course and match her if he was wrong, but he figured it was a tree or a large rock that had just rolled down that hill.

And if he was wrong he happened to have a vantage that would show her quite plainly when she crossed a certain point below, or tried to climb the slope to reach the trail he had left.

But reckoning that he was not wrong and that the unaccustomed racket was a diversion, he sat, and he waited, and reckoned when she came past him on her way down the trail he could lay hands on her and teach her quite well how she would fare in a real fight.

But there was no sound, no sound for a very long while; and he grew uneasy, thinking that she might in fact have taken some route completely off the trails—a climb up and over the hill, slower, but entirely possible to young legs and light, quick feet. She this moment could be doubling back to the cabin.

Or she had realized where he was now; and was lying quiet; and it was a matter of outwaiting her.

Damn.

He heard a noise then, a stirring of brush coming his direction.

He crouched in his concealment beside the trail.

"Master Saukendar?" The voice came from quite close now, just beyond the trees, tremulous and out of breath.

Damn, damn, and damn. He said nothing. He held his breath and waited, and heard brush break going right back down the trail away from him.

He broke from cover and plunged onto the trail in pursuit, having a brief sight of a ragged blue coat among the leaves. He doubled his speed, and she ran all-out ahead of him, dodging along the twists of the trail, her light-shod feet flying, up and over an outcropping of rock and around a turn as he came close behind.

He felt the trip-rope against his foot, he heard the sprung limb release. He saw the tree coming at him, did a turn and roll his muscles knew and his mind had outright forgotten; and a forty-year old body hit the rocky trail with a force that nearly knocked the wind out of him.

He rolled and got up again, bruised and outraged,

shoved the quiver back on his shoulder and picked up the bow he had dropped.

"Dammit, girl!"

"I didn't catch you, did I?" the worried voice drifted down the trail.

"Damn you to hell!" he yelled at her. And then caught his breath and his wits and decided on another tactic. "Truce. Do you hear me, girl? Truce for a bit. Listen to me."

"Will you not send me to Muigan?"

"Listen, girl. You're very clever. Someone *has* taught you, haven't they?"

"We did it for traps. When the soldiers would come."

"The hell."

"It's true. We did them. You aren't hurt, are you?"

"No."

"It wasn't a big tree."

"Listen girl . . ." He got another breath and calmed his temper. "It was a damned fine set. I'll give you that. You want me to give you a trial, do you?"

"You'll teach me."

"I'll give you a chance. With an understanding between us."

"What?"

"That you come into the house. That you do what you're told. That any time you want to quit, you tell me and I'll take you to Muigan."

"Do I have your word, master Saukendar? You'll take me for a student."

Another deep breath. "Yes. You have my word."

"Does that mean sharing your bed?"

He straightened back, feeling the ache in his bones. He had, gods witness, not thought of that in the bargain. Yet. "What if it did?" he shouted at the woods.

"Then we'll go on with this. I've gotten one promise from you."

"Damn your impudence!"

"I'm not a whore, master Saukendar. I'll cook your

WE DIDN'T KNOW—
WE ONLY BELIEVED—
NOW YOU'VE COME BACK

"Does it seem reasonable to you that a Regency continues—into an Emperor's thirtieth year?"

"No, m'lord," Shoka said.

"Not to us, either. Not to many of us. We were ready to make that objection—when lord Gitu overran Yijang and Hua. . . . Assassinations, elsewhere. Hired killers. Bands of mercenaries traveling under imperial orders. The *Emperor's* seal, and the Regent's orders. How do we stop such a thing? How do we prevent it—when every lord able to lead is apprehended, assassinated, when they strip us of men, even boys out of the fields—go to Saukendar, some said. Go to Saukendar. They *urged* me to send to you. This time he has to listen, they said. But if I had sent—and Ghita had known—you understand—" Reidi gave an uncomfortable twitch of the shoulders. His horse shifted again. "I had no true hope that you'd come. You'd indicated to the villagers—that you had no wish to hear from anyone. That you would refuse any such petitions—"

"You *were* watching me."

"It's my village, m'lord—as the Regent pointed out to me again and again, *and* threatened my life should you leave that mountain. Of course the word came to me. I tried to get a messenger down the road to you when I knew you'd left Mon. . . . We believed you'd come back to deal with Ghita and his partisans."

Shoka felt cold, cold all the way to the bones.

"There are men ready to follow you, lord Saukendar. There are men who've committed their lives to this— We didn't know the hour. We only believed. Now you've come back . . ."

"It's gripping drama, tightly focussed and inexorable as Taizu herself. Read **The Paladin** and you'll never settle for another ordinary sword-wielding female."
—Faren Miller
LOCUS

food and clean, but I won't do anything else for my keep."

He wiped the hair out of his eyes and, the sweat from off his face. He was offended. He also, no matter that she was a scrawny, scarred urchin, wished she had less virtue.

But she was not staying on the mountain, so it made no difference. She was still going to the nuns or to the village, and he had no mind to deliver her pregnant.

"All right," he said. "Those are the terms. You cook and you clean, and I'll teach you. And when you've had enough, you can tell me. I give you my solemn word. Is that enough?"

There was a moving in the brush further down the trail. In a few moments she came around the bend of the path, sweaty and scratched and filthy, her shorn hair standing on end and matted with twigs and leaves; but her eyes were shining.

He scowled at her, and slung his bow to his shoulder and waved a hand down the trail.

"You walk in front," he said.

Chapter Three

They were back at the cabin by noon—the girl had shown him where she had hidden her pack, which was one of half a hundred places he might have guessed if he had wanted to risk taking an arrow in the back, or risk her raiding him while he was raiding her hiding-place. Her basket rested in a tight little nook under one of the rock ledges frequent on his mountain, and where—he saw by the lack of sign on the ground around about—she had been canny enough to go on the rock if she had come and gone much there at all.

She had retrieved the ungainly basket, hauled it up onto the ledge where he waited, and taken it onto her back, walking ahead of him into the clearing much as she had walked into it the first time, a load of wicker borne by two skinny bare legs.

She shed the basket on his porch, and looked at him, the sweat running on her face.

"What have you got in that?" he asked, pointing at it with his unstrung bow.

"My blanket, my clothes, some food."

37

"Show me."

She unpacked there on the boards, rummaged out the hat, a pile of dirty clothes and blankets, the rag-wrapped shape of a sword; a few clay bowls, a tin pot, several small packets neatly done up with braided straw cord.

"What are those?" he asked.

"Brown beans," she said of one. "Mushrooms. Ginger root. Berries."

"Show me," he said. It seemed only prudent.

She frowned and untied the cords to show him, indeed, it was only what she had said. He went through the dried mushrooms, and they all seemed wholesome.

He took up the rag-wrapped sword, unfolded the filthy cloth from a plain, serviceable bull's-hide grip, and pulled the blade from the sheath.

"Not bad," he said, trying the balance of it. He put it back in the sheath. "But you're a long way from needing it."

She looked at him anxiously, and at the sword which he kept in his hand—which he fully intended to keep.

"First," he said, lifting the corner of a once-yellow quilt with the tip of the sword, "these need washing." He touched her arm with it, plucked at the browned-blue coat. "I trust you've found the spring."

A nod.

"Fine." He stirred the heap of clothes lying on the porch. The aroma was that of sweat, old laundry and mildew. He wrinkled his nose and went inside, leaned the sword against the wall, took a generous lump of soap in a leather wrapping, threw it into the washing-pail, and took a clean change of breeches and a shirt from the peg. He gave both to the girl, who watched from the doorway. "All your clothes, all your blankets, and your person, before you cross this threshold. Understood?"

"I'm very clean."

One hoped.

*　　*　　*

One hoped that scrubbing would work a miracle, but the figure that came trudging back from the woods had breeches knotted up with plaited reed about the calves to keep the hems out of the dirt; the shirt hung loose almost to the knees. She carried the huge basket, heavy, one supposed, with wet laundry; and the hair was still a mop, the skin was sun-browned now that the spots and crusts of dirt were gone—one had not expected the old-ivory and cinnabar-rose of the courtesans, but one still cherished a little expectation.

Decidedly not; and the scar, more the pity, was uglier and more inflamed after the scrubbing. Shoka felt a sympathetic twinge for that, in his own left leg.

He had not been completely sure she would come back from the spring. If she were in fact mad, she might start the whole business over again; and in that thought, he had not let Jiro out. But he had hung a cord from post to post of the wooden porch, and when she came up with her basket, he showed her that to dry the clothes and blankets on, while he went down to the stable and let Jiro out.

The old warhorse snorted and did a little flip of the tail as he skipped out into the afternoon sunlight, in much better humor. Jiro ran for a bit and finally lay down and rolled on his back as if he had just come in after a long day's ride.

So Jiro's world was back in order, with a stretch and a roll in the warm dust, and a good shaking afterward.

By that time, the girl had the laundry hung, and sat on the porch waiting for Shoka as he came up the hill to the house.

He shed the armor and changed to a light shirt and cloth breeches, gave a sigh of relief, and settled down on the porch while he set the girl to weed the garden—it was something she well knew how to do, he reckoned, and he was due a little work for his trouble, none of which he had asked for, especially considering he would be paying a year's wages for her sake to the nunnery at Muigan.

She did not object. In fact she worked very diligently at her weeding, a fetching perspective, while he drowsed somewhat at his ease and thought over such weighty matters as how much work he ought by rights to ask of her in return for his instruction; and whether she might be a decent cook; and, truth be told, what chance there was she might settle down and become a tolerably decent servant—as well she should serve him, he thought, as some cabbage-farmer down in the village, if she had no disposition to be a nun.

She was clever: she had proved that. A lady could never survive the mountain, but a peasant girl certainly could; and warm the winters and cook his food and weed the garden. . . .

He and Jiro could hunt and laze about the pasture, and he could build the cabin a little larger, working in wood being by much his favorite occupation. . . .

Revenge against lord Ghita. Gods, it was the kind of foolishness only a child might think of, who had been abused, who was crazed with grief for her family and the loss of everything familiar; more than that—he knew this from his own experience—her whole mad dream was only a place to go and a purpose to hold her sane when the world had left her nothing else.

She had only to see that there was still some good in life within her reach, and that her mad notion of revenge was impossibly out of any girl's reach and any man's, for that matter; and then she would use good sense. The mountain could offer her peace. Food, rest, a roof over her head and nothing to fear for the rest of her life.

If she was still sane, which was still a question.

Damn, no, she was a headstrong bitch. If he wanted a woman he could deal with the village for that commodity too: there were poor girls who would take to the life up here well enough, and be damned grateful for it. It was simply that this one was there in front of his eyes—bending over in the bean-patch—and that he had not so much as seen a woman in nine years. There were far comelier and far gentler and more reasonable girls to be had, any time he wanted a disruption in his life—perhaps a compliant, sensible young woman who would come and go occasionally, once a month or so, a small refreshing shower, gods witness, not a thunderstorm.

Pack her off to the nuns. A good harvest of furs could buy some village daughter from her parents, a girl of thirteen or fourteen, who would be quite happy to weed his garden and cook his dinners, and think his cabin on the mountain quite a fine, snug home when and if he chose to have her live there.

But—his mind slipped unbidden to other banished thoughts—have a child . . . gods, he had no right to have a son, to leave him a legacy of enemies and assassins and a peasant mother; or a daughter whose life would be brute drudgery with some villager. That was why, he reminded himself, he had taken no village daughter in the first place: that, and the fact that in those first years when he had never been certain of his own safety, a woman had only seemed a potential hostage for his enemies.

After that, once he had settled to the pattern of the mountain and come to believe that he was safe—by then he had grown so solitary, so wrapped in his reputation of infallibility with the villagers, so nestled into his place of respect with them—that to ask for companionship seemed too much intimacy with them and too much need to confess to anyone. Besides, any village girl he might take would be chattering about him to her relatives and spreading rumors that might well get to traders' ears; and from traders' mouths—to the heart of Chiyaden, attributing gods knew what ambitions to him by that time.

So the young girl so deft with the weeds yonder— wakened thoughts he had consciously, sensibly smoth-

ered for more years of celibacy than he had let himself
take account of.

Damn.

He shifted his position, leaned back against the post
by the steps, and watched her move and bend—not
forgetting the arrow which had flown past just this
morning; but finding that he had not quite become a
monastic in his isolation. Damn, he was not.

Even if she were a little mad, there were things to
recommend her—like the fact she had no kin in the
village to tell tales to; and like the fact she had come
with sense enough and skill enough already to take care
of herself if trouble did come.

Mostly—she was there, within reach, and no daughter of the village ever had come that close to him.

There was supper on the porch, where he preferred
to have it. Taizu had made rice with mushrooms; and
the thought of poison did cross Shoka's mind, but he
grew quite reckless today, a state of mind quite, quite
foreign to his methodical ways and his sense of order.

So the sun went down, leaving them in the dusk, on
the porch, with his given word and her anxious expecta-
tions.

"There's the porch or there's the inside," he said.

"I'll take inside," she said, and shot him a look. "A
corner to myself."

"I promised," he said firmly; and a light came to her
eyes, the shadow passed, the whole of her regard suddenly opened to him in a way that made no sense at all
for a handful of heartbeats—until he remembered the
faces in Chiyaden streets, the shouting crowds, the
adoration that he had believed in . . . until the need
came, and no one was there.

He flinched from it, stared off into the darkening
forest and nodded absently toward the indoors.

"Wash up."

"Tomorrow you'll teach me."

He looked at her, having achieved a cold distance

from the moment, heard what she was saying, and reckoned he was a fool if he did not get her to the nuns in short order.

"If you want me to teach you, girl, you'll start the same as every apprentice; the way you've already started. You work. You cook and you clean; and you learn not to question. When you've gotten that right, then you start exercises. And when you've mastered that, then we'll talk about weapons. Until then, don't let me catch you laying hand to that sword or I'm free of all promises. Do you hear me?"

"Yes."

Perhaps the look was still in her eyes. He was staring elsewhere, listening to the tree-frogs and the wind. He sat there a long time, until he had gotten her voice out of his mind; and her eyes out of his thinking; and until he had put Chiyaden at distance again.

He came to bed after dark, found his own mat, undressed and lay down to think, conscious of another human's presence in the cabin that no one had ever entered but himself—thought, in the dark, of the risk that he was taking. All the things that he had feared of her were still possible, including the chance, more credible in the dark and at the edge of exhausted sleep, that she was a demon more than usually adept at disguise: the villagers down in Mon knew that in the dark a demon had more power, and that if a man were fool enough to have converse with a demon and to share food with it or to take any favor from it, then that demon gained power; and when it got enough then it would drop the pretenses and show itself in its true form, with skull necklaces and fanged jaws and staring eyes. . . .

It was a fear a great deal easier to deal with than the more sensible one, that the girl was crazed enough someday to take offense and slip toadstools into his soup.

It was a lot easier to deal with than the fear that someone had sent her.

But he had learned long since that a man had to go to sleep on worries like that some nights, because the body and the mind could only go so far on half-sleep and one-eyed watching. One just shut one's eyes and trusted one might wake up if something seemed wrong: so far he had always done it.

He needed a dog, he thought sometimes. But one had never come along; and he had, in his reclusive way, asked not even that comfort from the village, and betrayed no worries.

Being a legend was a damned heavy burden, sometimes; but being human to people he relied on had always, since Chiyaden, seemed too great a risk.

He heard the girl stirring and opened an eye, but he had been aware of the daylight coming under the door and through the shutter cracks for some time now. He watched with slitted eyes as she got up, still fully dressed, and took the water bucket out the door. Industrious. He approved of that.

He had shown her where the latrine was. He gave her a little time, in consideration of her modesty; he thought about getting up and getting dressed while she was out of the cabin.

No, he thought. Apprentice she wanted to be, she wanted to be treated like a boy, then damned if he would inconvenience himself.

He got up, wincing—gods, the move he had made; and the flip and roll yesterday made themselves felt this morning with a vengeance, so that he ached all down his back, his shoulder, his bad leg. He took a stretch and swore—damned if he was going to hobble about and stagger in front of the girl. Damned if he was.

He wrapped himself in his top blanket, made his morning trip to the latrine and headed back to the rain-barrel to wash as she came up the hill from the woods and the spring, lugging a full bucket of drinking water. He watched her from the corner of the house and ducked back again for a quick rinse under the dripping-bucket that hung at the corner by the rain-barrel at the back of the cabin.

The cold water made his joints ache and set his teeth to chattering; he wrapped in the blanket and walked—limped, because the shivering made his bad leg uncertain—up onto the porch and back inside.

He shed his blanket then and dressed while she was boiling up a little breakfast tea. She did not look his way, more than a one-time glance and a flinch away from him. She worked with her back turned then—well enough. So she knew she was female.

He shaved, which he did not always; and she gave him tea—a novel and luxurious thing, he thought, to have a warm start on a summer morning. He sat on the porch and sipped his tea while she stirred about cleaning the cabin and rolling up the mats with a zeal for work he found amazing.

A man could get used to that.

But he remembered his resolve about the nuns, and his sound reason for it. When she was finished, and came out onto the porch to report herself ready for other tasks, he said:

"My horse wants watering. You'll find the bucket down by the fence yonder."

He walked down to the stable with her, handed her the bucket and whistled Jiro over to put a tie on his halter.

He fed Jiro himself. The horse had no disposition for waiting for his breakfast; but when Taizu came trudging back with the water he showed her where the grain was and how much to feed and how to latch the bin securely.

He showed her the shovel too, and where to put the manure til the sun could dry it for turning into the garden.

But that was no news to a country girl.

"You know you're planting the squash too close," she said, and with an earnest frown that made him think again that maybe the nuns were a mistake, "And the beans aren't much. You ought to let me pick the seed, master Saukendar. A gentleman wouldn't know the things I do."

But he said to himself that she would be gone before the moon came full.

She seduced even Jiro, after he calmed the horse down enough to get her near him, and he had showed her what to do with the curry comb. She found the spots he liked scratched; and in a little while Shoka, sitting on the rail, saw Jiro standing with his ears flat and his eyes half shut, while the girl worked away at the caked and dried remnant of the mud he had gotten into.

Shoka felt a little betrayed: he had thought Jiro might well put her right over the fence.

But pig-girl that she was, she had the hands, and Jiro even let her work with his forelock and his legs—not the tail: Jiro tucked it tight into his rump and she could get only the end-strands brushed, but his kick when she tried to get him to relax it was only perfunctory, a statement of territories. The girl did not even skip out of the way, she just stepped aside in time, and Shoka sat on the top rail with arms on knees and watched with the unhappy thought that Jiro was showing his age— getting a little gray around the muzzle, evidencing more than a little complacency in his retirement.

The girl ducked under Jiro's neck and Jiro did not react; but the girl kept her hand quite properly on Jiro's shoulder as she dodged through, too, the way he had told her to; and Jiro was sun-warmed and lazy.

The girl's help with the chores, Shoka thought, would give him time to do the repairs in the stable, but he was not doing that sitting here and watching, sun-lazy as the horse, be-spelled and letting the lazy daytime flow through his mind, thinking, when he thought at all, that it was a great deal easier just to sit.

*   *   *

He sat on the porch, watched her work and weed; and took the chance finally to repair the stitching on Jiro's bridle, work that agreed with aching muscles and the bruises he had.

And when, in late afternoon, she came up to the house all sweating and with her hair sticking around the edges of her face: "Wash," he said.

She bowed and went in and got the bucket.

"Clean clothes," he said. "And take the water bucket for filling: no need to make two trips."

She bowed again, on her way across the porch, went back and came out again with a change of clothes in the washing bucket, and the empty water bucket in the other hand.

And passed him and stopped at the foot of the steps. "Master Saukendar—shouldn't I take my lesson first?"

"Are you questioning my methods?"

"No, master Saukendar."

"You were panting when you walked up here. You haven't the wind to spare. When you do, there's a slope, up through the trees. Run to the top, run down again. Do it every evening before your bath."

"All right," she said; and set the buckets on the edge of the porch and started off at a jog.

He watched her go, watched her disappear into the trees; and knew himself how high that hill was and what a climb the top was.

He had an idea that she would stay that pace about a stone's throw, and then she would run and walk a little; and finally take the hill at a walk if she had even that strength left.

It would be quite a while, he thought, till she would be back; and he looked at the sky with a little concern: he had no wish to be climbing that hill himself even at a walk, stiff as he was, with the leg giving him trouble, searching for the girl lost in the woods . . .

No, not that one. She might not make it to the top, but he trusted her to find her way down again. Eventually.

He sat and drowsed on the porch through a gold and lavender sunset and into the edge of dark until he heard running steps coming down the slope; and saw her returning—soaked in sweat, and staggering up to the porch, a pale-faced ghost in the dusk.

But by then he was on his way to the door.

He did not say a thing to her. He walked into the cabin. He heard her drag the buckets off the porch; and he was hungry and annoyed at the prospect of a late supper.

But he hung up Jiro's newly-mended bridle on the peg by the door, lit the solitary lamp and stirred up the coals. He had tea on and the rice simmered with some of the squash from the garden before she came trudging in out of the dark with a bucket of wet clothes and another of drinking water.

"You're late," he said. "I expect supper at dusk."

"Yes, master Saukendar."

"Eat." He dipped up a bowlful and shoved it at her; and she took it with a: "Thank you, master Saukendar," and staggered out to the porch to sit down in the dark, where a breeze made it cooler.

He took his own supper out. "I want my tea," he said.

"Yes, master," she said; and got up after a second try and staggered after it and brought out his cup and hers.

"Eat," he said, when she sat there after, staring at the bowl in her hands and no seeming strength to lift it. "Eat, do we have food to waste?"

She dutifully ate, tiny bite by tiny bite, and did not finish what he gave her. "I'll have it for breakfast," she said.

He scowled at her, finished his, and said, "You can wash the pot before you go to bed."

She nodded, and got up and fetched the pot out of the cabin, staggered off the side of the porch and went around toward the back of the cabin where the rain-barrel stood.

He went inside, stripped down and was comfortable

in his bed in the dark cabin by the time she brought the pot in.

She was moving stiffly in the morning, but she stirred out at dawn, while Shoka lay in his blankets and caught a little more rest. When she came back and while she was making breakfast he went out for his own bath at the rain-barrel, shaved at his leisure, and came back to the porch again to find a hot cup of tea.

No complaint from her, not one objection.

Poor fool girl, he thought, sitting there sipping tea and watching Jiro cropping grass in his pasture down by the stable.

Not that she had run the damned hill to the top, he did not believe that for a moment; but at the least she had made a brave try at it. The stable was cleaned; the garden was weeded. He watched her this morning as she gave him his breakfast and carefully sat down on the rim of the porch with her own.

Poor fool indeed. Sore in every muscle. He rubbed the soreness in his own bad leg, and remembered the wound that had lamed him—the melee on the road, Jiro all but pulled down and trying to get up again under him, a blade coming from an angle where the breeches were not double-sewn, a blow that took his health and destroyed his belief in his own invulnerability.

He remembered another thing, when he thought of that; and while the girl was around back washing up the dishes, he went inside and rummaged among the pots by the cookpit, til he found the small clay jar with the beeswax stopper. It held an herbal grease he used nowadays for cooking-burns and sunburn. But it had other virtues. It was thanks to that salve he had healed as well as he had.

"Here," he said, when she came in, and he offered her the little pot. "For the wound." He indicated the line of it on his own face. "Morning and evening. It lets the skin stretch."

She looked at him with a little bewilderment, unstopped the jar and smelled it.

"Do it," he said. So she took some on her fingers and smeared it on the side of her face; and further down her neck where the wound was drawing. She gave one little sigh and a second, and turned a look of gratitude toward him—for what relief he very much remembered.

"That wasn't four weeks ago," he said, indicating her face, because that small discrepancy worried him.

"No," she said. "On the road."

Tight and clipped. She had no evident desire to talk about it; and did not complicate matters with confidences and tears.

Thank the gods. Sobbing women had always affected him; fools who expected rescue from their folly had always infuriated him; and considering that she was only a girl and a person of no high upbringing, she was remarkable, he thought, in many ways quite remarkable in her level-headedness.

One hoped to the gods she was not pregnant, that was all.

He waved a hand at her when she started to pass the jar back.

"Keep it. I get it from the village. Use it all if you need it. Meanwhile Jiro wants currying, the garden wants watering—we missed the rain; and when you're through with that, I'll show you how to deal with the tack."

"Slower!" he shouted after her, as she started her evening run up among the trees: day upon day of such running—and her time grew shorter, her wind grew better; but that headlong attack on the hill told him well enough how far she was going—about a third of the way up, he reckoned, maybe half. She had no idea how to pace herself. "Slower! You have to hold that pace!"

She slowed. He watched her from the porch until she disappeared among the trees, then turned his attention

back to his leatherwork, using a hammer, block and
punch, making holes for lacings in what would be, by a
few hours work, a good pair of shoes.

He had been saving that hide. But the girl could not
go barefoot, to the nunnery, to the village, or on the
mountain in the winter.

He had gotten her pattern, traced it on with a piece
of charcoal, and cut it in the afternoon. Now came the
stitching.

The soles were done by the time she showed up
again, sweated and coughing, and leaning with her
elbows on the porch.

"Off," he said. "Go. Wash. You're a sight."

She caught a breath and got up and looked at what he
was doing. The work was not at a stage that looked like
anything.

It was the last time he let her see the boots until he
had finished them, on the day after. They had started
out practical, and plain, but he had thought that a bit of
fox-fur about the calf was easy enough to do; and that a
little extra stitching on the front would make the top
resist stretching; and the pattern might as well go down
around the instep while he was about it.

He had never bothered making decoration for his
own: they were boots and the oiled-leather kept his feet
dry, which was all he asked; more, he had never had
the time. Now he took the time, now that the garden
was weeded, the stable was strawed, Jiro was well
content, and the cabin had become marvelously orderly
in the time the girl had been here.

So he set the finished boots on her sleeping mat the
evening they were done, while she was still out running
the hill; and waited patiently for her to find them when
she went in to cook.

She was very quiet inside when she had gone in, for
a long time, when there was usually the clatter of pots
and the making of dinner. She came out finally with the
boots in her arms and bowed formally. "Thank you,

master Saukendar," she said, in a meeker, more anxious voice than he had ever heard her use.

"Do they fit?"

"Yes, master Saukendar."

"Well?"

"Thank you, master Saukendar." She stroked the fox-fur.

Which was all the thanks he got, when he had hoped for maybe a little more, but it seemed she thought the gift was extravagant.

"Tomorrow," he said, "I'll show you the mountain."

She looked at him cautiously, with a dawning excitement in her eyes.

"I might do a little hunting," he said.

Taking her hunting with him was one way that he thought of not to leave her unwatched with Jiro and his belongings in the cabin: there were still times when he remembered, just as he was about to fall asleep of nights, that he knew nothing for certain about her, and that she might simply be a patient enemy, waiting her chance to do him harm.

He disbelieved that by broad daylight; but he did not disbelieve it enough to leave her in possession of the cabin for hours on end. In that consideration it seemed only prudent to find out what she did know about stalking—game or other quarry—and what kind of traps she might think of.

She would have taken her bow when he took up his from beside the door. "No," he said. "Not unless you need a walking-staff."

She gave him an offended look.

But she left the wretched bow and followed him into the woods.

He had piled up brush here and there about the mountain, and that was usually good for a rabbit now and again, just a matter of walking quietly and never touching the shelter itself, but setting snares here and there.

Taizu moved well enough keeping up with him, and she watched where she was putting her feet. She made little sound in the brush, evading the branches that might whisper against a passing arm or leg.

Not a farm-girl's skills, he thought. *Not* a farm-girl's way of moving.

He recollected the trap she had set for him, a damned skillfully set one.

That was another thing no farm-girl would know. Like we set for the soldiers, she had said.

He stopped finally to let the woods settle, moved up to a rocky slope and sat down; and in that idle time he thought to teach her a few simple hand-signs such as his father had taught him.

She repeated them for him, quickly, clearly, signs for actions and directions, and for the various animals that came and went on the hill.

Then he taught her the one for *man*.

"There are bandits yonder by Hoishi," he whispered. "And now and again a boy from the village comes up here with supplies. You've seen the village. The bandits— are different. I trust you'll know."

He caught a momentary expression as she nodded— something angry and hard and patient.

"If you see anyone that doesn't look like a villager, you don't lead them to the cabin; you don't get yourself caught; and you warn me as fast as you can. Understood?"

Again that look of intense concentration.

"Repeat the signs," he said. It was what his father had done to him, making him recall after he had stopped expecting it.

She gave them back to him and named them aloud, one by one, without a mistake.

Quick. Damned quick to understand.

It was a mortal shame that a girl owned the godgiven gifts that would make an exceptional student of arms.

But it was of no use at all to a nun, or to a farmer's servant—to know how to hunt. And he imagined how amused the court in Cheng'di would be to see him

crouched here in serious converse with a pig-keeper or
teaching a woman hunter-signs; and he imagined much
more what a joke they would make of it if he took to
teaching her more martial skills than that, or taking her
for a partner in his hunting.

But if it kept her content, if in the process of fulfilling
his promise to her he taught her to protect herself so he
needed not worry so much about her becoming a hostage or fecklessly guiding some bandit attack back to
the cabin—

Well, by the gods above and below, he did not have
court gossip to contend with any longer, it was not
Chiyaden he lived in now, and if Saukendar took a girl
to warm his bed and if it amused him to teach his girl to
hunt with him and to do men's work—then that was his
concern and none of theirs.

Let her immediate anger burn itself away in hard
work; and let her grow fond of the place and of him.
Then natural womanly impulses would take over, she
would give up her notions of revenge and settle into the
turning of the seasons and the planting and the hunting.

Damn, it was easy to get used to her.

She could be some use on the mountain; *she* had a
wit and spirit he had not imagined in any woman outside the court. She . . .

. . . was the first human being who had stirred anything in him in years, and he had no inclination to see
her go back down a road she had survived as much by
luck as cleverness—this time armed with a fatal overconfidence. Fools always perturbed him. Young fools
he personally could forgive, and principled young fools
he could even admire, remembering his youth and his
young notions of justice. . . .

But the world at large gave them no special grace,
the gods, if they existed, made no exceptions for good
motives; and young fools never understood that.

They came back again toward evening with a rabbit
their snares had taken: summer was no time to take the

larger game, in the months that meat spoiled quickly. Deer came across their trail and they let them go; it was past the season for berries, but there were wild greens to pick, and they came back cheerful with the makings of a fine supper.

"You see to the rabbit," Shoka said, putting his bow away. "I'll see to Jiro this evening."

Which he did, taking more time than he was wont to do on days when he hunted—but supper was arranging itself without his doing a thing, and he felt himself wonderfully at ease in his life.

He came up the hill to the smell of cooking, he sat down on the porch in the twilight as he had gotten very accustomed to doing, and had his tea and a bowl of savory rice and greens and rabbit.

And had the girl's not unpleasant company, as she talked about the woods and asked him what sort of mushrooms grew there and compared them to the mushrooms in Hua province. She named plants and asked if they grew on his mountain and he confessed he did not know all the answers.

"It was not part of my study," he said, "in Cheng'di or in Yiungei. I know the common names, and the mushrooms, and the ones to avoid."

She made a sound past a mouthful of rice. "I know. I can do that for you too."

Meaning that he should not send her to the nuns or to the village. So she was still eager to stay, even considering the work he heaped on her—

"It's good," he said, tapping the bowl. "Very good. You're an excellent cook."

Her face darkened, as if that had made her remember something or someone; and he thought desperately, searching for something to draw her away from that:

Ask her what? About her family?

Gods, no.

Her marriage prospects?

None.

"You did very well today."

She nodded.

Damn. One ploy down.

"You've hunted before."

A second nod.

"Gods, girl. Talk."

She stared at him, puzzled and disturbed.

"What," he asked her, "did you hunt back in Hua?"

"Rabbits. Mushrooms."

"Elusive and treacherous things. Who taught you to stalk?"

"My brothers." Her jaw knotted. "They're dead now."

Damn, again. There was no way to talk to her without touching something dark. Or maybe there was nothing but that, inside her, around her. He felt the coming night a little colder.

"So far," he said, between bites, "I haven't seen any reason to take you to the nuns. So far, I don't intend to."

"You said you'd show me how to make a bow."

"I don't recall I said that."

She stared at him, slowly chewing.

"For one thing, you don't haggle it. If there was any long grain in that piece of wood you ruined it. What did you use, an axe?"

She nodded.

"Where is it?"

"Lost it."

"Where?"

"Threw it at this man."

"Who?"

"On the road."

"I didn't ask where, I asked who."

"Man came up on me in the woods."

Piece by piece. "A man could get tired talking to you. Can't you *tell* a story, for the gods' sake?"

"You want me to say?"

"Entertain me."

"It was muddy and I got wet: I was going to make a place to sleep; but this man came up across the stream, and I couldn't talk, he might know I was a girl; so I grabbed up my stuff and I was going to leave, but he told me stay. So I said keep away. So he came across the stream and I flung the axe at him and I ran. I was afraid to go back for it. I figured he could be behind me carrying it."

He nodded. "Why not the bow?"

"It was wet. It was raining."

He sighed, rested his chin on his hand, his empty bowl in his lap, and looked at her, while she looked at him as if he had totally bewildered her.

Gods, what is this girl?

"He was going to come at me," she protested.

"I don't doubt."

She looked at him with misgivings then, as if confusions had piled up on her; she ducked her head and hunted a last few grains of rice on the side of her bowl.

"Girl," he said, "I don't know what happened back in Hua, but bandits have rarely bothered this place. You don't have to be afraid."

"I'm not afraid."

"You can't right every damn wrong in the world, even when it's your own wrong. Take that from me. People have come to me, asking me to come settle some grievance or another. All the stories are sad. But you know I can't help them? That's the greatest wisdom I've learned up here on this damn mountain. Manage your own troubles. Live peacefully. The sunrise and the sunset are more important than the rise and fall of Emperors. That's my whole philosophy. I give it to you."

She frowned and stared at her empty bowl.

"You understand me?" he asked her. He was not sure, sometimes, with her accent, that she did understand the language he spoke, or the words he used. He tried to keep things simple.

"I hear you."

"I didn't ask if you heard me, I asked if you understood."

"Teach me to make a proper bow. Teach me the sword. That's what I want."

"Girl, there are a lot of things I can teach you. . . ."

She shot him a wary, worried look under one brow, the kind of warning the man might have gotten before she flung the axe.

"Among them," he continued doggedly, "the gentleness a man ought to use with a woman."

She scrambled up to her feet, disappeared inside and came out with the bucket they used for drinking water, to set it on the porch the way she always did before her evening run up the hill.

"You can leave that off," he said.

"No," she said.

"I said to leave it off. Dammit, it's dark under the trees. You've hiked all through the woods; you can run tomorrow."

"I said I would run it."

"*I* say you won't." He put his feet down on the ground beside the porch, got up and walked up the three steps, a little stiff: he always was when he had been sitting cross-legged. "You also said you'd do as you're told; and you're not running in the dark." He saw the fear in her eyes, and lowered his voice. "Do I worry you? You needn't worry. Because a man says he'd like to show you a little kindness, do you think it's cause to run away from him?"

The fear did not go away. She only looked at him as if she were caught between choices, each one terrible.

"Girl, I wasn't celibate before I came up here; and if you think you look like a boy, and if you think I can share a cabin with a woman after nine years on this mountain and not have certain impulses, you've got a damn sight more to learn about men."

"You took me for your student, master Saukendar. What kind of man would lay hands on his student?"

"You're a girl! You don't change that!"

"Your word didn't say anything about that. You agreed. That's all of it."

"You listen to me, girl. You don't change nature. What you ask isn't reasonable!"

"You swore it."

"I was humoring a lunatic!"

"But you swore it. And it's your honor, isn't it, if you break your word the gods will remember it. You swore you'd take me for a student, and that you wouldn't lay a hand on me. Are you going to break your oath?"

"Fool! You won't last it out. There was never any hope of that. High time you realized it and started thinking about how you're going to provide a living for yourself."

"All you have to do is teach me. And I got here, master Saukendar, I got here on my own and you say yourself I'm good in the woods. I set a trap you walked right into, didn't I? And I've done everything you've set me to do, so you don't have any cause to complain about me. You teach me the same way you would a boy, and I'll learn the same as any boy."

"The way you run the hill?"

"The way I run the hill."

"Oh, come, girl, don't lie to me. You've never finished that course."

"I do!"

"Damn, you've never even seen the top of the hill. You sit down when you get winded, you rest till you think it's time and you run down, don't tell me you're going all the way to the top."

"Then follow me."

That stung: he could not run that hill himself, not with his lame leg, and he was sure she knew that and that she was deliberately making the point. He folded his arms and gave her a hard look. "Girl, you're trying me."

"I'm not a cheat."

He gave her a long, long stare. "You maintain that you're going all the way to the top. That you're not waiting it out. You're not lying to me."

"No."

"A truth for a truth: I expected you not to get half-way. Now tell me that you didn't, and I'll call it even and nothing will change. Students have pulled tricks like that since the sun was spawned. But by the gods if you lie to me eye to eye and I catch you in it, all agreements are off—and I will catch you, understand me?"

"I'm not lying!"

"Last chance."

"I'm not lying."

"Stay off the hill tonight. Get a good night's sleep. Tomorrow you'll need it. Or you'll tell me you've lied. Because if I find out you have—I'm free of anything I ever promised you. That's the end of it."

Jiro laid his ears back when the blanket and saddle went on; and he pricked them up again as Shoka led him out into the daylight where Taizu waited, sitting on the fence.

"All right," Shoka said, as Jiro worked the bit and tugged at the reins close-held in his fist. "I'll give you a head start. Down to the far end of the pasture and up again."

Taizu looked in that direction, the long slope of the shoulder where an old burn-off had left very few trees, part of the hill clear of woods had grown over with grass and weeds. He had hewed the saplings of the regrowth, burned and cut the stumps; used the trimmed trees for railing; and widened the pasturage year by year. Now it compassed all of a broad downward slope before it dropped away suddenly at the end and sides.

Taizu nodded and set off at a jog toward the railing of the pen, ducked under and set out at an easy pace across the pasture beyond.

He led Jiro over to the gate, opened it, led him through and swung up to the saddle as Jiro worked the bit and started to move.

"Faster!" he yelled at the girl.

She quickened her pace; and he let her get a good

long start across the pasture before he gave Jiro his head.

Jiro snorted and fought for more rein. Shoka held him in, feeling Jiro's uneasiness, seeing the way Jiro's ears came up with the girl a distant figure framed between them.

Faster and faster, Jiro fighting to break loose of the rein, the gap between them and the girl less and less. Jiro's ears went back. The warhorse knew one purpose to a chase and he had no compunction at all in a fight.

"Faster!" Shoka yelled.

The girl did not look back. She put on a burst of speed and Jiro ducked his head, fighting to get the bit.

"He'll knock you flat!" Shoka yelled. "Keep ahead of him!"

She dodged around one of the few standing trees and Jiro needed no rein to veer around and keep after her. The horse kept fighting for the bit, trying all his tricks as the girl reached the fence, hit the top rail with her hands, and dived back the other way, halfway through her course.

The horse fought to turn and cut her off, and Shoka took him wide, complete turn about, while the girl lit out on the uphill slope of the meadow.

Damn, she was not winded yet.

He put Jiro to a faster pace; and the girl took a dodge through a series of three standing trees, in and out among a handful of small, sharp stumps he had not yet cleared.

"All right, girl," he muttered to himself; and loosened up on the reins a bit, letting Jiro take the weaving course at a faster pace.

But the girl suddenly sprinted all out for the stable fence higher up the hill.

Damn, she was going to make it.

He gave Jiro his heels then, a full-tilt course uphill, to cut in between the girl and the fence at the last moment.

She veered off as Jiro's shoulder all but brushed her

and Jiro spun on his own, coming up on his hind legs as
Shoka reined back and then let up again.

Jiro dived after the girl, and the girl ran all out, for
the side fence, this time, then as Jiro closed that distance, cut across and tried to double back to the stable
fence.

"No, you don't!" Shoka yelled at her, and pulled Jiro
across to cut her off a second time, nettled and amazed
that there was so much speed left in the girl.

She changed direction again for the side, a sudden
sprint and a dart down the pasture, and he herded her
back again; another sprint toward the uphill, and he cut
that off.

The girl was drenched in sweat now; and reeled back
as Jiro came close with his shoulder, reeled back and
darted opposite to Jiro's right-hand cornering, shot
straight for the fence; but Shoka put his heels to Jiro
and Jiro stretched out in a run, cut between her and
the fence, hard-breathing and snorting as he turned.

She dodged back almost under Jiro's rump: Jiro kicked
and Shoka reined him aside, which Jiro took for a
full-about signal and dived again to head her back.

She turned again, stumbled this time; and kept running, while he took Jiro about and spun him into a full
turn to get Jiro under control before he dived after the
girl again; and the girl dodged back toward the fence,
stumbling now, while he reined circles around her.

He did not expect the final sprint that flung her for
the rails. She grabbed the fence, tried to go over it and
collapsed on her knees in the dust there, clinging to the
rail. She bent helpless for a moment, coughing, gasping
after breath, then shook back her sweaty hair and stared
sidelong up at him, one eye in eclipse under the mop,
the other glaring reproachfully up at him what time she
was not coughing.

Daring him to say that she lied. And he knew now in
his heart that she had not. She had run that damned
mountain, beyond any doubt.

He hated to be caught in the wrong. And doubly

hated, even considering that she was a fool and worse for everything she wanted, to have asked the impossible and pushed her as far as he had, twice over, to end up with her in the right and himself very conspicuously the villain in the exchange.

Damn. And he had put his word on the outcome.

"All right," he said finally, from the height of Jiro's back, "I'll teach you as far as you can go. But wherever you fail, you fail, and I'll hear no excuses."

She tried to straighten up. She hauled herself up against the railings and hung there.

"You'll cramp like hell if you don't cool down slowly," he said. "Walk up to the house, wrap up, I'll put some water on to boil."

She nodded, just that single move of her head. She climbed awkwardly through the fence and staggered off across the stable pen.

Damn, damn, and damn.

But he found himself seriously considering that she might make a student after all. She was fast enough and strong enough to learn far more than he had reckoned; and perhaps—one hoped—she would listen to good sense along the way.

Chapter Four

He did not sleep well that night. He kept thinking of Chiyaden, for reasons that he could not understand.

Perhaps, he thought, it was that he contemplated teaching; and teaching, he had to remember how he was taught and the things he had learned; and the learning of them had been in Chiyaden, and in his youth, and at his father's hand and at old master Yenan's, in the court at Cheng'di.

A great many of those memories would have been pleasant to recall, except he knew what his father's plans had come to. His father had set him, before he died, to serve the old Emperor in the Emperor's waning years— and, in his father's place, he had tried, earnestly tried, he had sacrificed everything he could in a personal way; he had defended the old Emperor against assassins; he had taken every precaution he could to preserve the Empire and the peace. But no martial skill had availed against the wilfulness of an heir who had conspired in the execution of his appointed caretakers and who had intended with everything that was in him, to see that Saukendar followed them to disgrace.

65

There was no wisdom that might have saved Chiyaden, except to wish that the Emperor had brought up a better son; except to wish the old Emperor had taught Beijun more, indulged him less when he was young, used a stronger hand to separate him from bad companions. . . .

Gods knew what would have served: he had tried to advise the old Emperor regarding his heir and his companions: his father before him had given the same advice, all disregarded. Maturity will change him, the old Emperor had said of his son. Responsibility will change him. Give him time.

In his nightmares he saw his friend Heisu under the axe; and the sensible lady the young Emperor had married—

—that *he* should have married, except the Emperor decreed Meiya for his son—

—Meiya sitting at the garden window with the poisoned cup in her hand, fragile porcelain, elegant as everything about her.

Damn, damn, and damn! Damn Beijun for a fool and himself—

Meiya had thought to the last, perhaps, that he would arrive in time; that he would cleave his way to her rescue. But no one had told him: the order was signed and sealed by the Emperor and the killers were on their way when she had drunk that cup, while he himself was two days away from the capital on a fool's mission the young Emperor had assigned him.

It could not have been the young Emperor's planning. Ghita's, beyond a doubt; Shoka had had nine years to live with that reckoning, that he had been caught for a fool, that if there was any adultery with the lady Meiya—

—at least of the heart—

He clenched his fists and twisted on his mat, and stared into the dark where Meiya's gentle countenance did not have the substance she did in his memories.

You have a duty, his father had counseled him, when

the old Emperor had proclaimed his wishes regarding his son's betrothal to the lady Meiya; the welfare of the Empire comes above every other thing. Think of your oath.

Shoka had rebelled against that decision: he had served the Emperor—and this was the reward of it, Meiya given to a fool, because the Emperor, in his slow dying, knew that his son needed strong advisers; and chose Meiya and through Meiya, her father lord Peidan; and besides Meiya, lord Heisu of Ayendan; and Saukendar, heir to Yiungei province, not least in that number.

His father had counseled him wisely in everything but this, that he give his devotion in due time to the new Emperor as to the old; that he persuade Beijun slowly to good sense; that he trust Meiya and Heisu and his own influence could take a self-indulgent, stupid boy and make an Emperor out of him.

This much was true, at least, that if he had arrived in time and carried Meiya away to exile, Ghita's assassins would never have given up; and that if Meiya had been with him on the road he would never have gotten this far.

But Shoka had heard the news too late for any such chances. In the years since her betrothal to the young Emperor, he and Meiya had grown apart, so that, far from thinking first of her when he had heard about her passing among the other deaths that terrible day, Meiya had seemed less in importance than Heisu and her father.

Later he had realized where his grief was. The soldiers like Heisu, the scholars like Baundi, the loyal guard and the retainers—they had run risks and most of them had had weapons and at least a chance to defend themselves. For Meiya of Kiang, immured in the palace, trusting to her wits, so gentle in her upbringing she could not have lifted a hand in her defense, there had been only the cup—a recourse delayed to the last moment that she had any choice.

It was that gesture that haunted his nights, the suspi-

cion that, lacking any reasonable prospect of mercy
from her husband, she had still hoped in someone; that,
and the fact that he had not even thought of her first
among the dead. Lady Meiya had sat with the deadly
cup in hand, watching by the garden window that looked
out on the southern road; and hoped to the last for a
lover she had given up fifteen years before.

They had put lord Heisu on trial for adultery in the
same hour they had invaded his apartments and dragged
him out; and Ghita's hand-picked judges had found
Heisu guilty on the evidence of lady Meiya's suicide.
That was the shape of justice in the new court, with the
old Emperor's ashes not yet cold. They had struck off
Heisu's head and mounted it at the north gate of
Cheng'di, the gate that looked toward Heisu's province
of Ayendan.

Shoka had known when he had heard the news, that
returning to the capital was hopeless, that there were
no allies to draw on: the plot was too thorough, the
Guard and the army itself subverted with gold and
promises: the order was out for his arrest as well, as
Heisu's accomplice in treason in plotting to seize the
throne. So the rot he had seen in the court had festered
and burst, and there was no rising of indignation among
the lords or the people, just a general scramble to find a
safe position in the regime-to-come.

That was why he had run for the border. That was
why he had saved his own life, after he had so badly
misjudged how far the young Emperor would go: the
young fool Beijun had quitted the court in a fit of anger
and run to Ghita for shelter from him. The young Emperor
had sought shelter from *him*, that was the fact; and that
Beijun was Chosen of Heaven and anointed by the
priests put a sanctity about him that, even in that hour,
Shoka had respected all too much.

Fool, he thought now. But when he considered who
else might have sat the throne, or who would have had
the force to hold it—there was no one . . . not after the
brutal example of lord Heisu; and not in the opposition

of the priests, the hired ones and the simple-minded ones who simply, doggedly, upheld the Chosen of Heaven, even when he was a fool. It was the will of the gods that the Empire was to suffer. It was the will of the gods that murder was done. Was not the Emperor the arbiter of right, the interpreter of the divine, the Bridge to Heaven?

As the priests went, so went the people, who hoped in the gods, and mostly hoped to be let alone: least of all would they fight against the priests. Shoka had understood that the first time a band of peasants tried to collect the reward on his head. He had spent his life thinking first of his obligations and his Emperor; he had defended the law; he had given up everything for the sake of Chiyaden and the Emperor in Cheng'di; and Chiyaden, in the end, had betrayed him.

So what do I have to teach you, girl? Wisdom? I've found none here either.

I had a dozen lovers. There was one love. I gave that up. I honored my father, she honored hers, we were fifteen: what do children know?

He could not forget the cup, lady Meiya, and the window, the way the stories told it—that solitary perfect image, as if he had been there, in that room, in that moment that she gave up hope—even though their converse in later years had all been plotting how to extricate the heir from his wild-living friends, how to circumvent lord Ghita and his cronies, how to persuade the dying Emperor to take at least some action to protect himself against assassination. . . .

If she had been his wife—

But Meiya had chosen duty too.

So she was dead and he was in lifelong exile, plagued now by a young fool of a peasant girl who thought that she could right the wrongs her family had suffered, that blood would account for her people's blood, or that the ghosts would not cease then to trouble her sleep.

One could not advise fools. Fools, old master Yenan

had been wont to say, have to mend their foolishness before they can listen. They have to know what truth is.

So that was the first thing—for a girl who did not want to be a girl, for a fool who wanted revenge that would profit her nothing.

That was the first thing that had to change.

Gods, he wanted to hit her. And he could not understand the why of that either, except that she was a fool.

That he wanted to sleep with her—with a scar-faced pig-girl—seemed like an exorcism, a coupling with a creature as rough and ungentle as he could imagine. Shoka's choice, not Saukendar's. Shoka's consolation. Not the woman he could have had.

Damn, better a woman who could take care of herself in the place he was condemned to live in, better a woman as real as the dirt and the summer heat.

Meiya was—what, twenty-two years ago?—when he had been young and whole, when he had believed there was right in the world.

This girl—Taizu—came to him like a second chance.

Teach her the sword.

Gods!

"Heel thus," he said to her, tapping the ground with the stick. "Toe." He pushed her foot into line, and walked around her, tapping an elbow, a knee, surveying her from all sides.

"Break," he said then. "Relax." And when she had drawn the first breath. "Resume your guard."

She looked at him, betrayed, and he thwacked her on the back of the calves.

"Resume your guard."

She wobbled desperately into position.

He thwacked her again, rapidly, on a misaligned toe, a knee, an elbow. Limbs jerked nervously into a half-remembered line.

He put her carefully back into position.

"Stand there a while," he said. "Until your body remembers."

And he went to sit in the shade and enjoy a cup of tea.

"Turn! Turn! Turn!" Shoka yelled, and the girl spun into guard position and spun and spun again, perfect in her alignment. She landed on guard and he brought his stick whistling around at her shins. She jumped over it and landed again on soft-shod feet, immaculate in her posture.

He took a tentative swipe at the backs of her knees.

She jumped, wrong move for that attack. The staff clipped her legs. She still recovered and landed.

"No," he said, and leaned on his staff with both hands, considering her, her reach, her balance.

There was only one student he had had—and Beijun had dodged out on his practices, whined when he took a fall, lamented the sweat and the exertion.

A line of sweat trickled down Taizu's face. She did not move from her guard. She waited.

"There's no more you can learn without the sword," he said. "There is a counter for that move. The sword is part of it. The sword makes the difference in your balance."

He walked up to the house without a word then, took the rag-wrapped sword from its place in the corner and brought it out where she stood waiting, in front of the porch.

He drew it and threw the sheath onto the porch. "Break," he said.

She came off-guard, wisely, warily.

"It's all right," he said, and held out the sword to her hilt-first. "Resume guard. Take it gently, gently as you can. I'll let you have the weight little at a time. Light with the fingers, understand?"

She nodded, came on guard with her face quite set and eager, but there was no grabbing at it: she took it exactly the comfortable way.

"That's right. That's one-handed. Second hand, now."

There was only one comfortable way, in that position. She found it.

"Exactly right," he said, with a sense of satisfaction the young Emperor had never given him, a feeling all but sensual. "Flawless."

She heard. She gave the tiniest of nods. But the muscles never varied.

"This is the weight. This is all the weight. Don't be aware of the sword. The sword is your right arm. Keep the body in position. Think of that position. Don't feel the sword. Feel your centering. When you feel it perfectly, go through your moves." He stepped clear. "Not until you're ready. Begin like the beginning: slowly."

She stood still for several breaths. The movement when it came was as perfectly centered as the resting-posture. Each step in the advance and turn was exact.

"Stop," he said, and she stopped in mid-turn, in a position she could hold for a very long while. He lifted his hand to a point in the air. "Bring your point to my fingers."

The steel touched.

"Now complete your move slowly and keep the point always in contact with my fingers."

He walked the half-circle with her turn, until her feet were in base position. "Again," he said, and walked it again. He did it seven times more, slow, stopping from time to time, at which she would stop, and her eyes never left his eyes, the way he had taught her.

Graceful, he thought. Beautiful. Not the face, but the perfection of the balance, the attention of the eyes— absolute attention.

"When you're ready," he said. "There should be no strain."

He drew back his hand, stepped back and watched her, amazed at the pig-girl who moved like a figure in a drifting dream.

His teaching, he thought. He was capable of creating something like this.

He felt the impulses in his own muscles, the remembrance what that movement felt like, rightly done. He had moved like that once.

But he could not do it now. He would never do it
again. He had constantly to recall that too.

"Again!" he said, and sat and watched while the girl
went through the pattern, sweating profusely now in
the late summer heat. He watched, and finally, having
made up his mind, got up and walked to where she
stood, panting, having finished the exercise.

He took hilt and fist in his hand and stretched her
arm outward. "Hold that," he said, and walked back
again to sit and work at the scraping of a rabbit-skin.
He stank of rabbit. She stank of sweat. It was one of
those sticky, awful days when the rains flirted with the
hills and left the air thick and still.

He watched her arm droop, watched her struggle
with the pose, and hold it.

But after a little the whole arm began to tremble. He
watched her closely now, the clamping of the lips, the
fight to hold the arm with the shoulder muscles and
finally with the back and the chest.

"Break," he said, and she hove her whole body into
an effort to let that arm down with control.

"Resume."

She tried, and got the arm up. It began to sink
immediately.

So he got up off the porch and held her hand, felt
her forearm and the elbow and the upper arm, and
said: "That's not enough. Find me two hand-sized stones."

"Yes, master," she said, and went and sheathed the
sword and went looking.

She still ran the hill. She weeded and washed and
carried water. But the strength of the underarm and
ribs did not keep pace with the legs and the back, that
was the difficulty.

So she brought him the stones, and he had found
himself two slender sticks of wood from the woodpile at
the back of the cabin.

"Let me show you something," he said.

"Master," she said earnestly; and he gave her one of the sticks.

"Come on guard," he said. He had never yet fenced with her. It was all exercises until now.

He moved very slowly, touched her elbow with the stick he held while she looked at him as if she was not certain whether she ought to do something.

"Up," he said, and put her arm in its worst and weakest position. "I'm going to hit you. Hold onto the stick."

He cut upward, wood cracked on wood, and hers went flying.

She clapped a hand to her arm.

"Numb?"

"Yes, master Saukendar."

He threw the stick away. "Give me the rocks now," he said, and showed her with one of them how to move her arm. "Do that," he said, "often."

He went back to his rabbit-skins, and the stink and the mess. She might have done the scraping for him; but most of the extraordinary work was done, meals happened, and he refused to abdicate Jiro's care to the girl—the horse was getting too damned friendly with her.

And Taizu did not shirk any part of the day: she was working or she was practicing or he was actively teaching her; and he found it easy as not to teach her while he was doing something else.

They hunted from time to time—hence the rabbit-skins and the opossum. They had tracked wild pigs and had a good notion how to come by pork for sausages, with colder weather.

The cabin had never been so comfortable, the garden benefited, and there was a kind of tranquility between them.

Not that he stopped thinking about her across the cabin at night. Not that the urges went away.

But things had settled to a kind of truce, in which watching her had its own rewards, in which he saw a slow settling in the girl's mind, a calmness beginning that he had no wish to disrupt. That was very much on his side.

A second time the stick went flying.

He dropped his arm and stood there a moment, then took her arm and felt of the muscle underneath, where there was more strength than there had been, but not enough.

He had thought there was.

"Go bundle straw," he said to her, measuring with his hands, "a mat this thick, tall as I am, half again as wide. And make five times that much strong cord to tie it. Bring it up the hill."

She looked puzzled, but he did not answer questions about such things. She went down toward the barn.

He took a stick of seasoned wood and his hand-axe and began to trim it.

When she came up from the stable, she carried a huge mat rolled on her shoulder, and she had straw stuck in the weave of her shirt and straw in her hair and mud on her knees.

He had a pile of shavings and a well-trimmed foil.

He pointed it toward the youngish tree that stood, first of the forest, within view of the porch.

"Wrap the mat around its trunk and tie it fast, top, middle, and bottom," he said, and went on with his plane, smoothing the grip on it. He wrapped the grip about with leather and cord.

And when she had finished he walked out to the tree and took the guard position, making three passes, left and right and left, against the mat that padded the trunk, before he stood up and handed the foil to her.

"On your guard. Left, right, left."

She struck as he had told her.

"Again," he said. And: "Again."

The cabin reeked with the scent of boiling herbs and grease, and Shoka wrinkled his nose at the stink and lifted rag after rag out of the mixture with a stick, dropping it into a pan.

Taizu wrinkled her nose too when he brought the pan over to her, where she sat on the mat, but it was only half-hearted resistance. "Off with the shirt," he said; and when she looked at him with profound offense: "No silliness, girl. Off with it! I've no damn interest in your body at the moment. I'm treating you exactly like you asked me to, and I've no patience with squeamishness."

She carefully turned her back and tried, wincing, to pull the loose shirt up and over her head. Her arms could not even manage that much.

He set the pan down, pushed the shirt up over her shoulders and shoved her face down on the mat, then took one steaming rag and laid it over her back.

"Ai," she yelled.

"Hot?"

She made a muffled sound.

He took the rest of the mess rag by rag and, starting with her shoulders, wrapped the greasy cloth around her joints, and around her neck and her hands; and flung dry rags on top, and finally a blanket, to keep the heat.

"I've made a pot of the stuff," he said. "You might as well just toss the rags in it in the morning. We'll be boiling them tomorrow night." He patted her on her well-padded, quilt-covered backside. "And don't worry about your virtue. That salve would kill a goat's appetite."

Chips flew, the axe-blows echoed off the fire-leafed mountains. Time to make sure the woodpile was ready for colder weather. Shoka felled two trees and sectioned them, Jiro dragged the logs out of the wood, and thereafter, Shoka had said, handing the girl the axe, "As well this as the foil. Excellent for the shoulders."

She never objected to the work he gave her. She attacked the logs the way she attacked the exercise, the way she attacked the hill. Her hair had grown to her shoulders now. It shone with health. The scar was bright only when she sweated; and he watched her now, with the sun on her and the autumn colors starting in the brush—thinking how the abundance of food and the sun and the healthful work had put a glow about her face, fleshed out her bony limbs, put strength into the way she moved, the habit of graceful action.

If she would only smile, he thought, if he could only get laughter out of her, or even anger, or a little less skittish modesty.

But: "All right," she would say, no matter how outrageous his demand, as long as he kept his distance from her.

Except she had looked at him strangely when he had been felling the second of those trees, and when he had asked why:

"Nothing, master Saukendar."

It was entirely unlike her, not like her usual inward-turned reticence, but an outward-focused one, one in which he was the matter in her thoughts.

For the first time in weeks he remembered his old suspicions about her, and thought how comfortable he had grown with her, how very casual he had gotten about trusting her at his back.

Measuring him. That was the look. And he caught her at it several times that day.

And that evening, when he sat down on the porch with his bowl of rice:

"What in hell are you looking at?" he asked her.

"Master?"

"Just then. What were you looking at?"

"Nothing, master Saukendar."

He scowled at her and jabbed the chopsticks her direction. "Don't give me that kind of answer. *Nothing, master Saukendar.* Your eyes were open. You were awake. What in hell were you looking at?"

She bit her lip and said nothing.

"I don't like secrets, girl. Did I talk to you about honesty? You said teach you the sword. Let me tell you there's more to it than chopping wood *or* necks. Let me

tell you there's an obligation to honorable behavior.
About time I taught it to you. Do you want to answer
my question?"

"I was noticing—you go off your center when you
don't have to, master Saukendar."

"What *about* my center?" He stared at her in vexa-
tion, thinking first she had taken leave of her senses,
and then that she was deliberately insulting him.

"When you were using the axe. You were off your
center."

"Damned right I go off my center. Has it taken you
this long to notice the limp?"

"I didn't mean that."

"What do you mean?"

She looked at him, swallowed hard and said: "When
you use the axe. You do it on a lot of things. You're
turning your knee and your foot. You don't have to."

Damned impudent brat, was behind his teeth; but his
own speech about honesty stuck in his throat. He was
outraged. He wondered, mad as it made him, about
that nagging stiffness in his back that had begun to
trouble him in the last year or so.

Is it age? he wondered, over a mouthful of rice.

Is she right?

"I don't mean to speak out of turn, master Saukendar."

He simply glared at her. She ducked her head and
ate her dinner.

But when he got up from the porch he wondered,
when he walked inside he wondered: he tried to feel the
extent of stretch in his legs and the line of his back and
could not decide.

He wondered the next day too, went back to the back
and split some logs himself, and damn, he *was* doing it,
curling the toes on his lame side, turning the knee
inward to save the leg not from pain but from the
memory of pain. That was the stupid truth.

He took a deliberate swing at the log with the leg
straight and felt not the pain, but the strain of weak-
ened muscles.

He looked up then at a movement by the front corner of the cabin, and saw Taizu looking at him.

Damn you, he thought, and knew beyond a doubt she understood why he had taken a sudden notion to chop the wood himself this morning.

Especially since she ducked guiltily back around the corner, as if she had not known what he was about back behind the house.

He thought about it every time he did something familiar—when he carried buckets, climbed the porch steps, when he stood up or sat down. He made himself use both legs equally, and he knew, dammit, he *knew* that she was able to see that he was walking straighter and damned well sure why.

So one was honest. So one was a gentleman. One did not beat the pig-girl for telling the truth she was able to see. One was even grateful.

One wanted to go hunting, say, for three and four days and not have her dour, calculating stare shot his way when he limped and when he did not. But he would have to come back then, either limping or not, either having begun to do something about his habit or not, and in either case to have the damned girl staring at him and knowing she was right.

So one just tried not to favor the leg, that was all; one refused to limp even on a cool morning when the old wound ached. One went down to the stable where the girl could not see, and practiced the exercises he had not done in years, until the leg ached enough to set his teeth on edge, and his back hurt, and he earnestly wished that he could make up an excuse to use the hot compresses himself; but that also admitted that she was right.

And he refused to do that.

Chapter Five

"There's a boy coming," Taizu said, panting from the uphill dash, not panic, just news: they had both been looking for that visitor ever since the first red had touched the leaves.

"Get out of sight," Shoka said, which they had agreed on, too.

The village tends to gossip, he had said, when he explained the matter to her; and gossip gets down the roads as far as traders go, and it's far, far better if I do nothing at all out of the ordinary. Let the village think you've gone. Let them think I sent you off like the others. And he thought, in a sudden cold flash, remembering the bandits: For the gods' sake don't let them know I've got a girl up here. . . .

Because of a sudden it had occurred to him that she was not the skinny waif who had come up the mountain—hair dusty and dull and bobbed, body bowed under that damn basket.

The girl he was looking at was clear-skinned and bright-eyed and better-fed, hair shining and shoulder-

length, her every move balanced on hips that had nothing to do with the way a boy's were set.

Damn!

And he had thought, in that same visionary moment,
that if the village sent up one of the boys who had been
on the mountain before, there would still be gossip
even if he never had eyes on Taizu.

Something's different, the boy would be saying di-
rectly as he got back to the village . . . because there
was a more prosperous look to the clearing this year, in
the way the garden thrived, with the beans staked up,
the little plot of herbs in neat rows—he could not put
exact words to it himself, except that Taizu had a way of
putting things in their place, and keeping things orderly, and she hoed and she weeded and even attacked
the vines that tried to creep into the clearing and wind
around the fence-posts and overgrow the path to the
spring: she put up pegs to hang things on; she racked
the hoe and the rake like weapons; she hung up the
onions in chains and the herbs and roots in bunches.

Not the same, he thought. Nothing was the same on
the mountain. And he could not imagine how he had
ever thought about turning the girl over to the nuns.

Now she slipped off around the side of the cabin to
take herself, he imagined, to the vantage-point upon
the knoll from which she would watch the trading.
Being Taizu.

And he took his bundled furs, an uncommonly good
lot of them, from the rafter where they hung, and
brought them out to the porch as the boy from the
village trudged up with his pack of rice and other
goods.

"Master Saukendar," the boy said—Shoka did know
him, but it struck him that he had never bothered to
learn the boy's name, a stocky, broad-faced lad, who
wiped the sweat from his brow and set the packs down.

"Boy." Shoka nodded courteously as the boy bowed;
and found himself wondering about the youth—his family, who he was, why he was for the last several years

the one the village chose to bring its gifts. But it seemed late to ask things like that and Shoka had no idea at all why it suddenly mattered, or why questions occurred to him that never had—

—except once upon a time Saukendar the Emperor's right arm had known everything in court, and kept an attentive eye on details; and nowadays Shoka the recluse had given up the court and all that went with it.

Damn the girl, anyway. It was more than the weeds she chopped away at.

So he kept his questions and his curiosity to himself. Questions from his side encouraged questions from the boy's side, and that was nothing he wanted. Questions about the world brought answers about the world, and he had stopped wanting to hear about it nine years ago.

So he brought out his furs, he cast them grandly in a pile on the porch and said modestly: "I'll want a few loads of straw, if you can. I've some patching to do."

The village never bargained. It got more in the way of furs than usual this year because he had had more time to hunt, and the good rains had meant an abundance of rabbits and foxes; if this year he wanted a load of straw, that should be no hardship, in the good harvest that it had been.

(Don't you let them tell you there's been bad harvest, Taizu had said fiercely. It's good this year, no way it's not.)

"Aye, lord," the boy said. "I tell 'em, m'lord. I bring it. Tomorrow, if you like."

"Good lad." So much for hard bargaining. He was grateful to the boy; and he saw the young face flush, the eyes dart toward his and lower again, shyly, as he began to unwrap the pack the boy had brought.

There was rice, there was salt, there were sausages, wonderful sausages, there were small pottery jars of preserves and other things lovingly made by the women of the village. He remembered other such gifts, small jars sitting on his shelves until the winter, when he allowed himself such luxuries. He *knew* this jar, for instance, that it was a ginger preserve: for years it had come in the same kind of small pot, with a wax seal; and it was as good as ever graced the Emperor's table. For years some woman had been sending him this, and he had never truly taken account of the gifts before, the fruit and ginger, the small pots of sauces and spices that relieved the sameness of his diet.

"This is very kind," he said, unaccountably moved. "This is wonderful. Tell them so."

"Yes, m'lord," the boy said.

Oh, gods, boy, he thought then, staring at the young face, *I'm not a damn hero, I'm not worth all this, don't you see?*

But that was not what the boy had come up the hill to find, so truth was not, finally, what he owed the boy.

"My mother sent you a shirt," the boy said, unrolling it from the pack.

"It's very fine," he said, fingering the embroidery. "Tell her I thank her." And, a little embarrassed, weighing the rice and remembering that there were two to feed: "I wonder—I could use a bit more rice—"

"I can bring that, m'lord Saukendar."

"I'd be grateful."

There were three more fox skins and a great number of rabbits and squirrels in what he gave them. He did not feel it was unjust.

Taizu had said it was not unjust.

And as the boy left, he clapped the youth on the shoulder like a comrade in arms, which the boy took well to.

He had never understood *why* the village worshipped him. He had never asked for it. It frightened him. And he remembered that peasants had tried to trap him and many villages had joined his hunters in Chiyaden.

For the bounty on his head, he had thought.

But not these folk.

Taizu was no different than any pig-girl he had ever seen.

And at the same time she was very different.

(Lithe body whirling with a flash of cane in hand, flash of bare legs, bare slim midriff and white shirt flying. . . .)

He had never understood the countryfolk. He had never understood the minds of people who worked the land and herded pigs and provided the things that turned up on the tables and in the granaries. He knew the importance of them in war. He knew the importance of supply and he understood the logistics of moving forces among such people, what force a band of spear-wielding peasants could contribute and what they were worth in a fight, with the bows they were entitled to, and what the laws were (when there had been laws) about what an officer could do and demand of the villages. But he had no notion why these folk down in the village of Mon should be faithful to him, except that they might assume more of him than he was and more than he could do. Which made him angry.

No, it troubled his sense of honor, because he had known in his heart it was going on all these years, and he had never let himself wonder about it or worry about the cost.

So he sat and stared at the boy's departing back as the boy went back down the hill, taking to the road; and he had not moved when Taizu came back to the edge of the porch.

"What did he say, master?"

"Nothing," Shoka said. "He said nothing. Except he'll bring the straw and a little more rice. So we won't run short. And we can patch the roof."

Taizu looked at him strangely, squatting down on her haunches there in front of the porch where he sat; but he got up off the edge and said that he had work to do.

He did not, in fact, know what that was, but he took the bucket of scraps and went and walked up into the woods and over toward the shoulder of the hill, where the smaller meadow was, and the thicket, where they put the bits and ends of squash and bean-pods. It made for more rabbits next spring.

Even a man from the court had not needed a pig-girl to tell him that; or what became of the rabbits that got to depend on them.

And on the next day he went down the hill as far as the appointed place, a narrow track on which Jiro could not help him; but Taizu went along.

There was a pile of straw bales, which the village had left on the last level ground; and there was a small cairn of stones, which protected the basket of rice.

He gave her the rice basket to carry; and he gathered up one of the huge straw bales and sent her up the hill first, because his lame leg gave him trouble on a climb like this, and he had no desire to have her behind him, waiting on his clumsy shiftings of balance and telling him: *You're off your center, master Saukendar.*

He made up his mind not to carry the load that way, in his slow campaign to correct his balance: he shifted the stress on muscles until he could feel the pain, and he was sweating, out of breath and feeling the pull in the old scar when he dumped the first load at the very edge of the clearing. "You can get that up the rest of the way," he said, and turned and went back down the track.

That gave him some breathing room, while she had to take the basket of rice as far as the cabin and then come back downhill and move the straw. It let him take the downward trail slower, limping all he liked now that he was carrying nothing, and swearing with every aching step.

He was a fool. He should have had the boy bring help and carry the damned straw as far as the stable. The boy would have done that. The boy would have been delighted to do that for the great lord Saukendar, who was too crippled to climb the damn mountain.

He cursed the assassins who had done it to him. He saw the dark, the melee, remembered the blow like it was yesterday and, worse, had himself to blame, for letting anger cloud his judgement and for letting a man come at him from the side.

One mistake in a lifetime. One mistake because he was more intent on killing than on surviving, because he was thinking of Meiya and Heisu and thinking that he would as soon die and be out of his pain.

One mistake because he was a man and not the paragon the legends said he was. And the *man* limped for the rest of his life and hurt like hell and was short of wind because he had survived that ambush, he had made it beyond the borders of the Empire, he had decided to live and he could no longer do the things that kept him in form. A little exercise helped. But it did not cure the lameness, did not cure the weakness.

Nothing could bring back Saukendar the way he had been. Nothing could make the years flow backward, bring the dead to life and make the pain go away.

And Taizu, damn her, overtook him before he even got down the hill, scampering down the root-laddered slot like a goat, cheerful as an otter.

She grinned at him as she took up a man-sized bundle.

That's too much for you, he started to say, because it was not the weight, it was the way the bundle caught on the trees along the trail and forced shifts in balance in the narrow track there was to walk on. It did that to him. It brought stabs of pain through his leg and a sick feeling when he took up the weight of another bale. *Damn stubborn girl. Let her find out for herself. Do her good.*

But she took out on the trail ahead of him, and widened the gap between them, so that he struggled to keep up with her, struggled and sweated until, at the top, the air he breathed seemed tainted with metal and the clearing swam in a film of sweat and pain.

Which he did not admit. He dumped his load just after her and said, grandly: "You seem to enjoy it. You go down and bring the rest."

He picked up the bales by the ropes, one in either hand, and carried them without a limp toward the stable, with the cabin and the trees and the stable swimming like a vision under water.

He dumped the load just inside the doorway, out of her sight, and sat down on it and held his leg and just ached in peace a moment, until Jiro came wandering in to investigate and nuzzled his shoulder.

He patted the offered cheek and got himself up on his feet.

He wished they had killed him, that was what. He had never done so before, but he wished it now, that he saw his youth was past, his future was here, and that future was less and less every year.

That was what the girl had taught him to do, to count time again, and to reckon the seasons, and to see the changes time had made in him, was making, until this year he failed to keep up with a sixteen-year-old girl.

He threw the bales of straw into the fenced end of the stable, out of Jiro's reach, then walked back down toward the trail and was part way down the hill when Taizu came struggling up with a load.

She was sweating now, at least, and panting with the climb; so he felt halfway chivalrous in saying: "I'll take it. How many more?"

"Two more."

"Go on back down," he said.

He took the load up, dumped the bale at the clearing edge and went down the trail again, to meet her struggling up again, but far, far down.

She stopped when he met her. She gave him her load and she started down after the last.

"No," he said, half-turning with the load, "that's too much for a girl. Go on up the hill."

"I can do it," she said, and with a sweat-drowned glance and a gasp after wind, got her balance on the slot of a trail and plunged back down the way she had come.

He stared after her, hard-breathing and exhausted, and with a bitter-coppery taste in his mouth. He stared for a long moment, then took up the bale and slogged up the trail, fighting the clinging branches until he faced the last slope, clearer there. He had gotten his wind again, and he was doing well enough, finally, except the hurt in the leg.

He shifted the ropes on his shoulders, sucked in a deep breath and took the last climb at a run.

He made it to the top, fell to one knee as the bale snagged on a branch, and for one pain-blinded moment had no strength to get the damn thing free.

He got up again with a furious shove.

Something ripped in the great muscle above his knee, and the bale shoved with his shoulder against a tree was all that kept him from falling down again under the pain. His mouth watered; his vision went hazy; when he came to himself he was still standing there braced against the tree and ropes about the bale were cutting into his shoulders. He did not know how he was going to move without falling down; but he knew that the girl would be coming up the trail soon and damned if he would let her see him like this.

So he got his balance again, pushing himself away from the tree, and he climbed the last little distance by pulling himself from branch to branch with his hands, until he reached the flat of the clearing and he faced the distant cabin on shaking legs, not sure the right knee was going to bear his weight at all in the next step.

It would, if gingerly. He walked—realized in his pain that the stable was closer, and he might take the straw there, but he wanted to sit down on the porch, that was all he could think of, and straight ahead was something he could manage: turning on that leg was like to pitch him helpless in the dirt, and he was not going to drop the bale and admit he had had to.

He got to the porch somehow. He threw the bale down. He sat down on the edge of the porch and felt the cold of the wind on his sweat-soaked clothes.

The girl was going to come up the hill and find him sitting here helpless: for the moment he could not even climb the steps to get into the cabin and take to his mat; and he had no intention of crawling up the steps and being caught at it.

Tomorrow—he thought—tomorrow the whole leg would stiffen. Tomorrow he *would* be crippled; and he contemplated the humiliation of his situation with the urge to go off into the forest, let the girl worry, simply hide himself away until the stiffness had left and then come back, claiming that he had been hunting—*None of your business, girl; I hunt when I feel like it*—

Like a fool, I do.

Like a fool I can hide the truth from you. *What's the matter, master Saukendar?* So he sat there to take what he had coming; and when he saw her come trudging up the rise into the clearing, a bale of straw first, and then a staggering small figure in a white shirt, he waited, rubbing the pain in his leg while she came closer, and finally said matter of factly as she threw her bale down by his:

"I've pulled a muscle. Boil up the rags, will you?"

She did not look at him then the way he had imagined, with amusement or with mockery, just with a little worry, a line between her brows. She was white and sweating. Her hair was stuck to her brow and cheeks. She looked as if she would like to sit down where she was.

But: "Yes, master Saukendar," she said, and went inside to see to things.

Damn, he did not want a girl's pity either, or her sympathy, and certainly not her feminine heroics. He hauled himself with a grip on the post by the steps and hobbled up the steps to the porch. But at that point the pain blurred his vision and the sweat stood cold on his skin, so that he just hung there awhile trying to breathe, until she came out again and he was caught in that condition.

She stared, a hazy image in his vision.

"The old wound tore," he said. "It's done this before."

Not in nine years, he thought to himself, and thought that he might have crippled himself for good and all with his stupid stubbornness. But he did not say that.

"I'll go boil up some water too," she said, and went back inside. "You could use a bath."

"I don't need your help, girl. I'll take care of the damn rags. Just let me alone!"

There was not a sound from inside. She did not come out, either.

"Do you hear me, girl?"

Not a sound. He recalled he had been through this game with her. And she had won it. It outraged him. He had crippled himself trying to take her advice and immediately as the little bitch saw him helpless she ignored his orders and did as she damned well pleased.

"See here, girl, if you want me teaching you, you *damned* well do what I tell you and leave me to myself!"

She appeared in the doorway. "All right, master Saukendar. If you insist. But the rags are heating. Do you want me to bring it out here or do you want it by your mat?"

"By the damn mat," he muttered, and judiciously let go the post and hobbled across the porch, about as much as he could do. She made to help him; he shoved her out of his way and with his hand on the wall limped over to his mat and fell down on his rump, the only sitting-down he could manage. The pain running from his thigh and his knee nearly put him out; and he thought of breaking the girl's neck.

But she brought him the greasy rags, and he bestirred himself to unlace his boot and work that off, and to pull his loose breeches up above the knee: then somewhere in the accounting she ended up squatting down to arrange a reed mat under his leg to absorb the oil from the rags. She fussed with the steaming cloths, rearranged what he did, since it did not meet her approval, and finally she stuffed a wad of quilts between his back and the wall, so he could sit in peace awhile and catch his breath between the more and the less of pain.

He was filthy and stinking with dried sweat and pain, the straw-prickles were all through his clothing, and he wanted at this point just to have his cabin to himself and his misery to himself, with maybe a jar of water by him and a few cold cakes or whatever there was, for whatever number of days it took to get over this.

But he admitted to himself that he was glad that she *was* there, and that he did not have to drag himself about to get the necessities, that the rags would get reheated as often as they cooled and that supper would arrive and there was someone to see Jiro got water. The last time he had been sick—

—gods, he had no idea how he had gotten water up the hill then: he never had remembered half those days, except finding himself on his face in the dirt, by the downed rails, down at the stable where he had decided to knock the fence down so Jiro could come and go where he pleased, and water himself from the rain-barrel or the spring.

And run free if his master died there.

He shut his eyes and rested in the coming and going of the pain. The next time he was aware of Taizu by him she had brought a pan of warm water and clean rags to wash his face, but he ordered her off and did it himself, stripping off his shirt and at least washing off the prickles that were driving him mad.

She renewed the hot compresses on his leg, and took the rags away to heat again.

It felt ineffably better after that second warmth had sunk in. He leaned back against the wad of quilts and rested half-aware until he smelled rice boiling and looked up and saw Taizu, in a clean shirt, cooking dinner.

He moved the leg tentatively. Mistake.

But he moved it again, and again, because he had nothing else to do, no other necessity weighing on him, and nothing to save his strength for. Taizu was there to water the horse; Taizu was there to cook his supper; Taizu was there to boil up the compresses, leaving him to tend his own hurt, and to keep it from stiffening.

He gritted his teeth and kept at it the next day, and sat on the edge of the porch and worked the leg with slow patience, thinking—

While Taizu was down at the spring fetching up
water—

That he was fortunate at least that it was not worse,
and most of all that he was not alone, because he knew
that he would have limped about and protected the leg
as best he could, protected it the way he had favored it
before. . . .

You're off your center, master Saukendar.

He had done it to himself once, because he had had
no choice. He had had to walk and carry and work, or
starve; and Jiro had needed care for his own wound.
He did not intend to repeat the mistake.

So he lay about with a woman to wait on him, he
rested on his back on the porch and drew the leg up
and drew it up a little more to the limit he could do it
without pain. Then finally, hurting and out of patience
and determined to see how far it would bend, he wrapped
his arms about his knee and hugged it to him, hard and
hard and harder, until he got another pain out of it
that half-blinded him.

But it was bending, he thought, more than he had
thought it would.

Then he got the notion that it might bend a little
more. The drawing that had happened over the years
was bad healing. Tear the damned thing. Give it more
flex than it had. Make it do what it was supposed to do.
So he pulled it harder, and harder, between bouts of
gray and haze. He had seen a fox gnaw its own leg in a
snare, to be free. He had not been sure whether it was
stupidity or courage. He still was not. He worked until
he was soaked in sweat, and wrapped himself in his
blanket and lay still and played the invalid while Taizu
was in sight; but when she was not he took the problem
again and again, a little gain this day, a very little gain,
but something: he was sure of it.

He made himself a stick to walk with. He was tolerably agile, once the leg was bound stiff, at getting up
and down off the porch, getting to the latrine, getting

to the rain-barrel to wash, getting about the cabin the
little that he must.

For the rest he kept the leg unbound, and lay about
the cabin or on the porch and worked it until the tears
ran from the edges of his eyes—while a fool girl who
was gifted by the unjust, priest-bribed gods with perfect balance and perfect health, stood out there in the
yard whacking away at a damn tree.

"Don't you think you should be up and about, master
Saukendar?" she chided him the fourth night. "Don't
you think you should walk with it? You told me—"

"I'm working on it," he said shortly.

But the next day—all her suggestions came at times
that if he did what he had intended to do in the first
place it looked as if he was moved by her advice, and it
maddened him—he took to walking without the bandage; and took to slow bending with the foot of his lame
side on the first porch step and the sound one on the
ground, time and time again, not caring now whether
Taizu saw him about it, because he was used to the pain
or the pain was less, he was not sure.

Knee straight over the foot while the leg bent, absolutely true. If the damned knee was going to stiffen, let
it stiffen in the bad directions, not the good one, let it
stiffen so it could no longer make the motion to the side
that would tear the sinews and betray the balance. This
time when it healed, let it not be on horseback, with the
leg out of line; or swinging an axe to try to build the
first shelter he had had up on the mountain; or simply
curling up to last through the pain and the cold, finally, because he had come to the mountain in the
rains, and sat under the scant cover he had been able
to contrive and tried only to keep from freezing until he
could limp about and put a little more solidity to his
building.

Thanks to the village he had not died in those first
days, thanks to the village who brought the supplies
that time within sight of his shelter; and he had not
even said a kind word to them for their trouble. He had

waited till the boys had left and then crept out of his
lean-to and carried them to cover little by little, in such
a haze of pain and fever as made those days hard to
recollect at all.

It was, perhaps, the only way the villagers of Mon
had known that he had lived, when they had come with
more food for him, that the food they brought was
gone; and that the shelter was larger. It had been at
least three visits they had made, laying their offerings
of food at the edge of the clearing, before he had even
come out to acknowledge them.

Damn, he had been crazed in those years. They
looked at him like he was a holy man and he was
nothing more than a rabbit content to burrow in and
nibble the gifts they threw, surviving till the hunters
came.

Even Ghita had decided finally he was not worth the
effort. Just not worth the effort and the lives and the
notoriety he might gain if they went on trying to kill
him.

Maybe Ghita had known that sending assassins against
him would have been a favor to him—to stir him up
and make him move. Maybe it would have kept him
going—longer—if there had been real enemies, instead
of just the fear of them. He had taken care of a few of
Ghita's men, early on. But his enemies could have taken
him—if Ghita had really cared to do more than send a
few assassins, he could have had him. And the village
would have paid dearly for helping him; perhaps lord
Reidi would pay—merely for tolerating him on his
border.

Damn.

Patiently, bend after bend, the knee exactly in line,
the foot on the second step this time. He bound the leg
when he walked; he swallowed his pride and used a
stick for balance, like an old man.

Taizu said not a thing more. He only noticed her
looking at him once, when he had advanced his foot to
the second step, and when he was bandaging his leg

again and splinting the knee. She just stood there and stared, and never offered a word.

Not even when he began taking further chances, and doing the deep bends that he needed the stick to get up from.

But he could do them. It was more than he had done in nine years. It embarrassed hell out of him, to be doing simple exercises, with a stick for help, when the girl ran the hill like a deer, when *she* clambered up onto the rafters and onto the roof to patch the leaks, when she did his work and her own and took care of him, and still practiced her strokes, day after day, like a maddening, willful fool, accusing him daily without meaning to accuse, reminding him that with all his pain and all his effort, it was a peasant girl he had to surpass.

Damned if he would not.

He felt compelled to a kind of honor with her, that he had to do at least that much or there was no reasoning with her, no moral force to any argument he could use against her mad ideas.

Damned if he would ask her to stay with him out of his necessity.

Damned if he would ask a woman to live with him on his terms if he could not ask it like a man with a choice.

And however much the sight of her tempted the mind nowadays, the body hurt too much to make temptation more than theoretical.

Chapter Six

Shoka squatted down deep and straightened slowly, without the stick, with the sword in hand, this time.

It hurt like hell. He was not sure but what it would always hurt, until he put himself in action and the muscles warmed.

A man could live with that, if it set his body straight and gave him back the youth he thought he had lost for good and all.

He saw Taizu's eyes follow that move, saw more than respect: a certain apprehension, as she held her own plain sword in her hands and waited.

"Your guard," he said.

She lifted her sword.

She was no novice now. She knew the patterns. He saw the correctness in her stance and felt the settling in his own muscles as he faced an opponent who meant business.

Woman she might be, but she tried, gods, she had battered away at that tree through three renewals of the straw matting, whack-whack, whack, whack-whack, until he heard that sound in his sleep; and he discovered a strength behind her arm even on upward extension.

Not to take lightly now. A fool would do that. She was fast, and he was years out of practice.

"Take it slowly," he said, beginning the patterns in the slow way that tested balance as well as form. No relying on momentum and strength to recover a mistake when one floated through the moves light and easy as the falling leaves. One had to be right or look the fool.

Taizu did not look the fool. Nor did he. He forgot the pain, for the pleasure of free movement, for the pleasure of watching his opponent in motion and feeling the answering stretch of muscles that still remembered, after so many years. Breaths puffed and frosted on the wind, steel passed steel without a sound.

He passed from feint to guard to strike in the same slow fashion, and saw, in exactly the right point of balance, the reaction on her side, no panic, just the right reaction, a move just out of his reach.

"Close," he chided her, as the sweep of his blade passed close to her arm. "Did you know where that was?" —Never ceasing his motion.

"Yes," she breathed, and her next step brought her blade circling around again, easy to evade.

"I'll show you another," he said, as he slowly turned in beneath the line of her attack.

She did not defend: he stopped with no more than the line established from his edge to her side.

"Do you see?"

"Yes," she said, holding her position. He broke his and walked around behind her, took her by the shoulders and tested her balance, marked a place in the dust with his foot: "Here," he said, then walked around to the fore and took her point between his fingertips, drawing her to the turn. Again a footprint stamped in the dust for her second step, and he led her about to a further evolution, full about, blade lifting. It was the most complicated counter he had ever shown her.

Twice more, guiding the blade. The feet came down impeccably on the mark.

Damn, he thought, thinking of his fellow-students in his father's tutelage, remembering the lessons upon lessons which had taught even the scatter-witted to go with the master, to keep the balance enough to defend themselves—but there was nothing scatter-witted about the girl. Tell that fool Beijun anything and the instruction flowed off into void and I-don't-want. *Don't think when I instruct you*, he had said to Taizu, as he had said to the heir in his time. *When I instruct you, I know, and you don't, so don't take your thoughts away from what I'm telling you. If there's a mistake at that point, it's my mistake, and I'll show you.*

Don't improvise to cover an attack you don't understand, if we're going slowly: stop the moment you recognize it and I'll instruct you your next move. There's a time you have to improvise. You know when that is. Don't learn the stop. Don't learn the bad move. When I'm instructing you, wait for the instruction. You understand the difference.

"Again," he said, without guiding her.

One, two, and three.

"Beautiful."

He took up his own guard then, and made the pass with her, came in and recovered the moment she began that evolution, with a turn of his own, slowly, slowly done.

"The pool reflects," he said. "My move and yours."

She repeated and stopped.

He stopped.

"Why?" he asked. "Have I changed my pattern?"

"No, master Saukendar." Softly, precisely, neither blade nor eyes moving. "But you won't let me go on doing that. What do I do now?"

"You're very forward." As softly, his own eyes on hers. But she was absolutely correct. "The next move is like the first. Practice the first, again. Be my reflection till I tell you otherwise."

One, two, and three. One, two, and three.

"The next," she said.

"Again," he said. And:

"Impatience is a flaw," he murmured as they stopped. "There's always just enough time when you do something right, no more, no less. Your sword has no blade. It has only your intention. When that goes astray you have no weapon. Continue."

One, two, and three. As master Yenan had taught him.

While the leaves fell and the garden turned to brown in the first frost.

"Up!" Shoka said, and sent the blade sweeping under Taizu's feet, spun it around in a turn that brought it for her back, lifted it to strike as she brought the correct counter back and held, reaching the end of the pattern.

"Now what will be the next move?" he asked her.

"You'll go low-line," she said.

"I might not."

"Harder to go up from that line."

"That's why I might do it. You might not expect."

"Dangerous, though."

"I'm the best. What will I do?"

"Some third thing. Not something awkward."

He was amused, pleased, but he did not laugh. He did not go off his guard with her. Those were not the rules in the faster game.

"What will it be?"

"You could turn back again and make me follow."

"What's the advantage?"

"Following takes attention. It ends when the opponent intends. Intention is the blade."

The old catechism, whispered on a frosting breath, under a gray autumn sky.

"Again," he said, and took the pattern from the beginning.

They were down to shirts and breeches. Sweat shone on her face and throat despite the cold; the white shirt clung and flared as she turned and struck and turned. He let himself go with the sheer beauty of the moment, the intoxication of movement, his and hers.

That was what she gave back to him. Teaching her, he taught himself. It pleased her. In time, he told himself, *he* would please her.

And there would be no more foolishness.

He pushed her toward the old tree that shaded the cabin. She refused that and tried to gain ground, away from the tree roots. "Ha," he said, and cleared back, giving her room.

Not pushing her, not forcing the novice into dangerous situations, not making a joke of her, for her pride's sake. He was honorable with her.

But she pressed it. Getting him to back away, she wanted to push him, and in an eye-blink decision he let her, for her sake, gave her the ground she wanted, backed.

She changed pattern on his second step.

He made the instinctive move and pulled it with a sudden lurch of the heart, saw her whirl and turn.

"Hold!" he shouted.

She stopped. He saw the blood on her sleeve. His heart was pounding in his chest. She seemed only confused.

"You're hit, girl."

She looked down at her body while the blood ran down the hand that held her sword, still not finding it, though blood spattered in the dust. He took her arm and found the cut while she craned her head over to try to see. Blood soaked the shirt. He grabbed it by the tail and whipped it up over her head as she protested and hugged it to her chest for modesty's sake.

It was on the back of her arm, a finger long, not, thank the gods, deep.

"I didn't even feel it."

"Fool." He shook her by that arm. "*Don't* try a trick like that on me again."

"I'm sorry, master Saukendar."

"It's shallow. It could have ruined you. *Hear me?*"

"Yes, master Saukendar."

He let her go and went and retrieved his sword-sheath, while she pulled her shirt back on and did the same, off the porch.

"Come inside," he said then. "Damn, that's a good shirt."

"I'm sorry."

He brought her inside, pulled the shirt up again and salved the arm for her and bandaged it. By then, he knew by experience, she was beginning to feel the sting in full.

"Does it hurt?"

"Yes," she said.

His heartbeat had settled and he was quite calm. He jerked her close to him by the cloth of the shirt she was holding to cover herself.

"It could have been your arm, you damned fool. Don't *ever* push me."

"Yes, master Saukendar."

"Go wash up. And wash the shirt. You're a mess."

She went. He frowned at her back and decided there was no damage done. But when he was washing up at the back of the cabin, at the rain-barrel, the moment came back to him again, that half-a-blink time he had had to react and realize he had reacted with an attack she did not know how to defend, one that would have, at full force, taken her arm off. He kept seeing it, feeling sick at his stomach.

He kept seeing it again and again: he looked at her from time to time as they sat inside at supper—not the porch, in the chill of this evening's wind—because the sight of her whole and hale was a cure for what he kept seeing in his mind: Taizu bloody on the ground, crippled even if he had been pulling his blows—

Or if he had not—

She looked at him between mouthfuls of rice, worried-looking, knowing, he was sure, that he was thinking

about her, that he might have something to say about
the situation; perhaps thinking that she had made some
unforgivable mistake, which was not the case. It was a
student's mistake. It was his—that he had stopped expecting her to do fool things like that.

He *enjoyed* teaching her, he looked forward to the
sessions, he took pleasure in the things he had not been
able to do in years, and it brought back his boyhood to
him—not the deadly years, not the duels, not the blood
and the pain, but the sheer pleasure of skill and excellence. His father's voice. Master Yenan's. The gray
dusty courtyard at Cheng'di, with the red-painted dragons on the gates. Faces of friends, most of whom were
dead.

Taizu, in motion in the sunlight—Taizu, at guard,
every line of her beautiful, from the slender turn of
ankle to the set of her hips to the sheen of her hair in
the light—

He had given her that grace. He could hardly remember the pig-girl. And the scar was part of Taizu. It
had a certain symmetry: it *belonged* to her, it was part
of the face and the person that he had come to depend
on being there, day and night—

Kill Ghita.

Gods. Leave the mountain, trek across the country,
throw her life away—

Like hell she would.

Like hell he would let her.

"I'm sorry," she said finally, in a meal that was all
silence.

He shot her a scowling look.

"I know what I did," she said.

Ask her, she meant.

Then they would talk about it, then it would be all
right and everything would go back to what it had
been.

Until something worse happened.

"What did you do?"

"I thought I'd be clever. I thought I'd find out if what

I thought was right, if why you learn in patterns is
because they're in balance with where your feet are,
and if you let me back you up then you were going to
let me follow right into what you wanted—so I thought
I could stop that by changing."

He stared at her, frowning, in long silence, following
every bit of it. Then he said: "You were thinking."

"I—" She pressed her lips together and was very still
for a moment, then nodded. "I'm sorry, master Saukendar."

He rested his arm on his knee, his chin on his arm,
and stared at her. "Listen to me, girl. You wanted me
to teach you. I have, so far. You're extraordinarily good,
for a woman. Probably better in the forms than most
that come out of the schools in Cheng'di. But that won't
save your life, you understand me? I gave you a promise because I didn't want you wandering off and getting
yourself caught by the bandits or starving on the road.
Look at you now. You're a damned pretty girl. Have I
done badly for you?"

Her lips were a pale line in the lamplight. "No,"
escaped them, hardly a move at all, and her nostrils
flared, her eyes moved in panic like a trapped rabbit's.

"Scared to death I'll make a grab at you. I haven't.
Not that it's been easy, understand. But I've kept my
bargain, haven't I?"

A nod of her head, after the same fashion.

"This isn't Chiyaden. A woman who lives up here—
had damned well better know how to hunt; how to use
a bow; had *better* be strong enough to swing an axe and
run a hill. The ladies in the court learn the sword and
the staff. There's nothing wrong in that. A woman ought
to be able to take care of herself—"

—it wouldn't have helped Meiya.

—If I had been there—

—If I had seen it coming—

"—and I'd gotten lazy in my retirement. I *enjoy* the
exercise. And if I want to teach a woman more than a
lady usually learns, that's my business. But when I

teach her, I have to teach her the other things too, like the good sense to know her limits."

"You promised—"

"You listen to me. If there's a mistake, it's mine, in hoping you'd have the sense to quit. I've treated you like a woman. If you think you backed me up—"

"I knew I didn't."

"Damned right. I should have pushed you right into the tree. That's what I mean. Maybe you're good enough to take a peasant or two. Maybe you could carve up a bandit. Most of them are rotten swordsmen. A lord's bodyguard is a different matter: every one of them a man twice your weight, a good span on your longest reach, *maybe* not as agile, but don't count on it—a man who spends at least an hour a day in the exercise court isn't a light matter for anyone, young miss, and even if you get one of them on *his* bad day, his three friends will take strong offense. Give me your hand. Give it to me!"

She gnawed at her lip and carefully put her small hand in his.

"Now push my hand to the floor."

She tried. She made him resist harder than he had expected, but he held, even when she threw her shoulder into it unexpectedly.

She sat back frowning.

"Do you want to try to hold *me* off?"

"You said don't engage."

"Sometimes you have no choice. Sometimes there are five and six of them and you haven't got a damn choice. Sometimes they come in numbers larger than that, and sometimes there's no room to back up, you've got to take the room. I've taught you the moves a woman can do. But there are some you can't."

"Try me."

"What you want is impossible, girl. A man doesn't have to be better than you to beat you. He just has to be stronger and half as good—and that means some damn door guard can lop your head off. That means some ox of a line soldier can bash a cheap sword right through your guard and if he doesn't get you on that one his partner will, from the back. That's the way it is in the world. You're not strong enough. You can't do everything with the blade and you can't evade everything that comes at you."

"All I have to be is good enough for one."

"You're out of your senses. You won't get that far, you'll die in a damn ditch, for nothing. *If* you're lucky."

"I'm not afraid."

"You're a fool, then! Or a liar."

"You swore you'd teach me. If you haven't been teaching me right, you're breaking your word." Her eyes glittered with unshed tears. "And you'd be a liar, master Saukendar."

"*Damn* you."

Her chin trembled. And she stared at him in defiance.

"Listen to me, girl. Listen. If I hit you all-out, as can happen, I'll break your bones. Right across the shoulder. First honest match, snap, there goes the arm. Is that what you want?"

"If you teach me so you can hit me, that's the way it is, isn't it? You want me to get killed."

"You damned little fool, I'm telling you it happens."

"You gave your word."

"I told you how that happened. Listen to me. You're good. You're very good. But you can't do the things you want. You can't change nature. Forget this crazy notion of yours. You've got a roof over your head. You've got a warm bed. You can stay with me as long as you like." He took a deep breath and took the chance, out loud, the way he had been thinking it—hell with his heritage, the things they would say in Cheng'di. Hell with the look his father would give him, if his father were alive to see it; but his father, thank the gods, had not seen a good lot else that had happened, either. "As my wife, or as close to that as matters for anyone. It's not a bad life here. Is it?"

"No," she said sharply, scowling.

"No, what? What are you going to do else? March on Gitu's castle? Be a damned fool? They'll cut you up for dog meat."

"You swore an oath."

"I made a simple promise! It doesn't count, to a madwoman!"

"No, you said you swore. And so did I, master Saukendar. I swore an oath too. And you'll teach me."

He gnawed his lip, glaring at her. "You're a damned hard-headed bitch."

"*I* swore. And I'll do it. And you will. You'll teach me the right way. You won't cheat."

"I didn't cheat!"

"What else is it, if you held back on me?"

"Damn you for a fool! You want your bones broken?"

"I want justice, master Saukendar. I want you to do what you promised. If you can't teach me any better than that, it's your fault, isn't it, master Saukendar?"

"Fool, I say! It happens. It happens to men and the best of them. What chance do you think you have? You get tired, girl, you get tired and you make a mistake, you get hot in the damn armor, you can't pick your footing, some damn footsoldier guts your horse—what in *hell* do you think you're going to do then?"

"You can teach me that. The way you promised."

"Fool," he muttered, and said nothing else for a long while. Finally he passed out of the mood to say anything, and went over to his mat and undressed, not caring about her sensibilities, deliberately defying her presence, and walked over to the hearth to pour a little rice wine and to heat it.

"Want any?" he asked brusquely, looking her direction. But she had gathered up the dishes and she was putting herself to bed, clothes and all.

"No," she said without looking at him, tucked under the quilts with her back to him and pulled them over her head.

"It's going to be a long winter, girl. Drink some wine

with me. We'll talk about the court. Talk about whatever you like."

"No." From under the quilts.

He stood there thinking ungentlemanly thoughts a good long moment, while the wine heated. Then he took the wine-pot and blew out the light.

"I'm going to my own mat," he said in the dark.

No answer from the other side of the room.

So he sat down in the dark and drank the wine down to the bottom, and tried not to think about her, the sword that had nearly crippled her, or Chiyaden and ambushes of ungrateful peasants.

He kept seeing that moment behind his eyelids. He saw the first man he had ever killed. He saw a score more after that, and the wreckage a sword could leave of a man. Good men. Maimed and screaming in the dirt.

He had himself another woman and he was as helpless to reason with this one as with the first.

He should have slept with Meiya, he told himself, the first time the idea had ever crossed his mind. There would have been scandal. A quick marriage. And Meiya, no longer virgin, before the Emperor had ever taken the notion to claim her for his murdering fool of a son, would have been safe from everything that had happened to her at the hands of her husband.

He should listen to no nonsense now, should take the direct course with Taizu, go over there and show her what a man's strength was worth against her prudery: she would warm after a night or two, would come to sense, would find a gentleman's ways different than the men she had known—

It all seemed very reasonable. Until he thought about Taizu.

Until he remembered what she would say to him at the critical moment:

You gave your word, master Saukendar.

"How's the arm?" he asked her at breakfast.

"It's fine, master Saukendar."

He ate a few more bites.

"I can do my lesson today," she said.

He said nothing.

"I'm not stiff, master Saukendar. There's nothing wrong with me. You mostly missed me."

"I pulled it, dammit. I laid myself wide open pulling it, I risked *my* neck stopping, let's get the thing right, shall we?"

"I wouldn't have hit you—"

"Then *what in hell* do you think you're holding a sword for?"

Taizu had her mouth open. She shut it, fast.

"All right," he said, glaring at her. "You want me to teach you like a man, you've asked for it."

The skirts of the armor came to her knees. "It's *heavy*," she said, swaying as he cinched it in with ropes about her waist, crossed around her chest, because it had to overlap to fit; and he had padded up her arms and her legs with leather wrappings and old rags, because the armor-sleeves and the shin-guards were impossible.

"You want me to teach you," he said.

"What are you going to wear?"

"I'm not worried," he said. "You're the one apt to lose a hand." He stood back, took up his sword and pointed at hers. "There you are. On your guard."

She staggered a little in the moves. But she steadied.

He put her on Jiro's back on the next day and let her have the feel of riding in that weight of metal, when before, she had only sat Jiro bareback when he was lazing about the pasture. She did not fall off. But Jiro was on good behavior.

"If you're going to be a gentleman," he taunted her, "you should know how to ride."

And *he* swung up in her place, took up the reins and said: "Pass me up my spear. You have a lot to learn, girl. We'll see how well you handle a rider."

It was more boiled rags that night.

"Do you want to quit?" he asked her.

She turned a dark and accusing eye on him, face down on her mat while he was putting compresses on the backs of her knees. "No," she said.

And he: "It only gets heavier with the wearing."

The arrow flew, the deer started at the sound of Shoka's bowstring and the arrow led the stag truly, arced straight for the heart—not hunting for sport, but meat for their winter, and they took no chances. The stag lunged at the impact, ran a few steps and went crashing down in a snowy thicket.

He cut its throat for good measure, and Taizu looped a rawhide rope around its feet and flung the other end over a branch.

Venison for the whole winter season. Hide and horn and bone for a fine pair of breeches and a knife-hilt and whatever else winter evenings could devise.

"I never had venison," Taizu had confided to him.

In truth, he replied, it was usually wild pigs. But there were two of them to feed this year, the stag offered itself, and between the two of them they could get their victim home again.

They smoked a great deal of the venison, made sausages, cured the hide, and hung the rest, frozen, from the cabin porch.

And on winter evenings, with the snow outside and Jiro snug in his stable, Shoka taught the making of arrows, the shaping of a bow—men's work; but it was what he knew, and it made the evenings pass and it pleased the girl and made the time pleasant.

Her eyes followed every move of his fingers; and his followed the light in her eyes and the little curve of a smile he could get from her nowadays.

And his thoughts followed her night by night. He tried her resolve from time to time, a little compliment, a brush of his hand while she was working.

She flinched and said, in one variation or the other: *No*.

So that was the way the winter went—from snowy day to snowy day, when they stayed snug indoors except the needful chores, like carrying water to Jiro and combing and currying him and letting him out for exercise and seeing him snug in his stable at night.

He showed her the way to spin out a bowstring, and how to tie it. He told her why certain arrows had certain fletchings and certain points, and how to choose the feathers and how to set them. He showed her—with the cabin's dirt floor padded with straw mats—a few of the elementary arts master Yenan had taught him, the turning of a blow with the fingers, the use of a bit of wood or the bare hand or foot to numb a limb or dissuade anyone who would lay hands on her.

Such things the nuns would have taught her. He reminded her of that; and she said:

"I wouldn't have stayed there long enough."

"Where would you have gone?" he asked her.

"I don't know," she said, evading the question. She would not look him in the eyes when she answered, so he made up his own: that she would have gone on the road and been a morsel for the stronger and the quicker, which he did not like to imagine.

He told her stories, and she told him, what the court was like, what Hua was like. They amazed each other, he thought; at least her eyes grew wide when he talked about the court and the Emperor's table where dishes came dressed in peacock feathers and roast pigs had sugar castles on their backs, wings of swan feathers and real rubies for eyes.

"We ate all right," she recollected, talking of Hua, and the things she said told him of a prosperous farm, a large family—my brothers, she said, and sometimes in her stories named names, like Jei and Mani. She talked about a deer lord Kaijeng's daughter had had for a pet until lord Kaijeng's hunters killed it by mistake, and then (there was none of Taizu's stories but had a sad ending,) she said that the lady and her husband were dead, that the lady had committed suicide and her husband had been killed in the fighting for the castle. She shed no tears for any of it. She only grew melancholy; and he thought about Meiya's death and was melancholy himself.

But he never talked to her about Meiya. She was a child. He was not, and he could not bring himself to confide those complex and painful memories to her, not even when he was a little drunk. He only brooded, and the silence was heavy for a while.

She was a little drunk that night, too, with the storm howling round. She gathered up her good humor and showed him a game they had played in Hua, when the snows came, but it was a game he knew, one they played at court. So that turned out to be something they both shared.

He remembered one world while he played with their makeshift counters, where he had played with ivory and jade pieces for high wagers, while she remembered her home, perhaps, and stone counters and a host of brothers and her parents. But they played for such things as Who Carries the Bucket and Who Makes Breakfast.

He suggested other stakes, but she glowered at him, and he assured her he was only joking.

"All right," he said, "if you lose you keep me warm tonight. Nothing else. No hands."

"I won't," she said, firmly. "You might cheat."

"At what? Besides, a gentleman doesn't cheat."

"Huh," she said shortly, arms on her knees.

"What does that mean?"

"I know what you want. And you won't get it. I won't let you break your word. So there."

"You're the loser," he said. "It's a cold night."

She shook her head. "You want to play?" she said. "Tomorrow's dishes against I curry down your horse."

"You do that anyway. That's no bet."

"Against who brings in the firewood next."

"All right," he said.

So they played that night while the snow fell on this coldest night of the year, and they drank a little more.

"Come on," he said, when she was staggering to her mat, and he was sitting on his, more than a little drunk. He patted the place beside him. "It's bitter cold. There's no sense being uncomfortable. I promise you, it's only comfort I'm thinking of. I won't do anything you don't want me to do."

"*No*," she was sober enough to say, and took to her mat alone, huddled up in a knot under the quilts in all her clothes.

Chapter Seven

The icicle at the corner of the porch grew spectacularly and fell finally with a considerable crash one afternoon, leaving a crystal wreckage in a remaining drift, under a warming sun.

There was mud everywhere, but the winds had shifted, burning off the snow at an amazing rate, and Jiro kicked up his heels like a colt, flagging his tail and cavorting around the pasture in a shameless display.

Hoping for mares, Shoka thought forlornly, considering the horse and the girl who tended him—her forfeit, carrying the bucket up the muddy trail from the spring, and currying the mud off Jiro, who would surely roll in it.

Hard winter, worse spring. He sat on the porch scraping the stubble off his chin, dipping his razor in a pan of hot water and sourly contemplating the warming weather that would have the whole hillside in a mating frenzy, the buds bursting, nature run amok to procreate and perpetuate.

Shoka sighed, looked from under a brow and a shaggy

fall of hair at the slim, far figure, and thought he had missed his best chance when they were both drunk at midwinter.

Sorry, girl, I didn't know what I was doing.

He imagined a morning after that event in which the girl would change all her opinions, all her intentions, give up her mad notions and devote herself to him completely.

Crash! went another icicle.

He did not, in fact, know what she would do if he laid a hand on her, but he did not, in broad daylight, think it particularly likely that she would immediately change her attitudes. He had never tried to think like a pig-farmer who had sworn to kill a lord of Chiyaden. But he tried a great deal lately to think like Taizu, and getting a few smiles and a laugh or two out of her was hard enough. Taizu—

—He could not think what she would do. But he doubted it would be peaceful *or* pleasant.

Damned fool girl. Damned fool girl who was a comfort he had gotten used to. And after nine years of celibacy—

Another sigh.

A man would want to say that getting a girl to bed was the most important thing. But that was a lie. The likelihood that she would be straightway down the hill and away from him—that was the thing he had thought about all the winter, that looking down that hill now, for instance, and not having the sight of her, ever; and having his supper of evenings in perpetual silence—was unendurable.

The longer she stayed the more accustomed she grew to him. The more she grew accustomed to him—

The ladies of Chiyaden had accounted him very handsome. And he tried, gods witness, to treat the little bitch with every grace he could make her understand.

Look at her—slogging along in the mud in one of the shirts they traded back and forth, barefoot and filthy to the knees, barefoot: it was the gods' own wonder she

did not get frostbite. But *she* had walked barefoot from
Hua, and likely the boots he had made her were the
first gentle care her feet had ever had.

Gentleborn students had to work to harden their
hands and their feet. Taizu's were hard; and she had
sword-calluses. Silk would fray on such hands.

But—he thought,—

But that went with Taizu. And there was only one of
her.

One still tried. It was a slow campaign. That evening,
over supper:

"We should go hunting again," he said. The deer was
long since scraps for the birds and the opossums, and
he had dragged it off that day, to keep the pests away
from the cabin.

She nodded, eyes bright over the edge of her bowl.

"You know, the ladies in Chiyaden use ivory chopsticks. They take smaller bites. Like so." He demon-
strated.

She laughed at him, a crinkle at the corners of her
eyes, as if all it had meant was a story, like the pigs
with ruby eyes.

"Even the gentlemen take smaller bites," he said,
figuring that if a gentleman was what she aspired to be,
she might at least acquire *some* courtly grace, "and they
use napkins instead of their sleeves."

What do they do with the rubies? she had asked
regarding the pigs. Taizu went straight to the heart of a
thing. And she was still waiting for a story. He saw that.

"Have you heard who invented chopsticks?"

"No."

"It was a greedy woman who couldn't wait for her
rice to cool. She didn't want to burn her fingers."

She looked at him curiously. "What province was she
from?"

"Probably Hua."

"That's not so," she said definitely, as if she would
have heard.

Then he smothered a laugh by filling his mouth and said: "Well, maybe it was Yiungei."

Taizu said: "Have you heard how the dog got in the moon?"

"I didn't know there was a dog in the moon."

"Of course there is. You can see it." She leaned and pointed.

"It's an old woman."

"The same that invented the chopsticks?"

"Probably."

"It stole this old woman's supper and she chased it with her stick. That's how it got there. It's a very hungry dog. It starves down to nothing every month, but the gods always feel sorry and feed it, so it never goes away."

That was a hopeful story. He laughed.

"I heard in Kiang province it was a rabbit. It jumped up there."

"Why?"

"Probably because the dog was chasing it."

She gave him an odd look.

"I swear," he said. "That's what I heard."

It should always be like this, he thought. She should always be here. Every evening. Forever.

"I think you're making fun of me."

"I never would. My solemn word."

She frowned at him.

He grinned.

She got up fast and headed inside.

"Taizu?"

Oh, damn.

"Taizu."

He got up and went after her. She was inside gathering up the rice-pot to wash.

"I wasn't making fun of you, dammit. Can't a man joke with you?"

"I don't know when you're joking," she said sullenly. "I don't think you've told me anything true."

"Like what?"

"Like everything in Chiyaden."

"Well, it is true. About the pigs and the rubies. And the ivory chopsticks."

She threw her bowl into the pot, and splashed water. "Are you through yet? I'll take your bowl."

"You're not going around back in the dark. A bear might eat you."

"Like the pigs. I can take care of myself."

"I don't doubt that. It's going to be a bad day for the bear. Come on back to the porch. You're being stupid. I never laughed at you. I was making a joke."

"So you were laughing at me."

"*I wasn't laughing at you!* Do you call me a liar?"

"No, master Saukendar. You're a gentleman. You wouldn't lie."

He stood fast in the doorway, with her with the potful of water in her hands.

And he suddenly thought that was a dangerous position to hold. He saw the thought going through her eyes. He gave her a look intending she see the one going through his.

Which left them standing there like obstinate fools.

"We can stand here all night," he said.

"Yes, master Saukendar."

He sighed, stepped aside, gestured her to pass.

"I didn't laugh at you," he shouted at her back. "You're being an ingrate bitch."

She walked down off the porch and around into the chill dark.

So he heated up the wine and poured himself a small drink and went to bed.

She came back quietly and blew out the light and went to hers.

She was very sweet in the morning. She made a special breakfast, with sausage. She said nothing about the quarrel.

He said nothing either, just stared at her while he ate.

She looked uncomfortable and went off to do the morning chores.

It was a sort of a victory, he thought.

They had practiced arms in the snow; they had practiced on the porch and up and down the steps—as well you learn what to do with a ceiling, he had said.

Now, with the snow lying only in shadowed nooks and the high part of the yard dry it was the yard by the old tree again, breath frosting on the air, and mud up to the knee.

You don't always get good footing, he said. You choose your ground if you can. Sometimes you can't.

Taizu went down on a wet patch, messily. He followed up with the sword to make the point, jumped back as she took a swipe at his legs and rolled and came up again.

"Damned fine!" he yelled at her, and brought his sword sweeping round to catch her shoulder—if she had not spun under and offered him the point of hers two-handed in a stop-thrust.

"Break, break, a hell of a sloppy defense."

"I'm alive," she said.

"You've bound your point skewering me! What are you going to do with the man at your back?"

"There's no man at my back!"

"Hell if there isn't! Don't give me any cheek, girl."

"It worked," she panted.

"Do you want me to teach you or do you want to argue with me?"

She drew a quieter breath and wiped her leather-bound wrist across her face. "Yes, master Saukendar."

"Which?"

She gasped another breath and took up her stance again.

His leg ached. He was out of sorts. "Slower now. Don't improvise. Hear me?"

She nodded. "I hear. Can you show me—how to do that?"

"You're not ready. You fell. Don't clown when you fall." He began a slow evolution, the beginning-moves again. "Teaches you bad habits."

"I wasn't—wasn't clowning. What am I going to do—when something happens—you didn't teach me?"

Then he thought about the spring; and the thaw: and thought in a flash of cold: *She's talking about leaving.*

"You're not ready yet. You're not near ready."

He saw the frown. He felt colder.

Show her otherwise, he thought; and watched her face, watched the smothered anger in the set of her mouth.

Pattern after pattern after pattern. While the impatience smouldered. He saw it in her. "Haste—kills, girl. —Remember that. —You have—a great deal too much of it—for your own good."

"What do I do—about a fall—master Saukendar?"

"Break," he said, finishing the patterned move. He was minded to quit. There was still a chill in the air. He had not been moving hard. His bad leg ached miserably. But: *Show her,* he thought. *Show the damn girl something she won't learn so fast.*

He threw his practice cane over to the porch, walked over and picked up his sword. She came and retrieved hers.

"Are you going to show me?"

"I'll show you," he said calmly. He walked back out to the tree and squared off against her, waiting. "Choose your attack."

She lifted her blade, careful movements now, bare steel. "Don't be cutting my feet off."

"I wouldn't think of it. Choose your speed."

She began, a careful, sedate pace, strike and turn.

He evaded, struck, evaded, struck, full about again. Damn, it was going to hurt. He chose his moment, chose his spot, shifted his weight to his good leg and went down hard, took the impact and used the force to rock himself up to a knee and to his feet with all his old speed.

She jumped back, spun and came in again, and he pulled his blow short, slowly, slower.

"All right," he said, panting. "You."

She looked at him. There was a frown of desperation on her face.

"Long winter?" he taunted her.

"I'll try." She lifted the sword again.

He lifted his and began the slow dance. "Use the force of your fall. If you fall, don't waste yourself fighting it. Fall. Curl up onto the right shoulder. Come up fast onto the right knee."

She took the fall. She came most of the way up and cut at him.

He stepped back, the knee caught, but he cleared the reach of her sword.

"You missed."

As she scrambled up.

She went down again. And lay there panting under the weight of the body armor.

"That's enough," he said.

"I can do it."

"That's *enough*, I said." He walked over and picked up his sword-sheath, sheathed the steel and picked up the cane. "Go take your bath."

It was a quiet supper, a deathly quiet supper.

And he wanted like hell to put a compress on his aching leg, but he had no wish to let her know that move cost him anything. So he drank a bit, measuring the amount of the wine left against the time till the villager came back. He went to bed without a word, and worked to find a position in which the leg did not ache.

It was worth it, if it put a healthy fear into the little fool.

Let her go on trying it. Let her bruise her backside and strain her gut and her knees.

He could *do* it with the armor, still. If the knee held. Damned if he wanted to demonstrate the fact.

*   *   *

"On your guard," he said.

Her sword came up. He kept the exercises slow, balance and precision. The wind had been warmer today, until evening. The sky above the mountain was gray and pregnant with rain. There was no twilight, only murk, and an occasional spattering of rain onto the well-trampled dirt.

She kept hurrying the patterns. He resisted. The knee ached. It always would when the weather turned like this. He might have known it was more than strain. And he had no wish to rehearse the pattern from yesterday.

"No," he said. "Patience. Patience."

She nodded. She kept the pace he set for at least three passes; and then he took it faster. And faster. Pattern and pattern and pattern and variation.

She threw herself suddenly into a fall then, and came up with a different line.

"*Dammit!*" He skipped back and swung the sword in temper and checked it.

As she did, her sword arm back, out of line, shock on her face.

He felt the sting of a cut on his leg, across the side of the thigh.

"Dammit!" he yelled at her as she got up. He looked at the wound: one had better, when one used the long-swords. One could be missing a limb and not feel it—yet.

Shallow, thank the gods.

"I'm sorry."

"So you drew blood. Congratulations. I'd have cut your head off. Hear me?"

She said nothing.

"You don't believe me, girl?"

"I believe you," she echoed back faintly.

He fingered the cut, which was running blood. And glared at her. Damned if she believed it. Damned if she did.

He walked over and picked up his sword sheath.

"I'll get something for it," she said.

"It's nothing."

"It's bleeding. . . ."

"*Let it be,* dammit." He rammed the sword home with shaking hands and gave her a direct look. Rain was spattering about them again, dark pocks on the dirt. "I gave you an order. You defied me. Now you're damned proud of yourself. Pulled a surprise. Now you think you're ready for your enemies."

"I didn't mean to."

"You're a damned arrogant little bitch, girl. I don't cry foul. I still have my leg under me. Better assassins have tried. I've pulled everything I've ever done with you. I pulled it then, which is why you still have your *head,* girl, and why I'm the one bleeding. It takes something to think through what I know and what you don't, and to keep on pulling back. I can see I was wrong. I *enjoyed* teaching you. I told you: you're good for a woman. But the first *man* you go up against is going to take your head off. I told you that from the start. You didn't want to listen. And I made a mistake. I made a grievous mistake when I thought that you'd come to your senses. I made another when I paced the teaching to what you could do. Now you think you're damned good. Now you think you're a match for men who've studied the sword for all their adult lives. Well, you're not. You go out of here the way you are and you're dead, for nothing, dead, the first time you try yourself against a common bandit."

"That's not what you said."

"I'm telling you *quit,* girl. I'm telling you use good sense and give up this whole crazed idea of yours. There's nothing to be gained back there. Kill the whole damned lot of them and there's more maggots to take their place. There's nothing you can do. You'll only come to a bad end and an early one and to no good whatsoever."

"You gave your word."

"I gave my word. I also put a condition on it. When

you've *failed*, girl, you've failed, and all the bargains are done."

"I haven't failed."

He drew a deep breath, looking at her, looking at his own creation staring back at him.

"Girl," he said, and drew the sword from the sheath again, "I wasn't fighting. I was teaching. You're about to learn the difference. On your guard."

She shook her head. "No."

"On your guard, dammit!"

"I can't hit you! You haven't got any armor!"

"You think that'll protect you. Hell if it will, girl. *Hell* if it will, from a proper strike. And I don't need it against a beginner."

She threw the sword away.

"Are you quitting?" he asked her. "Is the bargain off?"

"No."

He sheathed the sword and picked up the cane. "I'll give you one more advantage. Pick up the sword, or you've quit. Hear me?"

She bent and gathered it up again. The rain-spatter became a sudden downpour.

He came on guard. She did.

He let her worry; and let her settle. He gave her that grace, while the rain turned the ground treacherous. Her face was waxen-pale, her lips a set line.

"All right," he said, starting a slow movement.

"I can't hit you."

"You can try. You want to trade weapons?"

"No."

"So you know, girl. Just so you know. You want to get your own cane? You can. I'll let you."

She broke her guard and started to turn.

He attacked. She evaded him with a wild, off-balance spin and recovered her guard, wild-eyed and indignant.

"You believe your enemy?" he asked her. "That's damn foolish."

He attacked again, again, again, and brought the

cane through her guard, clipped her leg, clipped her arm and evaded a desperate return attack, spun under and brought the cane around hard into her side.

She fell. She rolled half-up again and he hit her again, two-handed.

The sword left her hand.

He hit her again. And a fourth time. She made a try after the sword-hilt and he knocked it from her hand when she brought it up. She rolled after it and he let her get most of the way up before he knocked her flying, skidding facedown in the mud.

She did not move then. He stood there with his leg shooting fire from knee to spine and his heart hammering with apprehension until she stirred, moved her feet and got her arms under her.

"This is what you could look for," he said. "You'd be dead. No excuses. No allowances. The world won't pity you. Damned if I'll let you walk out of here thinking you can take a man in a fight. You're not strong enough. You never can be. That's the end of it."

He threw the cane down. He walked past her in the rain, left her there to cry it out and come to terms with matters on her own, walked up onto the porch and inside, feeling the ache in the leg, finding, as he had climbed the steps, that his whole boot was soaked with blood; finding as he walked inside and untied his breeches to bandage his leg, that he was shaking.

The girl was probably going to heave up her guts between crying and cursing him. But he had not broken any bones. He had hit her nowhere that could cripple her. He knew that he had not. And the kind of thinking she had to do took time. Alone.

So he got down the pot of ointment and bandaged his leg and started the fire up, figuring she was going to need the rags when she came in.

Thunder cracked. Rain hit the roof in a gust.

She'll freeze out there.

He limped to the door and opened it.

She was gone from where she had lain. She was out

there in the rain, battering away at the tree with great clumsy strokes, left and right, thump-thump. Thump. Staggering as she swung.

Damn.

"Taizu!"

He was not sure she heard in the rain, in her state of mind. He swore and went out onto the porch. "Taizu!"

Thump-thump. Thump.

"Dammit, *Taizu!*"

He went out after her, in the sheeting rain, down the steps and across the yard. "Taizu, for the gods'—"

She turned about, cane sword in both hands. He stopped, seeing the anger and the shame in her; and the threat of violence.

"I could take you," he said, "even bare-handed. You'll never have the strength. It was a fool's choice. Do I have to prove that?"

She threw down the cane sword, there in the puddles and the mud, and with her hands and her teeth began to strip off the bindings of the armor as she stood, drowned in the rain. He did not help her. He only stood and watched as she flung it down in the mud. She looked to be crying, but the rain washed it away. She treated his armor like that. But he said nothing, just stood.

She took off the padding from her arms, the rain plastering her shirt against her, streaming down her face as she continued stripping the padding, down to her feet. Then he understood the move, the snatch after the cane sword. "*Without the damn armor,*" she screamed at him, and he dodged back, to the side, back again, but she gave him no room, no second to regroup.

"Dammit!" he yelled, remembered his own sword lying in the mud and feinted to one side, threw himself into a slide and grabbed it.

He cut at her legs; she cleared that sweep and he got himself room, hurled himself up and launched back in an attack on her blade, trying not to hit *her,* which consideration she did not return. She clipped his arm as he skidded. She skidded on her turn and he brought up short, square with her, even.

"All right," he said between breaths, and invited her with a disdainful motion of his other hand.

Tentative then, the exchange, a trial of position and guard, then an attack that startled him into a defense and a turn, into a quick flurry of passes that continued soundless and without contact for a moment.

Fool! he said to himself, and ducked under her attack and shoved her with everything he had.

She hit the ground downslope and skidded in the mud. She was halfway up before he caught up with her and slammed her back again with a half-pulled kick.

Her head hit the ground this time. She sprawled on her back head-downward on the slope with the rain beating down on her and her eyes white-slitted in the lightning flashes.

"You damn fool!" he shouted at her. "It's raining!"

She fought for breath, mouth open, and writhed over and slithered toward her knees.

His hand was waiting when she got that far. She glared up at him and he did not wait then, he took her arm and pulled her up, pulled her to him. There was no chill. Her body burned like fever, her sides heaving in the effort to breathe. "Come on," he said, and pulled her toward the cabin, up the slope. She pushed herself away from him to be free, and kneed him hard: the knee missed. He let her go, since that was what she wanted, and she fell to her hands and knees in the mud of the hill.

"All right," he said. "Lie there."

He stalked off, gathered up his gear from beneath the tree and took it to the cabin, up the steps, onto the porch before he looked back in the gathering dark and the lightning flashes and saw her sitting where she had fallen, tucked up, a small lump beyond the gnarled old tree.

"Damn you," he muttered, and dumped the armor and staggered back, grabbed her by the arm and hauled her up again, feeling the chill in her limbs this time. He held her arms pinned and hauled her along till it was clear she was trying to walk. Then he picked her up and carried her, stumbling in the mud, slipping on the steps. A stabbing pain went through his leg. He almost lost her there. But he made it to the door and kicked it open, got her to the warmth and light inside and collapsed with her on the floor by the fire.

She was shivering. He held onto her, his arms wrapped around her until she pushed away from him. Then he let her go and stripped off his wet clothes, dried his hair with a quilt and wrapped it about himself until his own teeth stopped chattering before he went back to her.

The water had boiled. He poured it into a bucket of cold water and put the oil-and-rags on to heat, then knelt down and started drying her muddy hair on the corner of his quilt.

"Let me alone."

"The hell." He grabbed her wet shirt and hauled it up over her head while she fought to hold onto it, teeth chattering. "It's not a rape, you damn fool, you're soaked. Get it off yourself, then."

"Let me *alone!*"

He jerked the shirt the rest of the way off. Livid marks stood out on her back, on her arms, old bruises and bruises yet to come.

He touched her poor back gently. He squeezed out water from the cloth in the bucket and washed her shoulders, washed her neck, while the shivering doubled her into a knot and finally passed, leaving her limp in his arms, her own arms folded tight as a shield against intimacy, her knees tucked up in a shivering that racked her whole body.

The breeches were running a muddy cold puddle. He pulled the tie and pulled them half off before she knew what he was about: he held her in one arm, lost the quilt from around him and got them down to her knees before her struggles got violent. He held onto her and hissed into her ear: "Girl, I'm cold, I'm tired, you cut me close to where it matters, and if you kick this damn bucket over I'll let you freeze in it. Settle down. Settle *down*, my word I'm not after your skinny body, you're all right, settle down."

He stopped pulling, she stopped fighting, and he wrapped the quilt around both of them and held onto her, just held her while she broke into a new spate of shivering, no hands where she would not want them, not that the thoughts were not there, but there were sober ones too—that he had pressed her hard enough, that things were already at the brink of no forgiveness with her, and that she stopped fighting now was the last little trust she had in him. So he held her like something fragile, and did no more than stroke her wet hair and sit there while his joints stiffened and one shoulder chilled, where the quilt would not reach.

He sneezed finally, and winced, and she moved.

"Let me go," she said in a faint voice.

He relaxed his arms. "There. You're free."

She struggled to get up. She hit the cut on his leg, and he grunted and took her by the arms while she was trying to disentangle herself without touching him at all.

He gave her the quilt. She snatched it around herself and averted her eyes from him, sitting with her back to him. The lamp was guttering, sending the shadows crazy.

"I haven't quit," she said in a thin, hoarse voice, and sent a chill of a different sort through him.

"I beat you," he said to her back, rationally, desperately, "with an attack you didn't know. I've been at this all my life. There'll always be one you didn't know. And I could have hit you with a hundred. Do you understand? There's no hope for you. No man will even fight you fair. They won't bother. They'll shoot you if you're lucky. That's what's true, never mind what you want. I can't teach you enough. I don't want to see you dead. You wouldn't believe me. You wouldn't listen. Listen now. You're good. You're possibly the most gifted student I've ever seen, *including* myself. But skill is worth nothing against men like that, against odds like that. I thought you'd come to the sense to see it. But you hadn't. You pushed *me*, and you're ready to push everything else; and you weren't ever going to see it until I pushed back."

She turned half about and looked at him from the corner of her eye.

"I haven't quit."

"Don't be a fool," he said.

"So you can beat me. That's no news. So what did you prove? That I was sorry I made a mistake? That I did make one when I hit you?" Her voice went to a croak and died. She turned half about, clutching the blanket around herself, himself sitting there in the cold with not a stitch on. But she stared off ahead of her with her chin trembling and the tears running down beside her mouth. "You didn't believe I could hit you again. I knew I could. You remember it wrong."

He smothered his anger, got up and grabbed a quilt off his mat and hugged it around himself. "There's truth in that. Not all of it's true. You listen to me, girl. The damn leg caught. I strained it, it went bad on me. I'm not what I was. But luck won't always run in your favor. And I won't help you kill yourself."

"If you stop now," she said, "I'll go with what I know."

"You'll get yourself killed!"

"Maybe I will." The voice croaked and broke again, the face, the unmarred side, like a white jade image in the guttering lamplight. "But I *keep* my promises."

That stung. He stared at her a long while, and when he spoke his own voice cracked. "We'll talk about it. Tomorrow, not tonight. Go lie down on your stomach. I'll bring the rags. Are you hurt anywhere?"

She shook her head, kicked off the sodden trousers from about her ankles and got up holding the quilt around her. She tried to clean up—picked up her drip-

ping clothes and his and put them in a pile by the door
on her way to her mat. For his part he got up, tied a
cloth about himself for decency and pulled on his remaining shirt for warmth before he put the rest of the
rags on to heat at the hearth and brought the hot ones
to her.

She made no fuss about it when he peeled the quilt
back by degrees and applied the compresses.

And tempting as it was to talk to her and try to
explain while she was quieter, he did not think there
was reason in her, not tonight. He picked a bit of mud
from her hair—she had made a mess of the quilt as well
as his armor that was lying out on the porch in the
storm; and he ventured to peel her wet hair away from
her face. The scar stood out plain on her pallor. And
she flinched from that slightest and only touch that had
nothing to do with treating her injuries, flinched and
turned her face the other way.

"Are you so angry with me," he asked, "only for
showing you the truth?"

She did not answer.

"Well," he said, "they chop heads for that in Chiyaden.
I can't say you're different than the rest of the world."

He rested his hand on her shoulder, gave her a pat if
only to annoy her and went to trim up the guttering
lamp-wick and fetch the second round of compresses,
cold, himself, and wishing he had someone to return
the favor.

Chapter Eight

She was moving moderately well in the morning. He was the one limping, and he sat down gingerly with his bowl of rice. They ate on the mats inside, considering the chill of the morning, although they had the door open, and the shutters, for light.

His armor was a sodden mess, still. That would take long work, to recover it from its muddy heap on the porch. He had wrung out their muddy clothes and spread them by the hearth to dry before he went to bed, and they had them to put on. The cabin was a shambles, the matting and the quilts muddy and stained with leaf-mold and blood, rags and buckets competing for hearth-space with the rice-pot.

He had cooked the breakfast too. He asked nothing of her this morning. He gave her no orders. If he asked himself why, he thought with the edges of his mind that he had tried her too far and done something wicked, pushing the girl to a desperate self-defense: and that was how he had ended up on the defensive, not that he was less than he had been, not that he had outright failed to defend himself, but that he had known damned well he was in the wrong and had no wish to hurt her in the bargain.

But, he told himself, she was not a student, she was a girl, and no one would have reasonably expected a girl to go berserk. No one of his skill should use his arts all-out against a woman—that was why his instincts had laid him open to a cut on the leg, that was why he had given ground. He could have taken the sword away from her. He should have. If it were a boy, he would have. He would never have felt that moment of dismay. He would never have taken the first step backward. Or the second.

Damn her.

He had set the empty laundry bucket in front of the door last night, as if it were carelessness; and tried to stay awake, or at least not to sleep too deeply, for fear she would try to escape in the night. Not for fear of murder. He had no thought she could succeed at that; and certainly he deserved better than that, even if she was a peasant and a woman, without any concept of honorable behavior. But he was mortally afraid of her trying to slip away and leave before he could make himself clear to her. It would be like her obstinacy to try to leave in the middle of a rainstorm. Damn her again.

He was a fool ever to have encouraged her. A fool to have taught her. A fool not to have taken her by force and ended her silliness. He could bring her to good sense. Pleasure itself could seduce her away from her lunacy.

That was what was the matter with her, anyway. Her first experience with men had put fear in her, driven her away from what was womanly and twisted all her thinking. He could cure that. No woman *he* had ever slept with had complained of the experience. She certainly would not.

Damn, damn, and damn. Give the bitch straightforward conditions. Tie her hand and foot if he had to. No more negotiations.

Why in *hell* had he backed up and gone for the sword, to match her even?

Could nine years take that much away from a man?

You're off your center, master Saukendar. . . .

She had said not a word this morning, not had her bath, nor had he: he had only pulled himself to his feet and dressed, opened the shutters for light and started breakfast before he brought her clothes to her.

They had had no supper, the morning was cold and wet, and she had dressed and sat down in a lump on the matting, not near the fire, not near him.

But the food brought a little interest when he gave it to her and sat down. She at least attacked it with appetite.

"I said we would talk," he said then.

She did not look at him. Or stop eating.

"I tried to tell you in words," he said. "You wouldn't hear words. You won't believe me. You insist to be a man. Then take a beating like one, take my advice like one, and listen to me when I tell you haven't the reach, you haven't the weight, you haven't the strength, and unlike a boy, you won't grow into it. You won't succeed at this. There are other things to do with your life. There are other things worth having."

Long silence. She took another bite and never looked at him.

"I want you to stay here," he said. "I'll go on teaching you. I'll teach you everything you can learn. But give up this notion of revenge. It's not going to buy you anything but grief. Someday you can be very good. Someday you might have a son or a daughter to teach."

She looked up at him the way a tiger might, glancing up from its meal.

"I'm very fond of you," he said.

It got nothing but that stare.

"Have I deserved to be hated?" he asked her. He had argued cases before the Emperor and before high magistrates and felt less at risk. "You came to my mountain, you disturbed my peace, you demanded this, you de-

manded that, you insisted I not touch you, all of which
I've granted; and now I deserve a look like that?"

There was a little tightening of her mouth. A blink.

"Or are you sulking because you've lost? *That's* not
manly behavior. Are we changing the rules today?"

The mouth trembled. The eyes flashed. "You caught
me by a damn trick. I didn't lose. You cheated."

"We're not talking about games, girl. You're talking
about killing a man. Is he an honest man? Not by
anything I know of him. So where is this talk about
rules and tricks? Where is any man that will fight duel
with a woman? Have you killed, yes. Meet you fair he
won't, for his pride's sake. Cut off your hand for carrying a weapon. That, he will. But I haven't taught you to
go killing honest men. They're the only ones who'd deal
fair. Don't *ever* take your opponent's word for anything.
That's the lesson."

Her face had lightened a little.

"But there's another one," he said. "And that's that
you're not equal to this. Give up this notion. Stay here.
I'm not a cruel man. Everything I've done, I've done
trying to stop you from a mistake. Stay and you'll see
I'm not the ogre I've been. I don't even say you should
share my bed, though I won't say I don't hope you'd
want to."

She shook her head.

"No," he read that. "But no to what?"

"No."

"Taizu, for gods' sake, *talk*."

She set her bowl down on the mat in front of her.
And stared at it and frowned.

"Taizu—"

She held up her hand, asking quiet. So he was quiet,
and waited, and after a moment she said:

"Are you going to interrupt me?"

"No," he said.

A moment more she stared at the floor, her hands on
her knees. Then: "You cheated to beat me. I didn't
expect that of my teacher. I should have, you're right,

and I won't forget it, master Saukendar. I wouldn't have trusted anyone else. Now there isn't anybody." Her chin trembled, and she lifted her hand, insisting on his silence until she had regained her calm. "I told you my bargain. I'll cook and I'll clean. And I'll stay another year. I haven't quit. You'll go on teaching me and you won't cheat me: teach me what I need to win. Whatever it is."

She's grown, he thought, dismayed. *She's learned that much. All right. Another year and more time, and maybe that's the cure for everything. Then she'll come to her senses. Otherwise she can find ways to escape. And damned if I want to track her down.*

"I haven't quit. It's still your word."

"You've failed, girl. *That's* the bargain."

"No. Till I *quit,* you said. You can't change that just because you say something different."

"Dammit, *quit* means when you can't learn any more. And you've gotten there. You're going to kill yourself."

She shook her head solemnly and looked at him with hard reproach, tears brimming.

"Dammit," he said aloud, "you could have a broken back. Or a broken skull."

"If you'd been able to hit me."

"If I'd been *able!* Girl, you're sadly mistaken."

"Maybe I am. I don't know. You said you weren't playing fair. Maybe you weren't telling the truth. Maybe you lied to me about that too. How do I know?"

"Damn your impudence."

"I haven't quit. *That's* the truth, master Saukendar."

He was quiet a time more, his breakfast cold and mostly untouched. He poked at it, and set the bowl down with a queasiness in his stomach.

"Are you going to keep your word? They never said you lied."

"I have kept my word."

"Are you *going* to?"

Backed to the wall. "Yes."

"Are you going to cheat me this time?"

"You need to learn respect for your teacher, girl. Your failures are nature's, not mine. I can't help your incompetence."

"You worked all year to try to stop me. What else do you call it, when you taught me everything so you could beat me and make me think I'd lost?"

"You *did* lose, fool. I did precisely what you asked. It's taken you a year to get smart enough to ask what you need, rather than telling me. Shut up," he said, lifting a hand for silence as she opened her mouth. "And listen to me. I gave you your say. Let's first of all have the habit of listening, shall we? You want to walk into a castle and murder a man. How will you do that? Walk in the front gate and say: *Here I am, a woman, come to challenge lord Gitu to a duel?* Is that your plan? It's got bad holes in it, girl."

"I wait till he's hunting. Then I don't have to walk in the gates."

So. We are thinking. So we teach her the right way, the slow way. Teach her prudence, for the gods' sake. That goes with the skills. It's damned well the thing she needs. Prudence, patience, and an understanding what she's up against. "Let's calm down and *think*, then, girl, about the real world, not your imaginings. So you meet him in the countryside. He's on a horse. He's got a good twenty other men around him. Better shoot him from ambush. That's your best chance. And then you've got to get out of there, because those twenty men are going to be after you. Have you got a horse?"

Her eyes were on him now, hot and dark and red-rimmed from recent tears. "I want to *kill* him. I want him to know he's going to die. I want him to see me plain."

His gut tightened in the face of a hatred like that. He tried not to remember when he had felt it; but it came back for a breath, in all its force.

"Listen. There was a boy when I was in training. His name was Abi. His family had enemies. One day he took a sword and attacked their house. The guards killed him. That's the end of the story. He never grew up. He never got smarter. His enemies are rich and his family suffered disgrace."

"Mine's dead," she said. He had walked into that one.

"Then at least think of your teacher and don't disgrace me by stupidity. *Someone* is responsible for you. And I couldn't teach you anything as long as you knew everything. You've lost your sense of balance, here—" He tapped his chest. "And everything's gone. Your courage is all because you don't mind dying. But you're likely to end up only dead, having done nothing you set out to do."

She scowled at him.

"First," he said, "plan to get out again."

The frown deepened.

"Think about *after*, girl. There *is* an *after*, of one kind or another and a revenge that leaves your enemies able to have their revenge on *you* is no revenge at all. Think about *after*, I say. Plan to survive this."

It was a strange expression in that startled look, a panic fear that touched him too, clear and sharp as if it were still alive—so that his heart sped and he felt the blood leave his hands. He was surprised by the strength of it, by daylight, surprised that a fool of a girl touched the old wound.

Her kin are dead. And it's as if the dead had deserted us in the street, in public disgrace. Or we'd somehow deserted our dead. I know where you are, girl. I've walked that road.

She gave him a defiant grimace. And thought her own thoughts, unreachable.

"Let me tell you something," he said then in a low voice, not ever having voiced such a thing before, having had no living soul to tell it to, and he was embarrassed now to be saying it—in the face of his own dead, to a peasant girl who would probably sneer and call him a coward. But it was sensible advice and it was true, and it was *not* what the ballads sang or the philos-

ophers said. "You want to know another thing I've
learned in nine years on this mountain, girl, it's that
there's no particular shame in being too smart to die
with your kin and your friends. I could have gone back.
If luck was with me I could have gotten to Ghita himself, and killed him. But I wouldn't have gotten out
again, and a dozen scoundrels would've survived me.
Damned if I'd give them the pleasure of having *my*
neck on the block. I trouble my enemies by living. A
dead man is no trouble at all. Neither is a dead girl
whose name no one knows or cares about. So be wise.
Live here with me. Become a rumor to disturb your
enemies' sleep . . . not a memory they won't even look
back on. You know what they'll say when you're dead?
She was some crazy peasant. That's all. That's damned
well all. And some other hound will take Gitu's place in
Angen and rule ten times worse than he did, to give
other assassins second thoughts. Nothing will get better. It may well get worse for what you do."

Her face grew pale. She was listening, he thought.
For the first time she was truly understanding what he
was saying.

Then: "No," she said, and shook her head vehemently.

"Think on it. You'll get one man. That's all. Maybe a
few of his guards. It's not payment enough. It can't set
anything right. Take my advice. Become a rumor. Rumors are much harder to kill."

Another violent shake of her head. She looked at her
hands and up at him, one eye from under a tangled fall
of dirty hair. "I'm not you."

"You can be the same. A mystery to them. Let them
wonder who you are."

Again a shake of her head, a taut, frightened look.
"No." She bit her lips and said, then, full of assurance:
"I'm not you, but the man that gave me this—" She
touched the side of her face. "I wouldn't be wondering
if he was dead. He didn't know how to use that knife he
had. He thought he did. A lot of them are like that."

"Some aren't."

"I'm still good. *I'm better than those men are.*"

"Of course you are." Still the whisper, closest confidence. He had her attention. He was gaining ground with her, he felt that he was. "What you don't have is experience—and a repertoire of tricks in case one goes astray. You ask me to teach you. That began last night. Let me tell you another thing. Whatever they did to you, that scar outside isn't your trouble. It's fear. It's the kind of panic that makes bad judgement and drives you to heroics. Get rid of your fear of men, girl. I don't say you should sleep with me. But I say that being afraid to—won't steady your arm or make good judgements. You're scared to death of me. You're scared to death of getting caught by these men because you know what can happen. That's not going to make good decisions. I don't think it's making a good one for you now. If you weren't scared of me, you'd think a lot more clearly. And you wouldn't run from me."

"I said what I would do for my keep! I'm not a whore!"

"It wasn't a whore's portion that I offered you. You think, girl. Fear makes mistakes. Fear makes its own reasons for a choice, when good sense would say it costs too much. Don't let fear push you. Whatever the fear is. Do you understand me? Until you overcome that— until you make up your own mind—your enemies are masters of everything you do. And you'll fail at the last. I've no question of it."

She turned away from him and scrambled to her feet, to the door, not looking at him, no.

"The sword is not the highest skill," he said. For a moment he was back in Yiungei, at home, in the court of pale stone. It was his father's voice. "It's a shadow of that skill. The substance is in yourself."

She looked back at him, angry and confused.

"The sword isn't the weapon," he said. "You are. Do you understand me yet? I can teach you the higher knowledge, but I can't say it's going to make sense to you. Don't frown. Show respect for your teacher. By

the gods, you'll learn manners before you learn anything. I won't have taught a barbarian."

"*Yes*, master Saukendar."

"Don't give me that tone. I've been patient. You're
treading very close to trouble this morning. You ask me
favors, you ask me to teach you, this is part of it. Go
clean up. And clean up this mess. I'm certainly not
going to."

She bowed, her mouth a taut line. And she went
without a word to gather up the cooking pot and the
laundry and a bucket and head for the spring.

One did not know what to do with a girl like that.
She *was* crazy.

He was, to agree to the things he had just agreed to.

So he thought, contemplating a cold bowl of rice and
a solitary breakfast.

He was afraid she might change her mind, afraid she
might not come back from her bath, afraid that, after
all, she would decide she knew enough and take out
one day, armed with her sword and her absurd notions.

She upset his stomach.

And disturbed his sleep.

It was the way with nagging problems, he thought,
that they could lie quiet all day and turn on a man in
the dark. If Taizu were not sleeping across the room he
would do what he had done on the worst nights, in the
early years and sometimes since: light the lamp and
find some work for his hands, and sleep during the day
till the ghosts and the demons had left him. But pride
afforded him no such refuge, and they had drunk most
of the wine.

What's the matter, master Saukendar?

He lay still, staring up at the roof with his heart
pounding, recollecting what hate felt like and what it
was to have lost everyone who mattered in the world.

And when he was not doing that he was reliving the
moment that he had backed up from a crazed girl with
a wooden sword.

Stupid, he chided himself.

Or he was wondering why he had ended up giving in to every demand she made.

Twice stupid.

He could not remember *what* he had sworn to her, that was the truth of it. *He* grew confused about what he had said.

One hardly knew what to do with such a woman. Beat sense into her, perhaps. One wanted to. But dealing with her was like trying to hold water in one's fist: the open hand, he told himself, was the only way.

So one kept the hand open. That was all. One took seriously the idea that she might go, in some fit of temper, and one hoped to teach her enough to save herself.

One hoped to teach her to rethink her notions and give up her idea of a personal revenge.

One had to maintain one's own sense of balance, and not relive those days. There was too much anger there, and too much pain; and it disturbed him that he had disposed of less of it than he had thought.

He had gone completely confused when she had come at him, that was what had happened. Her anger had been thoroughly imposing, and he was so very long from having used any of his other skills that he had instinctively, faced with a girl he had no desire to harm, realized that he was not in control of those skills and refused to use them. That was the truth he came to, in the dark, in long hours.

He had lost command of his art. That was the other part of the truth. The skills were there, but something essential was gone, whatever had ruled them and made them whole.

That was not her doing. It had been gone, he thought, from the time he had known there was nothing to be done. After that he had had confidence in nothing, and believed in no divine order, only chaos. If there were demons, and he believed even in them only by dark, the demons ruled the world, and always had.

So even having discovered the flaw in himself, he could not mend it.

Hell with it.

He should have slept with Meiya; he should have supported Riga in his bid to unseat the young Emperor; he should have taken every opposite course to the paths he had taken for honor's sake.

Teaching the girl, he took another—for honor's sake—if that was even what he had sworn in the first place.

Damn, they were all the only choices he had known how to make. If he had always been a fool he had had no choice about it, being a fool to start with; and if he had forgotten himself so far as to lay himself open to a girl with a stick, perhaps he had come down to a general disgust with living.

He had not felt that since the first years, not since that long night in the first winter, when cold and exhaustion and solitude had had the knife in his hands and gods and devils knew what had kept him from using it then.

He had been to the brink a few times since, but never at all in recent years. Not in this one, in this strange, different year when he had found himself taking a sudden interest in the world, when he had found the walls going down all around him, past and present and future. He had known the danger he was slipping toward, that he was laying himself open to more than sticks and a girl's temper.

Strange that a man could become so fragile. It was good that he could see it at least, and build back the walls and recover the skills he had let fall. That was the compensation she gave him. A man would be a fool indeed to let the chance pass, a little good time was worth the pain. And nothing he could win of her by force was worth shortening the time she might stay, or breaking the peace between them.

So he could recover his life if she left. *When* she left. It was a romantic fool who thought otherwise. He could buy some girl-servant from the village. There were always too many daughters. A village girl would fall down on her face and thank him for the honor of being concubine to a lord of Chiyaden. Hell with Taizu. Anyway. He could always find another pig-girl to teach. Maybe buy a pig or two to go with her.

Maybe, he thought on the contrary, the spring planting would rouse something domestic in his farmer-girl. Maybe he could buy a few pigs for her. Help her with the gardening. Maybe all his notion of making her quit had only made life here seem too hard.

Maybe he should take more of a hand with things and be gentler with her.

It was worth trying.

"I don't want any pigs," she said to his suggestion. "I'd rather hunt them."

So much, he thought, for that. But he took up the hoe and he went out to chop furrows in the garden, himself: Jiro had not lived this long to pull a plow—moving the occasional dead tree was enough for an old war-horse; and Jiro grazed placidly on the brown grass while humans sweated.

"You're putting those rows too close," she said, coming up from the stable.

He blinked sweat, wiped it off his face. "You could have said," he said with, he thought, remarkable self-control, "seeing I'm half done."

"You ought to be this far over." She measured with her hands.

"All right." His leg hurt. The hoeing was never his best job. And he had worked damned hard this year to get the rows straight.

"You're limping," she said.

"It's soft ground," he said. And swore to himself and started over.

The sword slid past her. "Turn," he said. "Give me your point. Now."

Her sword came around to his fingers. He led it. And

stopped. "Stand," he muttered; and stood holding his sword and meditating the lines of her stance, and the likely response to a move like that.

She *remembered* the moves he guided her to. She could repeat them. He shifted an elbow, improved a line like a sculptor in clay.

A smaller man, a lighter man, could turn a more powerful blow if the blade were angled just so, if the force slid along the steel; a swordsman of excellent balance could follow the force and slip under it.

It was not the way his father had taught. It was the art of master Yenan.

Forgive me, he thought to his ghosts. It was not pure form. It was a constant compromise, it demanded agility and the excellence of balance that, thank the gods, the girl had in unusual measure.

It took perfection of style and turned it askew, to do things more common to the inns than to the teaching-masters.

What has philosophy to do with pigs?

Or what abstract does she understand, except revenge?

"Again." He took up his guard. He followed the perfect, the schooled line, the natural course for the blade.

He brought the sword down solidly. It slid.

"Again."

Harder this time.

"Again."

With real force, his heart in his throat.

Steel grated and flashed around toward him and up again, in the wheeling stroke he had taught her.

It was, he congratulated himself, a move of some subtlety.

Her eyes shone.

With hope that turned his stomach.

Chapter Nine

The arrows thumped into the target one after the other, six, seven, eight. The archer stood, bow bent, feeling out the gusts of wind that skirled up the pasture slope under summer sun, and a seventh followed.

Center of the target, every one.

Small woman with an uncommonly powerful bow, one she had made herself, under his close direction.

Shoka stood leaning on his own and watching the concentration on the eighth shot, then quickly nocked an arrow on the carrying gusts and fired as she was about to loose the ninth.

She fired all the same, and as the two arrows hit side by side, turned an amused look on him.

"Damned good," he said, leaning again on his bow. "You don't spook."

"I know it's you," she said.

"Good. How do you know?"

She pointed off across the field where Jiro grazed placidly on the slope. "He knows."

He smiled. "Fair enough."

"But in Chiyaden," she said, "there won't be anyone I'll let on my flank."

Laughter died. "Well you shouldn't," he said, and took up his bow and walked away.

There was silence behind him, no sound of string or impact. Retrieving her arrows, he thought. For his part he went and hung up his equipment and picked a few squash for supper.

The leaves began to turn, as the boy came back, with more rice and more wine and a few jars of preserves. "Thank you," Shoka said, bowing politely himself, and the boy bowed and accepted his small list of wants, which were few for this coming winter.

A little straw. The cabin thatch held quite well. Rice and wine, a double portion. But he laid out for the boy a fine lot of furs and a little smoked meat besides.

So Taizu came out and watched the boy go down the mountain, herself squatting on the porch, arms on knees.

Not so timid now, Shoka thought to himself, observing her there in front of him, small figure with a tail of braid between her shoulders. More of curiosity than apprehension—

Perhaps Taizu did not even know the change in herself. He could see it, slow and sure, subtle as the changes in her body—shoulders broadened with muscle, legs strong and shapely, as she had acquired other, more womanly contours.

He had known half a hundred courtesans, soft of skin and pale and certainly never showing such an unfashionably broad back or taking such a graceless posture. Certainly Meiya never would. But, gods—

He whiled away the winter with stories, with moral tales master Yenan had told them: with, sometimes, stories of the court, and of things he had never told to any courtesan, nor any man either, when he came to think of it—duels he had fought, and skirmishes with the conspirators who had plagued the old Emperor in

his decline. He was telling the tales to someone outside
the court and beyond those politics, without family to
be offended, someone whose eyes flickered with understanding when he named this sword tactic and that, and
what his opponent had done right and wrong—not by
way of boasting, only pouring everything he knew out
to the only person since his father had died that he had
ever felt moved to tell these things.

She at least knew the reputations of the men he
named. That amazed him. "They tell stories in Hua,"
she said, amused and a little piqued, one night that he
said as much. And he felt strangely naked then, to
discover that a simple quarrel in the court had spread
so far and been embellished beyond all reason—in the
versions *she* recounted.

"Sorcery, hell," he said, regarding lady Bhosai's death.
"She was blackmailing lord Ghita. She drank from the
wrong teacup. I tell you, Cheng'di was like that. You
never trusted anything. They deserve all they got."

She looked at him, distressed.

"They killed the good ones," he amended. "But lady
Bhosai wasn't one of them. Lord Riga was. At least—"
He was whittling a filler for a crack the cold had
warped into the door planks. "I could have supported
Riga. He wanted to overthrow the heir. Dammit, if I'd
done it—" He peeled off one long hard curl. "Well,
someone else would have gotten him. Riga was a man of
principle. That was all. No great intelligence. Couldn't
be worse than the young Emperor. But he wouldn't
have lasted the day, once he declared himself. As it
was, Ghita found him out and killed him. I could prove
the one who did it. I couldn't prove the link to Ghita."

He looked up at her, at a face intent and listening,
asking him no questions.

"All of which is past," he said, and drew another
long stroke down the wood. "Past and dead. I don't
know there was ever a thing I could have done. Not for
myself. Not for—anyone else." He had never mentioned
Meiya's name to her. And he found her listening and

the night and the storm urging it was something she might understand, something that might explain a great deal to her, that he wanted her to know. But he could not bring himself to mention Meiya's name. Meiya had faded too much. And Taizu never asked, though that part, he knew, was a story the people knew.

"This was the inner court," he said, laying out sticks to frame the rectangle. It was still winter. Night was outside, and wind; and they worked over a good supper, a little wine. The stories became tactical problems, things he had witnessed. He set pebbles in the sand. "Gates." He stuck twigs upright. "Guards." A leaf with a pebble on it. "Lord Hos in his bed."

She gave a grim laugh. It was an attempted murder he showed her, one where the assassins had failed. Where there had been more tricks than lord Kendi's men had counted on.

"The walls are slanted, so. One can climb them with a grapple and a line. This wall has windows. Two."

"How big?"

"Big enough for a slender man."

She nodded, paying strict attention.

"So. Over the walls. In through the windows . . ."

"Is there a dog?"

"There's a monkey. It wakes."

"In the dark. The guards are going to be there in a moment."

"Have you left your line?"

"I did. I didn't take it down. I think I'd better get clear of there."

"I think you'd better. But there's guards here now—" He moved two twigs. "Armed with pikes."

"I have the bow."

"Can you take two?"

She nodded.

He moved more twigs. "So far you're doing better than the assassin. But two more guards have come up at your back."

"No arrows in my hand. I'd better get around the corner."

He planted two more twigs. "Sorry. You couldn't see them from the wall. They both have bows."

"The other way, down and roll, hit the doorway."

"The monkey's raising hell."

"The old man's awake. I'm down this hall the other way. The guards rush in. I'm there with the bow, at their backs."

"*Not* bad."

"I just wait for the rest. That's the other two."

"The man's little daughter runs into the hall."

Her face shadowed.

"Happens," he said.

"Not fair, master Saukendar."

"Will you die for that girl?"

She shrugged. "Let her yell. Like the monkey. She'll bring her papa."

"You'll shoot him in front of her."

"Happens," she said.

"Two more guards."

"If the girl's still yelling, good. Let them come in."

"They do."

"They're dead. I'm out for the wall."

"Hell, use the front gate. Take a horse while you're at it."

"There might be servants there too. I'm for the wall. I'm up and over."

He nodded. "You've left no witnesses but the daughter." And with calculated force. "Suppose she might come after you."

Her eyes shadowed again. "Gitu hasn't got a daughter. Not fair, master Saukendar."

"Nothing's *fair*, girl."

"Well, it's not poor lord Hos I'm after. It's Gitu. There isn't any daughter to worry about. If there was, she'd be well rid of him."

"He's got two sons and a flock of men-at-arms."

"That's why I won't go into his castle after him. Wait in the fields. That's the way I'll do it."

"You'll never take him with the sword. The bow, I'm telling you. It's your best weapon. Let me tell you another thing—" He drew a breath. "*Do* it and get away from there. Come back here. You'll be safe here. Plan to survive your enemy, dammit."

She had looked down the moment he said that, about coming back to the mountain. And that stung.

"I'm still the villain, am I?"

"No, master Saukendar."

"*Master Saukendar*. That's my court name. That's for talking *about* me. People called me Shoka, to my face. I'd rather you did."

"I'm your student, master Saukendar." Without looking up at him.

"I know. You won't sleep with me. I've got that memorized—it's not very long. That wasn't what I asked you. I just told you I've never liked that name. Saukendar is a damn fool. A story. Tinsel and air. Shoka is who I *am*, who I've been since I was a boy. Saukendar was what my mother used to call me when I was late to supper."

She gave a strange little breath. It might have been a laugh. She did not look up from her hands and her lap.

"I had a mother," he said. "Unlikely as it seems. Her name was Jeisai. She died of a fever. When I was twelve. After that my father had just house-servants."

She did not look at him.

"An uncle, an aunt, two cousins," he said. "I was late in my father's life. I missed my grandparents on his side. I do remember my mother's family. More cousins. Some of them may still be alive."

There was still no response.

"Even in court," he said, "we had kinfolk. It's not the sole prerogative of Hua."

No answer still.

"Damn, girl. —Taizu. If I haven't jumped on you in a year and a half, do you expect I'm getting too friendly because I talk about my relatives? I'm not a damn statue."

"No, master Saukendar."

"Shoka, dammit. You could at least call me by my right name."

"Master Shoka, then."

He sighed and leaned his elbow on his knee, hand behind his neck. "Gods."

She got up and fled to her mat, her side of the room, and sat there, not looking at him.

In a moment more she found use for her hands, braiding the rope she had been working at, the length of it pegged to the wall at the end of her mat.

"Girl. Taizu."

The fingers flew. The braid lengthened like magic. Never a look in his direction.

"You really try me," he said. "Dammit, I could come over there and be as rude. Where are your manners? You act like a damn rabbit!"

The braid lengthened another palm's-length. And her fingers stopped. "I respect you too much," she said without looking at him. "I *want* to do what makes you happy. But I don't want to sleep with you. I won't. That's all."

"Thank you," he said coldly. And then thought, with a little pain in the gut, that it was the first time she had ever confessed any fondness for him. And it was not the sort he had hoped to foster.

It was better than hatred.

It still made a cold bed that night.

They had practiced in the snow; they had practiced on the porch and up and down the steps, for practice with bad footing.

It was the yard by the old tree again, breath frosting on the air, and mud up to the knee.

Taizu went down, messily. He followed up with the sword while she slipped a second time on her recovery.

She had a handful of mud ready with hers. But she did not throw it.

He tilted his head to one side, looking down at her. "You should have," he said. "In your position nothing can be worse."

"I'd have to wash two shirts."

He laughed and offered his hand. "Up. Try it again."

She gave him her sword-arm and he pulled, helped her up, himself muddy to the knee. Helping her, he got it on his hands. And she contemplated the handful she had, shook it off and wiped her fingers on his shirt.

It took boiling to get their clothes clean. But he cherished that day, that he saw Taizu laugh.

There was still hope, he thought.

"Master Shoka," she said the next day, "can I have this?"

Holding the hide of the wild pig they had shot.

"Of course. For what?"

"For a shirt," she said. And laid a hand on her shoulders. "If I double-sew it, it gives me some protection. Without the weight. I think, after yesterday, I'd do better to have it."

He said nothing for a moment. Then he nodded grimly.

"All right," he said, and went and got the deer-skin, that was the finest of the skins they had. "No sense doing a patch-together."

So of evenings he carved small plates of bone, none above the size of a finger-joint, to fit the double-sewn lining of the armor he intended for her: pigskin outside, on the shoulders, soft deerskin inside, and little lozenges of bone sewn into the lining of the shoulders, down the back, and around the ribs and on the skirtings.

A woman's armor, light and flexible, to protect against grazing blows without sacrificing agility.

In the case of bandits, he told himself. Even if she might not go, it was worth having, in case the brigands from over in Hoishi ever tried them.

Damn.

Jiro grunted and rocked to the strokes of the brush, great fat lump that he had grown to be, well-fed and comfortable, and Shoka brushed til the winter hair flew in clouds in the sunlight that filtered in through the cracks of the stable walls.

Another year on the old fellow. There was more white around his muzzle, and Shoka tried not to see that. But when he was done he leaned on the horse's neck and patted him hard and wished—

Gods, for time to stop.

For death not to happen.

"I've got a fool on my hands," he said to the horse. Foolish to be talking to the horse. But he had, for years, because otherwise he never used his voice.

Until she came. And his whole life began to turn on that point.

"I teach her," he told the horse, who turned back a sympathetic ear, "because it's the only thing that keeps her here. Make her armor to keep her from killing herself. What else can I do? Eh?"

Jiro curved his neck around and lipped the hem of his shirt.

"Woman's a damn fool," he said, and scrubbed and curried with a vengeance. "She's not ready yet. Not near. She's finally getting the common sense to know it. At least she's come that far. *Men* are her problem. It's not Gitu gives her nightmares. It's every damn man who might look at her. Go out on that road. Looking for bandits. Gods!"

Horse and rider came rumbling up the rise of the summer pasture, and Shoka watched from the fence, elbows on knees, as Jiro took the crooked course toward the two men of straw and rags, as the sword came up, Taizu leaned from the saddle and hit one, Jiro veering about again—

Lazy horse, Shoka thought, seeing Jiro had gotten

into a rut. He knew straw figures when he saw them. School exercises.

But the sword strokes came very precisely on one or other of the lines of dye they had painted on the figures.

Back and forth, back and forth, from the straw-men at this end of the pasture to the straw-man at the other, till his rump grew tired with sitting and Jiro was lathered and hard-breathing.

"Suppertime!" Shoka yelled at her as she passed him and turned about again for the far end. "Walk him down!"

She drew in, Jiro bouncing and snorting and still ready to go for the targets. She got him down to a walk, and walked him down to the targets at the end, and to the rail, and reined in again.

A little space for breathing, he thought. There was a view from that vantage, out over all the valley, the whole of the mountain-skirts laid out to the west, toward the sunset and the gilded clouds.

But it was only that for the moment. He saw her gazing east, toward the dull, dark end of the sky; just sitting there for a while, facing that ill-omened direction.

He slipped from the rail, distressed, and waited until she finally reined about again. Then he wanted to seem not to have noticed, not to make any notice of it.

But she slowed Jiro again and turned him and looked back a moment more before she came back to the stable.

And she looked at him the same strange way, from the height of Jiro's back.

So he knew then that it was leaving she was thinking of. That the sun had begun to turn south again from its northerly wandering; and the fall was coming.

On a day like this she had come here. On an evening like this, with the sunlight gilding the edges of things. He remembered.

She said nothing about it at supper that night, on the porch. Or at breakfast, and still there was a kind of melancholy silence about her that told him that she was holding some debate with herself.

Perhaps, he thought, holding to hope, she was in the way of changing her mind. Perhaps that silence and that melancholy boded well for him.

He dared not ask and begin an argument: she was stubborn; she might go the opposite way out of habit. It was her sense of duty she was struggling with; it was—

Fondness, perhaps. A reluctance to leave what was comfortable; to leave a man who was at least her teacher. She weighed that against anger, against grief, against vows made by a child with no understanding of the cost of them to the woman she would be.

He had taught her to weigh things. Taught her to think things through, and the hardest thing in the world now was to keep himself quiet and pretend he had no notion there was anything amiss and just let her *do* what he had taught her and think down all the paths of the thing.

Trust her to use good sense at the last.

But he feared to go anywhere out of sight of the cabin, for fear that she might make up her mind without him of a sudden, and go, like the child she sometimes was, simply deserting him.

The very thought of that hurt.

One day and another one passed. He began to think perhaps he had read her wrong; or she had changed her mind.

Then he came back up the hill one afternoon to find her at the hearth, rolling up a packet of smoked meat in leather, with others by her.

"What are you doing?" he asked her by way of challenge: he already knew the answer.

She did not look at him immediately. She finished rolling the packet and put it with the others. Then she looked his way, as if facing him was very hard for her. "I'm going," she said.

"You're not ready yet."

"How long will it take? Till Gitu dies of old age?"

"Two years aren't enough. How long do you think a man studies with a master? Three and four. At the least. How long do you think Gitu's studied?"

She shrugged and turned and wrapped up the packets in an old rag and tied it.

"I haven't spent two years teaching a fool!" he said. "If the law catches you with that gear they'll cut your hand off."

She did not look at him.

"They'll catch you, girl. You don't walk like a peasant, you don't look like a peasant, you don't move like one, and you don't look like a boy anymore. Do you?"

"I can when I want to."

"Oh, *hell*, girl, not a chance. You're not shaped like a boy, you don't walk like one, either. *Or* like a peasant girl. So what are you going to do?"

She frowned. "Keep to the woods. Keep to the trails."

"With the bandits. A wonderful plan."

She stared into nowhere. "Can I take my mat and my blanket?"

He gave a wave of his hand, beyond talking for the moment. His breath seemed stopped up in his throat. He leaned against the wall by the door and folded his arms and looked at the floor.

"Can I take my mat?"

"Damn, take anything you want. Except Jiro. I don't care."

There was long silence.

She sniffed then, and he looked up and saw her crying.

"Well, you don't have to go," he said. "No one's making you. I don't want you to go. I'm begging you not to. How much plainer can I make it?"

She took up her bundle and went and dropped it on her mat.

"I'll stay here tonight," she said. "Tonight I'll sleep with you. There won't be any other time."

He drew in his breath, cold to the bones. "I don't understand you, girl."

"You said I shouldn't be afraid. So I want you to sleep with me. I want that to remember on the road. If I get a baby now it won't stop me. Nothing will stop me. I'll get there. I'll be as smart as I can. I'll come back here if I can."

"You'll do that and just walk out of here."

She nodded, calm now, and he stared at her in desperation.

Then he walked over to the corner shelf and got down his armor and flung it down by his mat. "Well, you might as well pack double, girl."

"No!"

"What *no?* I'm not leaving you to the bandits. Don't tell me that's not what you planned from the start."

"*I said no!*"

"Sorry." He got his sword and put it with his bow and quiver by the door.

"You're banished! They'll kill you!"

"So they will." He drew a breath and looked around him, at the place with its shelves and its accumulation of things that he had saved over the years, the familiar place, the familiar things. He felt a sense of panic, like finding himself poised on the edge of a fatal drop. But the step was easy. Very easy. He had learned that at the edge of duels, of judgements, of skirmishes. When there were no choices, one moved, that was all. He took down the whole hook of smoked venison and laid it on the hearth. "No sense to stint ourselves."

"Dammit, I'm not asking this!"

He looked at her and gave a smile, a laugh, a shake of his head.

"I'm not asking it! *I don't want you!*"

"That's all right. I forgive you." He found his leather breeches hanging from a rafter, pulled them down and tossed them onto his mat. "Have we got clean shirts?"

"Dammit!"

"You've learned bad language, girl."

"I don't want you to get killed!"

"That's a sensible ambition. Best I've heard out of

you yet." He took a spare shirt from the peg and threw
it atop the pile. "I don't want you with your hand
lopped by some magistrate. I'm along to settle questions
like that; and you're still learning. Something could
come up. Don't be arrogant. Take help when you need
it."

She wiped tears, crossed the room in a few strides
and started to snatch his armor up. He turned that
intention with a little move of his hand. And she knew
better than to carry *that* further.

"No," he said firmly. "Girl, you can take out down
that trail and try to leave, but I can still track you. So
can we save all that and start out together, tomorrow,
like two sane people?"

"It's my revenge, my life, my family. You have no
business in Hua!"

"You're *my* household," he said. "That's all. You want
this. All right. You've got it." He took her hand in his.
Hers was like ice, listless. "Let's do this in sensible
order. Get a good night's rest. Start out in the morning." He put his hand on her hip and she flinched.
"Changed your mind about tonight?"

"I—" Her teeth were chattering.

"Let me tell you: I almost married back in Chiyaden.
Lady Meiya and I—were lovers in everything but the
act. After that, I had no other women but courtesans.
I'm telling you the truth. A boy was in love with a girl
who became his emperor's wife. The boy and the girl
were fools—who never took the chance they had to be
happy. Honor meant everything to them, even when
she despised her husband. And gods know *he* despised
the Emperor. —Maybe we did choose right. Or maybe
I'm twice a fool to have waited with you—but I'm
used to waiting for women, you understand. And I'll go
on waiting until you come to *my* bed. If it's not tonight,
that's all right. If it's never—that's all right. Whether
we sleep together isn't the important thing. The important thing is the reason I'm going with you. The most
important thing is the center of everything I've taught

you. You know what that is now? You know why I'm going?"

She nodded, bit her lip and broke into tears. She hugged him and held onto him a long, long time.

A dog, he thought, would take advantage of a tired, distraught girl who had carried everything in the world alone. Even if he wanted to. Even if he figured it was a chance that would never come again and that she had no idea what she wanted.

So he held her like a brother and rocked her a moment and finally set her back by the arms and said:

"Let's have supper. Let's not go off like lunatics, after you've waited two years. I'm not putting you off. I'm just saying let's pack in good order and not start out tired. Tomorrow if everything's in order, day after if it's not. All right?"

She wiped her eyes, turned her face away, embarrassed, and broke away from him, not hard, just not looking at him, not then, nor when she squatted down and busied herself at the hearth, wiping her eyes from time to time on her sleeve.

He came and squatted down peasant-style where he could see her face.

"I still want you," he said, in the case she had mistaken that. Gods, it was true. He hoped he had not made his point too strongly. "I just don't want to push you into anything. You make up your own mind. All right?"

"I made it up," she said, between clenching her jaw and wiping her eyes.

"You're not scared of me. After all this."

She shook her head fiercely. Lying, he thought. And reckoned she had had her courage all put together and he had done the wrong thing. He put out his hand, rubbed the back of her neck. Her muscles were hard as stone. But she allowed the touch, and went on working, measuring out the rice, ignoring him.

"Hell with dinner," he said.

She shrugged his hand off, not looking at him, and turned and reached for the water-dipper.

"Hungry, are you?" he muttered.

"Everything in good order," she said, giving him his own back.

It was a damned nervous supper, out on the porch. Her hands were shaking. His were, though not so conspicuously. They said not half a handful of words to each other. She hardly looked at him; and he kept looking at the yard, the stable, the place that had been home. His thinking narrowed itself to the road, to reaching Hua, to a possibility of getting away from that and getting back to the road—he planned his retreats the way he had taught the girl, right along with the action.

And he chided himself for the morose turn of his thoughts. But it was a long road home again; and the ones who came home again—would not be the man and woman who had left. Not after the things they would do in Hua. Or that would be done to them.

She took the bowls and washed them, and he lit the lamp and made down a bed for them, both their mats together.

By that time she had come back again, and seeing what he had done with her mat, she looked apt to bolt from the door; but she set the bowls down by the door and looked at him, then went to her side of the room where he had piled their gear and undressed with her back to him.

He undressed and when she delayed, taking more time than the matter ought, he went over to her and put his arms around her from behind, feeling the tension in her from head to foot.

"It's all right," he said into her ear. "No lady ever complained of me." He ran his hand over her skin, soft as any lady's to his calloused hands, and felt her shivering like a rabbit. "There's no hurry."

Ten years on this mountain and he could hold off a little longer. He could damned well wait the little time she needed. An hour, two hours, if that was what it took.

"I'll get you some wine," he said, and slapped her a stinging blow on the rump, the way he had done a few times in their working together. She jumped. "Both of us, all right?"

She gave him a shocked look, halfway offended, he thought, in her young pride. He got the wine down and poured a potful. And gave her a little smile, seeing her standing there somewhat confused and worried-looking.

"This isn't a duel," he said, and nodded toward the mat. "Get on over there."

She went. She sat down crosslegged, her usual way, and he took a healthy drink from the pot, sat down and gave it to her.

"Big one," he said.

She gulped down two huge mouthfuls, and blinked and passed it to him.

He took a drink and passed it back. She took two more.

"That ought to do it," he said, and took one more himself. She was looking a little pale and sickly. "Come on," he said, holding out his hand. "Face about, the other way."

"What are you going to do?"

"Nothing. Come on." As she edged about with her back to him. He rubbed her back and her shoulders, and uncrossed his legs and pulled her back then into his arms. He felt the panic in her, arranged his arms to let hers free. "There." He ran his hand gently over her skin. Her arms rested on his and he felt her sigh, finally, like a long-held breath, her shoulders relaxing against him.

"Good," he said, and worked lower, keeping his mind from what he was doing, deliberately, thinking that this had to be a long, slow night. He talked to her, nonsense. But the shivers grew fewer, and less frequent, even when his hand touched between her legs; and finally she jerked, doubled up, and nearly left his hold.

Damned surprised, he thought. She had that look on her face when she twisted over and looked at him. He felt his own reactions getting out of control then.

"Come on," he said, pulling her up against him. She had very little trouble taking the cues. He intended to have her atop. She turned to get him there, and he was careful going into her, with about the last control he had.

She was utterly still for a moment. Then he began to move, and finished faster than he would have wanted. But she wrapped strong legs around him and wrapped her arms around him and held on, just held him, for a long, long time, until he finally, realizing he was lying on her, eased over and held her the same way, gently.

"Was that bad?" he asked.

"No," she said after a moment.

"Did I hurt you?"

"No."

He lay there quite still a moment, wondering if he wanted to go on with the questioning.

Dammit, it mattered. But he was not going to ask question by question.

She tightened her arms around his neck, hard, with her considerable strength—not hurtful: trying, he thought, to say things too complicated to explain to a man. And he embraced her gently, a little pressure of his arms, thinking things too complicated to say to anyone that young and that old.

He thought he knew what she was saying: too separate, too different; and both about the same, that it was nothing like the poets, nothing like a physical release, nothing that this could settle. It just started things, that was all, that made matters more complicated than they had ever been.

But she was glad to be where she was, he thought. Maybe she was glad he was going with her. Maybe not. Maybe she knew she was being a fool. Maybe he was an older, wiser witness than her notions wanted.

Maybe she had gotten fond of him, and he was more

than an older, second-choice man to fill in for whatever she had lost—or dreamed, in a young girl's way, of having.

A man got older. A man got wary of caring for things too deeply. A man got wiser and ended up on a damn mountain. A man could die alone up here.

There were a lot worse things than following a fool girl to Hua. There was a terrible end to it, of course; but lives always came to that, in some year; this spring's rabbit ended up a stain in the snow, but the world never cared, and the rabbit had no long memory of it either.

Chapter Ten

He had never expected her to get up from his bed with any different attitude: he had lived with Taizu long enough to know better than that: everything was ordinary with Taizu. She began to get up, waking him with her moving, she said she was going down for her bath, everything as matter of factly as if nothing had happened.

He reached out and grasped her wrist. "Well?"

"Well?" she echoed, worried-sounding. She was only a shadow against the light coming from under the door and through the cracks of the shutters.

"Was it all right?" he asked her.

A sort of motion of her head. He could not tell what. *Yes*, he thought.

"Don't I get an answer?" he asked.

She took his hand that was holding her wrist and pulled his fingers from her. Then she held that hand in both of hers.

They had made love again in the night. He was not sure who had started that. She might have. Certainly he had needed no reason, whether or not she had intended to come up close against him, and he had gone slower in the act this time, to give her the pleasure she had missed the last time. But he had fallen asleep again after, till she moved and waked him in the dawn.

She gave him no answer now, except the pressure of her hands around his.

Well, maybe, he thought, that was as fair an answer as she could give—no courtesan's glib *Of course, my lord.* Taizu thought about things. Taizu thought for days on a matter before she ever opened her mouth. He could imagine the pensive line between her brows and the fierce tightening of her mouth. Then she slipped away from him, grabbed up her clothes on the way to the door and fled in a flash of daylight.

So Shoka sat on the porch in the cool morning, with the polished bronze bowl hooked to the post, a pan of warm water in front of him, judiciously scraping the stubble from his chin. That he did most every day, when he got around to it. But this time he had put his scalplock up in its clip at the crown, the rest of it, still black and still thick as any boy's, to hang down his back. There were weather-lines about the face, sun-frown graven about the eyes and the edges of the mouth; but overall, looking at that image in the bronze, he saw an appalling similarity between himself and a certain younger man, and said to himself: *Haven't learned a thing, have you?*

He was finishing when Taizu came up the hill from her bath—she still preferred the spring, for whatever reasons; and he had rather the rainbarrel, which was not so cold a walk afterward. She looked at him sitting there in his old guise, her eyes widened, and she stopped there, with her wet shirt hugged about her in the chill.

He shook water from his razor and dried it, flattered and pleased at that look, that fed a vanity he had not known he had, and for which he was, all taken, a little regretful: damned nonsense, he thought, in the same moment, because it was not Shoka the man she was seeing. It was Saukendar the fool. The one the world knew.

But it did not please her.

What in hell's the matter? he wondered, and froze, afraid suddenly, and not even knowing the answer.

She was afraid, he thought.

Of what? Noblemen? Gods knew she had cause.

"Something the matter?" he asked her.

"No, master."

"Master, hell. M'lord, if you like. Shoka if you don't." He rested the hand and the razor on his knee. "About last night—"

"I'm cold. I want to get dressed."

"Girl, I'm more than fond of you, if you haven't figured that out. I'd have you for my wife, if you want that."

She looked at him still, so still, and drew herself up with one breath and a second, sharper one. She stood there a moment looking at him, gathering her composure. Then she bit her lip and ran the steps right past him.

"Doesn't that even get an answer, girl?"

He heard her stop. He heard her standing by the door, the little movements of breathing, against the hush of dawn.

"I'm not a lady."

He turned around where he sat, and looked at her, figuring some of what was going on, at least. "My *wife* is whatever she wants to be. My *wife* is a lady. That's what I'm offering, dammit. I *don't* think I've insulted you."

A long silence. She looked toward the dark doorway, not at him, a long, long time. And the hand came up toward the scar which, gods witness, he had not so much as thought about, not last night, not this morning.

That damned scar and everything that went with it.

No tears. He feared she was going to cry in the next moment, and his gut tensed up; but she kept her composure. And never looked his way.

"Master Shoka, please don't come with me. Let me do this. Then I'll come back and be your wife. I'll be whatever you like. Just *stay the hell out of my trouble!*"

He sat there, still, calm, while a girl cut at him in a way that no one on earth would do and walk away from—if he had not sensed the pain in her, and the woman's honor she had, not to take morning-promises of a man that he might be fool enough, having shared a bed with her—to mean for three and four hours.

"I put no conditions on anything," he said. "I couldn't stop you from coming here. Now you can't stop me from leaving this place. You see—*preventing* things is very difficult. So I taught you. So I let you go. And now you can't stop *me.*"

"Yes, master Shoka." A hoarse and hollow tone, as if she foreknew defeat and played the game for courtesy's sake.

"I'm no fool, girl. I passed my own adolescence a long time ago. Give me that."

Silence.

"That's what you think, is it? I'm a fool?"

"No, master Shoka."

Bitterness overwhelmed him, a sudden vivid recollection of Meiya's grave, carefully painted face, a meeting in a garden, in the palace: *Marry someone. For the gods' sake*— And a thought, sharp-edged, that Meiya had traveled into that hazy nowhere-land of legends, a damned romance the country-folk told in wintertimes. Saukendar and lady Meiya. As if he, plain Shoka, had no right to tamper with that, or change the ending.

Master Saukendar. . . .

—Dammit to hell, I'm still alive!

And if I want a Hua pig-girl in Meiya's place, isn't that my right?

I never wanted to be a damn legend.

"Dress," he said sharply. "Then get out here. Or if you've changed your mind about going to Hua, say. You're not obliged to be a fool, you know. Or if you're set on it, then we'll go today. Whatever you choose."

She went inside. He picked up his shirt from beside him on the boards, put it on, belted it this time, and looked up at a thump and crash of something from inside the cabin.

Temper. Yes.

He put his armor sleeves on and tied the fastenings, and the shin-guards, with their ties, before Taizu came out and dumped their rolled mats on the porch.

"Come here," he said, and pointed to the steps at his feet. She frowned and came that far. "Sit," he said, and added: "Please."

"What are you going to—?"

"Sit."

She sat, and he unbraided her wet hair and combed it, carefully—then faced her about by the shoulders and took his razor.

"What are you doing?" she cried.

"Come, come—" He took up one lock and the other, combed them back, then cut the next, making a fringe of bangs.

She squinted her eyes and wrinkled her nose as the hair drifted down. Three and four judicious cuts and he took a loop of metal and a pin and faced her about again, combing the long hair up to fasten.

"You're wasting your time," Taizu said.

"Why?"

"You can't make *me* look like a lady."

"That's all very well. I don't want them to take you for a bandit, either." He faced her about again, combed more hair loose about her ears, held her by the chin. "Damn, that's not bad."

Her mouth made a hard line. There was thunder in her eyes, and a trace of rain.

"It makes the scar show."

He pinched her chin hard. Shook at her. "What kind of thinking is that? Hold the head up. *Hell* with the scar and hell with them. People won't forget your face, that's sure. So hold your chin up. Who are you afraid of?"

"Nobody."

"What kind of words are you afraid of?"

"Nothing."

"Mmmn, it used to be *Sleep with me.*"

She jerked away from his hand and gave him a furious scowl.

He smiled at her. "You're damned pretty."

"You're a liar, master Shoka."

"Girl, girl, you've got it wrong: a man lies to a woman about *that* before he sleeps with her, not after."

That set her back. He saw the flare of her nostrils, the set of her mouth.

"Better pack before we get into too much of this rig," he said. "And get Jiro saddled. I hope you know he's not carrying much baggage. He's no pack-horse, and his full rig weighs."

Still the scowl.

"Poor old fellow," Shoka added. "You're doing a terrible thing to him, you know."

He said it to torment her. But he also felt it.

Jiro laid his ears back when the steel went on, and he blew himself up and threw his head and shifted and stamped, all calculated to make saddling him difficult.

"I suppose you know," Shoka said to the horse, and patted him hard on his leather-and-steel armored neck. "It's the road again. Back by spring, if we're lucky."

One could promise anything to a horse. Jiro never listened anyway. He only flicked his ears and sulked.

A man, Shoka told himself, ought to have better sense.

He unfolded his armor-robe from where it lay on the porch, and put it on—a little frayed, a little stained from where he had bled on it all those years ago, but the gold-thread dragons were still bright, their green eyes undimmed. Clouds and dragons on the robe, and red stitching on the breeches he was wearing, that color being faded, considerably—hard to tell what it had

been to start with. He tied his belts and sashes, eased
the body armor on and sighed, fastening the side ties,
while Jiro waited down at the stable, stamping and
fretting.

The silk weavings of the armor had been red once.
Those on the body-armor mostly looked brown—especially
since the mud. He finished the ties across the chest,
and looked to Taizu, who came out with their bows,
their quivers, her sword, and the bundles that were
their food and their pots and pans and their personal
necessities.

She came back in a second trip with her armor, and
sat down and did her own shin-guards and her sleeves;
but he helped her with the rest.

"Not at all like a bandit," he said to her. In fact, he
thought, he had done quite a good job with her gear—
small deer-horn plates stitched in patterns: her colors
were all tans and brown. But he found a red silk cording among the things he had brought from Chiyaden
and made her stand still while he tied it in her hair.

"You have to understand," he said to her. "A little
decoration makes your enemy know you're confident. It
makes him worry."

She frowned doubtfully at him.

"It's the truth. Who would you be afraid of? A scruffy
bandit? Or a man who takes care for himself and his
equipment? A ribbon or two and you look much more
substantial."

Bang. From downhill where Jiro expressed his impatience, a kick at the stable wall.

"You're damn pretty," he said, and touched the scar
on her face. "Wear it like a banner, girl. Like a challenge. You survived that. You're not ordinary. Hear?"

Bang, from the stable-yard.

Taizu gnawed at her lip. Not angry, no. Listening to
him.

"You're my student," he said. "You won't make me
ashamed. I have confidence in you."

"Then don't go!"

"Mmmn, it's not lack of confidence in you. Don't you think the whole of Hua province is too much for one girl to take on? You at least need someone to watch your back."

"You're making fun of me."

"No. I'm determined to get you back alive. I have a strong interest in that. You've promised to be my wife if you get back."

"I—!"

"I think that's excellent good sense. Look at what I can give you. A fine house. A whole mountain to hunt on. Good company. Are you sure you want to go to Hua?"

"I know what you're trying to do. You're going to be arguing with me all the way to Hua. And you'll step in at the last moment and kill Gitu. And I'll never forgive you for that."

Bang.

Bang.

"I have no such intention. I do plan to give you a little advice. I think that's only—" *Bang.* "—reasonable. You can have Gitu. I certainly won't contest you for a prize like that. Are we ready?"

Shoka did not look back when they left, leading Jiro. He knew what the place would look like: like home, only empty and dead—and sights like that were no comfort. Taizu did. And at least she cared.

Jiro laid his ears back and showed the whites of his eyes on the descent. It went by fits and starts, Jiro planting his feet in the narrow slot and eyeing the next steep, root-tangled turn: then a rush that ended with Jiro braced crosswise on what level ground he could find and looking with a misgiving eye at the next stage.

It had not seemed this bad on the way up, to Shoka's recollection. Or he had been seeing less on that day—when he had come to this place and decided on a certain mountain and led a much younger horse up it. It was a relief when he had all four of Jiro's feet on level ground again, with all four of Jiro's legs sound, and bearing that in mind he let the old fellow rest a while, content to walk, under the green leaves, until the trees grew fewer and they came to the fields.

Those had changed too—much nearer the mountain than they had been all those years ago.

"Are we going through the village?" Taizu asked.

He thought about that while they walked, the chances of going in secrecy, the chances that a man and a girl in armor might not be spied in all the weeks between this place and Hua. And he had worried about that since he had realized he had to leave the mountain—about that, and other things.

Maybe there was no real debt between himself and the villagers. He had never thought of one: they provided him food in trade for good furs, they were useful to each other.

But he kept thinking about the boy who came for the furs; and about the women who sent the pots of preserve; and the farmers who grew the rice, and it worried him, what they would do and what the bandits might do, once the word spread.

"We're going through the village," he said, and stopped and freed Jiro's saddle of the baggage they had slung over it. "Here you are." He handed her the roll of mats and bedding, and both their bows and quivers; and slung over the back of the saddle the rest of the packets that had not gone into Jiro's saddle kits, and tied that down. Then he set his foot in the stirrup and climbed up.

It was certainly, Shoka thought, a reason to bring the farmers running from their fields and the people from their houses—one of the odder sights that had ever appeared in the single dusty street: a gentleman in faded armor on a graynosed horse, with a somewhat undersized and over-loaded retainer. At first they had not even seemed to recognize him, or ten years had worked more change than he had thought; but then someone in the gathering crowd said: "It's master Saukendar!" and the whole village pressed about them, making Jiro anxious and crowding Taizu close to his stirrup.

But those were the young folk. The village elders came out to them, and bowed; and Shoka bowed from the saddle.

Are there bandits? he heard asked through the crowd. "Are the bandits coming?"

He felt a pang of guilt for that.

"What brings you to us, m'lord?" the oldest asked, in a voice like the wind in dry reed. "What can we do for you?"

"Honorable," he said, and bowed again, "this is my wife. Her name is Taizu."

Murmurs and bows. He could not see Taizu's face. It was, he thought, probably just as well. He imagined the scowl, fit to frighten devils. But she kept quiet, while the village women stared at her wide-eyed and the whole village wondered, in politely hushed tones, just where master Saukendar had *gotten* his wife and—in a little quaver of fear—just *what* such a woman might be.

Doubtless they were looking closely at her hands, to see which way the thumbs were on. And her expression, if it was what he thought it was, would lend them no confidence, Taizu standing there with her feet braced and her sword in both hands, crosswise.

There were bows, profound bows, the elders and the villagers to them both.

"We had not known—" the elder said.

He almost said: *You know her. She was the boy who came through here two years ago.* But prudence held his tongue—with the glimmer of an impious notion.

"My wife wants to see her homeland again," he said. "So I'm going away for a while." He heard the murmur of dismay and forged ahead quickly. "I've business to take care of. So I came to pay my courtesies to you, and thank you for your kindness—"

The elders bowed. The people did, a bending and a whisper like wind moving through a grain-field.

"But who will keep the bandits away?" an elder asked, setting off others asking the same question, a chorus of voices pleading with him.

"Quiet!" the eldest said, stamping the ground with his stick. "Quiet."

It took a moment. They were distraught. There was fear, there were looks toward Taizu, curiosity and resentment, and Jiro picked up the distress, stamping and fighting the bit: Shoka reined him tightly, for fear he would bite if someone came near—but no one was venturing that close.

"Pardon," the elder said, bowing. "Pardon, m'lord, m'lady, but who will keep us, then? The moment you go away, lord, the bandits will come down on us. They know we've been well-off, they know we've had good harvests. . . ." There was panic in the old man's voice. There were pale faces, wide eyes all around, and a whisper of profound despair. "Stay with us," people began to wail.

"Be still!" Shoka said, and everyone hushed, except the children, who had begun to cry. "Listen to me. You're also well-fed, prosperous, and there are more of you than there are of the bandits, who haven't had the courage to attack you. I trust you haven't forgotten the bow or the staff in ten years. Any of you who want to go up to the cabin and take anything, that's perfectly fine: but I'd spread the word to travelers, the demons will never harm anyone from this village, but no one else should go up there. There are terrible things. You've heard them howling on the ridges, demons with eyes like lamps and fingers like ice. But this village is safe from them. It has special protection, and anyone who steals in this village and anyone who does any violence against this village, that man will never be safe. My wife and I will come and find him. Hear?"

Eyes were very wide. People bowed, pale of face, and mothers hushed babies with their hands.

"Tell every traveler," he said. "Make sure they carry that word."

Again the bows.

"Good luck to you," he said then, and let Jiro move, the elders clearing out of their path with multiple bows, the people melting back behind them.

So they passed through the street, with Taizu walking at Jiro's head, with people hurrying along behind them to call out wishes for good luck and wishes for them to come back soon, with people rushing up to wave scarves at them and to give him ribbons and flowers.

"They think I'm a demon!" Taizu said when they had left the last of the villagers behind—a last dog coursing after them to bark and annoy Jiro. Taizu turned a furious face on him.

"With a look like that, no wonder."

"Dammit, I'm not your wife!"

"Demons can turn their thumbs around the right way if they cast a spell. Can't they?"

"It's wicked, what you did! You *lied* to those people!"

"About what? Don't you believe in demons?"

"Demons aren't to mess with!"

"Maybe the bandits will think the same. That's no loss, is it?"

Taizu's mouth was open. She shut it and walked in silence a while.

"I'm leaving them," he said, "to take you to Hua. It's not their fault. The only thing they ever had to protect them was a story about me. So it's only fair I leave them a story in my place. Isn't it? They're losing the furs I used to trade them. That's a lot of money to them."

"I know that!"

"They're losing my protection."

"That's not my fault! You don't have to go with me!" She turned around and waved her bow at him, so Jiro shied up. "Go back! Go away!"

"With you or behind you, girl. You'd be hell to track, but then, I could always just meet you in Hua. Come to Gitu's gate and ask if he's seen a demon-wife who's been looking for him. . . ."

"Don't joke!" She made a sign against devils. "You *lied* to those people!"

"I'm sure they'll put out rice and wine for the demons. I doubt the demons will object. Who knows, they might even protect the place."

"It's unlucky!"

"For the bandits, it is. Who knows, my wife might come after them."

"It's not *funny*, master Shoka!" Her face was red with anger. Tears shone in her eyes. "They'll get killed believing you!"

He regarded her sadly. "I know. But they'll fight better if they have hope. A lie is better than nothing. And a lie, lady wife, is all they ever believed in. What's better or worse in another fable?"

He shocked her. Completely. She looked away from him and walked on under her load, shaking her head. Eventually she stopped and looked back at him, and said, calmly, composedly: "Go back, please, go back—"

"Will you?" he asked, while Jiro, confused by this yea and nay, threw his head and worked the bit.

"No. I won't. But nobody knows me. They'll know you, and the soldiers will be hunting us, and we won't have a chance."

He smiled. "You're thinking. Good. So you've got me to look out for. And if you run off, the only thing I can do is go to Hua looking for you."

"They'll kill us both! *Please* go back."

"No," he said, in her tone, her exact tone; and she drew a long, trembling breath, turned and stalked on her way.

So he followed, at a pace Jiro found quite comfortable, beyond the fields of the village, beyond the further hills, where the trade road became a dusty track following the general line of the small river through grasses and rocks and occasional copses of trees. They were *in* Chiyaden now, in the province of Hoishi, on the track caravans went, from the kingdom of Shin through the barbarian lands of the Oghin to the civilized heart of the Empire, the Lap of Heaven. *Home*, Shoka kept thinking, and hating the thought, because *home* was back on the mountain, *home* had nothing to do with Chiyaden or its troubles, and he resisted that ambiguity. With all it meant.

They made camp that evening in the lee of a lump of rock, where the hills came close to the road, and where there was a spring and a wide place in the road where many a traveler had camped.

"This is too open," Taizu objected; to which he shrugged and said:

"So it is. Are you afraid already? Do you want to go home?"

"I *am* going home," she retorted, and sat down to unpack.

So he unsaddled Jiro, and set Jiro's gear carefully on the rocks to dry of sweat; and took off his armor and rubbed Jiro down with handfuls of grass before he thought about washing the dust off himself.

Sparks and fire glimmered where Taizu had coaxed a little fire out of their kit, feeding it with grass and small sticks and larger ones she had scoured up. He was washing at the spring when she came to fill their cooking pot with water.

"Wash," he said, feeling generous and wanting to make peace. "Take the armor off. I'll cook."

She was still not speaking to him, but she abdicated the cooking to him, and started shedding the armor—cause enough to be in better humor, Shoka reckoned to himself, and certain enough, coming freshly-washed and free of that weight to a dinner already done improved her mood no little.

"Mmmn," was all she said until the rice and the tea

were gone, and sighed afterward and just sat with the bowl in her hands.

"I tell you," he said then, "I won't talk about going back if you don't. Any time you want—we can. Do you want to?"

"You said you weren't going to talk about it!"

"So I'm not. I was just asking. Here. Give me the bowls. I'll wash up."

"That's not your job!" She stood up and took his from his hands and stalked over to the spring.

He untied their bedroll then. It was cool in the hills, even toward chill at night. He put the mats down doubled, two blankets for cover, and had bed ready by the time she had washed.

"I'm tired," she said, putting the bowls and the food away. "I just want to sleep tonight. Please don't bother me. All right?"

"Of course," he said mildly. "Whatever you like. But I hope you don't mind doubling up on blankets. It's going to be cold before morning."

She made a disgusted sound.

And when they lay down she pointedly turned her back to him.

All right, he thought, finding himself not so indifferent as he had hoped to be, and finally, uncomfortably, edged closer to her. The girl had thinking to do. At any moment she could change her mind and decide that she wanted to go back to the mountain, which was all to the better. So he could be patient.

He could not see himself being patient all the way to Hua.

Damn the girl.

He thought again of force. But Taizu had had that, had had much too much of that, gods knew, and she was not one to forgive a man's lack of patience. He had been patient two years. He could become ascetic with more patience than this.

Gods.

He stared at the stars. He got himself very well under control and said, quietly:

"You're not cold, are you?"

"No."

"I'm sorry about the demon business."

"Don't talk about it."

"Why?"

"Because I'm trying to sleep!"

"Do you believe in demons?"

"Of course I do. Stop talking about it! Do you want to make them mad?"

"Well, I don't. I lived on that mountain for ten years and I never saw one. Did you?"

"No, and I'm glad I didn't!"

"The village believes they're all through the mountains. And they aren't. If they were there I'd have seen them. Jiro would have smelled them."

She said nothing.

"Taizu."

"I shouldn't have slept with you in the first place. Now you tell lies about me in the village and you try to scare me."

"What does sleeping with you have to do with it? I thought you enjoyed it."

Long silence.

"*Didn't* you?"

"It was better the second time."

"You were helping. It does make a difference." He brushed a hand down her shoulder. "One never knows—how many chances there are. Gods know—you're supposed to enjoy it, Taizu. It's no good if you don't."

Silence.

"Dammit, you could at least answer a man."

"I'm trying to sleep!"

"Well, I'm not having much luck at it." He got up and shoved at her. "Get up. Give me my mat and a blanket. This isn't going to work."

"You said it was cold."

"So it is cold. A damn sight colder in this bed."

"I'm *tired*," she said, and sat up and put her arms around him, laid her head against him. "All right. It's all right. If you want to, I don't mind."

He was sorry then. He put the blanket around them and stroked her hair and held her, reckoning it had been a long way and a heavy load for a girl. Probably the armor made her sore in the joints. Gods knew it did him, and he had been on horseback all day.

"Just go to sleep," he said. "That's all a man needs, you know, a civil answer."

She put her arms around his neck and held on. He felt her shoulders heave gently.

"Are you crying?"

No answer.

"What for?" he asked finally. "Is it me?"

She took a fistful of his hair and hugged him tighter and shook her head. Whatever that meant. He heard her sniffing back tears.

"Tired?" he asked.

She nodded against his shoulder and did not let him go. So he sat there a while feeling awkward, but finding a lapful of Taizu quite warm enough against the night chill. He leaned his head against hers and sighed and prepared to sit there as long as comforted her.

But she patted his face then and said: "We can do it. It's all right."

"Dammit, girl." Because now he was out of the notion. "Be kind. Tell me once for all if you want to or don't. *Don't* change your mind again. You're wearing me out."

"I said yes. I mean yes!"

"Gods." He took her in his arms. He held her a while, feeling the exhaustion himself, and felt her shiver. "You're not scared, are you?"

"Cold." Her teeth were chattering.

He rolled her onto the ground and pulled the covers over. Exhausted, he thought. And scared.

So he held her close until she stopped shivering.

And by that time she was half asleep and he was.

"Hell," he murmured, "we'll try it tomorrow."

Chapter Eleven

Jiro sulked in the morning. A bit of exercise and an interesting trek through the hills was one thing, but he seemed to have a notion that home was getting further and further away, and waking up a good long way from his stable and his pasture put him thoroughly out of sorts. Being armored up again was not to his liking, and he more than laid his ears back, he cow-kicked and snapped.

Smart horse, Shoka thought, feeling a sharp pain in the leg this morning, so that it was hard not to limp, and picking up Jiro's saddle and slinging it on sent a stab of pain through the knee.

It was some satisfaction to see Taizu moving a little slower today, bending and stretching and grimacing as she massaged her shoulders and put the armor-sleeves on.

Decidedly slower this dawn than last.

"See," he said, "you should make love every night. It works the stiffness out."

She made a face at him. He grinned and threw the saddlebags over.

"I'll take one of the quivers," he said.

"I'm not going to argue."

"I could take half the bedding."

"I won't argue that either."

She never once suggested she ride—because, he thought, she knew that walking would have him limping in short order. And she never threw that up to him even when he provoked her, even when he was trying to wear her down and persuade her home again: she might have, he thought, except she was at heart kind, except she doubtless understood very well what he was doing, and put him off last night with some little justice on her side.

He remade the bedrolls separately, and came over to help her while she was doing her hair. He brought her ribbons the ladies of the village had given them, another red one and a bright orange.

She smiled at his gift, and tied them in with the first, and gave him a worried look, as if she was not sure she did not look the fool.

He smiled. Her eyes lightened.

So he walked off and mounted up, before a word could start another argument.

The day warmed and the road went smoothly, two ruts of silken yellow dust between the low growth of wild, late-summer grass. "Will you ride awhile?" Shoka asked finally, but Taizu shook her head and wiped a little trail of sweat from her temple. "No," she said. "Thank you, master Shoka. I'm all right."

"Jiro can carry the bedroll."

"No," she said cheerfully, light-hearted, even. She hitched the bedroll higher. "One isn't so much."

He had not once today said that they should go back. She had not spoken a cross word since morning. It was a seductive peace. It tempted a man to let it go on, at any cost.

But because the cost was Taizu he had no such intention.

* * *

There had been ruts in the road since yesterday, in the yellow dust; distinct and with the weeds and overgrowth crushed down here and there, broken, but not yet brown.

"There's someone ahead of us," Taizu said eventually.

"I wondered when you'd notice."

She turned and frowned at him.

"They could have said, in the village."

"We didn't ask, did we?"

"It would have been friendly of them to say!"

"I suppose. But I'm a lord of Chiyaden. Who talks to lords about such details? That's why we have retainers. There's a hierarchy of such things."

She scowled. "Well, then, lords must not know much that's going on, must they? *I'd* have said, and I'm a peasant. *I'd* think it was polite to tell somebody what was on the road."

"Of course you would," he said. "You'd run right out to a lord's stirrup and tell him."

"Huh. No. I'd let him *and* his horse fall through a bad bridge or meet up with strangers. If I didn't like him, I would."

Shoka smiled. "You would, too."

"Of course I would."

"Is that the manner in Hua?"

"We never let our lord fall through a bridge. We'd come and say, lord Kaijeng, you should fix that. Lord Kaijeng, strangers went through here."

"Lord Kaijeng was a good man."

"Did you know him?"

"Not half well. I met him a few times. He never attended court except the year of the floods. Then he was there to ask help."

"I wasn't born yet."

Shoka thought about that and gave a rueful shake of his head. "Well, I was in court then. It was in the old Emperor's reign. Lord Kaijeng came to report to the Emperor. I was impressed with him. He was a frugal

man. He asked remission of his tax for that year. He
bought six wagon-loads of rice and cloth and sent it
back to Hua to his tenants, so, he said, the farmers
could keep their strength up: there was a lot of rebuild-
ing to do and if the land was torn up, a well-fed people
were like troops to a campaign. That was his reasoning.
It impressed the Emperor so much he sent ten wagon-
loads of cloth and rice himself; and Hua sent back a
hundred percent of its taxes the next year, and sent a
gift of its best to the Emperor's table."

"I heard about that."

He could not see her face. The tone was easy. It was
virtually the first time she had been able to talk about
Hua. He did not want to press it too far.

"Pays to be reasonable with people," he said. "A lady
should remember that."

That got a scowl, Taizu walking half-sideways to glare
at him past the bedroll and the sword and bow and
quiver slung to her shoulders. "Don't you tell them lies
about me!"

"What do I tell them? Excuse me, good sirs, but I'm
Saukendar of Yiungei, escorting this farmer-girl back to
Hua so she can kill lord Gitu and marry me. I'm sure."

She shut her mouth and glared.

"Well?" he asked. "I think you'd better be my wife,
so far as the people we meet know. Nobody thinks
anything strange as long as you're decently married."

Taizu faced forward again, in time to avoid a large
weed. "If I didn't have you along," she said nastily, "I'd
lag back till night and then go past them in the dark."

"And get shot."

"*Wide* past them. Without making a racket. I'd be
perfectly all right on the road."

"I'm sure you would, but I thought we agreed we
weren't going to argue on that."

"I didn't agree. You did."

"That isn't the way I recall it. —See there?"

There was a dark spot on the farthest horizon, where
the road made a turning around the riverside. Taizu

looked, walking on tiptoe a moment and stretching to get a better vantage.

"Farmer-folk or traders," she said finally. "Wagons."

"Traders, I think. No few wagons. We're going to be all day working up to them, I think, catch up to them toward dark—"

"They won't like that."

"I certainly wouldn't blame them."

At least ten, eleven, Shoka decided, as the rolls of the land slowly concealed and revealed the caravan— which by late afternoon was surely watching them with some anxiousness. The river Hoi was on their left. The hills to their right hcve up bare-flanked, too steep and rocky for trees: the Barrens, the locals called this place, which lay on the edge of Hoishi and Hoisan, an anxious place to a soldier's eye—or a trader's, who doubtless, bound into the Empire, had wagons full of raw jade and maybe iron and precious metals.

So it was not surprising the caravan-guards lagged back to the rear, and faced them as they came, guards armored and mounted on wiry steppes ponies, with bows in their hands and arrows nocked.

"Go carefully," Shoka said, and lifted his hand to show it empty.

The guards made no such gesture. He expected none.

"We can go wide," Taizu said. "Just pull off from them, for the gods' sakes. They won't want us passing by their wagons and spying on them."

"It's our road, much as theirs."

"I don't want to get full of arrows!"

"And I don't want Jiro's feet bruised. It's rotten ground out there."

"You don't want Jiro full of arrows, either. He's a big target. You're on him. I'm beside you."

"Steady, steady. I thought you weren't afraid of anything."

"Arrows," Taizu muttered. "I don't like arrows."

"Well, they're not shooting, are they?" He kept riding, one hand held aloft. The caravan halted, one of the riders racing up the column; and soon enough a different man came riding back, a man in reds and grays.

"That'll be the caravan-master," Shoka said as two of the guards rode out from the halted wagons, a sedate pace, matching their own steady advance. "Let's act friendly, shall we?" And aloud: "Hello! We're fellow travelers. We'll pass you, by your leave."

The riders came scarcely within talking-distance and stopped as Shoka reined in.

"Travelers on the same road," Shoka said. "We'll ride past, by your leave."

"You're of Chiyaden," one of the guards hailed him back.

"That I am. Shoka of Tengu province. This is my wife, Taizu. And your master?"

"Master Yi. Master Lun Yi of the kingdom of Shin."

The speaker bowed; Shoka bowed; Taizu did.

So they gained leave to ride with the guards along beside the wagons, while the wagons stayed halted, and the caravan-master rode out to meet them.

There was tea, themselves and the caravan-master sitting on mats while the caravan-master asked them news.

"I have very little to tell," Shoka said. "My wife and I have been in living in seclusion on the edge of Hoishi, since the trouble in my homeland. I have no particular desire to go back, except my wife is homesick. So—" He shrugged, with no glance toward Taizu. "What can a man do? An unhappy wife or an unhappy journey."

The caravan-master slid a glance toward Taizu, and whatever he might have suggested for a nagging wife, died stillborn; his mouth went shut firmly, and a breath later he shrugged and said, "Well, I have *four* wives. And I have all of them to feed or I'd not risk this road myself, and that's the truth."

"Bad, eh?"

"Bad." Master Yi waved a bony hand at the road and

the land around. "Five attacks on this road this year. I travel with professional guards. You can see." Another wave of his hand, toward the caravan, the halted wagons, the caravaneers sitting in the shade the wagons offered, resting. There were at least fifteen guards, Shoka noted, who looked like hire-ons, by the plain, random style of their gear. "Costs me a fortune," master Yi said. "And it's not just in Hoishi. All *along* the road, from here as far as Ygotai. Bandits. Outlaws. You ride along fine as you please and whisst! arrows out of the brush. I tell you, I'd be nervous about traveling alone hereabouts."

"One worries," Shoka said. "As far as Ygotai, you say."

"*And* further! I tell you, bad times. *Bad* times. Time was, there was law up and down the roads. Nowadays you're on your own the moment you leave a town. Don't look for the local lord to keep up his highways! He's sent all *his* levies to Cheng'di."

"To the Emperor."

"To wherever the Emperor sends them. Mercenary guards everywhere. And no law. Good for trade in the capital. But terrible in the provinces. And a smaller caravan would be in serious danger. I tell you, you should have a talk with your young wife. You should have a serious talk, sir. Homesick is one thing. It's a very dangerous road. Very dangerous. If you'll take my advice, you'll go back to Mon and not spend another night on this trail, for your young wife's sake."

"We're all right," Taizu said sharply.

The caravan-master's eyes slid toward Taizu and lingered, carefully, with a little of apprehension as he took in details, one of which, surely, was the scar; and another of which was, perhaps, the overall look of her, in armor, with her little knot of ribbons and her hair shorter than a woman's ought to be.

He cleared his throat.

"We're honest," Shoka said. "You don't have to worry, master Yi. We're not spies. Ask me what you like about

Cheng'di and I can tell you—but all old news. We've been away for a long time; and we're anxious for whatever you can tell us."

Another slide of the trader's eyes toward Jiro, who stood grazing beside their baggage—one point in their favor, Shoka reckoned: Jiro's expensive accoutrements and his own accent and his costly if worn armor fit the story of a displaced gentleman-gone-rustic, and *that* fit the pattern of political troubles, while Taizu's scar, her diction—which had undergone some change under his teaching, but which still was not pure heartlands—and her unusual and very businesslike gear—meant, perhaps, something other than *bandit*, but still something worrisome.

If they were both men, one might say—mercenary. Professional. And one might worry about the smaller one with the scowling face as one of the crazy sort, the sort that might mean fights in camp and bloodshed before all was done.

Which made *him* crazier than his wife was and the both of them possibly more dangerous than bandits.

"What about the roads east of Ygotai?" Shoka asked.

"Good as far as Mandi. Then chancy. Is that where you're going? Where is your wife from?"

"Hua."

"Hua!"

"How is it there?" Taizu asked. Her fists were clenched on her knees. She bowed, being polite. "Please."

"I can't say. I don't know." Master Yi bowed too. "Everything I know is from rumor. But they say it's very bad everywhere east and north of Mandi. You'd be advised to listen to your husband. People are killed every day on these roads. Terrible things happen."

Master Yi fell silent, locked stare to stare with Taizu. He gave a twitch of the shoulders then.

"The regency is still in power?" Shoka asked.

"Oh, yes. Oh, yes. That doesn't change." Another odd look.

"We've been very isolated," Shoka said, and held up

his cup as the caravan-master's boy poured more tea.
"Thank you. —You've traveled this road recently then?"

"Twice this year. Our last trip before the snows. But
we met with a caravan in Shothai—" The master had
his cup filled. "And they plainly warned us. It's profit.
Profit. There's shortage in Chiyaden. Where there's
shortage, supply sells. That's my politics. That's all my
politics."

"Prudent man. Gods prosper you, master Yi. We
wish you well."

"I'll tell you," master Yi said. "If you won't take good
advice and go back—you'd be safer far to travel with
us. For a likely man like yourself, for your wife, no
charge, seeing you bring your own gear and I suppose,
your own food. Out of the goodness of my heart I offer
it."

Shoka bowed. "That's very generous."

Taizu gave him a furious frown. "No."

"I'll talk with my wife," Shoka said. "I'm minded to
accept, master Yi. It's a very kind offer."

"It's too slow!" Taizu said; and Shoka said: "Excuse
me," and bowed to the caravan-master, stood up and
seized Taizu by the wrist, dragging her up and off to
have a word with her on Jiro's other side.

"It's good sense!" Shoka said. "Speed isn't enough.
We can go as far as Ygotai with this lot! Use your head,
girl!"

"That man is already suspicious! If we stay around
he's going to go on wondering and pretty soon he'll
start figuring you could be wanted by the law and there
might be some money in us!"

That *was* a thought, audacious and crooked, decidedly a thought on Taizu's side of the slate.

"I trust *us!*" Taizu said. "I trust *you,* I don't trust this
master Yi and his people. They're barbarians! Gods
know what thoughts might get into their heads. They
could get scared if they get to thinking you could be
wanted! They could do all sorts of things and if we're
sleeping with them and eating with them there's no

way we can defend ourselves! I don't like it, I don't like
it, I don't like it."

She *knew* stealth. She had gotten from Hua to Hoishi,
alive.

And gods knew—outland traders might not know his
face or his gear; but someone they met on the road
might, and might talk, and an outland trader might get
ideas what his life could be worth in gold. . . .

In certain terms, he was more danger than protection
to Taizu; she was right in that; and that both galled him
and worried him.

"All right," he said. "All right. I'll agree with you."

She drew a quick breath and let it go without a word.

And he led her back to master Yi and bowed. "Master Yi, thank you, but my wife is shy of strangers, and
I've humored her this far. I thank you profoundly for
your good advice, but a married man, you understand
how it is with wives—"

Doubtless master Yi suspected how it must be with
this one. Shoka put on a rueful face and tried to look as
embarrassed as possible, not quite looking master Yi in
the eye, and not missing, either, master Yi's shake of
the head.

"M'lord, I trust you know what you're doing. I can't
urge you strongly enough."

"Women," Shoka said. He bowed again. "I certainly
admire you, sir." And as he walked away: "*Four* wives.
That's truly amazing."

"I recommend the stick," master Yi called after him.

Taizu started to turn around. Shoka grabbed her by
the shoulder and marched her over to pick up the
baggage. He climbed up to the saddle as Taizu thrust
her arms through the ropes of the bedroll and the rest
of their gear, and started off, with yet another bow to
master Yi.

"Not a word," he said under his breath. "Not a *word*,
Taizu."

She managed quite well, walking along with her head
down while they passed beside the caravan, picking

their way on the brushy margin, among rocks and in and out among the wagons as one side or the other of the trail offered sufficient room. Caravaneers stared at them. No few leered at Taizu, and two exchanged words in their outland tongue and laughed.

It was not easy, that passage. He thought fondly of taking that pair who laughed and seeing whether their humor extended to a beating. But satisfaction was much too expensive.

Down the long, long row of wagons, until they were well into the clear of the road, and rounding the curve of the hill.

Then Taizu turned half-about and said, indignantly: "They were making fun of you!"

"If we want them to report us to the nearest magistrate I can certainly go back and teach them proper respect: that should get our descriptions up and down the road as fast as anything I can think of."

"You didn't need to bow to them!"

"Dear wife, I thought I did rather well. We're well ahead of them, and if they mention us to the magistrate in Ygotai let's hope they report a doting fool and his spoiled wife who probably left their bones in the forest. I was Shoka to my intimates, not to folk at large, and I doubt they'll connect that name with Saukendar—but they might, if I'd cracked their heads. Wouldn't they?"

She still frowned, but she made no more argument.

"I didn't use the demon story."

"Oh, no, the *next* caravan through the village will pick that up, and we'll be famous!"

"Another reason why I thought you might just be right about making speed on this stretch. Their logical assumption is that we turned north at Ygotai, ahead of the caravan—*if* they realize it's me. We told them the truth about Hua. That's precisely what they'll think is a lie. So they won't look on that road."

Taizu turned around again as she walked, her expression thunderous. "On the other hand they just could believe Saukendar wouldn't lie."

"I hope I had a reputation for being smart. —Look out for that bush!"

She glanced back and skipped around it and the rock behind it. "All I can say is, if *I* was the magistrate in Ygotai and they told me about a gentleman clear out here with all that expensive armor, *I'd* be suspicious, and I'd know he was in some kind of trouble, and I'd know there wasn't any lord Shoka because that's not a proper name."

"He'd know there were a couple of mercenaries, that's what, one female."

"Who didn't want hire with the caravan."

"Because they had better prospects elsewhere. Gitu was hiring them ten years ago. I don't think he's changed. And you *m'lord* anybody with a full rig of armor. I'm at least a mercenary *captain*, and that's more than master Yi can hire. He knows that. If he believes the wife story, that's fine; if he doesn't he'll think we're mercenaries—"

"Who walked out letting those fools laugh at us!"

"They won't sleep well tonight. Mark me. That was stupid of them, letting us among them to see how many they are. That's why I *acted* the fool, and they laughed at the situation. When they get to thinking back on the style of the gear and the rest of it, they're going to have two and three thoughts on it, none of which agree, all of which are going to make master Yi damn nervous from here on, much more than if we were a simple pair of bullies they might have feathered outright. *We* walked away. They shouldn't have let us do that. And now I'm sure they're thinking about that and hoping we were fools."

She looked at him with her mouth open, walking sideways and backward. "You're so tangled up! You've told them so many things they'll suspect us for sure!"

"They won't know what we are. Till, as you say, some other traders overtake them. *Then* they'll know, and by then we'd best keep ahead of the rumors." He thought of plaguing her again about going back. And thought:

*Gods, there is no going back, is there? Ghita will know,
soon or late. And assassins will come again. Even on
the mountain there's no safety now.*

*Well, I knew as much when I began this. No helping
it. No helping anything now.*

*Straight in and straight out, and maybe, if we're very
lucky—go for the south and the mountains, and lose
ourselves there, where even the imperial guard won't
follow.*

Damnable mess this woman's talked me into.

The sun became a golden glow behind the hills on
the other side of the river, and a touch of gold at the
peaks of the hills that rose high on their right.

That went too, as they came to the place where the
river ran noisier over rocks, and where the hills of the
Barrens truly closed in.

Beyond this was not a place to travel in the dark, a
narrow place fit for ambushes, where the river flowed
in a riven, sometimes wooded gap and the ground was
stony and the hills were broken and tumbled on either
side.

"This is where we stop," he said, when a turn of the
hills brought them face to face with that.

"I did it by dark," Taizu said. "But I didn't have any
horse, and I hid a lot, whenever I could."

He shook his head, thinking of her with that damned
great basket, light as she had packed it; and her alone
in that place made for ambushes.

And he climbed down and led Jiro off where there
was still a little ground free of rocks.

"I've got an idea," Taizu said as they were boiling up
a little water: it was yesterday's rice and jerky, with
tea.

"Gods save us. What?"

"About the arrows. What we do—" She was sitting
on her heels feeding twigs of scrub into the tiny fire
while he sat cross-legged on their mats, close by. "What
we do, *I* go in first, just right down the trail, and I

make a lot of noise like a fool. And if there's anybody
there, you'll be behind me and you can pick them off.
That's better than both of us getting shot at or somebody hitting Jiro."

"No, they'll just shoot you outright. You don't look
like a woman, from a distance."

She gave him an offended look.

"I thought you *liked* looking like a boy," he gibed at
her. "There's nothing wrong with the idea, except making you the target. We *could* always wait for master Yi.
I knew this was ahead somewhere: I remembered it,
but I like the look of it less by twilight."

"I don't trust that man. I don't trust any of his people.
And they won't trust us. Like you said, they've had time
to think, and they'll want to have us back in their reach.
I'm almost more worried about them than I am the
bandits."

He frowned, thinking on that point, thinking about
Taizu, too, who he had long known was not dull-witted,
but by the gods, he began to see the journey she had
made and how she had made it.

Damn clever girl. Damned clever.

One had to take her very seriously. Even if his own
choice would be to go with the trader and crack skulls if
it came to it. Taizu in the field had all the patience she
lacked in other matters. Paradoxes.

"I knew a boy like you. Things were never real to
him until the steel was out. *Then* he used good sense."

"He's dead," Taizu guessed. "All your stories come
out that way."

He shook his head. "He's in holy orders. That's the
only thing kept Ghita's lot from taking his head—last I
heard. You know if you'd gone to Muigan, you'd have
ended up abbess."

She wrinkled her nose at him, and sifted tea into the
water.

"The nuns would have taught you the stick, you
know. Same as I did."

"Too many do-this'es. And praying." She made a face. "Not me."

"Celibacy, too. I don't think you'd have liked that."

She made another face at him. "I said, tonight. *After* supper. I'm hungry."

"Well, I might be out of the mood by then. Who knows?"

The look turned wicked. "Master Shoka, you haven't been out of the mood since I've known you. Here." She held out the pot to pour tea. He held out his tea-bowl and trusted her accuracy.

"It's *Shoka*," he said. "Plain Shoka, if you please."

A worried glance from under brows. The smile was gone.

"I wish you'd gone back, master Shoka. Now I'm afraid they're going to hear about you leaving the mountain. And then what?"

"They've tried before. They tried several times when I first came, when they'd found me. They stopped. It got too expensive for them."

"This time they might not stop."

"They might not. So we leave to the south. We go through the hills. We find another mountain further away."

She looked at him a long, long time.

"Your dinner's getting cold," he said, and popped a rice-ball into his mouth.

It *was* a cold supper, of course. She ate her own rice and jerky, listlessly, between sips of tea. He ate his with appetite, boiled up a second round of tea apiece, and leaned back to drink while she finished her dinner in silence.

"Admit it," he said. "You've gotten a little good sense thanks to my teaching. I won't say one word. You know everything I'd tell you. Plan a retreat. Always plan a retreat. I have one planned. Don't think I don't." Damn lie. He leaned his head back against the rocks, hoping that she was not going to find another excuse tonight, that her mood would not put her off. She slipped into that so easily. It took a few more years to put that much distance between a man and his dead, and to persuade him that the day and the moment were the important thing. "Enjoy life, girl. Or you let them kill you day by day. And I don't give the bastards the satisfaction. Take everything the day gives you. Enjoy the sunset. Enjoy the rain. Or a man who loves you. What the hell. I *don't* think I'm that bad. Am I?"

She looked at him over the rim of the tea-bowl, a short glance, and again, sidelong, thinking about it, Taizu-like. A small smile tugged at the corners of her mouth, and a brow lifted. "No, I don't think so." The smile disappeared. "I'm a farmer. I know how nature is. I've seen the goats and the pigs have a *fine* time. I had four brothers, two married." The mouth trembled. "And what I got was something different. You know? That doesn't surprise a farmer any. Goats aren't polite either. But hell! master Shoka—" She ripped up a handful of grass and flung it. "My bad luck. Isn't it? I'd like them to try now. That's what. I'd like that."

He exhaled a careful breath. Damn, was there no respite in her? "I hope you don't include me in that number."

She bit at her lip. "No, master Shoka. I just want you to know if you sleep with me, I'm not your wife, I'm doing it because I'm scared and I don't like being scared, so I do it until I'm not. But you think it's for you. And I won't lie to you. I don't like lying. I'm not a virgin. I'm not anybody's lady. It's my fault you left your mountain and I wish to *hell* you'd go back! If you'd go back I promise I'll try to stay alive and come back, and then I'll marry you, I'll do anything you want me to for the rest of my life. I just don't want you getting killed for me. I never wanted that. You're being stupid, and I hate that! I'm not what you think I am. I'm not your lady. I'm a farmer. They'll laugh at you if you say I'm anything else. Just like those people back there. And I won't have that!"

The face was perfectly in control, the hands on knees,

the whole posture tranquil. Only the voice trembled and broke.

He left that silence a long while. He found a twig of brushwood in his fingers and snapped it. "Let me tell you then, since we're being ruthlessly honest: I was a damn fool for not insisting Meiya sleep with me. Then she never would have married the Emperor. I was a greater fool to have believed there was something the Emperor would stick at, and not to have snatched her up and run for the border. But by then, you see—by then, she was the Emperor's wife. And they'd have brought an army after me; and she'd still be dead. But the fact is—" It was a thought that had been growing in him for months, a bitter thought, a thought that made desolate a good part of his life. "I don't think I'd loved her for years. I don't think she'd loved me—ever. We were kids. We were infatuated. I lost her to the old Emperor's order. It was romantical and I was desolated, and my pride was hurt. So what could I do but carry on with a feeling I'm not sure was ever real? You understand that? Probably what you're going through with me. You do and you don't. Yea and nay. But for me, then, it had to be real. She hated her husband. I was her friend. We never once slept together. If we had, I think it would have been to relive the past. To imagine there'd been something more than infatuation. The day she died—" He cleared a tightness in his throat. "She was waiting for me, I'm sure to the last, because I was her friend. Because she knew if anyone had come—I would have. But things between us by then were all politics and planning how to do this and planning how to influence one lord and another to do what had to be done—all politics. We weren't lovers, we were a faction Ghita had to break—myself, Meiya, lord Heisu. That he couldn't prove adultery on me— was because we'd been so careful there was no chance. That they proved it on Heisu—was because—gods only know—she might have. And I wouldn't blame her. I'd know why . . . because she treated me as too damned honorable. And she'd have known how foolish it was and how dangerous. But if she slept with Heisu—it was because she didn't give a damn for him, personally, only as a friend and adviser, and her husband never touched her. You see—there are things people do to each other as bad as happens on battlefields. That's my truth. You didn't choose what happened. I *made* the mess that I suffered from. So if I sleep with you—it's because I've gotten smarter over the years. I take the moments the gods give. I don't ask too much. I genuinely care about you. I've never slept with a woman I've cared about. Not one—until you." It grew too embarrassing, to be saying that to a very young, very tough-minded girl, no matter she was no child. He reached out and jabbed the broken twig into the fire, not looking at her, but at the fire that licked up, brief, bright flames and a few sparks in the gathering dark. "Anyway, that's my reason. It's not on your shoulders." He took another bit of brushwood and fed it in. "If I remember my maps, the hills in the south of Hua are wooded. Hard country to find anyone in. That's how I plan to get out. And you with—"

She had gotten up. He thought he might have upset her and she was going to walk off. Instead she came to his side and squatted down and took his hand and held it, arms between her knees.

"Let's sleep together. All right?"

He looked up at an earnest, firelit face, close to his own. His pulse quickened. "All right," he said, and closed his hand tighter. And thought of the woods not far away, and the nature of the land.

Hell with it. He started in with her ties and she helped him with his, and they peeled out of the armor like two youngsters in a hedgerow.

After which he covered the fire, threw the blankets around them both and said: "Let's not hurry. Let me explain the fine points of this."

"Just do it!"

"No, no, no, one doesn't."

"Mmmn," she said after a while, and let out a yelp.

The ladies of Chiyaden were more discreet. He could not say he preferred them at all, the more so as she got the notion to try her own ideas.

"Mmmn," he said. "Gods."

"That hurt?"

"No," he said, between breaths, and settled himself. "Now?"

Her nails dug hell out of his back. He had no care for that.

Jiro snorted. Loud.

He stopped. She did.

A pebble rolled, on the rocks above them. "Damn!" he whispered into her ear, feeling her grip on his arms. "Someone's up there."

Her fingers clenched, once, hard. "Mmmn," she said aloud, with cold presence of mind.

"Mmmn," he said in turn, and eased aside and felt in the dark after his sword, while she melted away after her gear, while Jiro snorted and stamped in alarm.

He *wanted* his armor, dammit, but his sword was all he could come by without a rattle. He hoped Taizu had sense to stay put.

"Mmmn," she said again.

He heard someone moving then, around by the side of the hill. At least one above. More than one to the right.

He heard his target, saw the shadow, and struck like a whisper. There was not even an outcry. Two objects hit the ground, one small, one large.

Sound from above. A stone rattled down, a series of rattles, as howls broke from human throats and shadows poured from the right.

He took the first three in that many passes: missed the fourth, trying to keep him from getting past, took the fifth and heard Taizu yell:

"Bastard!" —As something hit steel and flesh and a man yelped into silence; Shoka spun and struck and countered in what had started as fright and went to hot rage.

He heard the man charge down the hill-face, heard it coming and whirled and struck, whirled again with the sound of steel on his left, took another and launched himself for the pale figure enveloped in steel-shining shadows.

"Hyaaaa!" he yelled, drawing attention of his own, and cut his way through, heard a howl from Taizu, but not pain, a yell like an outraged devil's.

And the last few shadows took to their heels.

"*Cowards!*" she screamed after them.

Shoka let go his breath and felt himself shaking from head to foot, the old feeling that came with a fight, heart pounding, muscles charged to move. "Get a bow, dammit!" He grabbed Taizu's arm and shoved her back to the hill where their gear was. He ran and got Jiro from tether and drew him back close against the hill, trampling a detritus on the ground that had not been there when the fight started.

Taizu had done what he had told her, gotten to cover against the hill and gotten the bows strung.

Naked as she was born. "Are you hurt?" he asked.

"No. You?"

"No." He felt after his clothes. "Get dressed. We sleep turn and turn about. *Damn* them!" He found himself shaking for a different reason. For the memory of her out there surrounded. For what could have happened.

For what she had *done*, by the gods.

He hugged her against his side. "Scared?" he asked her.

"No." Her teeth were chattering. He felt her shivering. He held onto her, thinking . . .

Thinking that if she had made one mistake she would have died.

Thinking that then he would have fired the whole damn forest and gone for Gitu himself, and for Ghita and for the Emperor and his whole damn court.

He hugged her tight. "Want to go home?"

"Hua," she said.

Chapter Twelve

The sky cast a faint glow into the narrows, over a flat, rocky expanse littered with hewn bodies, bits and pieces. Not a wholesome place for the sun to come up on—the stink of death all around them and the day getting just enough to see what a longsword could do to a body, armor and all.

Not a good sight for a girl, Shoka thought, and then thought: but it's what she's chosen.

He rubbed dried blood from his hands, rubbed the stubble on his face and found the same. Saw Taizu waking, or never sleeping at all, her eyes dark, liquid slits in the shadow, her face dappled with filth like his own. Jiro stood still drowsing, close to them, in the same sheltering rocks.

They had not washed last night. They had armored up and stayed close to the rocks, and slept turn and turn about—*if* she had slept.

Scared, maybe. He hoped that she was. He hoped it was that simple, that natural a thing.

He reached out and tousled her bangs. "Better move," he said. "Early. Before our enemies want to get stirring."

He got up. She did, and looked around her, and got her sword and walked out among the dead, poked one body and walked on—stopped to pick up a dagger and sheath and thrust it through her own belt, simple, pragmatic looting of their enemies.

A grim face, stolid. It sent a chill through him.

But it was also practical, what she did. He shrugged and rubbed the blood off his fingers and walked through the bodies and pieces of bodies, looking for things of value.

A good dagger for her, a leather belt and silk cord—neither was to pass by: tack got worn and cords got cut. A couple of serviceable steel helmets. He had lost his in the fracas ten years ago and she had never had one. A gold locket. "Here," he said, tossing it at her. "But wear it inside. Stuff like this can get your throat cut—in more than one way."

She looked at what she had caught in her fist, open-mouthed in amazement. She did not put it on. She stuffed it in a bag she had taken from one of the dead.

A little silver. A little copper. A silver hair-clip. A silk scarf. That was the rest of their pilferage.

Nine bodies, in the faint light. He counted. Probably Taizu did.

"We've done no little service for travelers on this road," he said as he saddled Jiro and Taizu gathered up her load. "That's likely a good part of the bandits in Hoisan."

"Huh," she said.

At least she did not say—it was nothing. At least she did not say—she enjoyed what she did. He had seen both in boys in their first fight. But she was different. Like the wisest, maybe, who did what they did and kept their balance: that was what he had taught her— *Your soul has a center, girl, the same as your body has. Let nothing you do take you from that center.*

Where are you this morning, girl?

Or have you seen enough such sights in Hua?

Taizu walking among the dead. Taizu stripping weapons from corpses, coldly turning this and that bloody bit of a man to see if there was something to be scavenged—

Gods, what has Chiyaden come to, to breed a girl like this?

The road ahead by earliest dawn was an unpleasant ground of tumbled rocks, twisted pine, scrub and undergrowth giving way to tall trees as the gap widened.

A little forest, a little thicket, a great deal of rock, through which the road had to wind, taking much more time than Shoka liked, past rocks large enough to hide three and four men. "Don't talk," he said. "Jiro's ears and Jiro's nose is the best defense we have through this."

She nodded once. That was all, except when the road widened again and they went under daylight, beside the river.

Not the way Taizu had argued—with her out to the fore. The bandits knew there were two of them. They well knew it; and Shoka kept scanning the heights within bowcast of them, with his own bow strung, with an arrow held crook-fingered to the string and two more in his hand.

"I think they want easier pickings," he said finally.

"Maybe there never were that many of them," Taizu said.

He felt a prickle at his nape, strong enough that he turned in the saddle to look.

But there was nothing but trees and rock and the narrow clear area of the road.

He looked to the fore again, and wished with all his heart that he could put Jiro to a faster gait.

But there was no possibility of that. His weight, Taizu's, both in armor—their gear and the tack: Jiro could carry it, but no faster than he was walking; or run with it and kill himself.

So they walked, at a better pace than Taizu had yet managed. "Give me the pack," he said, and when she opened her mouth: "Hand it up."

She slipped her arm out of one rope, changed bow-hands, and freed the other, keeping only the quiver as she handed it up to him.

"Go," he said, then. "Move, girl. *Run!*"

She moved, took a steady jogging pace, and Jiro snorted and broke into a faster gait with never a touch of his heel—the old chase game.

That was the way they passed the heights, between rests in which they rested close against the rocks.

That was the way they came to the wider valley, by the waterside. Taizu came to a panting halt, the sweat and the dirt and the day-old blood streaked with runnels of sweat, her hair stuck about her face.

He felt as if they had passed a door—one without returning. And he gave a twitch of his shoulders.

"I'll carry the gear a while," he said. "We're not resting here. Keep going."

She looked at him open-mouthed, as if she thought this was some kind of revenge.

"Go!" he said.

She seemed to understand then. She gasped a breath and turned and ran.

They had to rest more often now—whenever they came to a rock that offered shelter. Taizu's breath came harsh and hard, and sweat drenched her. At the last she walked close by Jiro's side and held onto his saddle skirts, partly because she could hardly keep herself on her feet, partly to shield Jiro's chest from the vulnerable side as they passed the last of the heights.

Beyond that, with the land open again, she was stumbling with exhaustion, and when they were in a broad, clear space with their river again, she said, in a croak of a voice: "Master Shoka, can we rest a while down there?"

"Rest we will," he said, and got down from Jiro's

back and made her climb up, and walked, himself, with
Taizu sitting and swaying in the saddle—too prideful to
collapse, he thought.

But he insisted to make a fire when they reached the
ford and a little gravelly stretch where the river brought
wood and the sun dried it. He took off his armor and
washed with handfuls of the icy water, and she did,
some distance from him, and not looking at him.

He looked at her—squatting peasant-style as she
poured handfuls of water over her hair and her shoulders, managing to stir his interest even in that ungainly
pose—and he felt a moment of disquietude even then—
that she was so small, so set on her foolishness, and she
had grown so important to him. But that she would be
appalled at death and killing—he gave up that illusion
for good, and continued to be appalled in his own turn,
that she was so matter of fact about it.

Maiden-modest by daylight. And conscienceless as a
camp-follower. He thought he should be disgusted. But
that was not what he felt. What he felt was—

—attraction. And a thought that if she were a boy he
would think her extraordinary for that calm, and that
skill, and know here was that rare student too self-
possessed to do foolish things. A student well-set in the
Way.

As I've taught her, was one thought.

And the other—that it was feminine cruelty, of the
sort he had seen in whores of all classes.

One he respected; one he abhorred. He was not sure
what he was dealing with, or what he had taught; and
his body said he loved her, which disturbed him the
more—*You're off your center, master Saukendar. . . .*

Damn the girl.

He *wanted* to believe the best of her. He wanted it;
and yet—

Believing the best meant believing that she was capable of the Way; and that meant taking her in a completely different understanding than he had had with
any woman; believing the worst meant he was a fool,

lending his art to a student who would pervert it, even for a just revenge—and who all along had not been what a lonely man's vulnerable mind had wanted to make out of her.

Considerably off your center, master Saukendar. . . .

Demons he doubted. But that he might have bound himself up with a woman as destructive of him—he could not entirely rid himself of that thought. He had very little left but his reputation. And he had more than lent it to her. He had given it completely to her, to go into the world with, and to do good or ill with—

Perhaps he could take the age-old cure for demons and strike off her head where she sat, unawares, and go home, with his reputation intact: the village would make legends of his narrow escape from her bewitching.

But he had no wish to cut off her head. No wish to take her home by force, and no wish to wait on the mountain any longer, because now he would know what he was waiting for, and if there was never her again—then there was nothing, nothing, nothing for the rest of his years.

So here he sat freezing himself with cold water and wanting a woman who was the equal of any young fighter he had ever known—a thing which seemed vaguely to him like being attracted to some unusually comely boy—*and* she was simultaneously a saint who could be corrupted by his lust—or a conscienceless woman who would inevitably attach to his name, and be the end of all the reputation he had—

Not, he told himself, that it ought to matter to him. But, dammit, he had never asked to be a saint or a hero, and if the gods had cast his lot that way, and if he had tried to keep his name clean and not betray what people expected of him, then it was a *damned* shabby trick on the gods' part to send him a temptation like this one at the last—

Maybe he was *supposed* to do like the saints in the stories and cut her head off, and ride back to virtuous solitude.

But that was not what his flesh wanted to do and that was not what he had the fortitude to do and not what he had the conviction to do, not if she suddenly turned into the demon the village thought she was—if she suddenly turned about with fangs and staring eyes he would temporize with her and hope she would turn back again to Taizu. That was how bad it was with him.

He began to believe in demons after all, that she *was* one, come to carry off his soul and ruin him.

And he kept seeing her walking among the dead in the sunrise, cold as a devil's heart, prodding one and the other, turning a corpse to look for valuables—

No crime in that. It was only practical.

But she should have shown some remorse. Some fear. *Something as maidenly as her modesty.*

Damn, if she came to his bed with fangs and all he would want her. He could not understand how he had come to this state of affairs, or why living or dying would not matter to him, without her.

Possibly because it had not mattered for a long time before that.

That was a grim thought. But it seemed true.

He sighed, and splashed himself with cold water to wash the blood off from the night before and the sweat and the dirt off from today.

Damned mess, indeed.

They shared a little smoked venison, and a bit of sausage; Taizu hoped for a proper supper tonight, and she would, she said, cook up a bit of rice they could roll in leaves and have on the trail tomorrow when they got hungry.

"We're through the worst," he said, "till we get to Ygotai."

"Maybe," she said hoarsely, "bandits will give up on us."

"Don't count on it," he said. "But we might have convinced them to think twice about us."

"You always worry."

"I always worry. I served the Emperor. It's a habit."

She cut off a piece of sausage, and nodded soberly. "I worried. That's how I got this far. I thought you'd teach me so I wouldn't have to. That was stupid to think."

"It was a kid's way to think. You're doing much less of that."

She looked at him a long moment. Finally: "Those men weren't much."

"Did you expect them to be?"

"What about Gitu?"

"Much better than that. *Much* better than that. Gitu's studied. He's also ten years older than I knew him. He might have gone soft. But, I've told you, you can trust his guards haven't. Much better than those fellows back there with master Yi. Much better than the bandits. Don't expect otherwise. —Are you ready? Are you fit for more walking?"

"Yes," she said, and wrapped up their lunch; and gathered up their gear.

The land flattened out again and the road crossed over the little river at a shallow spot, up to Taizu's hips: she took her armor off and led Jiro across, using her bare feet to test the soundness of the bottom, while Shoka, astride, carried everything.

She went in up to her waist at one point, slipped and went in over her head. Jiro snorted and threw his head as Shoka kept him tight-reined and knew a heart-stopped moment till the river spat her up again soaked and outraged.

"Damn!" She still had Jiro's reins. And she added mildly: "Slick."

She led Jiro around. Shoka came across dry-shod, feet tucked up at the deepest part, and the girth wet. But Taizu was a mess.

Interesting view, too. He gave her the appreciative stare it deserved as she passed him up Jiro's reins; she looked down and pulled her wet shirt away from her body.

"Don't you *ever* think about anything else?"

He grinned. "Not with a sight like that in front of me."

She thought it was funny, then. A grin spread slowly, bright as sunrise and disquietingly wicked, before she laughed and swaggered up the bank to the flat of the road.

With a decided sway of her hips.

Like she had just found out her sex had a certain power—

—with a certain self-restrained and honorable fool.

The world would teach you otherwise, girl.

No, the world's already tried, *dammit. She's not fragile.*

Memory of her naked, pale dancer and bright steel, beset by shadows. Of her armored and blood-spattered, plundering the dead.

Of her arms and her body around him—

Of her going tense and panicked at the damnedest times—

And she walked now in her wet clothes with a deliberate twitch of very visible hips.

A girl trying out womanhood, trying out a sense of amusement about the mysteries and the to-do people made of it— Of course. With Taizu things were grimly serious—or not. Honesty—was grimly serious. And she would not, he thought, *not* deliberately cheat him.

I'm not your wife, it's because I'm scared and I don't like being scared, so I do it until I'm not. . . .

Fool. The girl warned you what she's doing. What does it take?

This morning she was a demon. Now she's a—

—damned tart.

She's—

—a kid. A scared kid who trusts me to treat her decently.

—*Master Shoka*—

He hurt. That was what. He had better sense than she did. He saw where they were going and he foresaw her lying dead on the road, foresaw himself giving a fair account of himself against whatever nest of trouble they had met. But himself lying on the road thereafter. And the farmers nearby saying: *Well, there goes a fool.* And the nobles in Chiyaden sighing and saying: *With a peasant girl. Whatever can he have intended to do?*

And others saying: *Maybe he went a little crazy, living off on that mountain.*

Boiled rice for supper, a decent fire, a good dinner. And Taizu fell asleep afterward, just—nodded off sitting there, her back against the rock, her rice-bowl empty in her lap.

It wouldn't be much good, Shoka thought; she had walked so far and run so hard; and she looked so damned innocent like that—

He put their mats by her, he said: "Taizu," and waked her before he took her in his arms—safest. "Lie down, you'll get a stiff back," he said, slipping his arms around her. She put her arms around him and muttered something, and nodded off against his shoulder.

Damn.

"Mmm," she said later, stirred and shifted over. He was not asleep, not quite. He had not dared in this place.

"My turn to sleep," he said muzzily. "Can you stay awake awhile?"

She brushed her fingers through his hair.

"If you do that," he said, "you're going to wake me up."

"I'm sorry," she snapped and shoved at him. "Go to sleep, then."

He blinked, rolled onto an arm, rubbed his eyes. "Don't ask profound philosophy of a man in the middle of the night, out of a sound sleep. What are we doing?"

Perhaps he embarrassed her. There was a long silence.

Damn, she had thought she was being seductive.

He fumbled down her arm and found her hand. "Sorry." She let him do that, so he reached further and rested his hand on her shirt, on her stomach, just friendly.

She took his hand in hers and put it up under, against her heart.

Which was all right for a while. Then the shirt went; and his did; and the breeches.

He took his time. And when he slumped down close to her ear and said, with all the deliberate timing of a courtesan: "Be my wife."

"O gods—" she breathed. And eventually, shortly: "No."

He muttered an army obscenity and sank off to the side, disappointed, discouraged, but not defeated.

A few more breaths. "You *say* I'm your wife. I sleep with you. What more do you want?"

He knew the answer. It was plain to him as day and night. But it was hard to say to a hostile woman. So he said nothing.

"What would your wife have to do?"

"I suppose what you do now. I've had no luck stopping you."

"Then why do you want me to marry you?"

"Because," he retorted, "if you don't they can cut your damn hand off for carrying that sword!"

"Well, you *lie* about it all right! I don't know why you couldn't lie to a magistrate!"

Caught, he said: "I suppose I could."

"So you don't need to marry me."

"I don't *need* to marry you."

"Then why? What would be different? That you'd tell me what to do?"

He asked himself that, not for the first time. "I wouldn't stop you."

"Well, *why*, then?"

He traced a line down her shoulder. And did not find it any easier for being down to his last excuses. "Because it'd please me. Because—" *Because after two Emperors and someone else's wife, I'd like to know someone loyal to me, as well as the other way around.*

She said, angrily: "It's stupid! You've gone crazy!"

She had her own hurts. He allowed that. His own pained him at the moment, sharp as the old wound when it ached, and he was not willing to get into an argument.

"Master Shoka?"

That hurt.

He turned his back to her. But she grabbed him by the shoulder and leaned over his arm. He was angry enough to have thrown her clear to the riverside.

But she said: "I just want to know."

It took forty years worth of self-control to be very calm and say: "Because it's decent."

"What does decent have to do with it?" she hissed. "Because master Saukendar doesn't like to be sleeping with his student, but his *wife* is all right?"

He took several careful breaths. He did not hit her.

"I just want to know why," she said.

"It's decent for people to make promises to each other, and keep them. I want—" *Once to have someone promise me something, and mean it.* "—to go to sleep. You wear me out, girl."

"Wear *you* out! *I'm* the one carrying the baggage!"

There was no romantic instinct in the girl. None.

She threw her arms around his neck, knelt there and rested her head against his shoulder. "I'm a peasant," she said. "The first time you see the ladies in Chiyaden you'll hate the sight of me."

"Damn if I will." He turned over and clipped her chin by accident. "Taizu, for the gods' sake—" He touched the offended chin.

"You will."

He was pushing too hard, trying to compel her. That was no good. It had nothing to do with the loyalty he wanted. "No," he said. "No." And sighed and gathered her into his arms, determined to go to sleep. "Let it be. Let it be. You don't believe me. And that's the end of it."

"What would I have to do? Do what you say?"

"Hush, go to sleep."

"Why do you want me to marry you?"

"Because I love you," he said. It was more complicated than that. But it shut her up for a while. Maybe she was thinking. Everything Taizu did was tangled.

Finally she said: "Are you going to say I have to do what you say?"

"No," he said, weary of this endless dicing of the matter; but patient. It took that, with Taizu. He *knew* her mind. They would be arguing when they got to Hua.

She was quiet a long time. He was half-asleep when she said, her head pillowed on his chest: "Can I think about it?"

He tousled her hair. "Do that." And tenderly combed it, since it had gotten leaves in it. "Don't sleep without waking me. Understand?"

"Mmnn," she said.

But he waked with the crack of a branch in his ears and the sun on his face.

"Dammit!" he said, and rolled over with his heart pounding, grabbing after his sword.

But she was there in the dawn breaking twigs for the fire.

He let his head down on his arms and got his breath.

"I didn't go to sleep," she said. "I couldn't sleep."

"Well, a hell of a lot of time we're going to make today." He got up and went off to the bushes, and came back and washed and shaved at the riverside.

She had breakfast ready when he sat down at the fire. So he ate, watching the riverside and watching the light on the water and thinking on as little as he had thought about in mornings at the cabin.

Except he missed the cabin. He wished he was there. With her.

He sighed and raked a hand through his hair. And patiently combed it and put it up before he set to putting his shin-guards on.

Taizu came and squatted in front of him, in shirt and armor-breeches, arms between her knees.

"Do you remember what you said last night?" she asked.

"What do you mean, what I said last night?"

She bit her lip, ready to take offense.

"I mean," he said, "I damn well remember what I said last night! What do you expect?" Damn, he had upset her. He was not his most diplomatic in the mornings. He threw the second shin-guard down and looked at her, at a very off-put Taizu, who had her jaw clamped. "Oh, hell!" Cross-purposes again. "It's not two merchants haggling over a load of salt, girl. It's not a financial arrangement. I've got nothing to give you—" He thought then, as he had not thought—what would happen to her if *he* were the one killed, and she were left, his wife, with his enemies, and that was enough to upset his stomach. "Not a damn thing I haven't already given."

"Can't you not swear at me?"

"I don't want to swear at you. Gods know I don't. All right, don't. *Don't* promise me anything." He picked up the shin-guard again and fitted it, beginning the ties. "It's all getting too complicated. I'm not trying to stop you."

"Then why are you trying to marry me?"

"O—gods." He rested his head against his hand. Looked up again with all the calm and patience he could muster, into two puzzled, earnest eyes.

"I want to *know!* You're asking me to do something, I want to know!"

Not surprising he made no sense to her, he thought. He made none to himself, nothing he wanted to bring into the light.

"What do you want out of me?" she asked.

He made the ties. He worked his arms into the armor-sleeves and tied the cords across his chest.

And she never said a thing to him. She just waited, arms on knees. Peasant-like.

So master Saukendar could get the lump out of his throat and get his balance back and manage some dignity. He *hated* being coddled.

Which was, he thought, close to what he was asking. Once in his life.

"I'm used to people *loving* me, girl. The whole world loved me. Love's damn cheap. You can buy it in the market *and* the court, two a penny."

She looked shocked.

"I'm too old for you," he said. "I was too old when you were born." He got up and felt the old pain, the way he felt it at every such move, always there. *I'm not coming back*, he thought again. *Not from this one. Why all this thought of permanency?*

"Master Shoka—"

Plaintively. Sharp as a knife.

He picked up the body armor and fitted it on, walking over to fetch Jiro.

"You're not old!" she yelled at his back.

And ran and grabbed at his arm, but he interposed a hand and a foul look, at which she was wise enough and respectful enough to stop.

So they took the road again, no different than they had begun.

Chapter Thirteen

The land became lower, the land became level, and rice-fields and dikes marked the beginning of farms, the tributaries of Ygotai.

And among the dike roads a pasture and a tolerably decent few horses.

"They belong to the judge," a farmer said.

"Stay here," Shoka said, and took the locket, the gold they had gotten, and the coins which he had, in the foolishness of their first acquaintance, proposed for Taizu's dowry.

And leaving Taizu to sit and guard their baggage by the dike-side, he rode to the judge's gate.

"My name is Sengi," he said, leaning an elbow on Jiro's saddlebow and looking down at the gatekeeper. "*Captain* Sengi, to see the judge—I understand he has horses for sale."

The magistrate was, thank the gods, not a man he knew or ever had heard of, a fat old man very nervous to find a mercenary captain at his gate; but a good deal happier to see that captain rattle a heavy purse and announce that he had given his remount to a friend and looked to acquire a serviceable animal—with tack.

So he left Jiro tied in the shade—calling out loud and friendly salutations to one of the judge's mares and generally giving grief to the judge's grooms—and walked out to the small pasture with the judge, to look at several fine mares, to admire their fine points, to talk horse-breeding, a passion of the elderly judge, and to agree with the judge's wisdom absolutely—which he figured might lower the price within his reach.

So one sat in the shade of the judge's garden, one sipped beautifully prepared tea—

—One remembered gentler times then, and felt a little pang, and felt the years shift back and forth in insane depth—

A garden, a path, a shade and a pool with an arching bridge.

His own house.

But it was forfeit. Confiscated.

"This is what I have." Shoka laid out the gold locket and the rings. And added a couple of coins. "I appreciate a fine horse. I'm afraid I know too well what they're worth. But the sorrel with the white foot . . ."

"Brood mare potential. You should have seen her sire. . . ."

"Certainly. But I couldn't possibly afford the bay . . ."

It took the whole damned afternoon. He imagined Taizu fretting and fretting out there on the road. He imagined a whole troop of imperial guards coming along and asking questions Taizu could not answer.

But there was no way to evade the old man, who asked him about affairs further north.

"M'lord, I've come in from Mendang. I've no idea. How are things in Hoishi?"

At which the old man temporized: "About what they have been."

"Cheng'di?"

"About the same. How in Hoisan?"

Cagey old wretch, Shoka thought.

And wished to hell he could get something current out of him.

But if he asked how were the crops, then the old fox would suspect something—a mercenary captain who went asking . . . might have banditry in mind; and the village judge was not the person to rouse suspicions with. So he drank the tea and talked over horses past and present.

He praised the old judge's favorite. He said—the truth—that he had seen the Emperor's own farms and—a lie—there had been none better. But he had no more gold, just a pittance of silver that he needed to live on.

They were down to bargaining for the tack.

Finally he turned out his purse and spent everything. Thank the gods he had left a little reserve with Taizu.

"That," the judge said, "is a *very* fine horse you have. I don't suppose you'd part with him?"

Eventually it was a three-year-old bay mare he rode back leading behind him, a creature with a white face, one hind foot white to the hock, one forefoot white to the knee, a broad, powerful rump and a good chest. Not precisely the most ordinary horse in the province. He would have preferred something less marked, but it was a good horse, the judge was anxious to sell her and he was anxious to get clear of the farm.

And Taizu, who came out from her ditch and her bushes to meet him—looked by her stance exactly the way he had expected, worried witless by now and thinking the worst; but it was a different look when he came closer and she had a look at the horse he had brought her.

"She's *beautiful!* But—"

"She's loud as a riverman's whore," he admitted. It had come down to two, one unremarkable in all points, including her bones. "I did what I could. This one's sound, she's strong and she's trained for a soldier. I'd rather you had her under you in a pinch." He gave her the reins. "Climb up on her. Try her out."

"Can we *afford* her?"

"Jiro clinched the bargain."

"*Jiro!* My gods—!"

"All our gold and Jiro's best try at the judge's bay mare." He patted Jiro's neck. "Poor old lad. Gave everything he had. Didn't you, son?"

Jiro was still unsettled. Jiro bounced and danced in place and worked to get the bit while Taizu made her acquaintance of the bow-nosed, white-legged mare. And the look in Taizu's eyes and the fever in her hands touched a horseman's heart.

"Up!" he said. "It'd be like the old skinflint to change his mind and send his house guard after us! Let's be out of here."

She put her foot in the stirrup, she got herself up, and the mare, skittish with Jiro and a strange rider, danced off sideways, but she steadied. Good hands. A good seat. Damn fine seat.

"I thought you could handle her," Shoka said. "After Jiro." He rode close and passed her the paper he had. "Bill of sale. Hang onto that. If we get separated I don't want them calling you a horsethief."

"Gods, she's beautiful."

"Damn, girl, *I* never get these compliments." He let Jiro move, down the dike road, and the mare caught up and paced neatly beside, an energetic clip, with a good deal of neck-stretching and eye-rolling and side-stepping between the stud and the mare. "Watch it, there!"

"Men," Taizu said. There was a tremor in her voice. A before-battle kind of shiver. Her eyes were bright. Her hands kept the reins under constant light tension, the mare trying every little shift, testing what was on her, flirting with the stud next to her, and finding out her rider was right with her every move.

Jiro for his part was a very happy fellow.

More than I can say, Shoka thought dourly, and thought back on the judge, damn him, who had flatly asked how he had turned to mercenary service, where he had served, whose hire he was in—

Sengi, m'lord, no, but my father was from Tengu, well, we lost our land, m'lord. No prospects. I'll be riding back to Choedri, north, hoping for hire. Maybe there. Clear to Cheng'di if I have to. You don't know what my prospects are there?

Damned spooky, he thought, damned spooky the way the old man kept looking at him, saying: *I don't doubt you'd find employment there. Where are you coming from?*

Caravan guard, m'lord. But I've had a belly full of foreign places. I'm coming home. I don't suppose—there's much change in the last couple of years. . . .

No. Again with that strange look. And: *Let me show you a mare you haven't seen. . . .*

Down the levies to the river again. The whole horse-bargaining had taken three times as much time as he had wanted and it was twilight by the time they came to the bridge. "I don't want to stop *in* Ygotai," Shoka had said before they had ever set about the matter of the horses, and now he cast a look over his shoulder, with more and more of a prickling at his nape. Thank *gods*, it was still clear back there.

"What's wrong?"

"A nosy old man."

"The judge? You think he knew you?"

"I don't know."

"Well, what did he *do?*"

"Questions. Too damn many questions. How are *you* doing? Can we keep going?"

"I can ride all night if we have to, it's not my legs. —What kind of questions?"

"Who I am, where from. My name is Sengi. I'm a caravan guard. A captain of caravan guards. I used to be a gentleman, you're my wife, the bill of sale is valid. We stay by that story."

"I *told* you we shouldn't deal with a judge! They always ask questions! He could have recognized you!"

"Village judges don't get to court. I never met this man!"

"Maybe *he* wasn't always a village judge."

"Maybe he wasn't."

"—Or, maybe—" The mare went dancing a few steps sideways and Taizu brought her back. "Maybe they've been watching for you to leave your mountain."

"All these years? That's crazy." He looked over his shoulder again, more and more regretting the strongly marked horse. "I'm a fool. I shouldn't have taken that damn horse."

Badly marked, the old man had said. *But look at her lines, not the markings. I can't sell her for the price she ought to bring. No gentleman like yourself would ride a horse so—irregular, and I don't want those markings passed down. . . . But for your purposes . . . to see her go to a gentleman's retainer . . .*

"Don't get attached to that mare. We can trade her off up the road. In the meantime we use those good legs of hers to put distance behind us."

"All right," she said, looking back herself. "She's in no trouble. It's Jiro I worry for—"

"We old men can manage, girl." He touched Jiro with his heels and Jiro had no trouble deciding he was going if the mare was. And vice versa.

There was a twisting way around Ygotai, by levies and dike-roads, among a few shabby buildings on Ygotai's outer edge—a town of some ten thousand souls, as Shoka recalled it from the Emperor's census; but the extent of the ramshackle buildings that he did not recall seeing, and the poverty—disturbed his sense of what should be. "These people weren't here," he said to Taizu as they rode, two mercenaries through the town slums; and people huddled under woven-work porches around their cooking fires—stopped their suppers and stared with bleak, worried eyes. Children did not chase them, there *were* no children, except those sitting close and inconspicuous by their elders. There was only a single impudent pack of dogs, and those were starved-looking, yapping and chasing the horses, but not far.

Mostly the people looked beaten and afraid.

"They're scared of *us*," Taizu said in a quiet tone. "We look like soldiers."

The houses were so temporary a strong wind would demolish them. The street was rutted, dried mud in some places, a stinking morass in others where gods-knew-what habitually ran. And always the stares, the desperate, mistrusting stares.

What's wrong in this place? Where did these people come from?

What's happened here?

We look like soldiers. *What in hell does that mean?*

"There's not much place for a camp," he said, looking over the land of dikes and rice-fields beyond the town. Easy for a supposed boy afoot—all too conspicuous for a gentleman, his retainer, and two horses.

"We'd scare farmers," Taizu said. "Mercenaries."

"Like we scared the townsmen," Shoka said as they crossed another bridge in the dusk. "I'd as lief be through this, far out into the country again."

"The road's safer. Stay out of the dikes on a horse, if we're thinking about stopping."

Dead ends. A maze of dead end paths. The farmer did not have to tell the soldier that fact.

So it was a grove of mulberries well after dark, where an orchard road gave them a little recess off the highway; and a bed under the trees, where no one might notice. The sky had turned nasty toward dark, a leaden gray that killed even the sun-colors, down to a pewter twilight and a starless dark.

And with the prospect of a drenching they shared a cold supper of rice-balls and sausage and a little tea, with a quick, small fire of stolen mulberry leaves and twigs.

"Why were they afraid?" Shoka asked then, in the dim light of that fire.

"Of *soldiers*," Taizu said, as if it were simple sanity, and he were very dense.

"Soldiers."

"Of the Emperor."

He shook his head. "You're dealing with a man who was past twenty when you were born, girl. Who was in exile when you were scarcely aware of the world. In my time soldiers weren't to fear. Not—at least—within the towns and villages, no credit to a little rowdiness about the camps—that's always been. But this was *fear*."

"The troops do what they want. The mercenaries do. They have papers from the Emperor. They're the law. . . ."

"The law my rear. The *courts* are the law, girl. . . . The *Emperor* doesn't hire mercenaries. . . ."

"The *lords* are the law."

"On their land, yes. Town taxes go to the Emperor, town problems go to the—"

"—Emperor's judges. But if you haven't got money you can't pay the fines and they take your pigs; or your house; or maybe the Emperor's soldiers just feel like a joke so they flatten your house and kill you. There's nobody going to tell who they were, nobody'll care to find out who did it if you don't belong to some lord— *he'll* get mad and go to the courts, but you don't go to the court if you haven't got money—"

He listened. What she was describing was not the country he had left. But it was plausible, if an Emperor were a damnable fool.

"—because that judge back there, either he's crooked and he's taking money, or he knows what could happen to *his* farm if he got afoul of the soldiers. That's the way it is, out here in the country. That's the way the law is. And if you're a peasant and you've got somebody like lord Kaijeng, they tax him till he and his lady could hardly keep the place up and they raid his farms, and they march all his men away to the border wars, and finally they just come in and kill him, and you don't expect the Emperor did anything about it."

"Does the Emperor really do *anything*?"

"I don't know," she admitted. "They say the Emperor does this and the Emperor does that, but other people say he just puts his name on things and he spends all his time with his concubines and his birds."

"Birds." Cages . . . cages of exotic birds, an immense garden where birds flew free, and fine mesh nets secured them from the sky. Plants and birds imported from nameless places, at risk of lives. The boy had spent a lot of childhood hours there, dodging out on his weapons-drill and his court duties. Not an evil boy. A spoiled, self-centered, soft-minded boy, feckless as the sparrows.

Who murdered. Who cold-bloodedly schemed with Ghita to be rid of his wife, his advisors, his tutor—

Because he was a damned *fool*, whose wishes and whose desire not to think were more real to him than the bloody result of his scheming—

Damn him! Damn him for it!

Taizu had worked herself into a rage. He had, even thinking about it, for different reasons. So it was a long while before he said:

"Is that the reputation he has?"

"Everybody says he's a fool. Spends all his time with his birds. Lords give them to him, if they want anything. There was one bird cost this lord thousands. And it died inside a week and after that the other birds in the garden got sick and a lot of them died. The Emperor said it was poisoned and it put a spell on the rest. Ghita had that man arrested and they took his lands— Tenei was his name, lord Tenei, up north—I think it was P'eng."

"That damn dog—"

"They came in to arrest him and his wife committed suicide, but he hadn't the nerve so his friend killed him and killed himself."

"Who else are the lords? Can you name them off to me?"

She leaned back against a mulberry tree, a shadow in the dark, and ticked them off on her fingers.

"I don't know who's in Hua, if it isn't Gitu. He's also got Angen, of course. Shangei, that's lord Mendi. . . ."

"My gods."

"I don't know anything about him. Except it was lord Heisu's place."

"Mendi's a dithering fool. Go on."

"Yiungei—" There was a little tremor of anxiety in her voice out of the dark. "That's lord Baigi."

"Ghita's lapdog. I knew that."

"Mengan district, in Yiungei, that's—"

"Jeidi?" It was his own district she spoke of, his own lands.

She shook her head. "Jeidi's dead. Peiyan."

"Not all the bandits are in Hoisan. Who in Taiyi?"

"It used to be Riyen. He died. It's some cousin—"

"Kegi."

"That was it."

"Just a name to me. Who are the best lords?"

"I don't know. Lord Mura. He was a friend of our lord. His name is Meigin. And lord Agin of Yijang, he was all right for a neighbor."

Two still alive. "Tengu?"

"I'm not sure. I didn't—care much then. I didn't care about lords. —I know Kenji: that's Mida."

Another one he knew, not a forceful man, a scholar.

"Hoishi is lord Reidi," he said, "last I heard. Much that you ever hear of him. I can't say I can complain of him as a neighbor, but I never crossed his borders. Now I have." He shook his head, feeling the same sense of desperation that had been with him down this road, too like—all too like—what he had felt ten years ago. "If Jiro could stand it, I'd say we should keep moving, but I won't break him down running, damned if I will."

"I wish you'd gone back!"

"It's too late now. There's no safety there—not for me, not for anyone with me. Not for the village if I go back there. This way it's on my head, and that's all they notice. Listen to me. I want you to listen to me very sensibly, Taizu: if soldiers do come on us, if there's no way to run, you leave me and you ride till that mare drops and you get off and walk—"

"No."

"*Listen* to what I'm saying, dammit! If they should call out the soldiers on us, I'm not saying it *will* happen—but if it does, it's because they've recognized *me*, not a kid from Hua—and there's no way in hell I can do anything at that point but make trouble for them. Most would stay with me—one or two might chase after you—you can outride them, you're lighter and that's a damn good horse, that's why I wanted her, other considerations aside. You can get clear. I haven't got a hope of it. So let's be sensible. They don't know you, they don't know what you intend. If *I'm* back in the Empire, they'll make only one supposition, and your only danger is getting caught in my company. Now, that's sense. If something happens to me, things are going to be stirred up for a while. You get out, get to the south, hide out till it's quiet—"

"You're making all this up, it's not doing any good, because I'm not going to do it. I'm not leaving you!"

He sat there quiet a moment, thinking: *I wanted loyalty.*

Damn her, does she ever do anything but when you don't want it?

He was scared, more scared than he had been since he could remember. He had *known* the first caravan to go behind them from Mon to Ygotai would carry the news of his having crossed the border: he had planned for that, planned to stay ahead of that rumor, even to use it: they would expect Saukendar to go due north to Cheng'di or into Yiungei, not to Hua. But what had seemed possible in Mon seemed less so in Ygotai, and the desperate look of the people and the evidence of profound changes in the land—made it all seem more desperate and more difficult.

And there was, since Mon, since he had breached the peace, no safety in return.

"You think the judge might call the soldiers," Taizu said, "and have them look out for my horse?"

"For your horse, for Jiro—a big red horse with a man

of my description. I'm not much less conspicuous, and
the Emperor's birds are more than show. A message
can fly from here to Cheng'di—damn fast."

"So. So—we just go fast, that's all."

"Where's the judge tonight? Where have his messengers gone? Where are the nearest soldiers and how
fresh are their horses, against Jiro?"

"Do you know that?"

"So we hide! We hide until they think the judge is
crazy."

"Where?"

"I'll find a place. There's hedges. There's thickets."

"We're dealing with two horses, for the gods' sake.
You said yourself, if we get into the paddies, there's no
way—"

"You listen to me, master Saukendar, you from the
Heavenly City: *I* got out all right, didn't I? This is the
country. You see this orchard. You see that road? It's
not fast. We'll have to wade. But I'll bet the soldiers
won't do it. We get back among the paddies and back
into Taiyi province—"

"There's a river. Jiro's carrying armor."

"Well, if we cross by dark and we split up his tack
and let my horse carry half—"

He sat there thinking about his reputation, about a
single, sharp fight on the road, a way for a man to go
out with some credit and some satisfaction on his
enemies—

And thinking with a little rise in his spirits—what
Shoka-the-fool would have done in his youth, and risked
everything for—having no hero's reputation to lose.
Right through the rice-paddies, the fox's way—if he had
a guide who was more than wishful thinking—

"You think you can find a way through to Taiyi?"

"I know I can."

"They'll track us. *Horses* don't come and go down the
paddy roads."

"That's fine. Water covers a lot. Horses can wade the
same as we can."

"Then let's do it by dark. Before the rain starts."

There was a moment of silence as he got up. A pitiful small grunt as Taizu gathered herself up.

There was more than that from Jiro, who stamped and shied around at being saddled up—and at being loaded this time not with a rider, but with the armor and the packs.

Shoka carried the armor when it came to climbing the main dike. He handed it up to Taizu, who set it on the ground, and he climbed the bank himself and pulled on Jiro's reins. After which Jiro came up in a rush and knocked him flat.

"Dammit!" he breathed, on his back on the ground, in the mud of the dike-side. And he turned and struggled to his feet and up the slope with his leg shooting pain up the inside.

Taizu tried to help him at the last, a shape in the dark that loomed up at the top. He shoved her. She was in his way, it hurt, and he shoved her. Then because he knew he was in the wrong he got angry at her. "Dammit, don't get in front of me!"

It was misting rain. It was wet, it was slick. Jiro was exhausted and panting with the treks through mud, they had scarred the flanks of more than one dike in a trail a child could follow, and the turns along the roads, every choice of paths—their zigging and zagging along the dikes, sometimes a long arm, sometimes a short one, sometimes simply where they could manage the climb, became a nightmare of moonless, starless choices.

He picked up his sodden armor from where Taizu had dropped it, while she was picking her gear up and putting it back on the mare's saddle. His leg hurt, gods, it hurt. He piled everything back on the saddle and tied it, thank gods for the cord they had gotten from the bandits.

"We've got to go down again," Taizu said suddenly in a hoarse and shaky voice.

"What do you mean we've got to go down again? We just came *up* this side."

"We're wrong. We're going wrong. I know we are."

He was freezing, with the wind driving against his wet clothing. His boots were double-weighted with mud. Jiro was in no better case. And at every turn it had been: *I know, I'm sure. I know where I'm going.*

"Look," he said hoarsely, "look, girl, you *don't* know where you're going. What are you trying to do, keep going until one of the horses breaks a leg? Let's get off this damn dike, settle down and rest till we get some light, so we can see where we're going."

"We're all right," she said. "We just got fouled up back there, we've got to go down again."

"We don't know where we're going, we're damn well liable to wind up north again for all we know—clear back to the damn road!"

"No. It's this way."

"You haven't got the moon, you haven't got the stars, *you can't dead-reckon your way across this maze—*"

"I've got the wind!"

"The wind shifts, dammitall!"

"And the *feel!* The way the land is, the way the dikes run, I know what I'm *doing*, dammit, I *know where east is!*"

"Oh, gods," he groaned, as the shadow that was Taizu started down the dike-side again.

Leave the bitch. *Let* her hike out there in the dark until she knew she was alone.

It was too damn cold to stop. His teeth were near to chattering.

"Damn her," he said to Jiro, and untied the baggage and the armor and tied it on his own shoulders.

He hurt so much already there was hardly worse. It was Jiro's legs he worried for—an old horse, under his own armor, a cold night and muscles gone weak with chill.

He fell on the slope; he hit the water and the mud and for a moment could not get his feet under him or get a breath. He made it. It was the bad side. Oh, damn, it was. But he got himself to his feet. Jiro was standing there on four feet and whole.

"Come on," he said, finding the reins. And he kept
going, as far as the other end, where Taizu swore they
could go on dry ground and trust the paths a while.

"Let my horse carry it," she said. "She's all right.
She's all right, master Shoka."

"So am I," he said in what of a voice he had left. And
added: "But Jiro's too old for this."

They put his armor up on the mare's saddle. Taizu
started off again.

"We're lost," he said to her back. "We're lost. You
know that."

"We're all right. We'll get out of this. It can't last too
much further."

He swore a steady stream of line-soldier obscenities
and limped after.

The sun was edging its way up a murky sky when the
dike paths came to a line of trees; and as they came to
that ancient stand of willow—

An uncrossable expanse of river.

Taizu stopped, when they came over the dike face to
face with that—stopped. Her shoulders slumped, and
she turned around with a look of absolute desperation.

"It's all right," he said. "It's all right. We've come
back to the Hoi, that's what we've done. You've led us
true east. We're all right."

Her lips trembled.

"The river's on the *right*. We're back where we started!"

"No," he said. "No! We crossed the river Hoi, at
Ygotai. It's the same that flows past Mon. It's *our* river,
after the Yan flows into it. It goes down to the
Chaighin . . . *Maps*, girl. The benefit of maps, remember? The Hoi and the Chisei come together at the east
end of Hoishi. . . . Taiyi's straight ahead. Straight ahead
as we're going."

Tears started down her face. She came and put her
arms around him and rested her head on his shoulder,
just stood there, shivering.

"You led us right," he said. "You brought us east. It
was east all along."

Chapter Fourteen

Shoka wiped his nose and drank the pleasantly steaming willow-tea with his supper—old mother willow and her sisters gave them a shelter, a canopy of ground-reaching branches that enveloped them, the horses, a level, tolerably dry bank, and a little of the river edge. Sometimes barges and boats passed, bound from Ygotai onward to trifold Mandi, which sat astride the Chaighin where it and the Hoi became the Great River, and flowed on to distant reaches of Sengu and Mendang, and remote outposts where barbarian traders came. And sometimes those boats came back upriver bearing, one supposed, goods from Mandi's bazaars. A rough place, Mandi, a country place, lacking the graces of the imperial city—but prosperous with the trade from the joining rivers and from the outside.

Strange to think that that large city was not so far away, when they sat in their willow-tent sneezing and coughing and warm, thank the gods, the willow tending to confine the smoke so they dared a tiny fire now and again, and shielding them from the wind and the misting rain.

"On the whole," he had said to Taizu, that first morning, "we're quite well situated. Let the furor die down. Let them wonder where we are. We don't seem in any danger of being discovered, no one walks this shore, they go by boat—so I can't think of a better place for the moment."

And Taizu: "I hope the north river isn't this wide, without going back—"

"It's not." He sneezed, and wiped his nose, and seeing how low Taizu's spirits were, got himself a willow-wand and sketched her the wedge shape of Hoishi, with its two main rivers, the Hoi and the Chisei. And Taiyi, the other side. "The Chisei never is much. A soldier knows these things. His supply depends on them. I've neglected your education in maps, girl; maps are the essentials of any campaign—"

His voice was going. They had rubbed the horses down when they had first made their camp, they had cut grass on the dike-side, numb with cold and staggering with exhaustion, and seen that Jiro and the mare had a breakfast. Then they had stopped, tucked up in the quilts their mats had managed to keep dry, both of them cold as corpses and holding onto each other. Warmth came, warmed bodies, warmed limbs, enough to shiver a while, enough for Shoka's leg to start hurting again, an agony that would have kept him awake if he were not so mortally exhausted. As it was he simply clamped his jaws and tried to think of something else, waiting for exhaustion to win out, determined not to give way to the pain in Taizu's hearing. But she made a sound, a kind of steady, hurt whimper with every breath, until he stroked her wet hair and hugged her and she stopped, evidently realizing only then that she was doing it.

Poor girl. There was no strength, he thought, could have carried her; it was the simple, stupid vitality of the young, who had no experience to tell them what was possible.

And seeing her moving around, with the afternoon, a

man had to move again, and see to his gear. It was her job, washing their clothes. But it was not the cabin on the mountain, it was the field again; a man took care of his own things if he had no servant. And he did not.

There was no way all the dirt would ever come out of the cloth or the leather. "We'll look like mercenaries for certain," he said, while she used a pot of oil soap to try to restore their tack and the leather of their clothing.

"It's a mess," she said.

"It's always a mess." The leg hurt enough to distract him from the rest of his stiff muscles. "I think I tore something in the knee. I'm not sure whether it's good or bad."

"We haven't got the rags. Except these."

He looked at the oily rags she was using, heating them over a tiny fire in a tin pan; and the ache was enough to blur his vision, the thought of warmth on the joint enough to make his speech thick. "We can try it."

It did help. It helped so much he lay back on the ground beneath the willows and shut his eyes and opened them to find the whole world gone dim.

Twilight.

Taizu sitting by him, waiting.

That was how the willow-tea.

And the map-drawing in the fading daylight, Taizu watching the lines he drew with that thinking-frown on her face and her lip caught in her teeth in that way she had when she was desperate and worried.

Terrified.

"We can go two ways from here," he said. "Back along the Hoi till we can cross; or up to the Chisei. West or east. Your choice."

"If I wasn't with you," she said, fists clenched, "master Shoka, I'd be on into Taiyi."

He shook his head. "You'd be dead back on the riverside. With a good number of bandits to your credit. But you'd be dead." He saw her chin trembled. He thought of home again, on the mountain. He thought of the assassins and the armies, thought of sleepy lord

Reidi in Keido, who might be forced, finally—to do something about the exiled lord Saukendar, if only to loose messages north.

Thought of the villagers of Mon, who had fed him all these years, lying dead for no fault but relying on him.

Thought of a young fool who tried too much and did too much and who, damn her, had cleaned their tack and their armor and washed their clothes and made him tea and now had the gall to call him useless and an encumbrance.

It must be the pain. His eyes stung, and he massaged the aching leg.

Her hand rested on his. She leaned forward and put her arm about his neck, her cheek against his. "Please let's go home. Let's go home. I'll marry you."

He put a hand up to push her back. "For *what?* To keep me from getting you killed?"

He saw the glistening on her cheeks in the last of the light. "It doesn't matter what happened," she said. "It doesn't matter anymore. I'll be your wife. Please let's go home."

Whatever she did—was always at the wrong time. He thought that again: that it was always the right promise at the wrong time.

Damn honor and *damn* the pride that made men fools. Take what she offered. Take her across the river to the wilds of Hoisan, find another mountain. Have sons and daughters.

Damn the things he had taught her, encouraging the woman he loved to put a premium on honor, and pride, and all the things that made men fools—

But, he had thought, she had come to him already equipped with that. And she had compelled him to teach her. And believed in him, beyond the point she knew him in his mornings and his out-of-sorts days, his worst days and his lameness and all his faults—

She was the invulnerable one. She was young. She was all those things.

And it took his weakness to stop her and make her

plead with him, never saying it: *Don't kill yourself. I can't stand to watch you. I'll marry you.*

He touched her face. He said: "Did I teach you this? Pull yourself together. Plan your retreats. If you want to go back across the river and think a while—we can do that. But I don't say you should give up. I don't say you should ever give up. We can go back a while. That's another part of soldiering. You reconnoiter, you gather information. We've created a little stir, so now I'll tell you what we do, we go back into Hoisan, we wait for the rumor to get to the capital, if it will; we spread the word—like I said, remember?—that I'm at large. That the woman with me has a grudge with Gitu. Let our enemies lose sleep. Let them grow thin worrying. Let the time be ours. You and I—we can be with them—we can be with them closer than their wives of nights. That's what I'd do."

Like I've always done. And gods know if they even care.

Taizu rested her head on her arm, one hand at the back of her neck.

"All right," she said.

In that beaten, weary way that had never been Taizu.

The morning came with a gentle damp in the air, an autumnal chill next the water. A boat passed. The voices of the rivermen and the splash of oars pierced the stillness.

They lay close beneath the clammy quilts, for nothing other than warmth, and Shoka tried to keep his coughing still—wishing not to disturb Taizu and not to attract notice. But Taizu coughed too, and it was a long time before either of them stirred out, to make a breakfast their throats were too sore to enjoy, to cut grass for fodder and tend to the horses, and to huddle in damp quilts and reckon their situation—how much food they had, how long they could avoid discovery.

Jiro and the mare made acquaintance—too much noise and too much stubbornness for two fevered, exhausted human beings to trust; and the mare too close to her own home to trust she might not bolt—excepting the attraction of Jiro, who was less inclined to desert them and go kiting off to the dikes—excepting the horses were as sore and tired as their owners, willing to rest and fill their bellies while their owners huddled in a nest of blankets that would not quite dry and coughed and sneezed til their sides ached.

"It was like this in Shangei," Shoka said, in what of a voice he had left, "the year we had to ferret the rebels out. Never stopped raining."

"What rebels?" Taizu said, a croak of a voice that might have been a man's.

"Lord Mendi had a nephew," Shoka said, and tried to tell the story, except he took to coughing, and it never would stop until Taizu brewed up willow-tea and he got a little warmth on his throat.

He coughed when he talked, so did she, and mostly their noses ran. So they heated up the rags they had, turn and turn about put them on chests and backs and throats, drank willow-tea for the fever and the sore throats and mostly stayed under covers, while the boats passed, and the rains spattered on the willow-leaves, and winds swayed the trees and shook down water to keep the blankets damp and keep their clothes from drying.

The third day it was better. Taizu trapped some minnows on the riverside and made a hook and used some of their saddlery cording; that night they had their fill of fish and rice with wild herbs, risking a larger fire than usual. A man felt he might live after that supper; and he said:

"I think tomorrow night we might ride back to Ygotai."

She said nothing for a long moment. His heart began to beat faster, because he reckoned that she was not thinking about Ygotai and the south, but about slipping off north tonight, and leaving him and the horses and everything behind.

Except she no longer looked like a peasant. She had

not her basket to hide her sword, her shirt was too fine, her shape was not a man's: she could look the peasant squatting on the riverside to fish, and wave at the boatmen and feel quite smug in her deception while he suffered in hiding—

But not on the road, not under close scrutiny.

He had time to think of that. He almost said it out loud, but she sighed and said:

"Yes. We could."

It was not the absolute affirmative he hoped for. He thought of saying: *Well*, will *you*? But that would start her arguing, and arguing could send her off to Hua. So he nodded placidly, as if he had never had such a thought. "After moonset. We might have trouble at Ygotai. But once across the bridge—there's no worry."

"Where will we go?"

He shrugged. "Wherever we find pleasant. It's what I say: let our enemies worry." He coughed. That was still with them. "Wherever it is, high ground and drier."

There was fish for the next day. They were almost out of rice, so they saved that. And come dusk of that sunny, warmer day, they saddled up and put on their armor and tied up their hair—"No need to look like brigands," Shoka said.

"It's dark," Taizu said. "We're hiding. I thought no one was supposed to see us."

"No need to *act* like brigands, then," Shoka said; and made her stand still, sulking as she was, until he had arranged her hair. Then he turned her around and made her lift her chin. There was a furious scowl on her face. And her eyes glistened.

"Where's your center?" he asked her quietly.

She gave him no answer for a moment. It was a dangerous moment. Everything could break.

But she said: "Next year. *Next* year, master Shoka."

Not husband. "Am I divorced, then?"

A long, deep breath. "No." Her voice still broke into hoarseness. "I don't break my promises. *Any* of them."

And she walked off to sit on the riverside and wait for full dark.

So he came and sat by her on the rocks. Cranes were flying in the dusk. From somewhere there was the smell of smoke. But they had had that before. Perhaps it was all the way from Ygotai, perhaps from some farmhouse they had never found.

"We'll find a place in Hoisan," he said, "set up a camp just like the bandits. We'll set ourselves for winter. We won't plan to stay there. Let them send after us. —I'll tell you: you're better than most. And you're getting smarter."

She said nothing. She only stared at the darkening water, dusky profile against that shimmer. He saw her look toward him, and expected her to say something— but her head lifted subtly, her shadowy face showing dismay at something behind him.

His muscles tensed. He did not turn at once, thinking someone might be there. He waited for her to cue him, and she said:

"Master Shoka, the sky. . . ."

He did turn. The sky beyond the willows, above the dikes, held a red taint like a beginning dawn. And the smoke had been there all along.

Fire. A huge one.

"That's toward Ygotai," he said, getting to his feet. The ache in his knee bothered him still, but it was inconsequence of a sudden, against the cold suspicion of disaster.

Taizu headed down the shore, around the willows, up the slope of the dike. He followed, slower, feeling the climb in his knee, slipping on the grass, seeing the glow brighter and brighter until he reached the crest and saw the red with no bright rim of near fire.

Not toward Ygotai. At Ygotai. Not some burning straw-stack. Much, ominously much more than that.

"It's in the town," Taizu said.

"Come on," he said. "If we're going to get through, let's make a try at it."

She followed him down the slope and down beneath the willows where the horses waited. They led the horses up again, a slanting course up the tall face of the dike, and mounted up, facing toward that glow.

Taizu did not speculate aloud. He did not. But he put them to a faster pace than he would have, thinking that if the fire was accidental, some cooking-pit blazing up to catch a house—it might still draw the soldiers the judge had talked about; and if they came there early enough in the commotion they might pass, two shadowy figures on horseback, along the fringes of calamity, to the bridge and across, while the town was still occupied.

It might be, aside from the calamity of the property-holder, a piece of luck too good to let pass.

But he feared otherwise. He feared shapeless things—like rumor and birds. . . .

The further they rode, the brighter the glow, the more pungent the smoke, until there appeared a seam of yellow fire along the horizon, and it was abundantly clear it was more than one house or one barn.

"It must be the whole town," Taizu said at that sight. "The whole *town's* burning."

He thought of accident. He thought of their transit through the place.

And the bridge, which was one narrow bridge, and the way anyone who wanted to escape the province south would have to go—if they had no boat.

They might perhaps give up the horses, and hope to steal a boat at Ygotai's riverside. They might cross the Hoi, and be afoot in Hoisan with only their armor and their weapons. —Give up Jiro and the mare, in the hope that they could get away and escape the traps laid for two riders....

If it had to be, it had to be, dammit. The old lad would find his way, he hoped, to the judge's mares, and not to the hands of mercenaries. He was only a horse. Dammit.

"There's boats," Taizu said. There were, several of

them, running dark on the water. Then more and more
as they rode, until they reached level ground and trees
came between them and the river.

People ahead, afoot, without armor, people with baskets and bundles, fleeing the nightmare of fire and
stinging smoke. Shoka reined back, confronting that
movement around a turning of the road, and the mare
danced anxiously past and around again under Taizu's
hand.

"It's townsfolk," Taizu said. "Running from the fires."

Worse and worse, Shoka thought. Much worse. The
fires involved houses, barns. He had a surer and surer
feeling of disaster. That *damn* horse of Taizu's.

It's our fault. It's our doing.

"Come on," he said, and rode forward, slowly. People scattered from them, through the trees, people
shrieking and crying.

It's the soldiers, he heard.

It's the soldiers.

And when they had come closer to the town, they
caught sight of riders passing against the light of burning houses; and saw people lying dead, pale blotches on
the firelight ground. *It's the soldiers.*

"Damn them," Taizu said, in a hoarse, demon's voice.
"Damn them!"

He reined in, caught up the helm that had rattled
useless by his knee till now, and put it on, making the
ties carefully, precisely, while Taizu put on her own.

"The bridge," he reminded her harshly. He drew his
sword, and sent Jiro ambling forward, the mare beside
him.

The steel of Taizu's sword rasped out of its sheath.

That damned white-legged horse . . .

"Let's go, girl."

Faster now, running flat-out, the whole night narrowed to what came through the face of the helm: fire,
clouds of smoke, the bright fire of a burning barn, the
black shape of an abandoned cart— He whipped a

glance rightward as they bore left down the street, and saw it clear from that direction.

"Master Shoka!"

Riders in the way ahead of them. He went clear and cold, measuring the strides, their horses' and Jiro's. And hers. "*Haii!*" he yelled, and gave Jiro a kick that the old lad was well-trained to. Jiro surged forward and Shoka laid about him with a vengeance, one, two, three men out of their saddles before one got past him.

Not far. He heard Taizu yell.

Four, five, before Taizu caught up with him and they broke through to the riverside road—

There were no boats beside, except one burning, with the light flaring out on the waters: with the light showing the road ahead.

And a troop of foot guarding a barricade ahead.

He spun Jiro sharply to the right, hard about with a yell at Taizu: he had not *seen* the bows, but he *knew*—he swept Taizu up as she reined the mare around; and rode, down the rutted shanty street, past the burning wreckage of buildings.

Four riders ahead. He gave Jiro his heels again, and yelled at Taizu: "*We're going through! Stay with me!*"

He took two men out of the saddle and did not appreciably slow down. He wheeled about for a third and got him off Taizu's back. "Get the horses!" he yelled, and herded one riderless horse against the wall, but it and Jiro took exception to each other, a teeth-bared encounter that was going to cost dangerous time. He let it go. "*Never mind!*" he yelled at Taizu. "*Get the hell out of here!*"

She had snagged a horse. She nearly came out of the saddle trying to hang onto it, the animal backing wildly. It slipped free.

"Never mind!" he yelled at her, and the mare bolted into a run as Jiro came past her.

"Where are we going?" Taizu yelled. "Where are we going?"

"Hell if I know!" he yelled back. "We can't make the bridge. Out of here!"

There were carts on the road ahead, in the dark. People left them and ran when they came by. There were soldiers plundering one.

"Stay back with that damn horse," Shoka said to Taizu, and rode up on the soldiers alone.

"What are you doing?" he asked them.

And killed both of them.

When Taizu caught him up he was waiting quite calmly, quite numb, thinking over the archers on the bridge, the ruin of the town.

"We can go west," he said. "Down the Yan. Toward Dai, as far as Muigan, then cross south."

"All right," she said in a thread of a voice. And then, in a creaking squeak. "I'm sorry about the horse. I'm sorry. I couldn't hang onto it."

"It's not your fault," he said, very quietly, very reasoned. "It's mine. The best thing we can do for these people is get out of Hoishi, as far as we can. As loudly as we can."

She said nothing for a moment. Her face showed between the steel cheekplates of the helm, the metal shining with the distant glare of the fire.

No protests, no arguments. Just that grave, large-eyed stare. And a sniff and a discreet wipe at her nose.

"Probably it's a good thing you stay with that horse," he said. "Attract all the notice we can. We get out of this if we can. I'm not going back to Mon. We're not going anywhere but to the border, and over." He turned Jiro's head to the road, started them moving. "We save the horses for times we have to run. And we'll have to."

There were no more soldiers on the road, just peasants, farmers out of Ygotai and gods knew where—folk who abandoned their belongings as riders came by, threw them on the roadside or left handcarts standing and fled, dragging children or carrying them. In some cases they hid very near the road, old folk, perhaps, desperately afraid.

But before long they passed beyond all such refugees, onto a clear road, across a flat, wild land.

They were on the Keido road, Shoka reckoned. There were hills westward, that would make pursuit harder and give them a chance—as long as they could keep the horses sound: that was his greatest concern, and for that reason he wanted to keep to the good road as long as they dared, as long as it tended generally toward the hills. They kept an easy pace, rested the horses when they tired, keeping, Shoka figured, only a minimal distance between themselves and the trouble flowing outward from Ygotai toward Keido.

"It's going to be hard tomorrow," he said when Taizu protested they were stopping too often. "Get your breath now." He sank down by her, Jiro's reins in hand, and found his own stomach empty and aching. "We're doing all right. Don't worry."

She was scared, he thought, sitting by her in the dark. It took a great deal to frighten Taizu, but she was living a great deal with memories tonight. He longed for daylight, and dreaded it; and saw it coming in the dimming of the stars.

"Sleep," he said. "Can you?"

A sigh beside him in the dark. She leaned against him, a grating of armor-plates, hers and his, and she put her arm around him. In a little time she went limp that way, and he lay back on the embankment, in the grass, trying not to fall asleep himself, or lose track of the horses that grazed on their leads, the leads wrapped about his left hand. It would be so damned easy. And he was being a fool, he thought: the young could go so much longer.

But he knew how to sleep in the saddle. If she was rested she could shepherd him while he caught a nap. They could go off the road in the morning, cut across the rocky highland fields—leave tracks, gods knew, thanks to the recent rains, but he *wanted* to be tracked, if not closely; he trusted that the peasants who had hidden from them would describe them to anyone who asked.

And draw their pursuers away from Mon. Gods hoped.

He moved finally, pushed at Taizu. "Sorry. We can't stay longer."

Dawn was coming—a gray definition of trees and rocks, a seam of red along the east that was not burning Ygotai.

Taizu moved, and looked around her. "How long?" she asked. "How long?"

"It's all right. We're still ahead."

He said.

But when he checked Jiro's girth and climbed into the saddle:

"Oh, damn."

"What?" Taizu asked.

"Riders," he said. There were, three of them visible on the crest of the hill ahead. Taizu climbed hastily up to the mare's back and had a look for herself.

"What do we do?"

He was not himself sure. He looked at the land ahead, the rough land to either side. He started Jiro moving, in that strange nowhere calm of hours like this before hostilities, two forces camped close to each other.

He wished Taizu were not with him. He wished—

He was not sure.

More of them came over the rise.

Twenty, thirty now.

"Gods," Taizu breathed. But he kept riding and she did, calmly, slowly.

The road out of Keido, he thought. Lord Reidi's home. A Hoishi town burned at the hands of mercenaries and an army came down the road from Keido. Perfectly reasonable: the lord wanted to know the reason. But not reasonable that the town burned at all. It was a good part of lord Reidi's income.

"I don't know what we're into," he said. In the dim gray light he could see banners. The white showed

most. If it were indeed lord Reidi's men, it would be a
black lily on a white banner; and there was white enough.

"Taizu."

"I'm not going anywhere you don't!"

"Easy. Easy. *Whose* are the mercenaries back there?
Who do you think?"

A pause. "I don't know." There was an edge of panic
in Taizu's voice. "They could be from Keido. I don't
know whose they are."

"Taiyi?"

"I don't know."

"The peasants are going *toward* Keido."

Taizu was silent a moment. "Likely they're going
everywhere. But where they thought it was safe. . . ."

"I want you to do something for me. Just stop on the
road. Let's give them a parley signal—"

"No."

"Shut up and do what I tell you. One of us. One of
them. If they do something else, I'll be coming back in
a hurry. Just stop in the middle of the road and wait.
Hear me?"

"I don't like this. Let's get off the road. Gods, there's
more of them. . . ."

There were ranks behind the ones in the lead. It was
a cavalry on the move.

"Stay here," he said. "*Do* it, girl. You might string
your bow—in case. But don't be obvious."

She reined back. He tapped Jiro with his heel and
Jiro took a breath and collected himself. He held that
in, took his sword and laid it crosswise of the saddle.

Slow advance then. He reached a point outside bowcast
from both sides and stopped, and waited.

Chapter Fifteen

"**L**ord Saukendar," Reidi said, his wrinkled face—not so much changed, after all these years—showing the worry natural to a man at such a meeting. But the old lord came forward in person, once his retainer had told him who it was—came forward himself with no guard, elderly as he was, while his retainers drew his troops up at rest on the hill.

"Lord Reidi," Shoka said, and bowed in the saddle. "I appreciate your courtesy."

"You're after more than courtesies, m'lord."

"A free road. Your leave to pass. Perhaps your advice."

"What advice is that?"

"What's happening in Hoishi?" Shoka nodded his head back toward Ygotai. "What kind of craziness is loose in Chiyaden these days?"

Reidi stared at him as if he had lost his wits.

"So I see I've asked a foolish question," Shoka said. "Am I at fault?"

"I had a report from Mon. Another from a judge—regarding a horse. Unfortunately—I'm not the only one

who'll have heard. The word's out. It's going north of
here. The Regent's men have been scouring all along
your track. And evidently they've attacked *me* as your
ally."

Shoka let go his breath. "You've been a good neighbor, m'lord. I'd never wanted to cause you grief. Now it
seems I've caused more than my company may be
worth to you. What about the other lords? What about
Hainan and Taiyi?"

"*What about my town*, m'lord? What happened at
Ygotai?"

"Someone set fires. Someone killed a great number
of people. The ones who escaped have taken to the
roads. I don't know who fired the town. I rode through
when I saw the fires—my wife and I—"

"Wife!" Lord Reidi looked past his shoulder, his jaw
clamped like an old turtle, his eyes glittering sharply.
"What are you doing to us?"

"My wife has a grievance with lord Gitu. From Hua.
Relatives. I thought to have a quieter ride than this, by
night, by the back roads—take care of the matter and
out again, with no grief to Hoishi. It seems I'm sadly
mistaken. So I ask you for your advice now—and I
offer you my help—if there were anything I can do to
make amends."

"You don't know," Reidi said with a shake of his
head.

"My lord, no, I don't." Softly, quietly. Reasonably,
while his heart was hammering away and he was poised
to move. "Would you explain?"

Reidi leaned his hands on the saddle and heaved a
sigh. "The Emperor, lord Saukendar. The Emperor—
and the Regent. Does it seem reasonable to you that a
Regency continues—into an Emperor's thirtieth year?"

"No, m'lord."

"Not to us, either. Not to many of us. We were ready
to make that objection—when lord Gitu overran Yijang
and Hua. Both likely to support us. Your—wife—has
told you nothing about that matter."

"Tell me."

Lord Reidi's brow arched, rearrangement of a myriad wrinkles. "I ask your honesty, m'lord."

"You have it, my lord. I believe I have yours."

There was long silence. Reidi's horse shifted under him. That was all.

Then Reidi said: "Gitu has hired thousands of mercenaries in the last two years—with the imperial treasury. Fittha and Oghin, while we fight their like on the border. While they take our young men to fight in the Imperial army. And there is no Emperor to rally to. Ghita's sapped the wit he did have. Ghita's assassins have taken Meigin. . . ."

"Damn."

Reidi gave him that one-sided stare again. "Why did you come back?"

"A man can be a fool at any age."

"In what respect, m'lord Saukendar?"

"Perhaps—to hope there was something changed here."

"There is no Emperor."

"Dead?"

"Effectively. There was a chance. There were those of us who would have brought him to the throne— His thirtieth birthday seemed the propitious day—"

"Hua. Two years ago."

"Hua and Yijang. Which fell to Gitu's mercenaries in the same month. Assassinations, elsewhere. Hired killers. Bands of mercenaries traveling under imperial orders. The *Emperor's* seal, and the Regent's orders. How do we stop such a thing? How do we prevent it—when every lord able to lead is apprehended, assassinated, when they strip us of men, even boys out of the fields—go to Saukendar, some said. Go to Saukendar. They *urged* me to send to you. This time he has to listen, they said. But if I had sent—and Ghita had known—you understand—" Reidi gave an uncomfortable twitch of the shoulders. His horse shifted again. "I had no true hope that you'd come. You'd indicated to the villagers—that you had no wish to hear from any-one. That you would refuse any such petitions—"

"You *were* watching me."

"It's my village, m'lord—as the Regent pointed out to me again and again, *and* threatened my life should you leave that mountain. Of course the word came to me. I tried to get a messenger down the road to you when I knew you'd left Mon. I take it that no one reached you."

"They were too late, if they got through at all. Re-garding what, my lord?"

"Your intentions in leaving Mon. Did *Kaijeng* send a messenger?"

Did he? There was a sudden chill about his heart. *Taizu?*

Damn, no!

"His daughter?" Reidi asked.

"No. I've said. —What would you have expected me to do—leaving Mon?"

"I would say—lord Saukendar—we need you. We *believed* you knew that. We believed you'd come back to deal with Ghita and his partisans."

He felt cold, cold all the way to the bones.

"There are men ready to follow you, lord Saukendar. There are men who've committed their lives to this— We didn't know the hour. We only believed. Now you've come back, we have a leader the other lords will take the risk for—"

He rode quietly back to Taizu, whose face—

Gods, the things Reidi had surmised could not be true. Not with that look, that bewildered, worried look she gave him as he reined to a stop in front of her.

"What do they want, master Shoka?"

"They want me to help them," he said. "It seems— the moment we crossed the border—the rumor started north that I'd been *called* north by some conspiracy, to lead an attack against the capital. The local garrisons of Ghita's troops moved to try to prevent me; the rumor

may have reached Ghita by now, by messenger bird—
and if it has—" Blood flashed to mind, and poison:
Ghita's assassins: the cup in Meiya's hand. Deaths far
and wide across Chiyaden, the last possible friends.
The numbness seemed all the way through him. "—if it
has, then orders are coming back from Ghita by now,
the Guard is moving against everyone who might be
disposed against the government— Reidi, some of the
other lords—they'll fight. They've had enough. They've
committed themselves to this—too far to look innocent.
That's the problem. They want me to go to Cheng'di;
and I want you—please, please listen to me: I would
much prefer you go to Keido and stay there—"

"No."

"Girl, we're not talking about bandits in Hoisan.
We're talking about imperial troops, an entirely different kind of fighting. You'll have your chance at the end
of this. But not now. Please, go to Keido. Lord Reidi's
wife will—"

"No."

"I'm asking you. You can be useful there."

She shook her head. "No. You *taught* me." Her head
came up, that chin set. He thought: *If not with me,
then behind me every step of the way.* . . .

"What did I teach you?"

"*Honor*, master Shoka."

"Where did I teach you a fool idea like that?"

The chin trembled and steadied. "You wouldn't let
me go alone. Now you won't go away from lord Reidi
and let him go alone against the soldiers. That's what."

Memory painted him gruesome scenes, terrible ways
to die. He tried to shove them out. But hell if he could
hope she would be reasonable and go to Keido; at
bottom, he was only grateful she was not talking about
an independent assault on Gitu.

"Then I need you to listen to me," he said, to fore-
stall that before she thought of it. "I ask you—don't
surprise me, Taizu. Don't do things like going after

Gitu. Later for him. I trust you. I can't say that about any of these people I'm fighting for."

She looked perplexed and worried. Well she might.

"They'll swallow me," he said. It was the only way he could think of it, the people like one vast dragon. They wanted Saukendar; Saukendar would save them; Saukendar owed them everything. Saukendar was whatever they decided him to be. He always had been. Shoka had lived in the belly of the dragon most of his life. Now the dragon wanted him back and all that could keep him out was a girl saying, "That's nonsense, master Shoka. You're a fool, master Shoka."

The body that was Saukendar could go on fighting long after Shoka was nowhere at all: he was confident of that; but Shoka would go with her, Shoka had no other reason to live; and Shoka was ready to hear her say no, and go away, not even knowing what she took with her—being a young girl, and not understanding a man who had never, but a few years of peace—existed.

"What are you talking about?" she asked him.

It was nothing that even sounded sane. So he said: "Just stay with me."

"Is that—marry you, again?"

"No," he said. "It's something different. —Besides, I thought you had."

She bit her lip. "I did, and I'm going with you. You can divorce me if we get to Cheng'di. Meanwhile there's none of the ladies in Chiyaden who'll be any help to you along the way."

"Who said divorce you? I worked hard enough getting you to agree!"

"You just remember I said that." Her jaw clenched. Muscles bunched, making her chin look uncommonly fragile. "You remember that in Cheng'di."

"Then you think damn little of me," he said.

"I'm no lady!"

"*The hell with them!*" he hissed, smothering it. "The hell with Saukendar, wife. Don't you do it to me! For gods' *sake*, don't you do it to me!"

She stared at him with wide, offended eyes.

Kaijeng's messenger, lord Reidi had surmised. *A scheme to get me back across the border, involved with their plots again?*

The very thought left him cold.

But the wound that scarred her was real. Her anger was real. Everything she knew and all she did was real. He wavered on the edge of a vast dark and Taizu with that shocked, hurt stare—was the only thread that saved him.

Right now she thought he had lost his mind, and was no little angry at him. Good, he thought. *Good for you, girl.*

They came among the first of the refugees from Ygotai by full daylight, and it was very different when the people saw their own lord's banner; and when they understood that the tired, travel-stained riders with him were Saukendar and his wife.

Shoka heard the murmurings, saw the change in the people's eyes, saw the respect they gave him. *Poor fools,* he thought. *Your houses are burned; your neighbors are murdered for me. Damn you for looking at me like that—*

But if one tried very hard one could ignore the stares, one could blur the faces at the edge of one's vision, one could tolerate the old woman who came and scared hell out of Jiro trying to touch him, babbling something about the old Emperor, and the way things used to be, and how she knew Saukendar would set things right.

One could blur one's vision and make one's heart cold and tolerate it, even if it rubbed the soul raw.

They got some satisfaction for it at Ygotai, among the burned sticks and rubble that had been a prosperous town. They found a small band of mercenaries, which Shoka expected: and he had already sent thirty of Reidi's men wide around the town to lay an ambush while he and Taizu rode with Reidi and the other hundred of

Reidi's men down past the town and onto the dike road
where the garrison had put the barricade across the
bridge.

It was appallingly easy. They *gave* the mercenaries
the way out down the main street of the town and
chased them all the way to the ambush out on the road,
in which they had one minor wound; and the one of the
mercenaries that looked apt to escape, went tumbling
off into the ditch with an arrow in him.

"Good," Shoka said coldly, calmly. "That'll let us gain
a little ground before the word spreads. M'lord, you say
you'll go north: are you ready to go now, this hour?"

Reidi looked gray. His white hair flew in wisps. He
looked as if the affair around him was more than he had
bargained for. But he got his breath and nodded. "Yes.
My wife—the system we have— We can get word to
the others. The birds—we breed them, you know. Exchange them. That's how we've planned it. When the
day came—we'd loose the birds . . . to every one of
us."

They had the mercenaries' few horses for remounts—a
good chestnut gelding to give Jiro relief and a bay to
change off with Taizu's white-legged mare.

It was the ferry on the Chisei that Shoka figured for
trouble. So it was more than the horses they borrowed:
it was the armor and gear off the dead mercenaries, and
when they got as far up the road as the Chisei it was not
lord Reidi's men in view, it was himself and five of lord
Reidi's best on the mercenaries' horses, in the mercenaries' gear—fifteen more on foot. "You're not going,"
he told Taizu flatly when she stuck her lip out at him
and glared. "You're too damn *short,* girl, you don't look
like anybody they know, so shut up and take orders like
anybody else in this company."

She mended her manner then.

And he led the chestnut gelding down to the river
where lord Reidi's men were hauling the rope-drawn
ferry back across the river.

Small guess why there were no ferrymen. If they had had sense they had run; if they had had no luck they were dead; and if there was not a band of mercenaries on that other shore the enemy were fools.

Slow going: the men playing infantry hauled on the rope, Shoka and the two with horses in charge had the horses to keep steady.

Easy to figure why the ferry was lodged on the far side of the river, and what might have been the fate of the farmers who had tried to flee to Taiyi.

It was a low shore, a dirt road going up from the ferry-landing; bushes beyond, a little stand of saplings—yellow earth, pale grasses, the haze that was not autumn.

Beyond the Chisei, the heartland, of which Hoishi and Hoisan and Mendang were only the outliers. Pan'yei. The lap of Heaven. And the air stank of burning.

Hell of a homecoming, Shoka thought, and swung up to mount as the bow of the ferry bumped the shore. The gelding had no notion of going. Shoka kicked him hard in the flanks and the horse shied up and scrambled off in a scrape and thump of hooves on board and mud. Up the slope, no more than an energetic man might do. He saw the mercenaries break cover of the thicket and bar his path with bent bows and arrows they hesitated to fire.

That was their mistake.

It took some little time to ferry a hundred men and as many horses across the river. Shoka shed his borrowed armor and sat in the shade of a more substantial tree well up on shore while Jiro and the mare rested with eyes shut, not even interested to graze. Neither was he interested in the food Taizu pressed on him; but he swallowed it down, muttered, "I'm done, girl," and stretched himself out to rest on the cool ground, that was all he wanted.

Mostly his head was throbbing, his leg ached, and he saw blood when he shut his eyes, he saw terrible things.

But he could trust where he was. She was there, she told him she would not sleep, and as long as she was awake in the daylight, then he was safe and he knew his way back to the world.

Taizu, nodding away with her sword between her knees, Taizu, in her strange leather armor, with the ribbons in her hair. As long as he saw that he did not see the blood, and the dark would stay away.

"Get away," she had screamed at some man of Reidi's, who had come up asking questions. "He hasn't slept since yesterday, let him alone!"

Whoever it was and whatever it was, waited, and would wait, he reckoned, wandering that dark place.

There were shadows there. He fought with them.

The old Emperor was there. *My son is a fool*, the old man said.

Everyone told you so, he said, out of patience and disrespectful of the old man.

He stalked out of the imperial hall without courtesies. The guards for some reason did not stand in his way.

It was his father he was looking for, it seemed it had been a long search, and fraught with more and more anxiety.

I have someone to show you, he would say.

But when he thought he had found his father, sitting in the courtyard at home, his father vanished, and there was a shadowy army on the field in front of him, and the sun in his eyes.

And Taizu squatting in front of him and saying: "M'lord. M'lord, you've got to wake up now. Please. Lord Reidi says."

He squinted at her and shaded his eyes with his arm, not sure for the moment whether he was awake or not, with a feeling of anxiety for the men—how many of them?—waiting for him—where? how long ago? or when? His heart hammered while he tried to sort then from now and recollect if there was something he had promised, something he was urgently supposed to recall.

But it was only Taizu moving between him and the sun, and holding out a steaming cup of tea.

He struggled up to put his back against the tree and took the cup in a shaking hand and drank. The shade had passed from where he had slept. He blinked and tried to take account of where he was, saw lord Reidi walking up on them, the men gathered a little distance away, seated, the horses at tether.

"M'lord Saukendar," Reidi said, standing at the edge of the sun, shadow against the blaze of light. "Forgive me, but we're in a precarious position here—a hundred men—here against the river— The mercenaries—"

His head ached. He squinted, trying to do Reidi the courtesy of looking at him. An anxious old man. An old man who risked everything being here, in the kind of situation Reidi had spent his whole life avoiding. Shoka felt no fear at all. He remotely wished he felt something, except exhaustion, or that something was as important to him as the wish for another hour to lie down and the wish Reidi would move a handspan over and block the sun from his eyes. He motioned with his hand. Reidi moved, flustered at the mundane request, and Shoka let his arm fall and leaned his head against the tree.

"We're all right," he said. "Rest here a while, go up to Choedri, hope lord Kegi's stayed at home—"

"We don't know where the mercenaries are," Reidi said. "M'lord Shoka, we haven't crossed the river to sit here with our backs to the water. . . ."

Textbook soldiery. "Men and horses can do only so much, m'lord." His voice was hoarse, and it cracked, point proved, he thought, if the old man listened to anything but his own growing panic. "We have cover, they don't know we're here—we're just the guard they set here. Let them come. We'll move at dark."

It was not what Reidi wanted to hear. Reidi stood there and gnawed his lip and finally said: "We're a hundred men, m'lord Saukendar."

"You say we'll be more after Choedri."

"I don't know. If we'd gone back to Keido, if we'd occupied Ygotai—"

—my lands and my family would be safer, I'd be on familiar ground—

"—the others would rally to us—"

"Making the Chisei a battleline." His voice cracked again. "I'd rather one closer to Cheng'di. Or *will* the other lords join us? Will the officers of the army? Or will the levies fight for us—or for the Regent? If you have any doubts of that, m'lord Reidi, best we all go south and keep going."

"To the ruin of our lands."

Shoka closed his eyes. "We'll move, m'lord, but with our numbers, dark is better. If anyone wants the ferry, a few of your men can help them, and get among them. No need for a lot of noise. If someone's due to report, they may come to investigate. Put a man up that tree over there. Wrap him up in a cloak, let him look like a lump, and let him watch the road. I'm going to sleep a while. So's my wife. I'd advise you and your men do the same, by turns. Pick the scared ones for sentries. They won't sleep anyway."

Lord Reidi was one of the latter, Shoka reckoned by the look Reidi gave him.

"Dark," Shoka said, and Reidi gave him a curt bow and went away.

"You'd better sleep," Shoka said to Taizu then; and Taizu came and sat down by him and snuggled down without a word.

Poor girl, he thought. He reached up to his shoulder and touched her cheek. It was the scarred side. He rested his cheek against the top of her head, felt her arm go over him. He saw the cabin then, when he shut his eyes. Saw her in the morning, in that damned over-sized shirt, with the water-bucket, trudging up the hill. . . .

"M'lord!" someone hissed, and Shoka came out of

sleep toward twilight, Taizu waking, the man saying
something about riders coming.

"How many?" he snapped back.

"Five, six—"

"Then take care of it, dammit!" He rubbed his eyes
and got to one knee in the dusk. "Dammit, where's my
armor!" Petulantly, because his throat had made it come
out that way.

"It's over here, master Shoka." Taizu, on her hands
and knees. As horses came nearer and men rode into
their midst.

And bowstrings sang, one, two, a dozen.

Bodies hitting the ground. Shoka groped after his
sword. But it was over. Lord Reidi's men caught the
horses. Shoka stumbled to his feet and walked over to
the scattering of bodies, kicked at one. Through the
neck. That man was not talking.

Nor were the others. Lord Reidi's men were elated,
having proven themselves formidable, he reckoned. At
least none of them had gotten away.

Sometimes he was sick at his stomach at something
like this. At the moment he was still muzzy with sleep
and wishing he had not gotten up so quickly and wishing it were not indecent to ask for a cup of something
hot at such a juncture. "It's all right, it's all right," he
said to a nervous lord Reidi. "None of them raised a
fuss."

*Raised a fuss, my gods. I want to go home, that's all.
I want the mountain, I want Taizu and me and Jiro,
there, safe, tomorrow morning.*

The sun and the moon and the stars while I'm at it.

*Damn, I want my own porch and my spring and the
view out the front door. . . .*

He walked back and sat down to put on his shin-
guards, his own armor this time, fitted to *him*, not the
mercenary's rig—while lord Reidi followed him up chattering about the necessity of getting underway, of his
fears of discovery, about the risk they were running.

Yes, m'lord, no, m'lord, hell if you don't know your
choices by now, my lord. . . .

"Send some of your younger men out," Shoka said,
"if there's any reasonable chance of them making it.
Hell with the pigeons. Have them spread the word
where it counts most, in person, where they can answer
questions and give assurances, and hope your allies are
committed to this."

Lord Reidi went to do that.

He tied the cords about and put on the armor-sleeves.
Taizu was there to help him with the body-armor. Not a
word from her, not a complaint, only a grim, jaw-
clenched calm.

He took her by the arm, said, close to her ear: "Are
you all right, girl?"

"I'm fine." Tight, between the teeth.

He put the arm about her, held onto her a moment,
scared for her, scared for himself.

"Plan your retreat," she said into his ear. *"Plan your*
retreat, isn't that right?"

"Damn good advice. I couldn't think of better. Wish
to hell we had the men to leave for a garrison."

Then speed . . . speed and silence, in lieu of num-
bers. . . .

They were on the road by dark, and with a good
string of remounts, thanks to the mercenaries on this
side and that of the river. No stopping, Shoka had
decreed. The handful of lads Reidi had picked had gone
out, with Shoka's instructions in their ears, a good half
hour in front of them, but none of them to Choedri.

"We'll deliver that message ourselves," Shoka said.

Chapter Sixteen

The stars were dimming, the sky eastward appearing to darken over the low hills when they reached the ford at the Tei—"Damnable thing about roads and rivers," Shoka muttered to Taizu as they rode, "roads go to fords and fords are where your enemies can find you. I don't look for that kind of luck twice."

"It'll work again," Taizu said, "no reason it shouldn't."

He hoped so. Privately he placed much of his hope in the handful of young riders that had gone out from their company west to Jendei in Hainan, to Maijun in Feiyan, and east to the lords of Sengu and Mendang and Taiyi, at Mandi on the Chaighin, along the river road. There were three of them, going fast in that direction, one more speeding back to Keido to put Reidi's lady Aio current of the situation, for her to send messages with her birds, one more on to certain friends in Mura and Hua and one straight north to Kiang, to the farthest reaches of the Empire. Multiple of everything, an agreement to duplicate all messages, because there was no guarantee of any single message getting through, whether it came on horseback or by air.

But if they did nothing else—the lads with their fast riding and their dodging through the back roads might convince an enemy that two fugitives on horseback had gone any of a half dozen directions; while a large, noisy band of motley-clad riders going right down the roads might, the gods willing, be mistaken for one of the mercenaries' own companies.

Keep moving, move fast, keep the enemy thinking while their situation changed by the hour.

Run the horses to the safe limit, change the remounts through the company, change the light and the heavy riders, walk and cool down, gather breath and go again. . . . He and Taizu traded oftenest, for Jiro's sake, the old fellow loping along with no more burden than his tack for most of this night, but he had come the farthest and he was the oldest.

Damn sure he was not riding the old lad when they hit the ford, a belly-deep wade and a muddy climb to the shore, up among the trees.

"What company?" a voice shouted out of the dark above them.

"Aghi," Taizu hissed to him; and: "*Aghi!*" he shouted out, with no idea in the gods' creation whether that was a valid name. "*New hire, up from Hoisan! What's your company?*"

In case anyone wanted answers they might not know.

A long pause. Then: "*One of you come up,*" the watcher shouted down. "*Afoot!*"

"*What's your company?*"

"*Don't!*" Taizu hissed at him, "*don't go up there.*"

As the answer came down: "*Sachi's!*"

"Is that valid?" he asked Taizu.

"Don't go up there!"

"Shut up. If you come up anywhere near the head of the column I'll loosen your teeth for you. —*All right. I'm coming.*" He climbed down from the saddle, handed his reins to Reidi's captain and said, "When you hear me shout, come up that slope like thunder."

He left the captain with the horse's reins as if the captain were his servant: but it gave him the chance for a word.

"*What's the delay down there?*" the watcher shouted.

"*I'm coming up.*"

Now he felt his heart beating faster. Not fear yet, just that things sharpened their outlines around him, memories of this road ten years ago, how it turned, if he had not confused it with others like it, if floods and time had not changed it: bend to the right and the left and the trees up there.

He walked it, finding the turns what he remembered, a winding climb among trees. Archers, he thought, and hoped Taizu believed him.

He saw the shadow of men ahead of him, subtle sheen of ambient light on metal.

"What captain, before Aghi?"

"*I'm* captain of this company. And *damned* if I stand here playing riddle-games in the dark. I'm on orders, I've got my pass, and you'd *damn* well better have yours handy, son, and mind your mouth with me, *I'm short of sleep and too damn long in the saddle to put up with some ass no-rank who wants to play games with me!*"

He heard the company start up the slope. He saw the confusion in the figures in front of him, heard the guard-chief shouting, "Dammit!" and backing off a step—

He was already moving, a rolling tumble on the leafy ground as arrows hissed; hands on his sword hilt and out with it into a smooth swing as he came up on his feet and launched himself for the only place the archers would not aim—face up against their officers, one, two, and three, a head flying, a man crippled, and the third giving him two, three passes before he made a mistake backing up and stumbled on a tree root.

Shoka wanted a prisoner. No time for this one, with arrows flying and the company coming up under fire.

He whipped the sword across an opening in the man's defense and took the man across the arm, across the neck: he was dead before the pieces hit the ground.

Horses broke through, crashing up the trail, through the brush, going every which way, bowstrings thumping, swords meeting steel and men screaming—men and one shrill yell he well knew.

He dived into the brush and laid low, figuring his main danger at the moment was his own side.

"M'lord?" he heard then, plaintively, as the noise died down, a feminine voice; so he gave a whistle back, gathered himself up, and heard a sound by him, someone breaking away to run through the brush.

"Get that one!" he yelled, and heard a rider take out in pursuit, dark body racing right past him in the thicket, to fetch up short. But whoever it was left the saddle and raced after the noise.

"Taizu!" he yelled; and got, "I'm here!" from the vicinity of the horses. Then he remembered she had a horse in lead from her saddle—thank the gods it was not Taizu crashing off through the brush. He came back to the clearing, hearing the sound of someone crashing about out there, but no sound else.

The white-legged mare showed even in that dark. He found Taizu, and Jiro, in her charge. "Are you all right?" Taizu said.

"No problem," he said, taking Jiro's reins from her hand. But he heard a sudden stillness in the brush, where a man of theirs had been, and knew their man had gotten smarter and gotten down and still to listen or they had just lost a man, one or the other.

In either case they had let a man escape them, to run for his superiors and spread alarm.

He whistled, the signal he had instructed Reidi's men to obey for recall—too much risk and too much delay in hunting through the brush for an enemy better than his fellows; and everything to gain by putting distance between themselves and the mercenary camp, wherever it was.

A horse whinnied out of the dark, off beyond the woods. "*There* they are," someone said.

Hare off into the dark into what could be ambush, where there was already a man loose and unaccounted for.

Hell.

"We've got some kind of courier here," a man said, displaying an ivory chit from the purse on one of the bodies.

"That's one message not going through," Shoka said, and swung up to Jiro's saddle. "But there's one loose that is. Come on. We haven't got time to go through things. Let's get out of here!"

"Pei's not back, m'lord!"

"Pei may not be *coming* back! It's Pei's problem! We don't know what the hell that man can raise. Let's move! Now!"

"M'lord," Reidi's voice protested sternly.

"This is *war*, m'lord! —Come on, Taizu!"

"Don't be so sudden!" Reidi said, as horses milled and backed and his men who had dismounted to search the dead scrambled to mount without his orders. "A man of mine is—"

"*Dead*, m'lord Reidi, or he'll catch us up on his own! Are you with me? Do you take my advice? Or not?"

"Dammit—"

"Are you coming, m'lord?"

"All right," the old man growled. "All right—"

Shoka clapped his heels to Jiro's sides and Jiro surged into motion, full-out down the road; Taizu on the white-legged mare was right with him and the whole company sorted itself out behind.

"Keep low!" he yelled at Taizu as they broke through the screen of trees and out into the open.

But there was nothing in front of them but open land, and the first red seam of dawn on the right.

The man they had left did not overtake them. "Assume the worst," he said to lord Reidi, riding close to the old man when they settled to a saner pace. "My condolences and my apologies, m'lord, for your man back there, but he didn't answer my signal and we're on the gods' thin tolerance as it is—and I'd rather trust something more substantial."

"The gods favor us," Reidi declared thinly.

Ruffled religiosity. He was back in Chiyaden. He swallowed an acid witticism and said: "I trust so, m'lord, but I don't test their good will by haring off sidelong when they give us the road we need, m'lord. . . . They *take* their sacrifices, and they ask us to go on—"

Pious asininity, old man, you lose men, that's all, and you give an order and you hope to hell the one who goes knows what he's doing, my lord, or you lose him—

No damn time left. No time.

As the sun came up in a cloudy east and the horses labored under the going.

And a band of riders appeared on the hill.

He saw it in the same instant that outcries of alarm broke out from the company, as men reined back and threw the column into confusion. "Come *on*," he said; and it was Taizu by him before it was anyone.

"You get back," he said. "Take to the bow, rear rank. You haven't the weight."

"That's banners, husband! That's banners up ahead, it's a lord's ensign!"

He saw that, too. He heard what she had said to him. His heart was beating with a heavy rhythm, in time to Jiro's footfalls. Red banners, white device; blue with gold.

Red of Feiyan. Blue of Hainan.

"Up with the banners!" Reidi ordered, and Shoka did not gainsay that. The black and white of Hoishi came up on its pole, unfurled and snapped in the wind.

"My lord Saukendar," said Maijun of Feiyan as they met afoot, their riders around them, banners fluttering and cracking. "My lord Reidi," with bows and like courtesies from stout Lintai of Hainan, the son of old

Jendei. "My father would be here," Lintai said, "if he could ride at all. There are—" Diffidently. "—four hundred men behind us, afoot. Light-armed, traveling at their own speed. We met your messengers on the road. We'd already set out. They're on to Yiungei."

"Gods' speed," Reidi said piously. "Brave lads."

Trust the birds' speed, Shoka thought: it *was* good news, that the birds had been sufficient to rouse two provinces, as much as anything. That the riders were already headed north was a second bit of hope. But not enough. Five hundred heavy cavalry with Maijun, four with Lintai, maybe three, four hundred peasants back there somewhere, and, Shoka thought, amid the general elation of the three lords and the troops: *Not enough to beat the Guard, too many for mobility.*

Enough to keep the south off our backs, and stir up the east, if they'll take orders.

Reason had never been Maijun's strong point: Maijun of Feiyan was of that generation he knew, a man who made up his mind and spent all his subsequent thought justifying his opinions.

But it was the moment, emotion was high, he had Maijun's attention, and Shoka said: "My lords, you couldn't have come at a better time. I don't know what's coming at our heels, but we've stirred things up behind us. I'm going with a small force—*speed*, m'lords, and surprise, to get us across the Hisei before they know where we are—look like one of the mercenary squads and cut right through their defenses, ourselves the edge of the axe and your forces behind us—as if we were one of their own bands falling back from your advance, dust and noise and all."

"Dangerous, m'lord Saukendar!" Maijun of Feiyan said. "Danger from our own partisans as well as the Guard—"

"No time to wait. We hope those partisans are *there*, m'lords."

"There will be, m'lord Saukendar. Messages are out. They'll answer."

Hope to the gods they answer. I don't like this. I've never trusted another man's estimations. I've never gone blind into a thing. Damn, it has a queasy feeling. But stopping's worse. "Then expect we'll have the way open. Whatever's with you can follow us."

"If the people can *see* you, m'lord, if you're more than a rumor to them—the people need to *see* you—"

"Tell them *you've* seen me. Tell them I'm going straight up the road—" He lifted a hand toward Choedri. "—and they'll find proof enough where I've been. If they're fast enough, they'll take advantage of it. If we're *fast* enough, my lords, we can keep them revising their plans till we're up their throats, at which point your light-armed folk and your heavy cavalry need to be there. We're already inside their perimeter. If we slow now, Ghita's hired soldiers can come at our backs and hit us from all sides. If we get as far north as the Hisei there's my *own* province to draw on, and the lords northward and the troops off in Kiang; if we have them, then we've got the Regent front and back. He'll pull back behind the Chaighin if we don't give him time to organize at the Hisei. Speed, my lords, and flexibility. Right now we're mobile enough to get in there and get out again if he gets his defenses up too fast: that's all we can count on. But we have to have you up there at a pace that won't exhaust your infantry. If you'll do us a service, trade us for some of our weaker horses."

Everything trembled on a knife's edge, yea and nay with these lords. Maijun's eyes shifted from him to Reidi, to all the company about, and lingered on Taizu with a peculiar expression, before they shifted back to him.

"Pigeons," Maijun said. "The Emperor's own birds. Faster than any horse, m'lord Saukendar. If the Emperor's men have any afield—"

"I'm betting they do. But it's still less risk than getting us bogged down in an engagement too far south for the northern lords to feel the urgency of it. Every league we gain toward their territory is that much closer to their hearts, gentlemen, and if they don't know we're more than a rumor of an insurrection, they're not going to commit to it. Let the people see me, that they'd better, they'd better see *us*, my lords, they'd better see the Regent back away, they'd better see us driving toward the capital, that's what has to happen, or we'll be damn lonely in a circle of Ghita's hired troops, and our heads will be on the block, gentlemen, yours and mine alike. —Lord Reidi, it's a hard ride we've had this far; now we've got relief, I'd not think less of you if you'd leave the hard riding to younger men and join these gentlemen—it's no less danger, but it's a damn sight less hard on the gut."

The old man set his jaw. "There's nothing wrong with my gut, m'lord Saukendar."

Shoka nodded, in one part relieved, in one part thinking, *I've tried. Poor brave fool.* "Then we'd better move." Before someone could open his mouth and start discussing, gods help them; and the lords start objecting and thinking, gods doubly help them. No knowing if there *were* messenger-birds flying north and east; and what murders might be happening and who might be arrested by now in the north and what traps laid at the Hisei, if Ghita had his hand on things as closely as he might.

"Do we have the horses?" Shoka asked.

"Yes, m'lord," Maijun said.

"My gratitude." He bowed to the lords and walked among the men, singling out the worst of their mounts. "This one," he said, of a horse that had been coughing; "the sorrel, there," of one he knew was always hindmost. He did not presume on the lords' generosity by giving them too many culls, but he picked out eighteen that were in difficulty, traded them out to lord Maijun's men with profound thanks.

But Jiro he kept; and as well, he thought, to keep Taizu's mare: she was sound, and hell with the loud markings, she had battle-sense, the old judge had told the truth—no shying and no bolting, and that was more than he could swear to in the remounts.

He took Jiro's reins from Taizu then, and got up to Jiro's back while the rest of the men mounted up. But when the lords met him, their men mustering behind them with banners and all, he saw anxiousness in the look they gave him, that set his teeth on edge.

Then as they met face to face, the two columns, Reidi and his men, and him, he saw it was not himself they were looking at, but to the companion on his right.

A woman in armor. Of course it troubled them. Of course they took second looks and wondered *was* it a woman or a too-feminine boy. . . . Or they had heard *that* too. Reidi's lads, Shoka thought, and said, doggedly polite, "Taizu, my lords. My wife."

Anxious looks none the less, glancing from her to him. And respectful bows from the lords and whispers among the men.

"We've heard," Lintai said, too quick for thought; and Maijun kept his jaw clamped, more discreet, and bowed.

"My lady."

Shoka winced, uneasy at that *My lady* to Taizu's face; and felt more uneasy at the signs the troops made as they rode past, the touches at amulets, and the close and furtive looks they gave her.

"Don't scowl like that," he hissed at her, once the lords were out of earshot. "Smile, dammit."

She smiled. She turned her head and smiled deliberately, showing her teeth, and nodded at the passing riders as both columns got into motion. And, looking back, scowled at him.

"They've heard all the way from Mon!"

"They heard from Reidi's men! Don't scowl!"

"Tell them I'm from Hua!"

"I told Reidi! I could have, then. Would it change anything? Has it made any difference? —Lord Reidi says you're Kaijeng's daughter. . . . That you came to trick me into fighting—"

"*That's a lie!*" The whisper almost got beyond a whisper. She looked fit to strangle. And that indignation of hers cut through a last few threads that, he realized only that moment, had been bothering him. "Do *you* think that?"

"I don't. I've even stopped checking your thumbs when we sleep together."

"It's not funny, dammit!"

It was not. It was far from harmless, to either of them. He was quiet for a long moment as they rode, while Reidi's man furled the banners and they became mercenaries again. "You're my wife. There's a price for that. You say, wait til we get to Cheng'di and I may change my mind. I say . . . you're my wife, and I wish to the gods I could unravel everything back to the start, I wish I'd not thought—"

"—what?" she asked after a moment of silence.

"—not thought I could *use* the rumor. Spread a bit of confusion, make it so fantastical people wouldn't believe, the court wouldn't take it seriously—or enemies might not follow us home, if they did believe it— Damn them."

"Well, tell them the truth!"

"I *have*, I'm telling you. *You* can tell them the truth, and it won't help you. Nothing will stop what people want to believe." He looked at her indignant face, at truth and honesty brimming over, and felt a pain around his heart. "I'm a fool. I thought you knew that. You tell me often enough."

"It's not funny, master Shoka!"

"I'm not joking. I know what it costs. *Damn*, I know what it costs." He saw her going away from him—saw her, even if they lived, deserting him . . . to save herself; and even that would generate rumors; and leave him—wishing himself dead . . . pining away, like the damn fools in the ballads he tried to evade. But even a real heart could break, after so much and so long. He clamped his jaw and stared at the rolling hills in front of them, that led down and down to Choedri—that they were going past, soon, quickly: Saukendar's thoughts, going on in coldest good sense, telling Shoka-the-man that what he wanted and what he hoped had no place in the world and there was certainly no leisure for his worries now. The rumors were a weapon, he used even Taizu, he generated fear about him, he bullied the lords because they were wrong and he was right, and there was no other course but the one he took, Saukendar had no doubt at all, nor fear, nor pain for the things he did.

Except when he heard the girl by him say, meekly, "Master Shoka?"

He did not look at her. It hurt too much.

"M'lord? —What am I supposed to call you? Nothing feels right."

"Anything you like," he said, too harshly. His hoarseness tried to come back. He wondered, cooly, distantly, if he wept in front of Reidi and his men, if *that* would shake their confidence. But that coldness took hold, and would not let him go. Not now, it told him, not with lives at stake.

(*Die in this, dammit, and they'll say how a demon led us—*)

Taizu said nothing for a long, long time. Men came around them. There was no privacy for talking.

But when they changed horses again she came up beside him and touched his arm. "I'm sorry," she said.

"Sorry?" He was bewildered. "For what, for the gods' sake?"

He confused her too. He saw that.

We may be dead in the next hour. She's a kid. A girl. What in hell is she doing in this? Why didn't I stop her?

"Have I done anything you said not?" Men were mounting up all around them. "Have I?"

Straight to the heart. "You *ought* to be out of here," he said. And remembered that there was no safety for Saukendar's wife. Anywhere. Ever. "Damn."

"*What did I do wrong?*"

"It's my fault."

"It's *not* your fault." She was trying to whisper and her voice kept cracking up a notch. "Dammit, *I'm* not your fault, I'm nobody's fault but mine, don't you tell me anything different! What did I do?"

He looked at her, sorting through that step by step. They might have been back on their own front porch. The cabin. A year ago. For some reason he felt his balance settle, dead center.

"Nothing," he said, taking Jiro's reins from her. "Not a damn thing. I've seen far worse." *Damn, why can't I say it straight?* "Few better. I just *like* your neck that length. Take care of it for me. Listen. If this goes wrong—if I'm killed—"

"Don't say—"

"Go to the country. *Get* Gitu. Pay the bastards for this. Does that appeal to you?"

A dark fire came into Taizu's eyes. Her head came up a bit. She nodded, very faintly, very surely.

Not crazy. No. It was as if a wall had come down that had been there for days, and they were looking each other in the eye again, without needing to dissemble or look away.

A horse snorted. Men were waiting all around them. They were standing there like fools.

"We've got to move," he said gruffly, and turned and climbed up to Jiro's back, while Taizu swung up onto the mare.

Saukendar and his demon wife, they would say. She has him enspelled. She came to him on the mountain, she bewitched him, she agreed to help him against his enemies, so long as he would keep her for his wife and make her a lady of Chiyaden; and she would never, ever take her real shape, except, perhaps, if he was unfaithful, if something broke the spell—

He saw how the men looked at her. He saw how they cleared Taizu's path, and some of them stared at her behind her back. Taizu had *that* to bear with—not malice, gods knew. No one had had experience dealing with a demon, but then—if a foxwife or a demon fa-

vored them, and was clearly bespelled to Saukendar
and on her good behavior—then . . . there were good
demons as well as bad, and a well-disposed one was an
ally as valuable as Saukendar. She might take her demon-
shape toward their enemies, gnash her teeth, turn their
knees to water with the glance of her eyes, strike with
twin swords of lightning and twin spears of fire, calling
up wind and storm—

They expected things like that, the way they expected unicorns and gods in little-trafficked places; and
burned their incense-sticks for the happiness of their
dead; and wore their charms for luck and to keep their
souls safe in crises. So why would their demon turn on
them, how could things go amiss if there was Saukendar
to wear like a talisman, no different than the luck-
charms about their necks and ankles.

Damn them for too much faith, and for putting it on
him.

And most of all for putting it on Taizu.

The fields around Choedri were tilled: the land showed
order, the work of farmer folk not one of whom was in
view. There was not an ox or a cow in sight—everything
away from the highroad, Shoka figured, everything back
in the hills, in the folds of the land, or shut away inside
the walls of Choedri castle.

"Pray the message got through," Reidi said when he
remarked on that eerie vacancy. "Lord Kegi is one we
can rely on, if they haven't come down on him—"

"I'd think he'd have sent south," Shoka muttered,
more and more uneasy. "Feiyan had time to get to us,
for the gods' sake."

They had a couple of men riding point, about half an
hour ahead, in the guise of ordinary travelers, unar-
mored and with nothing martial about themselves or
their horses. *Be respectful to whoever you meet,* Shoka
had advised them, *mercenaries or Kegi's men. You're
townsmen from Ygotai. You're on your way to ask help
from the regional authorities.*

He hoped the men could carry it off. He hoped the men were still alive up there, concealed in the folds of the land, the small woods. Now and again they would find a blot of flour in the road, which was the scouts' way of telling them it was clear as far as they could see.

But there were too damn many little hedges and hills.

"Another mark," Shoka said, more and more anxious; and almost wished, at the start of a wooded stretch, that the white blotch had not turned up in the road. *If you hit a bad stretch, one of you lay back for safety and wait till your partner has it clear. Don't make a mark you're not sure of.*

Damn, I don't like it.

"Split the column," he said to Reidi. "Lay back. We'll go through. Damn, doesn't Kegi believe in clearing back his right-of-ways?"

"We planned these overgrowths," Reidi said. "To use."

"So can the enemy," he said curtly; and waved Reidi back. He thought about sending Taizu back, and reckoned, if something went wrong, she was better with him than with a confused and desperate remnant.

The column split, half hanging back.

He put Jiro to a quicker pace. His half of the company kept moving, a brisk pace under the forest shadow, a clean, well-kept road. Another flour splotch.

Then a bending of the road, and a hedge of sharpened stakes dead in their path.

Horses shied up, steel came out. "Dismount!" Shoka yelled, pulling Jiro close against the trees beside the road. He was out of his saddle when a handful of men in Taiyi colors appeared at the barricade.

"Stop!" lord Reidi's lieutenant yelled, still on his horse in the middle of the road. "Stop! This is lord Saukendar—"

It was about time, Shoka thought, to disentangle himself from the thicket and hope Reidi's man was not about to get an arrow through the gut. "Careful!" Taizu said, her voice shaking. She had slid off and

ducked down beside him, bow strung and arrow ready.
But Saukendar could hardly look the fool, hiding against
a bush, so he acted one, and gave her Jiro's reins—no
sense getting the old lad shot—and walked out to the
middle of the road with the other fool.

They *were* lord Kegi's men. They had the scouts,
credit to them and none to the embarrassed scouts,
who, ungagged and set at their liberty, went back with
lord Reidi's lieutenant to explain matters; and Kegi's
men were duty-bound to run ahead to the castle and
advise lord Kegi it was all true, the lord Saukendar had
come back, the provinces of Hainan and Feiyan and
Hoishi had risen, their lords were out with their personal guards and their people were on the march. . . .

That was when Shoka heard about the dragon which
had heralded his return, a huge beast which had appeared near Ygotai and left its tracks along the dikes,
great scars of claws and its immense body dragged in a
winding course across the paddies, marks anyone could
see.

Shoka looked at Taizu and saw her standing there
with her mouth open as if the next moment she was
going to deny everything. But she just stood there,
with Jiro's reins and the white-legged mare's, at the
edge of the road; and he said:

"Taizu."

She brought him Jiro. He took the reins and she
stood by him without a word.

There were mercenaries in Tengu, northward. Most
were on the Hisei, at Lungan.

So lord Kegi's men warned them. Bad news, Shoka
thought. He *wanted* to be pushing ahead. He *wanted* to
make as much ground as he could, make it sound like a
larger advance than it was—bluff and commotion being
the best allies they had at the moment.

But fatigue had his vision blurring, and sense said
stop, now: that there might be no more chance to stop
past Choedri.

"Come to Choedri keep, lord," Kegi's guard urged him. "Our lord will be anxious to see you."

Shoka considered it, longed for a real bed and a hot meal; but prickles went up and down his back at the thought of entering into anyone's walls. Reidi had sworn to Kegi's good will. But Reidi had sworn to the scouts too.

"No," he said. "My apologies to your lord, but I've taken an oath—" Gods, what a pretentious lie! "—not to take any shelter before the Hisei. Ask your lord meet us by his gates this evening, if he'll be so kind. Myself— lord Reidi—we'll rest on his side of this woods till dark. We've had a damned long ride to get here."

"My lord," they said, "yes, my lord." And the captain in charge ordered the barricade moved, dispatched a messenger to his lord, and once Reidi and his men had caught up and come current of things, saw them to the far edge of the woods, a slope that overlooked the broad plain where Choedri sat.

More, he offered them what little food and water his company had, and half his men for a guard while they rested, seeing the road behind seemed secure enough.

"Can we trust it?" Taizu asked, quietly, aside, when it came to taking food of them. She was hoarse. He felt the same, as if, the imminent danger past, his wits wanted to scatter and raw suspicion wanted to take over, like something cornered.

He was being irrational, he told himself. It was the surest indication that he was not thinking clearly, when he began to doubt everything, every sound around him, and the pure water they were handed; and a sensible, well-prepared ally whose captain seemed more than competent.

"Hell if we've got a choice," he said.

Chapter Seventeen

It was not a lord's entourage that came up from the plain before dark, it was an expedition, banners, carts, rumbling along in a racket that more than woke Shoka an hour or so into his sleep: for a heart-stopped moment he imagined a whole battalion coming on them, but the banners were the personal banners of the lord of Choedri, vassal of Deigi of Taiyi. The guards stirred about to welcome their lord and lord Reidi roused his entourage—

"There aren't that many of them," Taizu said under her breath, disappointed at their numbers, and Shoka thought the same.

"Supplies," he said. "Likely the rest are back at the town. It wouldn't make sense to march them up here and back again." But he felt the ache in his bones worse than when he had lain down to rest, and he felt a moment of despair for reasons he could not name— except there was so damned much fuss about the approach. *Fool,* he kept telling himself, *fool to be here, fool to take on all this commotion—and not enough men in this place to take the field, not unless this is a damn sight better organized than seems likely—*

Go alone, get close to the enemy, get through the defenses—

He had called Taizu a fool for headlong notions like that. *Look at me,* he thought, and imagined her thinking those thoughts and chiding herself for them and imagining master Saukendar must have some secret plan for going along with these lords, these keep-bound lords all but Reidi and Maijun successors to the ones he knew—and all the while master Saukendar's mind was so muddled with exhaustion and dealing with others' plans and plots that he could not see the chance to do anything but rush ahead of the tide till bone gave and wits went scattered on the winds—

Plan your retreat—

Minimal force—

Superior position—

The lords of ten years ago had given way to new lords, untried in the field, and gods knew what had changed or what survived along the track to Cheng'di—

Or where Ghita was, holding what; or how many mercenaries the imperial treasury could buy—

The lord and his baggage train rattled up—decidedly *not* the portly lord of Choedri he had known—a thin, bookish sort climbing off his horse, who—gods!—dropped a scroll from his sleeve and nearly collided with the servant who dived to retrieve it—

Scroll clutched to him then, handed him by the same servant—"My lord Reidi! My lord Saukendar!" the presumable lord Kegi said, and, brow wrinkled anxiously: "It *is* lord Saukendar—"

"Yes," Shoka said, and taking a deep, resolute breath: "M'lord, I hoped you'd come."

—with ten times the men. . . . Which I hope are down there, m'lord.

You could have spared the books.

"I've brought food, spare horses, all we have— Rest, please! We'll see to things, we'll have you a good supper, have the horses rubbed down—my doctor has a salve—"

While the servants were noisily pulling things off the wagons, hauling out firepots and cooking-pots and bundles and jars of food, confusion like an upset in an anthill. Shoka stood blinking as a meal began to happen, and the doctor and a small clutch of servants took immediately to the horses—a whirl of servants and cooks: *Gods save us, food and efficiency— There is hope of this man. . . .*

Which was enough to loosen his knees and blur his eyes and remind him he was exhausted and at wit's end. "M'lord," he said by way of courtesy, "forgive me. I'll leave things in your hands." That with his last sane breath; and he dragged himself and Taizu back to their blankets at the roadside.

Kegi might murder the lot of them, he thought. Kegi, so convincing to Reidi for years, might be a spy. He was new in his office. The Regent had to have acquiesced in his accession to his post. Anything could be a trick, nothing could be trusted, but they had gone as far as flesh and bone could go without rest and sleep.

If we eat his food, as well sleep in his keeping. Reidi trusts him. Taizu doesn't object. If there're no honest men left in Chiyaden—what are we here for at all, and what chance have we in the first place?

Upon which thought he sank toward dark, grateful to let go for a while more.

But he saw through slitted, hazing eyes the motion of lord Kegi's men about them, saw them stop and saw them stare and whisper together—

What are you looking at? he wondered. Stares he had had all his life; and whispers behind hands—

But he heard the word *woman*, and then he knew the gist of it, and what they whispered, and why.

The demon-wife, the ensorceller: the rumor still spread, Kegi's messengers, this time. They saw a man snared, they whispered together, they wove details to

suit their fancy—and Taizu if she did hear made no
sound and no complaint.

He hated it. He had always hated it. Damn his
moment's whimsy, damn the whole madness they were
involved in—

Gods knew how much she heard: whispers wondering at the scar on her face, about where he had come by
her, at how much *wife* meant—the story growing by
the hour and the day, people whispering about her—
who had so much expected of her and so little resources
left; and no forty years' experience to armor her.

"I know," he whispered into her ear, wrapping her in
his arms, the hell with the curious and the gawkers.
"Rest. Hell with them. They're crazed."

"They'll get us killed," she said, the first objection
she had raised.

They. These people. And *us*.

No one achieves perfection, master Yenan had said—
how many times?

But on the mountain they had touched it. Everything
on the mountain had been better than this. It always
would be. And it seemed more and more remote from
the place they had gotten to.

"Go down to Choedri," he said. "Wait this out. This
isn't your kind of fight. I didn't teach you this."

"No," she murmured, working closer to bury her
head against his shoulder, and he pulled the blanket
over her to give her the dark she was hunting for. "Not
Choedri."

She was close to sleep. He was. They had had the
argument again and again. He knew the steps, one after
another. "Where, then?"

"Sleep." Patiently, wearily, with a sigh against him, a
tightening of her arms.

Horses can't take much more, he thought. *Too little
resources. Too few men. Should have gotten Reidi and
his men back across the river, into Hoisan. I should
have done everything from there. . . .*

If I had the strength—if the horses did—

She knows. I taught her better than this. . . .

*She hasn't said a word since we took up with Reidi.
Since I asked her—stay with me. . . .*

Fool, girl, say it! Damned fool!

*I've known—I've known it. Too many well-intentioned,
too many brave, without sense—*

*Too late to turn this around. Too many committed,
too many in too far—*

There's no damn help in good intentions—

*—should have learned that, dammit, should have
learned that, ten years and the land's not the same, the
land's bled too long, the fighters are dead. This is
becoming a disaster.*

*No hope when we count our numbers in the hun-
dreds and we're this close to Cheng'di—*

He slept, while he was trying to work that out . . .
sleep like a roll off a cliff, just enough time to know he
was going, thump! and gone, until he smelled cooking
and woke by firelight, with Taizu's armored body up
against his, and Reidi's lieutenant saying, close by them,
"Lord Saukendar, please, there's dinner. My master
thinks you might want to wake now."

Another little dark space. "Lord Saukendar?" the
voice said, persisting.

Saukendar would have been awake the first time.
Saukendar would not be caught that deeply asleep.
Shoka dragged his weary limbs up to a sitting position,
raked his hair out of his eyes and rubbed his eyes at the
firelight glare and the sting of smoke.

He coughed; it was the cold ground; and blinked
again, finding Taizu no quicker at least—finding the
very ground unsteady under him until he had had a
moment to collect himself.

He should be scared, he thought. He had been fretting over their situation when he had fallen asleep and
he should be worried now, except he could not remember the details of matters and he found himself lost in a
kind of haze in which everything had equal importance—
Ghita, their numbers, the horses' condition, the season

of the year, his memory of the way ahead, that led to
Lungan and the great bridge—

His own calmness amazed him. He sat a moment
letting his vision sort itself clear and he still could not
muster any emotion about the chance of attack. Nothing was clear yet. Nothing made sense. Nothing was
urgent, and it might have been ten years ago, himself
suspecting nothing of the stirrings in the capital—

—Meiya, perhaps, taking account of things that night
and realizing, because Meiya had always been alert to
such things, that his absence and Ghita's shifting this
and that man's duty in the palace might mean harm—

Meiya had sent for Heisu in the night. That much he
knew—

On that thin charge they had had Heisu's life; and
she had had recourse to the cup—

"M'lord." Taizu's voice, Taizu's hand on his. He had
no more interest in remembering Meiya. It was the hall
he saw around her that he tried to bring into focus, the
exact recollection of the palace in a detail that he had
not had in memory for all these years. He was there,
and all Cheng'di was outside, the land beyond that,
every detail of the road. . . .

"Don't," he said to her. It was very close, all the
recollection, Cheng'di to Lungan, and the bridge
there. . . .

That.

He sat there a moment. He built the entire water-
front at Lungan in his mind, the great bridge—the
walled garrison beside it on the esplanade, the street
beyond, where it went through a town of red tile roofs
and buff walls, of prosperous shops. Trinket-sellers and
vendors who cajoled the travelers bound for the Gate of
Heaven, in Cheng'di. The road outbound, across rolling land and rich pasture. . . .

"M'lord," he heard someone say, but it was not Taizu.
"Let him alone," her voice said fiercely. "He's heard
you."

And closer, working backward from the great bridge

over the Hisei, nothing more than the shallow, slow-moving Paigji, crossable at virtually any point until it joined the Tei, well past Botai. . . .

"The Paigji ford will be open on our side," lord Kegi said, by the firelight, over a plentiful supper of pork and rice and honey-cakes, and Shoka listened, between mouthfuls. "I thought—" Kegi was a soft-spoken, nervous man, and the scroll, gods help them, was the works of general Bogi'in, six hundred years ago. Kegi had made a study of that book: the old lord had died, cousin Kegi had succeeded to the seat at Choedri, and while his overlord had not yet responded to Reidi's bird-sent messages—nor would respond, Kegi said, until he was sure others were moving—Kegi had taken the field with nothing but that damn musty scroll for advice, that and his priest, his cook, his horse-doctor, and the men of his personal guard. It was Bogi'in this and Bogi'in that— "I thought, by what I read—it seemed good sense—lord Bogi'in said roads were the thing, Roads and Rice—"

Shoka regarded the man with dismay. A classroom came back to him, master Tagyan—*roads and rice*, and the lazy song of cicadas; the council-rooms, the late Emperor's voice stern and incisive, regarding the incursions of the Fittha raiders and the security of remotest Feiyan—

"Open—on your side of the ford. How many of the Regent's men on the other?"

"Constantly four or five, on both sides."

A cold chill ran through him, imagining the five from the other side, alarmed, taking flight and alarming the countryside all the way to Cheng'di. No damn use except intimidating the peasants, and counting the traffic. Not a way in hell the mercenaries could hold that border. The Paigji was too shallow, the crossings too numerous to guard.

"You've ordered attack," Shoka said.

"Discreetly," Kegi said.

"My gods," Reidi said.

"My lord," Kegi said to Shoka, nettled, "your arrival in Chiyaden is already a matter of rumor. And speed down that road is surely worth the risk of an alarm— The lords will rally to you. The Appearance of Strength and Confidence—"

Shoka looked at Reidi and saw a face set like a statue's. Not panic. The old man was too disciplined and too politic, considering the men not far out of hearing; but his lieutenant was in the circle, and that man was frowning.

"When will they make this attack?"

"It should have been made by now. At dusk. The Advantage of Superior Numbers—"

One breathed very carefully. One nodded quietly and said, quoting Bogi'in, "Speed and Stealth, m'lord Kegi. How many men do you have?"

"The Regent's policy—" Kegi said, "of taking levies from the provinces—I'm sure lord Reidi has told you—"

Men conscripted and sent to the border wars, to provinces remotest from home, notably to the frontier up in Kiang—lords stripped of all but their personal retainers, even young men essential to the field work and young merchants from the towns, completely untrained for combat. For the defense of the Empire, the young Emperor had said. While Gitu hired a private army with funds far above what any lord of Angen ought to have; and the Emperor, with Ghita's hand firmly guiding his, hired more mercenaries—*to maintain the strength of the army at home, with so many men away at war—*

"How many men have you got, m'lord?"

"Mounted, a hundred," lord Kegi said. "Myself, my personal guard. Lord Jendei is with us— I had a message from him, and m'lord Reidi—"

With all the lords that have joined us, with all the rest—at best, less than two thousand men. Where are your allies, man, where are the rebels and what do they know, against the mercenaries? Where are all these conscripted soldiers in the Guard that ought to join us—if things are what you say?

People will save their lives, that's the sum of it. Did Bogi'in write that, fool?

"Weapons," Shoka said. "Nature and number. What do you have?"

"Bows," Kegi said. "Spears. —They took most of our horses, m'lord Saukendar. The mercenaries were down here four days ago, they marched away every man between sixteen and forty, except those I could plead were my guard and my servants; even boys out of the fields, and they—"

"There's a long ride between us and Lungan," Shoka said quietly. "And one can cross the Paigji virtually anywhere. But the bridge at Lungan—"

There was profound silence at the fireside, quiet enough that the snap and spit of the fire wore at the nerves. Kegi was sweating. He had that much sense.

"I couldn't prevent them," Kegi said. "I sent a message—to Hoishi and to Feiyan—"

"It didn't catch up with us," Reidi said.

Moving too damn fast. The statement hung there, for anyone to understand. *Ghita knows. He's moving to strip us of support. Does he know yet how close we are?*

And how few we are?

"The Hisei and the Chaighin," Shoka said. "The two dragons about the walls of Cheng'di, my lords. A barrier and a trap. If they bar that bridge, as well they can, then we're put to swimming the Hisei—or ferrying an army across, an army we haven't *got*, my lords, so we can't rely on it."

He could see Taizu's hands, that worried a twig to death, white-knuckled. He imagined the thundercloud look on her face, imagined the biting of the lip.

Damn right, girl. Damn right we're in a mess. And this—scholar—attacks the guard at the ford, to help us on our way—

"Keep your guard, m'lord. I'd rather a change of horses."

"M'lord?"

"Jiro's a conspicuous color. He stops here. I can use about ten men, bay horses, mismatched armor, nothing conspicuously good."

"Nine," Taizu said under her breath.

A sensible man would have his wife *carried* down to Choedri. But small luck for Choedri, he thought, holding onto her.

"Nine men," he said, and looked at Reidi and at Kegi. "I'll want my horse back. I value him. The mare too. Bring them to Lungan."

"Nine men—" Reidi possibly understood what was toward. Perhaps even Kegi did.

"And I want a bird, m'lord Kegi. One of the Emperor's birds . . . "

The dovecote, the aviary, the gawky young Emperor tending his birds every morning . . . personally.

"M'lord?"

"*Have* you one of the Emperor's birds, lord Kegi?"

"Yes, my lord," Kegi said.

"And a writing-kit?"

That, of course Kegi had. The Necessity of Records. Bogi'in had devoted an entire section of his book to that matter.

Shoka rubbed Jiro's bowed nose and got a butt in the ribs for his sentiment; but it was hard to walk away, imagining—he told himself he was a fool—that the horse knew desertion when he saw it, that the old lad could smell it in the air, hear it in his voice.

He moved fast when he took up a remount's reins and stepped up into the saddle—last of all their small company. He bade a quick good luck to the men he was leaving and put himself out in front of his company, in the dark of the woods and the night.

Fool, he told himself a second time, because he felt himself that much further from things he knew, too far away now to get back again—too lost to think of home, too much changed, except that rider that came up beside him—

Fool for taking her along in a business like this, fool not to send her back, lie to her, give her some charge that would keep her busy long enough—but of the ten he had, she was the one he wanted by him, she was the one who would never cross his moves, never misstep, never leave anything to chance—

So they were mercenaries, that was all, dirty and haggard and riding away from the disaster to the south.

And it was not the Choedri ford of the Paigji they headed for, it was the one east of there, off the road—no road for wagons or traders, but the sandy Paigji had such places up and down its course, it always had had, and the whole border between Taiyi and Tengu was a sieve as passable for Ghita's men to launch an attack south as for them to slip north.

If Ghita did attack—there was no holding Choedri. But what Ghita would come seeking would not be there.

Reidi understood. He had made Reidi understand. Seven days, he had said.

He hoped Reidi understood.

"Ghita?" was all Taizu had asked, before he had explained a thing, by which he knew she guessed what he was doing.

"No basket," he had said. "Mercenaries. We need the horses."

Taizu had nodded soberly and said: "No ribbons either."

And, "No ribbons," he had agreed, amused despite himself.

Listening to which conversation, any third person had to know they were both crazed.

Sword, bow, and the plain, desperate look of hired soldiers, Taizu's hair flying loose around her ears, a barbaric topknot tied atop, amulets about her neck, her face smudged with dirt and a mercenary's grimy sheepskin coat over her armor—part of the spoil of the lot at the ferry: no casual glance would find a woman under that mop, or expect more than a wiry, smallish youth in the company of men as disreputable.

The nine were a handful of lord Reidi's men, reliable and steady; and one Jian from Choedri, that Kegi had sent— He knows the roads, Kegi had said.

And thank the gods Jian, who had a girl the other side of the Paigji, knew the back trails and found them the shallows he had promised them, a solid bottom, an easy belly-deep wade for the horses at the worst, hock-deep in most of it, and a peaceful climb up a game-trail into Tengu province.

Not riding straight north, toward Lungan, in the line of march they had established, but to the ferry in Anogi, two days' ride down the Hisei.

"I'd ask," Shoka said to Taizu finally, when the morning was breaking, and they were well across the Paigji, "knowing you wouldn't go back to Choedri—there's a straight ride on west—"

"No," she said. He sighed. "Unless you do," she said after a while.

"No," he said, from the gut, and thought about it. Again. But there was no way out except a coward's way, for both of them—unacceptable. And he knew that. "Hell of a mess, wife."

"No worse than Hoisan," she said. His student. The girl with the basket, who had known traps before he taught her, a woman born to times when pig-girls learned ambushes and the bow. He *saw* what had become of Chiyaden: he imagined what growing up for a peasant girl might have been, in these years.

"You were fighting in Hua," he said, "—how long ago?"

"At least six years," she said after a moment. "Seven, I guess. Everyone hid out, every time the soldiers came over our border. There's a lot of hills in Hua. —Till the soldiers got to burning us out. Then lord Kaijeng—my brothers were with him, mostly—said fight any way we could. And my brothers when they were home, they taught us. When the castle fell, when lord Kaijeng died, my brothers came home then. But there wasn't much anyone could do then. Nobody was in charge. The soldiers ran right over us."

"They had to," Shoka said, thinking of how Hua sat, a hilly place apt for rebels, touching Angen's borders. "If they couldn't put you under, they couldn't hold Yijang or Sengu, Mendang or even Taiyi, and without Taiyi, no hope for Hoishi—everything's connected, all the way up to Yiungei, one great loop they couldn't hold, if little Hua embarrassed them. You were damned important."

This, for the girl who had never studied maps.

She might be thinking it through. Or she might be thinking about her home. Finally she said: "*Gitu's* not that important. What they were afraid of then, the reason they had to run us over—they've got to be afraid now, don't they, unless they can catch us? If they go attack the lords and their people back south—we're not there. But they'll know where we were. And not where we'll be. They'll try to kill *you*. They haven't won if they don't. So we lead them all over."

"Damned smart. Damned bloody. That's the trouble with young thinkers."

She looked at him. He could tell that much, with the sheen of starlight on her head, on her shoulders. She had not asked a question, had not challenged him once—in front of witnesses. By now she was likely choking on questions.

"How do we do it, then?"

"We embarrass Ghita," he said. "We make him retreat, we make him a fool. It's a damn dangerous game. Does it scare you?"

"People *know* you," she hissed. "They're talking, master Shoka, don't think they're not. Everywhere people have gotten to, everywhere those birds get to. Ghita's not sleeping tonight. Neither is Gitu—or the Emperor. We'll keep them awake at night, the way you said. And eventually they'll do something stupid. And people will stop being afraid of them."

"I'll tell you," he said, "there are too many of us to strike deep and too few of us to strike wide, that's what we're doing out here. They're too damn slow to organize and gods know—" *Gods know what any of these men are worth in the field.* But he did not say that, considering their companions on this trail. "Ghita's been ready for this for years. Maybe too ready. Maybe he'll jump too soon. Maybe he'll follow us, who knows? Or maybe he'll be smarter than that and do something we haven't figured. That's always the trouble with planning things."

Taizu was looking at him again, shadow-shape thinking thoughts he could not read.

She was not the crazy one. Perhaps she had only seemed to be, all along, and her craziness was simply a sane girl's dealing with a man who had gone a little mad in his solitude, or who had always been a little mad, serving one Emperor and the other. It had felt that way to him—that their whole course had felt increasingly wrong, and that Taizu had the same opinion, that she had been biting her tongue and watching, *waiting* for him to produce a miracle or come to his senses, and she had not really known which.

I've taught her—to be clever. I've chided her about foolishness and fools and taught her how to win a lop-sided fight. She was seeing it, dammit, while I let Reidi and Kegi plan my course, Kegi—of course the fool; but Reidi—

Reidi so damned competent, so much more plausible, with things done and the course laid—

But the flaws were in the very start of it, flaws in intelligence, flaws in assuming too much help from frightened people—

This isn't a time for Kegi's sort. Virtue's a damn poor substitute for battalions—

"Who knows?" he said. "The pigeon may get through."

Don't trust Ghita, he had written to the Emperor. *Run for your life.*

And signed it without flourish or titles:

Saukendar.

Chapter Eighteen

Shoka applied the point of the dagger to the back of his hand, then quickly, as blood spurted, applied the result to the bandages that crossed Taizu's cheek and jaw.

"Ugh," she said as the blood soaked through. The eyes made a grimace. The mouth was hidden. And the bandages took on a convincingly gruesome blood-soaking.

"You got an arrow through the face," he said, "knocked out a couple of teeth, messed up your mouth, you can't talk, just grunt. We'll soak that bandage once a day. It'll look fine after a couple more." He wrapped a cloth around his own left hand and let one of Reidi's men tie it. A stain spread through that too.

The men Reidi had lent were a lord's retainers, stiff-backed and proper—in a gentleman's presence. He explained things in terms of slovenly discipline and debauchery, he taught them *yes* and *no* in the border patois, and the men he had picked were southern in the first place, with the country Hoishi dialect, which was as far toward the outside westward as Taizu's was east and, at its thickest, obscure to another Chiya, let alone a foreigner— *Speak country,* he had told them, *thick as you can. The Fittha will think you're Oghin and the Oghin will blame you on the Fittha*— —The last in a passably outlandish northwestern brogue, that got a look from Taizu. *Keep them confused.*

There were valuable things they had come by—among the spoils of the mercenaries at Ygotai and northward. One was an ivory plaque, a courier chit. From Aghi's company, it said.

And there were names. Taizu knew— They raided us often enough, she had said. We got to know who was who with Gitu's lot. I can't say who's alive now and who isn't, but they're real names.

Taizu sat now on a rock with a bloody bandage covering half her face, drinking a little tea, which stained the bandage, so much the better.

"Here," she said, through the bandages, offering him the cup, and he took it, grateful for the warmth after the bleeding. His hand was shaking. He should, he thought, have used one of the horses. But they needed their strength: *he* was sitting, at least for the next day or so; and a human hand was easiest to get the blood where it was needed, soaking already-wrapped bandages in a credible pattern. A ghastly wound. Well enough to account for silence from the wild-looking youth in the sheepskin—and to cover a very smooth chin.

Full daylight and no sign yet of anyone on the back-roads. A little stop for hot tea and last night's cold rice, and to horse again. The men looked sober by sunlight, haggard, unshaven, possibly now realizing that they had ridden off to a different kind of danger than that their fellows faced who had stayed with Reidi and Kegi in the south, the kind that required less immediate courage, but steadier nerves in a crisis.

Possibly, Shoka thought, the men were amazed that Taizu sat there to be made up in bloody bandages, instead of shape-shifting herself; but no one asked—which just meant, he reckoned, that they made up their own reasons, which he had rather not ask, or even imagine.

Damn, the capacity of people to believe when they had to—when otherwise they had to know it was just themselves and no one god-blessed or special who had to ride into Anogi and romance their way past the Regent's hire-ons.

He had *rather* have had a demon or two, himself, given a choice.

But for a second choice, in a crisis where wit counted, he had as soon have Taizu.

It was a tired handful of mercenaries who rode down among the scatter of brown board buildings and fisher-shacks below Anogi southtown—that was what Shoka hoped the town saw, eleven men in motley armor plastered with yellow dust, and horses whose color had started bay and gone to ghost-yellow like their riders; one rider with a bandaged face, the cloth crusted with dirt and old blood and new, and that rider slumping wearily in the saddle among the rest, some of whom had lesser wounds. Not a prosperous group—and all the attention the town of Anogi paid to them as they rode was a surly glance and, continually down the street, the quiet latching of shutters and doors.

Click. Thump.

Through the town and down among the mercenaries on guard by the river—a slovenly camp, gear scattered around an evening-fire of boards, outside the ferry-man's hut—

"It's hell back there," Shoka said, squatting there with a bored mercenary squad leader while his men waited on the ferry to come, doing a little trading for rice and a little dried fish— "Listen, don't be robbing us. That's a lousy piece." He indicated the thin one, and the man threw a broken bit of fish onto the dirty sacking, looked up at him with a that's-the-limit kind of scowl. "I'll tell you," Shoka said conversationally, "I'm from Bagoi, myself, and I'd just as soon be back there.

Nothing but damn lies. *They won't fight*, the captain says. Hell. They cut us up. They fair cut us up down south."

"Where are they setting up?"

"No damn place, no damn place, that's what's going on down there! Whole place is coming loose around the edges. I don't like it. Me and mine, we'd *like* to cut out down by Mandi, get the hell out of here, but we ain't got paid, that's what, and it's going to be a hell of a long winter—"

"This Saukendar—this warlord that's supposed to've come in. You seen anything of that?"

"I dunno. I dunno what went through us. We ain't seen nothing except where we was supposed to find ours, there was theirs, and all I know, the captain's dead, there ain't no pay and I said to mine, We're going north, that's what—north, over-river, go up, get clear and get somewheres we get paid, damn right— Get enough money ahead we can get back home if this goes bad—"

"You think it's going that way?"

"Hell, I dunno, I dunno." He saw with relief the ferry pulling in toward shore. He folded up the sacking scrap around the fish, stuffed it in his bag and got up. "I tell you this—it ain't a bad thing to know where the road out is right now. We ain't spending from now on. That's how I think it is."

The mercenary gave him a worried look.

"They're headed up straight north," Shoka said. "Lungan, that's what I think; that's where they're coming across, coming right for the capital, and then watch the whole damn place come apart. I'd rather face regular soldiers than any damn farmers picking at you from hedges, I'll tell you that. But it ain't like you'll see any action here . . . not much chance. . . ."

As the ferry pulled in.

Eleven riders and horses: there might have been townsmen and farmers with notions of using the ferry this morning, but no one came up to share the space. The horses went anxiously down the small board pier to the loading area, had to be tightly held when they felt the heave of the water (Jiro would have walked on in grand disdain, even after all these years) and one thanked the gods there were three stout-railed stalls on the deck, or one of the horses at least would have drowned itself, most likely the black-stockinged bay with the scarred chest. (Good riddance, Shoka thought of that horse, considering matters all along the trail. But it settled, with its head firmly lashed to the high rail.)

The real town of Anogi inched closer as the ferrymen plied the big oars—a free-moving ferry, this, the Hisei being too big and too trafficked to be crossed with ropes—a kind of barge that described a crescent-shaped course from shore to shore, a compromise with the current, while larger and smaller craft bound downriver went straight courses past, fishing boats and cargo boats and such. Business had not stopped at least: there was that much normalcy about the river, as if there were nothing at all going on to the south—but then, people who lived by trade, had to trade, and soldiers ate rice and used cloth and iron. And fishermen had to fish: the world might be askew and disaster threatening, but those boats had to go out so long as the weather permitted.

"You shouldn't talk to them," Taizu muttered, as they held close to the stall rails, keeping the horses calm while the ferry pitched in the wake of a passing barge. "You took a chance. You always said, don't take—"

"I bargained us another half a fish," Shoka said. "I thought that was damned sharp of me."

"Don't joke! There's too many of them!"

"We're fine. Don't look worried."

"Don't look worried! What else—"

A riverman came past, running toward the bow, and Taizu swallowed it down fast. They were coming in at Anogi proper, which loomed up in tiers above the riverside, the two halves of the city somewhat skewed

from each other across the Hisei—but that was the way
the current brought the ferry ashore, and that was the
way the two halves had grown.

"Poor boy," Shoka said. "Don't try to talk. You'll
open that up again."

Taizu glared at him.

"Trust me," Shoka said, and rested a hand on her
shoulder. "We're doing just fine. Aren't we?"

"Not if you go talking to soldiers!"

"But I *was* one," Shoka said. "Don't worry about
that part. Where are the damn levies from Choedri,
that's what I'd give a lot to know. Maybe off at Anogi
garrison. Maybe in Lungan or beyond it. It's not something I can ask without telling too much. But I used to
have resources in Lungan. We'll see if anyone's left."

"And if they're scared enough of Ghita—"

"There's that risk. There's always that risk. People
change. Loyalties do. Don't think I haven't thought
about that."

"Who are you going to talk to?" she hissed; and
choked off whatever came next: the riverman was coming back past, headed astern in the general commotion
of putting in at the landing.

"Old acquaintances," Shoka said under his breath,
and looked out over the bow of the ferry aimed toward
Anogi north.

He thought of the old man and Lungan in about the
same breath. He wondered was Jojin still alive—whether
an aged grammarian had been too political to survive; or
whether Jojin's priestly connections had saved his neck.

Two days on the road and he had gotten nothing from
the ferry-guard, back there on the Tengu shore, of
anything he did not know or could not have guessed.
The general situation was all too old to gossip about,
the present details too intricate to navigate in blind
questions with a man who could raise a general alarm—
that was what he had sensed when he had abandoned
his attempt to get news and skirted around the edges of
matters.

So he had gotten back to the matter of the fish, very quickly, and tried to answer nothing and gather what he could by implication.

About Saukendar: yes, the mercenaries north of the river knew he was abroad.

About trouble, even a collapse of the south into chaos: that certainly worried them but they had no trouble believing it.

About a mercenary unit coming northward bereft of its captain: everything he had claimed to have done, escaping a night attack, coming north to report, had seemed reasonable to them. Thank the gods.

Two days of their seven were gone. And he was not as far along toward Lungan as he would have wished.

Nothing was as far along as he would have wished. He had wanted one of the birds to take along. If there had been a reason he could have thought, to justify a band of common soldiers having a pigeon-cage strapped to some horse's rump, he would have done it. But there was too much that could go wrong, a bird like that escaping or being let fly with a false message—was too dangerous. Hence the simple pact with Reidi, and a schedule that had to be kept.

Don't go charging blind into Lungan, he had said. Be ready to improvise. Don't follow instructions over the edge of a cliff.

He trusted that the man who had set up so much of this over the years had the wit to improvise in a crisis: he trusted the old man desperately, he hoped that Reidi's physical strength would suffice under the strain, he hoped that Reidi would have the moral force to prevail over fools like Kegi and Maijun. It was a great deal to hope of an old and hitherto sedentary gentleman, and for a dizzy, foolish moment of his own he had even wondered if Taizu would be capable of that kind of judgement in command—he was that short of talent, and she had it, he thought, she had the imagination and the sense that could make a correct decision in any situation except battlefield tactics, *if* she had had the simple years of living to let her understand cowardice and greed and glory-grabbing on her own side.

She was learning. He had seen the flicker of her eyes, he had seen her listening in councils, clench-jawed and silent, he had seen the little tensions that came and went when in their own small company, someone suggested something he himself had to refuse—*she* understood.

Damn fine, girl. Damned fine all the way we've come together.

I should let her go now.

Then he knew that he was thinking about dying.

Plan your retreat, master Shoka. . . .

He felt the pain in his leg, old ache, never quite absent in this long riding. He remembered cutting wood, and the frown on Taizu's face. He remembered that frown when the ferry bumped against the shore and the officer of the guard on that side of the river came up asking for names and business.

A quickening of the pulse then; and he put his mind into the essence of one Sengi, mercenary, late of Aghi's company, who carried an ivory courier chit and who had made fast time ahead of trouble. "They said report in," he said to the guard captain; and then, taking a deliberate chance: "They said higher-ups better talk with us, if we know anything they'll want to know. Where do we go?"

"Everything's at Lungan," the guard captain said. "Everything's out of there."

"Same place *they're* headed," Shoka muttered, slipping the chit back into his belt-pouch. "Fast. They're coming right north, they've picked up forces out of the west. Some of that lot. Probably been in it from the start, and there's too damn many of them, hitting all over. The rumors are wild down there—there's supposed to be a dragon down in Taiyi. A demon with Saukendar's army. I tell you it's crazy."

"Anyone see it?" The captain looked Fittha. His armor was hung with amulets and his wrists had braided horsehair charms against spells. "What kind of demon?"

"Hell if I know. If it was there I didn't see it, but I don't want to either. They have to get the priests busy, that's what. They'd better do something, damn, they better get those prayer-sticks lit, *I* ain't going to go have a look for it, not me, no."

The captain scratched and rubbed at one of his charms. "So what are the companies south doing?"

Shoka shrugged. "I dunno. I don't know who's moving out there, I didn't see anything. What hit us was in the dark and fast, and we got out alive, that's all. Except we know Hoishi's gone. We got reports up from there; Hoishi's one of the ringleaders, and we saw banners from out west. So what I know, I don't know who knows, but I figure somebody should, fast, before it gets across the Hisei. So I'd better get on the road and move."

"That one won't make it there," the guard captain said, with a nod toward Taizu, who had her horse ashore and who mounted up with every indication of exhaustion, the horse shying off and circling—*My gods, from behind!*—until Taizu hopped around in a drunken stagger and clawed her way up with the horse between her feminine backside and the captain's stare. "Better leave that one to hospital."

"My cousin," Shoka said. "I told him. He won't. Afraid of us getting separated. And I promised his father I'd get him home." Shoka climbed up to the saddle and reined back. "Lungan. We'll make it. Wish I was staying. Here's a hell of a lot safer. . . ."

The horse wanted to move. He gave it a touch of his heels and the rest followed, clattering up the stone landing and onto the streets of Anogi.

Everything concentrated at Lungan.

Ghita too?

Where in hell is the Emperor right now?

Or that damn pigeon.

Taizu pulled up beside him. She said nothing. His heart had nearly stopped when she had to climb up on the horse again with the captain watching. "That coat's not long enough," Shoka said. "Be aware when a man's behind you."

"I saw it," she said between her teeth. "You think he saw?"

"You covered up. I hope." Anogi streets unwound around them, riverside market, a road that lay toward town-edge, and they picked up the pace a little, bunching together, stringing out to pass a cart, together again as they headed up the river front, past docked barges and small vendor boats.

All the while he kept thinking it was not going to work, that the guards were going to start thinking about Taizu's mannerisms or recall something in his accent and start wondering. He kept expecting pursuit, as nervous as the men with them, and not daring to look over his shoulder more than a man might, who was trying to keep a small band together on a city street.

But there was the city gate ahead—a mere landmark, Anogi long ago having sprawled beyond its old limits, so that the wall was built up in houses and shops and the gate had become nothing but an arch to shelter beggars.

An ungodly number of beggars, the halt and the maimed, some of whom, doubtless, had been soldiers.

Or farmers.

He felt anger at that thought. He saw the numbers—he saw the wounds, the kind of wounds that swords made, he saw the hate directed at them in that ride through shadow—

—for foreigners, for hired soldiers, for ten years of oppressors.

He thought of Taizu, glaring up at him as he stood on his porch.

Justice, master Saukendar.

And he thought, hurting this time, *Young fool, I can't help you.* . . .

But they were not far from Lungan; or the Regent. And he was *angry* in that moment, with a sense of outrage Taizu had stirred in him, but no one else, for years.

Shadow to sunlight, and the last sprawl of the town in front of them, people going about their business, just dodging the mercenaries in the street, that was the way people lived—except for the scarcity of young men on the streets.

There had been young men among the beggars, there were a number of young men in the yellow robes of monks—

But not otherwise. And the women swathed themselves in scarves and shapeless coats, tired-looking, worn and cheerless, even the young ones.

The ghosts of laughing girls flitted across his memory, bright colors, flirting eyes, steps that danced. . . .

The women of Chiyaden, the young women, going stoop-shouldered and fearfully about the riverside—

Taizu, in front of him at the porch steps: *Teach me, master Saukendar. . . .*

Taizu, in the rain, flailing away at the tree, Taizu lying in the mud, under the lightning-flashes—

—Taizu with that demon's look on her face, white and wet and terrible—

—Riding beside him, absolute in her intentions as he had never known how to be: *Justice, master Saukendar . . .*

He was not sure what justice existed in the court at Cheng'di, but he had a notion what justice he would take from the fools who marched the youth of Chiyaden off to border wars and plundered their own land and maintained their power with hired soldiers—

Who used the young men of the provinces as coin to buy alliances, supporting one barbarian king, fighting another—and called it affairs of state—

Cut off the head of this monster and that was only half the battle: the rest of its coils were threaded through every province of Chiyaden, and apt to die hard, working destruction as far as mercenary bands could reach.

But no worse than he saw around him.

There was no way to extricate that beast from the land; and gods help the people when they struck the blow.

Gods help the people if they did not.

That was the way he kept thinking, with every stride the horses took. Five more days beyond this one, and Reidi was going to put his neck out and with him every hope of opposing Ghita's regime.

Five days beyond this one and that bridge at Lungan had damned well better be open. He knew no way, this side of the river, to get one of the men back to Reidi in time to say otherwise, and he wished to hell he could, now, strongly suspecting, by everything he had heard from the Fittha, that Ghita was well warned and prepared to draw a battle-line at the bridge at Lungan.

That said something about the north, that Ghita reckoned the Imperial Province well in hand, so that he *could* hold at Lungan, without worrying about anything coming at his back. So much for the hope that the Imperial troops in the province might mutiny, that some wave of rebellion might come in from the borders, at least sufficient uncertainty to make a difference: in that case Ghita would pull back behind Cheng'di and across the Chaighin, to his own land in Kenji and Angen, where he could virtually section off Ayenden, Shangei, P'eng and Yijang, where the mercenary forces were thickest and where his supporters held lordships—a slow, nasty kind of war, but better than fighting it out in the heart of Chiyaden.

But Imperial troops had evidently not defected, the Hisei and not the Chaighin was the line of defense Ghita chose, and the Emperor and the capital were firmly in Ghita's hands.

Decidedly *not* what he had hoped for.

The sparse traffic on the Lungan road had a desperate look, a few traders, anxious gentry in fancy, flower-painted carriages and countryfolk in plain farm carts, or just poor townsmen walking with baskets and bundles. When they saw soldiers they pulled over to the edge of the road and inched along, or stopped altogether and made respectful bows from which they did not look up at all. Taizu just rode coldly past them, watching, watching all the while, wary as he had taught her to be, sharp eyes above the mask of filthy bandage, while the men, some of them, rode silent and avoided looking at the people: ashamed, Shoka thought; or feeling too much.

Himself—he tried to figure out what he felt, who—he could not shake the feeling—might have come earlier, might have planned better, and, by the gods, on his side, might have had a damn lot more help from these same people—if any number of them had been willing to take matters in their own hands. He was not sure whether he loved them in the aggregate or wanted to do them violence; or wanted simply to ride off and let them talk their way out of their disaster, the way they had talked the emperor to the throne and Ghita into power and himself out of favor and then turned around and deified him right into the mess he was in, his whole life carried one direction and another on the breath of the people; and all the virtue he had went to refraining from what they deserved—

—except Taizu was one of their number. And he could not forget that, whenever he saw some poor soul struggling along with a basket or bundle, all that was valuable, all that was possible to save out of a lifetime. The lords fought, the banners flew, and the gray lines of desperate people trekked the roads, with their meager world on their backs.

Taizu believed less in gods after knowing him. She began to know what the people's heroes were made of—exaggeration, desperate wishes and superstition—and still stayed with him, caught in the same nets, while at the bottom of his heart he was terrified that she would get up sane one morning and see an ordinary, lame, forty-year-old man with a nasty disposition and too little patience with people.

He hated power over people. He truly hated it. And sometimes he hated *them*, that was what he was profoundly ashamed of, hated them because they thrust off

all the virtues they admired on some poor idol, and
stopped expecting them in themselves.

He wished he *did* have a visible god or two to shove
matters off on—but if the gods were accessible, it seemed
only fair not to do to them what he complained about in
others: as well, then, to shut up and carry matters on
his own as far as he could. Then the gods might be
happier about coming through in a pinch. That was the
sum of his religion, and he was thinking earnestly about
it this afternoon, on the way to getting all of them
killed.

*Well, Celestial Lord, I'm not sure this mess is solv-
able. Ghita's invited the foreigners into the heart of the
Empire. He's a fool. Of course the foreign kings are
helping him, while Chiyaden's army fights their wars.
But there are far too many of them, aren't there, Ghita's
gotten himself into a trap he has to understand by
now—too much unrest to trust the army home, so much
he needs the foreigners to keep order, and he has to
know if they find a leader of their own, it won't be a
border war any longer. So he has to keep the border
war going not only to keep the army officers busy,
but keep things stirred up so his foreign allies need
Chiyaden's army. He can only do that so long, before
the whole stack of bricks falls down.*

*Chiyaden will pay for what he's done, down the
years. We've shown the barbarians too much about us.
They know our foolishness. Mend that, Celestial Lord,
and save us from our own short-sightedness: that's what
we can't do ourselves.*

It was the only conversation he had had with the
gods in ten years; but this afternoon he was down to
that. He had no notion yet what to do, what they were
going into, what their enemy's preparations had been—

And all along the road they were passing people who
might have that information, who had come out of
Lungan or its surrounds. The refugees, he thought, the
people who shied off from them on the road—knew
things that were life and death to them; and might, if

he told them the simple truth, carry that rumor back to mercenary units on the road behind them.

He watched one cart on its way to disaster, a girl with a baby, a young boy, an old man—the cartwheels squealing under the misaligned load of household goods and the old horse working hard to make headway.

On impulse he blocked the dray's path with his own, and, seeing the fugitives panic, bowed in the saddle, courteous and not crowding them himself, but his anxious company drew close on the side and behind him.

"It's all right," he said in soldier patois, and held both hands in plain sight. "We just have a question or two about the road ahead. Come all the way from Lungan?"

Heads nodded.

"Is the Regent at Lungan?"

Terrified stares.

"Where's lord Ghita?"

The eyes hardly blinked. Only the old horse moved, restless under the stressed shafts.

"Dammit, answer me!"

"Lungan, lord. In Lungan." From the grandfather, who looked fit to collapse. "All the soldiers are there."

"Fortified?"

"Yes, lord, fortified."

"Where?"

"The camp, lord. Around the camp."

Too much fear. Too little knowledge. Anything they said might be a lie, they would agree to anything he suggested, whatever would please him. "Go on," he said, and reined out of their way. He added, sorry for them: "I'd go wide of Anogi if I was you and I'd spread that word up and down the road. There's a garrison there. I just wouldn't be in that town, if things get bad. The mercenaries are apt to loot and run straight down to Mandi. Pass the word. Go north of Anogi, keep to the country roads. You'll be a damn sight safer."

Still the huge-eyed stares. The baby cried and the girl put her hand over its mouth, hugged it against her.

"Go on," he said.

They started the horse up. The cart rolled past.

"And throw a third of that damn junk off," he yelled over the squealing of the wheels. "You may *need* that horse."

There was no likelihood they would take either piece of advice. He staring past his shoulder at tragedy on an unstoppable course.

"Can't depend on anything they say," Taizu said, walking her horse up beside him. "They're too scared. They'll never talk to a soldier."

"Damn fools."

He knew better than what he had just done. He felt angry with himself, angry with them, for reasons varied and too scattered to make sense of.

If you were there, Taizu had said to him a long time ago, *you'd set things right.*

Of course I would.

Like climbing a cliff. It was the looks down that took a man's stomach, the occasional realization where he was and what he was doing and what he had to work with.

A while more down the road, thinking and thinking, watching the people they passed for any sight of weapons. But there was no threat in the wagons and the carriages, in the people who ran from the trouble they foresaw, who drew aside in terror from a company they took for Oghin mercenaries. Very few young men, very few; exempt as some lord's servant, some lord's tenant farmer, a widow's son, all the various reasons a household could give for exempting a boy from conscription. And from those very few, nothing but bowed heads, averting of the eyes, as if they were terrified every moment a soldier's eye was on them that they might have that exemption revoked.

Of course conscript the young men out of the central provinces, *especially* from regions around the capital, especially from the towns and cities, where discontent fomented and young men gathered in taverns and tea-shops.

And damned if those that were left were going to risk their precious exemptions. So they would do nothing, dare nothing; but one could panic, accosted by soldiers, one could turn out to have a weapon.

So it was one of the women he rode down on of a sudden, when they next came on a knot of refugees—the hindmost, who struggled along under a bundle too large for her, and who had no hope of running. She looked up when he reined across her path. It was a tolerably pretty face. Or at least it might have been, except the dirt and the sweat and the fear. "Girl," he said, holding his fretting horse still, and saw out of the tail of his eye that the next to last straggler of the little group had delayed, an old man with the cart who looked as if he wanted desperately to do something—and was not sure how much a moral act was worth.

"Girl, just a few questions." In a cultured accent this time, pure courtly language. "I won't delay you, I won't hurt you. Who commands in Lungan?"

"Lord Ghita," she stammered.

"Is he there, personally?"

A definitive nod. Fear in the eyes, but a re-estimation, too. *Who are you?* that look said, scared, but with perhaps the sudden notion that she was not talking to a mercenary.

"Who's attacking him?"

"Lord?"

"Who's attacking Lungan?"

A hesitation. The horse pulled at the bit, and he held it hard, waiting for his answer.

"They say the lords south."

"Who's leading them?"

"They say lord Saukendar. They say there's demons. They say—"

"What, girl?"

"He's come with their help." A quick swallow, as if too many words had gotten out. Her mouth trembled and she clamped it hard, her face quite pale.

"Where's the Emperor right now, do you know?"

A desperate move of her head. *No.* She looked at him, at his hands, at his face again.

And the old man still lingered, at the edge of his vision.

"That old man yonder looks like he'd like to help you. Do you know him?"

A frantic glance. "No. No. I don't."

"I'd travel with him if I were you. He's worth something."

"Lord?"

But he let the horse go then, and it walked on, his waiting company closing around him at that pace, a long day, tired horses.

"Ghita's in Lungan," he said, "and they know I'm involved in the south. The rumors have gotten north."

"M'lord," the squad leader said. Which was about all the conversation he usually had of the men. But they were steady and none of them were slow-witted. Not one of them made a suggestion. They talked, when they rode close to each other or when they stopped for a rest, in quiet voices, sometimes with looks his way or Taizu's. Sometimes they looked a great deal worried. They did now.

Wondering what we're doing? Shoka thought. *Wondering how we're going to get into Lungan and what we're going to do and what they're along for?*

So am I, man. I'm working this out as I go. Or maybe I have an affinity for women with baskets.

There was a wall and a hedge for shelter in the last of the dusk, an old shrine, which the men thought lucky: they made sacrifice of a little rice, a little wine, and paid their respect to the gods and their ancestors with more fervency, a couple of them, than might be likely in foreigners.

Asking the gods for help, maybe. Or for the welfare of wives and parents they might not see again.

But no one was there to see: the refugees had thinned out to a very few after dusk, and no one stayed near them. No refugees and no sign of other units, which was the thing he had worried most about—running into some other squad, real mercenaries inbound or out-bound from Lungan. None so far, and either they had hit the pace that might keep them isolated on the road, or inbound troops were getting very few now and no one was coming out again.

So it was a plain, decent supper, a camp with a little leisure to sit and catch breath instead of falling straight-way to sleep. "We could gain a little time," Shoka had told them when they stopped, "but I know this road we're on and I know Lungan, gods know I know it. We can stop now, get some sleep and get there by noon tomorrow, and if there's any traffic coming in at all, that can help us. I'd just rather not answer close ques-tions if we can avoid it; and if we have to, better we do it on a good sleep. Take a little wine. Whatever lets you rest. All right?"

"Yes, m'lord," the squad leader said. His name was Chun.

"I don't think I've ever served with better," Shoka said after a moment; and the men looked shocked for a moment, then, with Chun, made deep bows, murmur-ing, "my lord," one and all of them.

There was fervency in the look they gave him, in the dark, in the light of their little fire. He usually hated looks like that. But not at the moment. It came from both sides, he thought. That was the difference. Chun. Eigi. Jian. Panji and Nui, cousins. Liang and Waichen, Yandai and Wengadi. They did not, thank gods, look to him for miracles, just sane orders. And they tried, they kept trying—maybe because there was a woman in their midst, even if she was a demon.

"Um," he said after a moment, clearing his throat, and got up and walked away, wishing then he had not said anything. It was a trap. They had no reason to be impressed with him. He had no right to use them. He forgot, *forgot*, dammit, the sense he had gotten to, to keep himself away from people, not to attract their attention, not—with the little virtue he had attained—to make them into instruments. Not to be used, himself; and not to use others. And not to make them love him.

Dammit.

Why can't I learn? What makes me do such things?

Taizu stood by him. Taizu touched his sleeve. "Master Shoka."

It stung. He took his arm away.

"Master Shoka." Again the touch at his arm, urging him toward the shadows of the hedge.

He drifted that way with her, into the dark, and stopped there, with no present inclination to talk, even to look at her. But he put his hand on hers where it touched his arm.

"Is everything all right?"

"Of course it's all right." He kept his voice down. *I have no idea what I'm doing. I have no plan. I have no idea where our enemy is. I've led you all into a damn mess I can't see out of. Of course things are fine.* But that would scare Taizu, and scared, she might make a mistake, and making a mistake, die for it. There was no sanity anywhere.

She put her arm around his. She rested her head against his shoulder. That was all. And he thought about the bridge, sorting through images and memories, every crossing he had made of the Lungan bridge, every detail he could recall of its construction, whether Ghita would go so far as to dismantle it—at least the center. Or how many Imperial troops Ghita had at his disposal, and how far down the ranks he had replaced officers with his own men. . . .

"Can we sleep together?" she asked.

He drew a ragged breath, thinking about the men back there, about people too close to him, people tearing him apart. Taizu hugged his arm.

Never since the willows. Not a single chance. They had been sleeping together, right enough—stinking of blood and dirt and horse and smoke, so exhausted they fell unconscious two breaths after they lay down and

waked stiff with whatever position they had fallen into;
and he had felt apt to the same kind of collapse tonight,
until she said it and he reacted—to a woman muffled to
the nose in blood-caked bandages and sweaty armor.

He hugged her against him, same as hugging a rock.
And said, fingering dust-rough, tangled hair and a bandaged cheek— "We can't unwrap this. We'd never get
the dirt back right."

"Just let's do it."

"Scared?"

"No." Short and sharp. She shivered in his arms.
Hard. "Dammit."

He knew that reaction. He held her a moment. He
walked her along by the hedge, into the deeper shadow
of a mulberry and the old wall. He set her down and
they started undoing ties. "We can't undo all of it."

"That's all right," she said; and: "Oh, damn," she
said, when sleeves and armor got in the way.

"Simple tactical problem. Patience. Patience always
wins, that's what my master used to tell me. . . ."

There was no finesse in either of them: short, fast;
and afterward, he felt his heart fluttering, the whisper
of the leaves a thin, surreal sound over Taizu's hard
breathing. He felt her touch on his cheek.

In case there was no more time. Because it warmed
the body, occupied the mind, blotted everything out.
And she was too smart to cozen with assurances. Or to
come to him with any. She was just there, and he could
think again, if he were not too far gone with exhaustion.

He shut his eyes. He was home again. The leaves
whispered overhead like rain on the cabin roof. "Remember the winter," he murmured into her ear. "The
monkey and the daughter."

"I remember." Muffled through the bandages and
thick with sleep.

"I wish I could tell you I've got a plan. I haven't.
We're going in to figure one out. That's what you're
along for."

She said nothing for a while. Then: "We can get Ghita."

Straight and simple, putting it together the same way he had. Nine men whose lives were expendable—hands and backs and swords when they were needed. Themselves—minimal force, straight to the balance-point.

That was granting they got through the gates.

Chapter Nineteen

The gates at Lungan were the narrow spot, Shoka had figured all the way. In the long peace, towns had spilled past their gates if they had them at all; but Lungan with its bridge was the gateway to Pan'tei and to Cheng'di, the very heart of the Empire, and the old Emperor, acting as chief of engineers in his father's time, had ordered the gates refurbished and thickened, the walls heightened, built the walled market that was also the bridge garrison at need, built the gatehouse on the Anogi road in case it ever needed to be manned.

It was now. Absolutely.

They adjusted their pace and picked their company going in the narrow gate—a pig-seller with two animals done up in slings and a returning slops cart all in the same general area, and Shoka reined around the slops cart, hoping to clear the questions of the gate-guards.

But a guard shoved a spear in his horse's path and shied him up. "Where?" the man asked. Fittha, taking them for Oghin, likely, and willing to give them grief.

Shoka had the courier chit. He stopped his little column in the gateway, creating a deliberate roadblock, with a flock of goats not far behind them. "Captain's business, coming up from Anogi."

The man examined the chit. Damned if he could read it, Shoka thought. He took it over to his officer, as bleating goats began to leak around the nervous horses. The officer came back, and the company, on previous orders, backed and shifted in what could be restlessness on the horses' part, but contrived to block the gate. Goats bleated, dogs barked, and the slops cart was probably in it somewhere.

"Clear the gate!" the officer yelled. And a stream of something foreign.

"Aghi!" Shoka yelled back and pointed at the chit, maintaining his company right where it was.

"Pig!" the Fittha yelled at him. "Report to the camp, second on your left, straight on, move your ass, pig!"

And shoved the chit at him.

Shoka took it and sent his horse off fast. His company followed. *Stay to the background*, he had warned Taizu. *You're too much question as it is.*

But she came up beside him as they clattered along the street and around the second corner, by a tea-shop with shattered screens and a crowd of customers that got hastily back to the walls and out of their way.

Used to dodging soldiers, apparently. A squad was coming from the other direction, and they went single-file for a moment.

Get in, he had listed the points for Taizu and all the others, find out whether soldiers come and go on the street, see if there's a way to sink into the city without reporting through Ghita's command or getting shut into that camp.

So when they got further down the street that led to the bridge and found soldiers no uncommon sight any-where along the way, Shoka slowed the pace and finally took them around a corner, on a row of cheap restaurants. The air stank of cheap beer, overloaded sewers and the wind off the stockyards.

"Good as anywhere," Shoka said, and stopped and got down. Taizu dropped to her feet beside him, a spatter of something noxious, as the rest dismounted and gathered around. "Food and drink, someplace for the horses—" He looked up at the advertisement of lodgings and looked further up at a rickety stairs.

Not the most prosperous place in town. Officers would lodge in finer places. Common soldiers would set up in tents, off in the camp they were supposed to go to. But mercenaries being mercenaries, they came and they went, and officers counted on payday to get them on the rolls where they could be accounted for and assigned: that had been the system ten years ago, not the official procedure, but the actual one.

And tent space being limited, if some mercenary squads put up in hostels, that had been winked at, so long as the town magistrate sent no complaints to the higher-ups.

He hoped, as he led the way into the dingy restaurant, that that was the way Ghita's officers ran the army.

Trail-cooking was better than the garlicky, oily mess the *Peony* dished up. They picked at it, picked out the edible bits, ate the rice, drank the cheap wine and took a collective breath.

Three rooms, stables, meals for the lot of them. "The innkeeper's going to be damn happy," Shoka said. "He was scared when I asked for rooms. I said we were real quiet, I didn't let my company get drunk, and I pointed out with all the soldiers in town he might be glad to have us laying claim to the room down here, we were a real asset—keep the place safe and all."

"What about the camp?" Taizu said.

"We'll take a walk about. I had a talk with the

innkeeper—got a little sense where things are—being
new in town. Ghita's here, all right, quartered in one of
the big houses. The camp's where the line-troops stay,
but there's a lot of billets about town, those that can
afford it, mostly cavalrymen, a lot of damage—damn
loose discipline. I asked him if he ever got soldiers in
here, he said not usually, it used to be a lot of workers
from the slaughterhouses and the tannery down the
street, they were used to the smell and a lot of the
other teahouses didn't like the air about them—"

The men had never understood his levity, all this
ride long. This time they seemed to, slight, shy humor,
down-glancing.

Only Taizu—by the line between her brows—was
not smiling. She ate, pulling the bandages with the
fingers of one hand to get food into her mouth, drinking
and soaking the filthy cloth while she did.

Impatient. Worried. Eyes darting to every movement in the room. He reached out and nudged her leg.
"Easy."

She drew an audible breath. "Time," she said in that
guttural mutter that was her public voice.

"We're doing fine."

A dart of worried eyes. He imagined the rest of
the expression, the thrust of the lip. *You're lying, master
Shoka.*

He put a leg over the back side of the bench. "Come
on, boy. Let's take a walk. —You fellows stay close
here. Finish your lunch. Get some sleep."

"Where are we going?" Taizu asked as they walked
the twisting stone street, past tea-shops and pepper-
vendors and shops with hanging poultry and strings of
garlic. People jostled past. War was in the offing, but
business went on. Wives were stocking larders. Men
were carrying past sacks of rice. The prices white-
washed on the boards outside shops were predictably
outrageous.

"The camp—take a—" He saw her eyes dart to a passing cart. "For gods' sake, what's the matter with you? Stop jumping at everything!"

"I'm not jumping!"

"You're nervous as a—" *Virgin in a whorehouse*, the expression ran. "Calm down, dammit."

Another dart of the eyes, a man with a load of lumber. "I'm sorry."

"Just take it easy. You want questions? I don't."

"There's too damn many people!"

He looked her way, grabbed her by the shoulder and hurried her across the street, dodging the yellow streams that ran between the pavings. "That's what makes a city. Doesn't it?" The panic was infectious. It was a weakness in her he had never reckoned on. Damn, she had never been in a town larger than Ygotai; they had touched no more than the edge of Anogi, ahorse and bound out of it as fast as they dared. On the road she had watched the people with that kind of attention, eyes checking every movement. Crazy-dangerous, people would think.

It was everything he had taught her in the forest, tracking every move and every sound that came strange to her, but everything was strange here and there was too much of it, too fast, all at once.

"Shut your ears," he said. "Be blind. Trust my eyes. You're watching too much, too hard. Just wait for my cues, all right? Like in practice. Don't react."

"Yes," she said quietly. Her stride changed, became easier.

"Just a lot of people. Civilized people. They don't jump at you. Not in broad daylight. Just a lot of racket on these damn cobbles, covers a lot of sound. Echoes off the walls, plays hell with your sense of where things are. New place, new senses. You'll get used to it."

You'd better, he thought. *Damn fast.*

Take her back to the tea-house, leave her with Chun and the rest—

She can't handle this. She's going to make a mistake. First man who startles her, she'll jump—

Berserker. That's what she gives off.

Taizu in the dark, naked shape among the bandits, blade flashing—

Everyone's her enemy but me. All the way from Hua—hiding and running—and two years learning to hear a leaf drop—learning my footstep in the dark, on the dirt, on the porch—

Anyone else—anyone she can't identify—dead. She's that fast. And react is all I've taught her.

This is a mistake, her being here is a mistake, we ought to turn around now and go back—

Horsemen were coming down the street at their backs. She did not turn and look. She was settling, he thought. Of course she was settling, she had never failed, not in any move he had taught her.

Walk her around, let her see the bridge, get the feel of the town, ask a few questions, go back to the tea-house for a drink and have a talk with her in the room. That was the sensible thing to do.

The air smelled of the river before they got as far as the market, and the masts of river-craft, sparse as they were, stood against the pale gray of the water.

A girl from Hua had to stop and stare when she saw it. A boy from Yiungei had done the same thing, contemplating riding that great span on horseback.

Later the youth, learning the marvels of its building, how many workers had died, swept away in the current, how many attempts had failed, how often the footings had given way and wrecked the effort, and how the Imperial Engineers under the then-prince's direction had spanned the treacherous currents first with a pontoon bridge and then with stone carried by barge, to the one favor nature gave them, the subsurface island in the center, and across again, building the stone sections and filling them with rubble—until the great Hisei flowed docilely through stone arches, whole boats able to pass beneath.

"The old Emperor wanted to bridge all the rivers," Shoka said, "but in these times—gods know if it's wise."

"Two carts can pass on that thing!"

"That they can. With room between."

"What are we going to do?" There was an edge of panic in her voice.

"Don't worry about the bridge right now. It's not the important thing. It can't be, yet. Just stay calm." He walked her on, where the bridge street gave out on the old market, familiar enough ground ahead for a farmer-girl, he thought. The camp was on their left, towering walls of buff stone that closed off the esplanade as far as the river-edge. Not yet for that, he thought, looking down the aisles of tents, dislodged from those grounds, filled the paved esplanade where jugglers and trinket-sellers and artists had made carnivals in peacetime, amid a host of sit-down drink-sellers and pastry-makers. Not nowadays. The whole bazaar had been displaced. Best just wander around a little, get the temperature of the place.

If there was anyone desperately worried these days, it was surely the merchants with bored, off-duty foreign mercenaries walking among their displays. He and Taizu got looks—rough-looking, the dust washed off while they had been up surveying the rooms, but even a washing-down had failed to get the cracks between the plates and weavings of the armor; and the armor-robes had gone to a kind of dim patina of dirt and grease.

—"Better we clean up a little," he had said to the company. "Get a little trail dust off."

Which the company had known how to understand. Only Taizu's bandages had escaped washing—and Taizu with her filthy sheepskin coat, her topknot and her bandages was easily the worst, the latter by now stained with food, trail dirt, an appalling amount of old blood

and a small circle of new—Eidi had contributed that
this morning as they were setting out, to make the
wound seem recent, for fear someone might question it
otherwise.

But the looks it drew here gave him second thoughts
—a ghastly wound, a soldier from off a fighting front.
People shied from it and stared for more than fear
of pilferage, and doubtless whispered after they had
passed.

War-jitters here too, the same as on tannery row.
And a *lot* of soldiers on guard by the bridge.

What are we going to do? he imagined Taizu's question. She felt steadier, as if her focus had come back.
There was noise and confusion on all sides as they
walked the quayside. Someone chopped a chicken close
by them and Taizu glanced that way—but any soldier
might. At the next aisle a whore importuned them.
Taizu stared.

"No," Shoka snarled, and the whore yelled out something about boy-lovers as he pulled Taizu past.

A sweetmeat at a booth in mid-market, a cup of wine
in an area that smelled less of the fish and poultry-
sellers. Taizu sipped through her bandages, returned
the cup to the vendor.

Horsemen came through, *not* mercenaries. Banner of
Angen, red circle on black.

Gitu.

Taizu went completely still. Not a twitch. Then she
moved again naturally, put the cup up.

"Through?" A male hand reached for it, four, five
soldiers moving up to the drink-vendor. Shoka drew in
his breath, heart speeding, but Taizu nodded calmly,
and before he could get her out:

"Where you in from?" one asked.

"South," Shoka said, edging in, trying to catch Taizu's
expression past the bandages, with the panic feeling
that she might just, if he got tied down in the first
chance they had had to find out vital information—walk

off down the row and vanish in the crowd. He put his hand on her shoulder, and felt the tension. "Up from Taiyi."

The mercenaries were all attention. "Bad down there?"

"Damn bloody awful." With a shrug. "Lost half the company."

"Buy you a drink," the one said, and threw out half the contents of his cup, put it back, and indicated the edge of the market square, the sit-down wine-shops. Meaning he and his wanted the rumors.

"Lost all our money," he said over a cup of hot wine, too worried to feel the alcohol he had at lunch and after, thank the gods he had *had* the lunch. It was Taizu he was worried about; but if worry burned it out of him, Taizu had enough going in her, he reckoned, to burn off twice her capacity, and she was steady as he could ask—not a tremor in the hand that carried the cup, no gulping down the wine, just measured sips.

"I've been twenty years hereabouts," Shoka said. "Not this recent stuff. I hired on to a lord, personal. I was just a kid, Juni's age, here. Traveled with a caravan, got to Ygotai, I thought I'd seen a city." Not too much confidence too fast. He spilled the bits and pieces he had cobbled together, reason for a mercenary to speak the language and forget his own. "Hell, Lungan in those days—I came up looking for hire, I mean, in those days, there weren't that many places you could get, but I got a post with this old gentleman—just watch his horses. And pretty soon I was in the house guard. Ten years with that old gentleman. Then this. Captain killed, no damn pay— So I get up here, hell, I report what I know. Do I get any damn pay for risking my ass? I should've cut out down to Mandi, get the hell *out*, before this whole damn thing comes down—"

"What's the story down there?"

Shoka took a breath, shook his head. "I know too much."

"Like what?"

"I can't. Can't talk." He put a leg over the bench, gathered up his sword. "Come on, Juni. We'd better get back."

"You're drinking our money, you sit down. What've you heard?"

"It's not heard, man, it's *seen*." He settled back again, leaned confidentially across the table. "That's what they don't want spread. . . . And not a damn *copper* for it!"

Heads leaned forward. Shoka looked around him.

"The whole south's coming up here. Every damn province has come in with the rebels, and they're *moving*, they've gathered up more men than you'd think was *in* the south—I've seen them. I've seen things—" He dropped his voice and looked around, as a waiter passed. "We're sitting in the middle of this damn city—you know who this Saukendar *is?*"

"Warleader. On the outs with the Regent."

"He was damn popular. These aren't happy people. I'm telling you, twenty years in this country, and I know something, I know something scares hell out of me, sitting here in this town. This whole damn country's boiling up around us—that's what I'm feeling, all these damn streets and every window just watching— I was in the riots back in P'eng. . . ."

They shifted on the benches.

"It started over a cart in the street. The people up in P'eng, I saw them kill this poor sod of a regular with pitchforks—"

They were weaving when they walked away. Shoka kept a hand on Taizu's shoulders, but two drunks could hold each other up.

"You did fine," he said, squeezing hard. "You did fine, boy."

"I didn't *do* anything—"

"That was the fine part." A second squeeze of her shoulders. "Good. I'm proud of you."

"I'm *all right*."

"I know you are. We're going back to quarters, try not to get picked up for drunk and disorderly."

"Do we get him tonight?"

"I'll have a look at it after dark."

"We."

"No 'we.' You're too damn easy to spot. I'll handle it, I'll map everything out for you. You'll be along when it's the real thing."

"I don't trust you!"

"What kind of talk is that?"

"You're the best liar I know of."

He was still thinking about that, along the row of booths and along by the back way, among the restaurants, decidedly the best way for two drunken soldiers to slip back into the city streets.

Straight on down the row and around the corner, face to face with a foreign-looking man in a fur-trimmed cap. Whose eyes widened.

"No, you don't!" Shoka grabbed the man and shoved him up against the wall, holding him by a fistful of expensive Shin brocade, thinking about murder, just a dagger in the gut and silence thereafter—no matter he had drunk this man's tea and shared his fire.

Master Yi was evidently thinking about that too. He was shaking, his teeth chattering. "I don't know you," he said, "I swear, I don't know you!"

He was a fool not to kill the man. He knew that. A damned fool with thousands of lives riding on him. But it was an old man, a scared man, who pried weakly at his hands and looked as if he was going to die of shock.

He jerked the trader into the shadow of a wagon, less in the way of witnesses. Master Yi was gasping for air, and it was not even a close grip he had on him.

"Master Yi!" Taizu said, female voice, whisper gone too high.

"I never saw you!" Master Yi protested. "I don't know a thing, I swear, I don't want to know anything—"

"What's my name?" Shoka asked him. "Tell me my *name*, Master Yi!"

A shake of the head, vehement. "I swear, I don't know!"

Someone came near, decided otherwise about going down that particular aisle.

"You know, Master Yi."

"Are we going to kill him?" Taizu asked.

"No, no, no," Master Yi said. "I swear, I swear!"

Shoka fingered the gilt braid and the fur on Master Yi's coat. Master Yi stood absolutely still.

"You know we can't afford to have you spreading lies," Shoka said. "What's my name, Master Yi? I'm sure you followed us. I'm sure you noticed a sudden dearth of bandits. We did you a favor. Now you spread gossip about us."

"I gave you hospitality!"

"That might be worth something. The truth might. You're a trader. I trust you know when the market's changed."

"Yes, m'lord!"

"Who?"

"Whatever you want me to call you, m'lord." A dart of the eyes from him to Taizu and back again. "I'm a subject of his majesty of Shin. I don't involve myself in politics—"

Shoka took a good pinch of expensive fur. "You've heard the rumors. Haven't you? You've heard all the rumors. Let me tell you, foreigners aren't going to fare well here, not at all. You know what's across that bridge?"

A shake of the head, widened eyes.

"An army, Master Yi. —And do you know what's *this* side of the bridge?"

A whisper: "Mercenaries, m'lord."

"Something *else*, Master Yi."

"What, m'lord?"

"The *people*, Master Yi, the people. And my agents, here, there, wherever they need to be, all through the city. You know how dangerous it might be—for any foreigner. On the other hand—a foreigner who proved he was a friend—might find—*imperial* gratitude."

"Please." Sweat rolled down the trader's face. "What do you want?"

"Why don't we go to a quiet place?"

Guards came and went, slow patrol, up and down in front of the walls and the gate. Curved, elegant roofs rose up in tiers, porches lit with lanterns in the dusk. Guards there too.

"It's big as a castle," Taizu whispered.

"Almost," Shoka said, measuring the wall with his eye. And feeling the ache in his leg, that came with a cold night, a lot of riding and walking during the day. For a moment, considering that obstacle and the guards, he despaired. Too high, too far, too well guarded. He pushed Taizu back and retreated into the shadow of the winding lane that offered a view of the Lieng estate, where Master Yi waited in the nook of a much poorer gateway.

"What are you going to do?" Yi whispered. Dragged from the market to mid-city, spying on the Regent's headquarters . . . Master Yi was not a happy man.

Not alone in that state, Shoka thought sourly, and calmed himself with a glance at Taizu. No panic. Just the confidence master Shoka, after all this, was going to come up with something remarkable.

Except master Shoka could not scale a wall any longer.

"What are you going to do?" master Yi reiterated, at a higher pitch.

"Just be calm. I know what we need. Let's go."

"You're going to break in there."

He turned and laid a very gentle hand on master Yi's sleeve. "Master Yi, you *know* what we're going to do. And you know what your choices are. I see no reason, if you're the cause of a disaster to us—not to elaborate your part in this when the authorities ask questions. Do you understand me, master Yi?"

A speechless nod.

"Good. Good. I suppose you've got some friend at the market that has a pushcart he'd let you rent."

It was nothing unusual that rattled up in the alley back of the *Peony* and stopped, a cart with two huge well-capped jars. A man pushing, an assistant panting along beside: nothing particularly remarkable that two tired soldiers came home about the same time as the slops-wagon arrived, in the night. "That's fine," Shoka said to the older of the pair. "You're done." Bad choice of words, perhaps. He patted Yi on the shoulder and picked up the bundle the cart carried besides the jars. "I owe you."

"I just want to get back!" Yi said.

"Taizu."

Steel came out. Yi and his servant looked that direction, flinging up hands that in no wise would protect against a longsword.

"Just walk upstairs, master Yi. You'll be safe—with men of mine. I just don't want a fuss right now. Understand?"

Chun was watching from the stairs. Chun came down, doubtfully, but when he nodded to him, Chun drew his sword and came on down to the alley. "Captain?"

"Just an old friend I want you to keep track of for a few hours. Give him a little wine, a little dinner. He's had quite a walk. His man here's a pleasant enough fellow. But I'd see he stayed seated. I promised the innkeep we wouldn't be brawling."

Upstairs. Downstairs again with a long bundle this time, two rag-wrapped slop-men, who shoved the bundle onto the cart beside the jars and set off again.

No rule against a couple of soldiers going about with a bow, maybe, counting that everyone was going about in full kit and rattling with swords, but in a city this anxious, in the Regent's neighborhood, it was a weapon that could get a second, calculating stare.

Slop-men never did. "It's something no one wants to notice," Shoka had said. "They come and they go. *Especially* to the big houses. At night, so the master never has to notice at all."

"No worse than pigs," Taizu had said. "I've shoveled a lot of it."

Rumble and rattle across cobbles, half the width of Lungan. "Damn potholes," Shoka said, as the cart bucked and jolted against his hands. Numb to the wrist as they turned up the street next that of the Lieng mansion, his leg aching. They were in full kit under the rags, Taizu without her bandages, with her face muffled up with a cap and a dirty brown scarf against an edge of river chill in the night, Shoka with a thick scarf and ragged layers of robes—perfectly comfortable if one were not wearing two stone of armor under it and pushing a damn rickety cart loaded with two jars that made it impossible to see the rough spots ahead. Sweat poured on Shoka's face. "I can't say much for the Regent's streets, either."

"Could be mud and raining," Taizu said cheerfully— who had walked free as a lark all the way, and doing a great deal better now that the streets were clear of day-traffic. They met the occasional night patrol, the occasional other service-cart, the occasional drunk; and a scattering of others with midnight business, mostly in groups.

But this street was conspicuously patrolled, conspicuously vacant of traffic, and lit with lanterns, a long, lonely way up to the lane they had spied out as the servants' access.

There were soldiers at the turn. *Don't notice anyone,*

Shoka said. *If you want to go invisible, it's a two-sided thing. Invisible people don't look at anyone when anyone's watching: that way no one looks at them.*

So he kept his eyes on his cart, kept himself in a quiet little fog, the way he had told Taizu: *There's a time to see everything. There's a time to see nothing. No one will attack us without warning. Who'd do a thing like that, to some poor slop-men? We're too humble and too dull for soldiers to challenge, don't even be expecting it until we get to the scullery gate.*

No challenge from the sentries at the corner. He took a look around the jars and aimed the cart down the middle of the lane, with the wheels rumbling and chattering.

Right up to the gate.

"Evenin', sir," Shoka said. Three guards, one leaving the curb to look them over.

"You aren't the ordinary," the guard said.

"Bashed his foot," Shoka said. "He asked me swing over from my regulars an' take care o' his."

The guard grunted and opened up the gate. "You wait. Man brings it out."

Damn. "I don't mind, sir, we can fetch it."

"Ain't the rule." The one guard turned his back. And went sailing into the wall. The second and third closed in, drawing swords. Shoka dodged one, whirled past and took one with a knee and an elbow, bending him over, passing him to Taizu, as he spun again and knocked the third guard flying into the cart.

The first man let out a yell. Shoka kicked him, grabbed his sword from the bundle off the cart and Taizu grabbed her bow and quiver.

Into the scullery-court, then, fast as they could scuttle, and up a stairway to a garden terrace.

"I'm *sorry* about that!" Taizu whispered as she crouched down beside him in the shadow of a potted pine and nocked an arrow.

"Damn, I've gotten soft! Stay here!"

He sprinted along the terrace, across the shadow-bars of the pines and the lantern-light of the porch above. The hue and cry was spreading. Shouts racketed off the walls and lost direction in the porches.

He knew Ghita. Nothing but the best. Center of the mansion, second or third level, in regal quiet and elegant splendor.

Damn mistake not to have knifed the poor sods out by the gate. It would have gained a little—not much, but a little.

Up a wooden stairs as lanterns flared above. He ducked low, dived off the stairs into a clump of juniper as guards came thundering down the walk, headed for the scullery gate.

No question whether Ghita was awake by now.

And one good thing about the guards: they made so much thumping on the wooden porches he could run full out. He scrambled up onto the stairs, up onto that porch and right through a fragile window-screen, crash! right into the second-level hall.

Guards ran to stop him. They spread themselves out. That was a mistake. One-two, three, four, and five—an arc of blood spattered across a fresco of mist and mountains. He ran the hall, shoved open the doors at the end.

More guards in a lighted hallway, a startled cluster of screaming women who had no time to scatter. He took one guard and the other, that second man down with a crippling wound, howling—

A man in front of him. A face like a mask of terror; brocade robes, trailing hair. Not Ghita. He *knew* the man, memory said, and a heartbeat later knew the boy inside the soft, plump face.

The Emperor himself. Beijun.

"Shoka!" the Emperor breathed, under the clatter of arriving guards.

From the hall behind. A good score of them.

"Shoka, help me!"

He froze, sword lifted, guards behind, in a dead-end room.

And whirled and charged on the last instant, cut his way left and right and never looked to see what he hit, only where he was going. The leg burned as he ran, tore, gods knew what.

He ran, grabbed a corner, swung onto a stairway and took it with desperate abandon.

A matching screen. He hit it with his shoulder, rolled off the sill with his hip and somersaulted onto the wooden porch—

No fear of burglars, had lord Lieng.

Right off the porch onto the junipers, thank gods for the armor. He clawed his way to the low wooden fence, swung his leg over, and pelted along the terrace with the shouts of guards in his ears and of a sudden the sharp whisper of arrows passing him.

She was there, she was waiting for him in the shadow of the wall, and guards were dying behind him.

"Shed it!" he hissed as he reached her post. He stripped the rags off, pulled a bamboo pin off an armor strap and furiously grabbed up his topknot and pinned it. She threw down her bow then, dumped the quiver, the rags and the hat, and scuttled down the stairs with him, down to the scullery court.

Soldiers came in the open gate. "Up there!" Shoka yelled at them, pointing with his sword. "*Move*, dammit, they're up there! —You and you, get that gate!"

The soldiers poured past them. The designates turned to close the gate.

And died quietly.

"Damn," Shoka said, and walked over the body that blocked the doorway, out onto the sidewalk by the cart. There was one man moving faintly, of the injured. One was gone. One lay still.

They walked down the lane to the corner, where a sentry stood.

"One got out!" Shoka said hoarsely.

"Haven't seen a thing!" the sentry said.

Shoka pointed with his sword, uphill, beyond the lights. "We'll check up this way!"

It was just that easy to walk away, into the alley, sheathe the swords, and vanish into the maze of Lungan streets.

But he had to tell Taizu then: "I didn't get him. I couldn't get that far. —I ran into the Emperor."

"Here!"

Soft, terrified face. *Shoka, help me!*

When his arm had trembled on the verge of murder. *Help me!*

Gods, that he had the gall!

Chapter Twenty

"Chun?" Shoka asked, arriving with Taizu at that door in the *Peony's* upstairs hall.

"Captain," came from the other side, muffled, and a bar lifted and thumped. Chun opened the door. The men were on their feet, anxious: so was master Yi and his man, but Jian whipped out a sword and master Yi and his man sat right back down again.

Chun shut the door.

Shoka folded his arms, leaned against the wall and stared at master Yi, stared at him grimly, a long, long, considerate moment, while the men asked him questions he made no attempt to answer.

"I'm sure you understand," he said when the questions had died away into deathly silence, "master Yi, —we're talking about life and death here. I'm sure you know—I've gone to a great deal of inconvenience to keep you safe. Another man might just have cut your throats. *Do* you understand, master Yi?"

"Yes, m'lord," Yi stammered.

"You can go."

341

"Please—"

"Don't *worry*, master Yi. You or your man. Unless somehow the Regent's men can trace that cart or the jars. I'm afraid it's in an inconvenient place right now. We'll have to depend on you to cover it with your friend. *I'd* tell him someone stole it. I don't think he'll want to know more than that. I don't think you do."

"No, m'lord." A whisper, in a room where a whisper was audible.

"I wouldn't let them trace it, master Yi. You're a wise man. You know how the police are. It doesn't matter whether you're in with us or not. You procured the incriminating cart. Your friend knows you did. I suggest you tell *him* how dangerous it would be to file a theft report—because I'd hate to see you arrested, a foreigner, being asked questions you can't answer. Ignorance is much the safer course—because we'll be watching you, master Yi. You can depend on that. You see we've kept you alive. We will. *We* remember favors. They don't. Think about that, master Yi."

"I will. I will, m'lord."

"Make your friend believe it, master Yi. Tell him how dangerous it is. Tell him what he can be involved in. You have time, if you leave now. And I trust you can guarantee your man's silence."

"Yes, my lord!"

"Go *on*, master Yi."

Master Yi hesitated a moment to look at the men around him. Then he got up and his man did, and Shoka stepped aside from the door. Chun opened it and master Yi bowed his way out, rapidly, herding his man with him.

"We missed him," Shoka said after the door was closed. "We had to get out. But we found the Emperor."

Faces showed their shock.

"Here and in secret," Shoka said. "We met. He said, Help me. And by that time the guards were coming. I couldn't stay to ask him against what, or whom. My guess is, Ghita's worried about what he'll do, left in the

capital—worried, maybe, that he might take power into
his own hands. I don't know. Right now we've got to
get moving."

"Yes, m'lord."

Shoka looked at Chun.

"Captain," Chun amended.

"Let's get out of here," Shoka said. "Are we set?"

"Two streets north, captain," Eidi said. "Place called
the *Felicity*."

A sharp lot, Reidi's men. A word passed while they
were changing clothes and putting master Yi under
guard, and everything had shifted, money had passed,
Eidi had kited off quietly and arranged them another
bolthole while they kept this one paid for as well. The
Peony's owner did no bed-check on his tenants; and in
this neighborhood, it was not likely he would dare
double-rent the place or bother the horses, not dealing
with clients of their sort.

"By twos and threes," Shoka said. "Down the alley.
Just what you have to have. Afraid we can't take the
mats, just the blankets. We don't want to be that
conspicuous."

Heat landed on Shoka's back: he clenched his teeth
and tensed his arms, face down on the floor, while
Taizu fished rags out of the pot and applied them with,
he was sure, a certain satisfaction for what he was
suffering.

Thank gods the escape had been downhill.

Another rag. Breath hissed between his teeth.

"Hurt?" she asked.

"No."

"Sorry. That was the bottom of the pot."

They had the room with the small stove and the
cooking-pot, the *Felicity*'s one elegance. Chun and the
lads had the other, a little crowded: not bad, captain,
Chun had said.

If the landlord knew how the rooms split up, it
needed no guesses what he thought.

"You've got a bad bruise back here," Taizu said.

"Lucky it's not worse than that." He knew the one she was talking about. "Damn bushes."

"What are we going to do?"

He started to draw a deep breath. It hurt too much. "Reconnoiter. Again. We moved. We'll need to know what Ghita's doing. I don't know what the Emperor's situation is, but you sure as hell don't bring your Emperor to a battlefield. He's *changed*. He's not well. . . ."

"You *can't* feel sorry for him!"

Another breath. Nothing made sense. *I tried to teach him. I don't know if I could have done better. Maybe if I'd had more patience. . . .*

Innocent people died for him. More will die, because of him. Damn, why did I stop? Why in the gods' name did I stop?

He saw Beijun's face, white, swollen, terrified—but not of him. Not of him, despite the sword. As if he saw him as a rescuer.

Taizu touched his back, rested her hand on his shoulder. He opened his eyes to be rid of Beijun's face, looked straight ahead at the brown boards, the dingy yellow brick of the wall, the post that held the roof off their heads.

"Ghita!" Taizu hissed. "That's what you said!"

"Damn right." He propped his chin on his fist. "The question is how much to tell around town—about the Emperor being here. There's a chance they'll kill him tonight."

"And blame you."

"If Ghita knows it was me, he'd be damn tempted. And once the word gets out I'm here—there's some danger. There are a few people in this town who've seen me up close. Ghita's surely not going to be surprised at anything I do, but I'll bet he's asking the Emperor some real close questions tonight. Real close."

"Like—the Emperor was in on it, with Reidi?"

"With Reidi and with me."

A silence. Then, quietly: "Damn."

He twisted around to see her face, saw the frown. "Damn what?"

"Damn Ghita and Gitu and the Emperor and everybody with them! They kill people and burn their houses and they get away with it, and you can feel sorry for them!"

"I've had two students. One was you."

"The other was the Emperor?"

"He thought I came to help him." *Like he'd been waiting all these damn years. Like Meiya at the window, believing I'd come.*

What did the young fool get himself into?

Did he run to Ghita?

Quiet morning. Very quiet—the way the conversation at the tables in the *Felicity's* common room fell away when mercenary soldiers came downstairs, the way soldiers gathered in knots on the street—talking together.

"What in hell's going on?" Shoka asked, of the small group a few doors down from the *Felicity*. Alone. Taizu was back in the room, a matter of no little argument, but things were getting close, he had reasoned, she had a fresh new bandage (a discreet, almost-healed kind of bloodstain he had contributed) and she was too brightly conspicuous for a morning when people were asking questions—like this one.

Which got raised eyebrows and an estimating look, before a Fittha said, in a low voice, "They broke in at headquarters last night."

"Rebels?"

The mercenary spat to the side. "Twenty dead. They're saying the Regent was asleep upstairs. Slept right through it."

The hell. Shoka put on a bewildered face. "How'd they get in?"

"Service gate."

"Had to have help," another man said.

"Shit," Shoka said, and walked off shaking his head.

To another group, outside the *Peony*, he said, gruffly, his best officer-voice: "Any of you heard anything about the Regent?"

"What?" an officer asked, regarding him cautiously.

Shoka nodded toward the side of the building, drew the officer that way. "One of my men picked up a rumor the Regent's dead. They say they're hiding it. They're afraid there'll be a riot."

"*Who* said?"

Shoka scratched under his stubbled chin. "Oghin. Over on Flower Street. *You* ain't picked up on it?"

"No."

"Hell. Just checking it out. Men're asking *me*. They're saying the rebels got somebody on-staff. Maybe real high up. That the whole thing was inside."

"Shit."

"Yeah. What *have* you heard?"

"Just it was up from the kitchens, got the gate open, got maybe twenty, thirty of 'em inside. But they're saying they ain't got that number of bodies. Ever' one of them was on staff."

"Hell. And how many of 'em *still* on staff, walking around searching for the assassins?"

"Ain't us. My money's on the Guard."

"Hell. We got out of Taiyi, cut to pieces. I got half my company dead. Sent us up here, said the line was here. I ain't seen a line, and the HQ can't even hold its own wall, what kind of shit is that?"

The Fittha scratched and held onto one of his amulets. "They pay."

"Yeah," Shoka said. "So far. I'm hoping he's alive. What've we got, if he ain't?"

The Fittha's face shadowed.

"Why in hell ain't they said?" Shoka asked. "That's what makes me nervous. You don't know what these damn pig-lovers are going to do. They better put out some patrols. . . ."

And collaring a yellow-robed monk in an alley near

the bakers' street: "You! You know an old man, a scoundrel named Jojin?"

There was dismay on the monk's face. "No." It was outright shock for a moment, amid the natural panic at being held by the throat against a wall.

"Tell him, if you see him—in Celestial Light monastery, if he's where he was—that the boy who took the plums is sorry, and he's in town. *Remember that!*"

"I'll remember it." The monk was about fifty, old enough to be a religious monk, not the sort who got their divine enlightenment around soldier-age. And he was curious enough to stare Shoka in the eyes.

"Do that," Shoka said.

Not hard at all to find a whole caravan in the market—in a town no one could freely leave. A lot of people in the market, not much buying but a great deal of talking in small groups, with a quick and anxious glance and a silence when a soldier walked by, or when a soldier came and fingered expensive things on a wagon's let-down counter.

Easy to get a merchant's attention then, in the little knot of men close by.

Easier yet when the merchant recognized him.

"This yours?"

The merchant came over fast.

"Where's Yi?"

The man did not want to answer that. Plainly.

"You'd better find him," Shoka said. "I don't care what he's told you. You'd better get him. Tell him his friend's here."

The man left in a hurry. Shoka browsed, picked up a trinket for Taizu. And walked back alongside the wagons, watching where the man went, up the steps into the centermost of that little cluster.

So he followed, up the steps, into the dim inside, where two frightened merchants stared at him.

"Hello," he said, folded his arms and leaned his shoulder against the wall.

"Get out of here!" master Yi said. Not to him. To his

associate; and that man darted for the open door and
outside.

Shoka walked over to the alcove at the front of the
tiny wagon where Yi sat on his pillows, and carefully
squatted down with elbows on knees—the sword at his
back hindered further courtesies. So did the bruise on
his backside.

"How are you doing this morning?"

Yi stared at him.

"I just thought I'd check," Shoka said. "Don't be
anxious. I trust you got everything taken care of. How's
your friend?"

"Scared!" master Yi said testily.

"Everything's fine, then," Shoka said, and picked a
sweetmeat off the low table. "Mmmn. Don't worry. But
the real reason I came: I'd advise you just have a
bolthole in mind. Just rent a place somewhere in town,
get some of the nicer pieces out of the wagons. . . ."

Yi looked anxious. Abruptly he cleared his throat and
rubbed his hands together. "Considerate, m'lord."

"I told you. I return favors." He picked another
sweetmeat from the bowl. "Mmmn. So you knew me
when we met on the road. I *don't* suppose the village
talked about me."

"I knew when we'd gotten to Ygotai, when we talked
about the bandits—all of them dead—"

"Quite a night, that was. So you spread rumors about
us all the way."

"No, m'lord! We weren't the only caravan. Rumors
were everywhere."

Pigeons, Shoka thought. And said: "Just call me captain. —What rumors?"

"That you'd come back, m'lord. I knew—then—who
we'd met. But by then we'd gone too far, we couldn't
come south again—we were afraid what we'd meet
going back, so we kept going. We hoped Lungan was
safe."

"Wrong about that. And I don't suppose they'll let
you go down to Anogi."

Yi shook his head. "We're trapped here. Myself not the only one. They've confiscated our horses, they give me a paper they swear will make it good—but we can't move these wagons without our horses."

"Terrible mess."

"I want to see my wives, m'lord, *all* of them, that's all we think about now, just how we're going to get out of here and home again, damn this trip! I don't want to be involved any further! Don't ask me anything!"

"Captain."

"Captain, m'—" Yi choked it off. "*Please* don't ask me anything."

"Just pass the word among your men: tell them what I've told you. We're here in force. You can tell that to anyone else you think is reliable. The fighting's coming in the next few days. And you'd be wisest to get to the west end of the waterside and stay there when it starts. Don't worry about the outcome. *We* have help."

"Yes, m'— Captain."

"Word is back from the north," Shoka said lazily, taking another sweetmeat, "the army is coming home. On *our* side. You can pass that word too. It's just as well people know it. And just as well the mercenaries hear it the same as the people do. You understand." He picked out another couple of sweetmeats. "Have you a paper? My wife would love these. You don't mind, do you?"

"No. —No, of course not." Yi snatched up a cloth napkin and gave it to him, frowning. "Have all you like."

"She's delighted with such little things." Shoka dumped the bowl into the napkin, looked up into Yi's eyes and saw the cold fear. "Really. You'd think otherwise. I know I wasn't sure what—well, I wasn't sure I could keep her, you know, *satisfied.*" He cleared his throat and wrapped up the candies, devoting his attention to that. "Came up to me at dusk, she did. Gods! Damn near killed me. Seems she'd been watching me, in the mountains. Seems she had this personal grudge with

Gitu of Angen, and I was the way she picked to get here."

Master Yi's eyes were absolutely round, his under lip caught in his teeth.

"I wasn't sure," Shoka said, "I'd survive the honor. But she's a damn good wife in a lot of ways. Cheerful. Stubborn as hell, terrible temper—but *damn* good in bed. You could guess."

Master Yi plainly did.

"There's a certain—difference making love with her. Especially in thunderstorms." Shoka gave a twitch of his shoulders. "But she's a good ally in a thing like this. Damn good. And I wouldn't be in Gitu's place right now. Would you?"

"No," master Yi breathed.

"Limb from limb," Shoka said. "You don't cross her kind."

"What did he do to—?"

Shoka shrugged. "Had to do with some pigs."

"P—"

Shoka lifted a brow. "She's rural, you know. I've got a bargain with her. She helps out on this and she and I—you know. I think she's halfway in love with me. And I don't mind. She's damn good in bed and I've gotten used to her—little peculiarities."

Master Yi stared.

"Ah, well," Shoka said. "I explain that because you've met her, and you know—certain facts. I *wouldn't* be standing in her way—when things break loose. In case you should be in that position."

"No," master Yi said. "*No,* m'lord."

"You spread that word, master Yi. She's damn hard to control. Sometimes she doesn't understand where to stop. That's why only our enemies should be in the streets. They may see things—you understand."

"*Yes,* m'lord."

"Shutters barred. That's safest. Just stay inside and don't look outside." He tucked the napkin into his belts. "She *will* like this. I'll tell her who it's from."

* * *

"A walk around the block!" Taizu cried, with Chun and the others in the *Felicity*'s upper hall. "My gods, where have you *been?*"

So much for Taizu's reserve in front of the men, who, with mutiny begun, gave him dour, worried looks.

"I told you not to worry." He dropped the napkin into Taizu's hand. "Have a sweet."

"You said—"

"Wife, —"

Taizu glared above the bandages, opened the napkin and popped a sweetmeat into her mouth, possibly to restrain herself, as Chun opened the door to the room the men shared.

"Settle," he said. "I'll tell you what I've learned."

The men and Taizu sat. The napkinful of sweetmeats went the round, man to man. And by afternoon, in the *Felicity*'s commonroom, Jian, lounging there in ordinary clothes, had picked up a collection of rumors.

One, Ghita had been killed by, variously, shapeshifting demons who had slaughtered from ten to fifty of the Guard; or by twenty to thirty assassins led by or ordered by Saukendar; or by a conspiracy among the Imperial Guard officers, who were, variously, dead, in hiding, secretly in power, secretly negotiating with the rebel lords southward—who were, variously, ten to a hundred leagues south of the river, allied with, variously, one to fifty demons, the bandits of Hoisan, assorted mercenaries, and one to three dragons which were variously, the soul of the Old Emperor, the guardians of the Hoi and the Chaighin and the Hisei, or a mountain dragon which had been stirred up by the demons Saukendar had been consorting with for ten years.

Two, Ghita was alive and Saukendar had been killed in the attack, or had escaped, or was presently on his way to the capital, or had been captured and was presently held prisoner by the Regent, or was loose in the city with from twenty to two hundred rebels and a number of shapeshifting demons.

Three, some priests had declared the dragon auspicious for the Regent; but certain others had been heard to say it was an omen of calamity.

Four, the whole rebel army had crossed the bridge disguised as mercenaries and peasants and tradesmen, and was waiting some signal, when it would launch an attack on the camp and on the headquarters.

"One could wish," Shoka said, chin on fist, listening to the report from downstairs. "But not likely. I had a look. They're damn careful who passes."

"I could," Taizu said, lifting a brow, more cheerful, having glowered through the reports about demons and dragons. He knew how she would do it, by that look, remembering the basket. Probably the men had more fantastical notions.

"We'll manage without that," he said. "We'll know when we need to." They were careful naming names and details even here, in guarded privacy—because bad habits, he had told the men, otherwise encouraged deadly slips in public. "I'm going up to the bridge tonight."

"Us," Taizu said.

"You're too damned obvious."

Taizu held a lock of hair across her upper lip. He scowled at her.

"A boy can't grow a mustache like that."

She dropped the hair. "Basket," she said.

"The hell."

"Well, I'm not staying here!"

She had gotten all too easy with the men. She sat now sulking, he could tell it past the bandages, the all too conspicuous bandages.

"You're too easy to describe, wife. You want to see all of our heads on Lungan gate?"

She said nothing. She just looked at him. And then he worried, seeing her trekking right along the street behind him.

"We'll think of something," he said. In fact the thought of her across town and alone worried him—Taizu with her fear of cities, her inexperience in such simple things as walking through traffic.

None of which would stop her once she made her mind up. Nothing ever had.

"Someone's in the hall," Jian said. A board had creaked on the stairs, and there were quick footsteps.

"Eidi," Chun said as Jian sprang up to get the door: Eidi was the one of them on watch.

A thump at the door, a low voice: Jian unlatched the door and let Eidi in.

"Captain," Eidi panted, with a bow. "They're saying the Regent's going to give a speech, in the camp, to prove he's alive. That everybody's supposed to report in. That we're—that the *rebels* are in sight the other side of the river. That the Emperor's come in and he's going to be in the camp with the Regent."

That last was the bit that surprised him—that Beijun was alive. That the Regent made the move he did—

"Ghita's making his move," he muttered, and rubbed his neck, under a greasy fall of hair. "And our friends could be here a day early; or scouts could've spotted their camp; or engaged them; or Ghita knows damn well where they are and he's hoping to get *us* to move on a fake report and commit ourselves too early."

Worried looks surrounded him. "What do we do?" Taizu asked.

"I'm thinking," he said. He was, desperately—sat there with arms on knees, staring at the age-grayed boards of the floor, and figuring how to establish reliable contact with Reidi.

Dry, age-grayed boards.

"It's our turn," he said smugly—he could not help it. Things had gone amazingly well, considering he had improvised continually. *And* gotten the targets out into the open.

Maybe, he thought, considering it was Chiyaden at stake, the complacent gods were waking up.

Or maybe a certain old monk was praying them out of bed.

In his younger, more pious days he would have worried about a thought like that.

It looked like a parade, the general flow of soldiers toward the camp this late afternoon, all carrying their gear and their bedrolls; groups on foot and groups on horseback—but for a parade, Shoka thought, it had a scarcity of cheering onlookers. What citizens were on the streets or looked on from windows or shopfronts, just stared glumly at the forces that were, ostensibly, their own.

They had the remaining bow—Chun carried it and the quiver wrapped in the sole sleeping mat that had covered it on the way from the *Peony* to the *Felicity*.

Only blankets otherwise: everything else was still at the *Peony*. They were a poor-looking company that trekked up the street in the tail of the afternoon.

A gong crashed in the distance. All up and down the street soldiers looked up from their conversations and their preoccupations, and the heads of townsfolk turned, everything in the city attentive to that one sound.

"Must be Ghita," Shoka said, and after a moment more of walking: "Bringing the Emperor into camp. Where assassins can get at him. Or *we* can. It's a trap. Both ways it's a trap—to draw us out early and to draw us into Ghita's reach."

A few more paces.

"So what will we do?" Taizu asked.

The summons to the camp. The Emperor for bait.

Hell.

Chapter Twenty-one

A narrow lane cut in on the street near the market, like any of a score such alleys, except its clutter of refuse and broken shutters. It went in the general direction of the camp and some of the drift of soldiers toward the summons might take that darker, winding shortcut behind the riverfront buildings. Shoka took a glance back down the street, saw that a few bands still followed them, but the traffic was thinning.

So they took that way. And there was no one behind them yet to notice, he made sure of that, when they took a lane back north again, a twisting gut of a street that cut further south, in the long run, just about the time it got to the vicinity of the camp.

The men were doubtless impressed. Himself, he only knew the lay of the town, a memory of maps—years ago—that the streets here tended to a diagonal, that the Old Emperor in his youth had seized a row of warehouses fronting the harbor and bricked up its windows and its harborside doors, as cheaper than building a thirty-foot wall.

And any street in this quarter that did not go through,
ran up against that barrier, the northern wall of the
square riverside enclosure that was the market in peacetime and the gate-garrison in anxious times, and that
wall was the sealed face of old warehouses and brothels.

But the tenants had moved back in again—at least
the warehouses. The brothels and the taverns sought
more trafficked places. The city's poor nestled in the
decay of the neighborhood's whorehouses.

"There's the wall," Shoka said, nodding up toward
the thirty-foot face of buff stone that sealed off the end
of the street between two leaning ramshackle apartments, past a tangle of hanging laundry and illicit built-
ons before it became again the back wall of those
buildings.

As the hammer of drums and the sound of trumpets
announced an imperial arrival on the other side, and
the poor folk on this side looked with fright at a motley
group of soldiers where no soldiers would tend to come,
and scuttled out to grab children and get doors and
shutters between themselves and trouble.

"Get that door," Shoka said, as a girl, baby in arms,
ran for a door a woman held. Chun and Wengadi vaulted
the porch railing and bashed the door out of the woman's hands as Shoka came up the steps.

"Please," he said, in the northern accent, and bowed
with utmost politeness to the terrified woman. "We're
after the loan of your upstairs. Please."

Eyes widened. The terror was still there. But there
was a different look to it.

"Ye're with Saukendar. . . ." As if that was no bad
thing.

"Here." Taizu closed her fist around a gold amulet
she wore, part of the mercenary's gaud, and took it off
over her head. "Get! You can get killed around us! Go!
Get clear! Get everyone out of here!"

"Come on, dammit!" Shoka followed Chun and
Wengadi up the narrow stairs, past wobbly balconies,
past graffiti'ed erotic frescoes, and up and up to the

topmost level, where a weak door gave on a dark little hole, someone's apartment, a stinking lot of clutter, a low ceiling with birds nesting in the rafters and a scant light coming through the roof tiles.

Damn mess. Some dirt poor grandmother made party to what could get her killed, if the soldiers came searching.

Reidi, for gods' sakes, look alive over there!

"Up," he said, and Jian and Wengadi scrambled to grab a plank that had served as a table, and braced it against the brickwork and climbed up to knock roof-tiles aside, letting a blinding light in from overhead.

Jian and Wengadi swung down from the low rafters. Then came the anxious part. "I'll do it!" Taizu said. "I don't weigh so much!"

"You don't know what you're aiming at," Shoka said. He slipped his sword, his kit and his blanket roll off, tossed the encumbrance out of the way, and with a deep breath and a rush, ran the slanted board to grab hold of the dusty rafters. From there he edged over to climb higher on the beams, and put his head out into the fading daylight, chest-level with the tiled roof.

"Those tiles are old!" Chun's voice came up to him. "Be careful!"

But he was looking out beyond the immediate prospect of the untidy camp spread out at the foot of the wall this roof sheltered—was looking beyond the camp's further, riverside wall, across the Hisei, where the bridge was, the distance-dimmed hills where Reidi ought to be . . . if Reidi was there at all.

And closer then, thirty feet below him, too close, with only head and shoulders above the tiles, to see the gate that let out near the bridge, or the tents up against the foot of the wall, but the further ones spread, between their mandated aisles for movement of troops and horses, in a tangle of overlapping guy-ropes and tent-edges, no neat, precise rows, but a motley city in canvas and goat-hide and whatever material and shape the mercenaries had brought with them or plundered.

Pirates and brigands, ensconced where the precise, pale tents of Imperial troops had been, for Imperial visitations; or more often, the stripes and bright colors of Lungan market, in the Empire's better, more tranquil years—a safe, enclosed bazaar where a few police and strong gates could mean an honest trade and a scarcity of cutpurses and thieves.

There was the muster of troops—a dark gathering around bright torches, lanterns, lit against the gathering night; banners; and the rostrum which Ghita would use. The procession had already passed. There were figures on the podium, small and glittering with gold.

He levered himself up gingerly, trusting his weight to old tiles and old wood.

"Damn fine view."

"Here!" Chun said from below. His bow came up, strung for him. He worked around to get his knee under him. Tile grated and slipped under his hip. He flattened and the slippage stopped.

"Captain?"

"Shut up! I'm all right." In a shaky voice, mindful of a thirty-foot drop and an enemy camp below. He eased up again, listened for the grating of tiles and carefully settled his weight on one knee, then drew a whole breath and leaned to take the two arrows that Chun passed up to him.

On his knees he could see the tents and the aisle below as well as the further quarters of the camp. Long shot. A fair amount of wind coming almost squarely at his back, a little off to his left shoulder. He took a good brace with his foot and his knee, then drew the bow, calculated his shot and arced it high into the camp. Ranging shot. He saw it drop nearly to the far wall, with wind and starting-height to help it. He did not need the second arrow.

"Come *on!*" he hissed at the dark opening beside him. As light flared, and a third arrow came up to him, this one with a blazing wrap about the point. Well-soaked: it fluttered and spat in the wind as he took it up and drew for a shot high and wide. Heavier point. It would drop more quickly. A trace of fire flew across the dusk, dimmer than the torches.

"Here!" Chun said.

Another arrow, and another, into the tents. As the first one blossomed into fire. In a too-tight jumble of canvas. In a good northerly breeze that would sweep fire to the far walls, and carry burning wisps of canvas swirling in the air, inside four high walls with a far distance between fires and the two water-wells.

He saw the troops scatter from the gathering, he heard the thin voices shout orders as smoke rolled up, lit from spreading fire. He kept shooting as long as arrows came up, trails of fire across the sky, till Chun clambered up to put his head through the opening and survey the spreading fire that glared off walls and off the smoke, soldiers running to save what they could of gear and personal belongings. They were mercenaries. Everything they owned was in those tents. But there were eight, nine points of fire in the camp, and two of them bracketed the gate. Horses screamed in panic. Riders fought to get them to the gate. He picked up an ordinary arrow and fired into a mass of running men below him.

"Get *down*, m'lord!" Chun pleaded with him.

About time, he thought. He moved to do that, and the tiles slipped, a grating slide toward the edge.

But a hand grabbed him as he slid, and hauled him down through the opening in a shower of tiles, onto a collapsing cushion of hands and bodies.

"Dammit!" Taizu yelled.

"We got him, we got him," Chun gasped, and Shoka fought his way to his knees amid the tangle, realized part of the difficulty was the bow he was still holding on to. He let it go, grabbed for a post and hauled his way to his feet. "I'm all right," he said. "Let's get out of here—" —as he grabbed his sword and his kit from under bits of tile. He reached again to get the bow, but Taizu grabbed it up, unstrung it, and wrapped that and the quiver in the mat that had concealed it, while Wengadi gathered up the firepot and the rest of the evidence.

Down the stairs, past doors still shut; and out into the street again, down another lane.

And across the main thoroughfare, where people gathered in bewilderment, under a sky lit with fire and smoke.

People spotted them and scattered, fast.

But a rock hit Jian's shoulder.

"Damn!" Jian yelled.

"Down with the Regent!" someone shouted.

"Come on!" Shoka said as Chun started to turn around. "Get *out* of here!" He grabbed Chun and ran, as stones flew out of the dusk and rattled on the pavings around them.

Horsemen plunged around the corner ahead of them, soldiers coming pell mell from the riverside and the camp—

—looking for the source of the tiles and the fire, Shoka reckoned, and finding rebellion in full flower.

The street was suddenly empty back there except for rocks and bricks, the soldiers scattered in pursuit of rebels.

"We can't help them!" Shoka said. "They're on their own! Come on! Back to the *Peony*, get the horses!"

"Captain," the innkeeper panted, following them down into the stableyard. "I kept 'em f' you, ain't nothin' missin'—"

"Good," Shoka threw back over his shoulder. "Then you're safe. *Get back inside*, master innkeeper!"

"What's happenin'? What's happenin', what's burnin' uptown? Is there fightin'?"

"There will be, just lock your doors and stay out of it, man!"

Chun was hauling the tack out of the owner's kitchenshed, and Waichen and Liang were already saddling, throwing blankets on horses stable-bound too long, stiff and fretful.

"I been friendly to the army!"

"Just shut *up*, innkeeper!" Shoka grabbed his own tack out of Chun's hands and turned and glared up. "Better start figuring out what side you belong to! They're crossing the bridge!"

The innkeeper shut up. The door banged. Shoka hauled the gear up to his horse and saddled with economy, no haste, no nonsense either. Taizu's horse had the stall next.

"You keep to our center," he said. "Taizu, hear me? Don't get reckless."

"I've done all right," the faint, feminine voice came back to him. "Haven't I?"

"We got a damn bunch of —" —rabble, he almost said. Old ways, old thinking. "—bunch of fools can't tell sides out there, for gods' sakes, just stay close. We're going across that bridge, we're going the smart way, we don't need any damn heroics."

His hands were sweating on the girth. He had the shin-guards on and the gauntlets and the helmet with him, they had picked that cumbersome gear up in the room upstairs, along with their other two bows and the several quivers. The owner of the *Peony* had that to his credit at least—no pilferage: an anxious man, a worried man—

Damn, he has a right to be, who am I to blame him?

He backed the horse out, climbed up into the saddle and walked it circles while Taizu and Wengadi and Nui got their horses saddled. "Be careful out there," he told the men. "Citizens don't know who the hell we are. Remember that. We just get out of here, cross the bridge if we can, or if you get cut off, dismount, lie low till it's over; if *that* doesn't look good, remember the east gate and run like hell. We've done our part. Just get out alive. Hear?"

Chun got up to the saddle. Taizu did, and Nui, while Wengadi led his over to the gate and opened it.

The smell of smoke was on the wind. The *Peony's* lanterns overwhelmed any glow of fire from the south.

Wengadi held the gate for the last of them and they pulled up to wait on the street while Wengadi mounted up, leaving the *Peony*'s gate to bang against the post.

Black figures showed in the lantern-light up and down tannery row, small groups who did not stay to the walks, but who gave a group of horsemen an uncomfortably apparent attention.

"Let's get out of here," Shoka said, and sent his horse off for the corner and up the cobbled street, which was deserted beneath the light of infrequent lanterns and a ruddy sky. Dark buildings, shutters open to the night and not a light showing above. Just the lanterns that made anyone on the streets a target, and, south of tannery row, torn-up cobbles and a body lying on the pavement.

He put the group to all the speed he dared on the uneven ground. The racket of shod hooves came back at them from the walls on either side, drowning thin shouts from the distance. More horsemen came their way and cut off ahead of them, down a side-street.

Patrols. Flying squads. Deserters or looters. Gods knew. He took the chance for a look back to make sure of his own group. They were riding close, all of them, keeping with him, not down the middle of the street, but over to the side, where they at least had occasional shadow and where they made a less convenient target for half the street at least.

Two blocks to go to the esplanade and the bridge. A shadow showed on a balcony across the street. The echoes came back crazily from them and from somewhere else. More bodies on the street, paving stones and rocks littering the cobbles. One of the horses caught-step and stumbled, sending a bit of brick skittering across the arch of the street into the gutter.

Suddenly rocks were landing around them and a lamp plummeted from the balcony and shattered, oil-fire spreading around the cobbles, throwing light, shying the horses. "Come *on!*" he yelled, and kicked his and kept going. Something hit his back. The gelding jumped

under him, lost its footing on the oil and skidded while
rocks hailed around him, hitting him, hitting the horse
as it scrambled for balance and skidded again.

"Dammit!" he yelled as it tried to bolt, as missiles
kept coming, crashing around them. One horse was
down—Eidi's. He tried to get in the saddle as it scrambled up, and just held on as the horse fled the barrage
in panic.

Then more horsemen came charging in from the
riverside, right into the middle of it, more horses skidding. Eidi had his horse stopped, Chun was through,
with Wengadi and Jian. Taizu came out of the confusion, with Liang and Waichen. Nui, then, and Yandai,
with Panji clinging to his saddle-leather and running
along beside.

"Get to cover!" he yelled at Panji. "You can't go
double, get to cover!"

More riders were coming, men on foot now, a tide
hemming them about as the street filled with soldiers
trying to tear up shutters for a barricade.

"What in hell're you doing?" Shoka yelled, reining
into the middle of it.

"They're crossing the bridge!" an officer yelled back.

"You're stopping our own troops, fool! Order from
headquarters! *Keep this street open!*"

"*The hell—*"

Shoka whipped the sword out and across, and the
officer went staggering back, screaming.

"Get that down!" Shoka yelled, and pushed his horse
into the press. "You're cutting off our own men, you
damn fools, get it *down!*"

He was not alone now. Chun was with him, Eidi on
his horse and pressing up close to lend their weight to
the deliberate push into the soldiers trying to establish
the barricade, with men still pouring in from the other
side, knocking the panels aside, shouldering and shoving the horses, until the barricade-makers dropped their
effort and let the shutters fall to be trampled, joining
the retreat down the street.

Shoka kicked his horse ahead, gaining ground as he could. "Run for it!" he yelled at the retreating soldiers till his voice cracked. "East gate, go, go!"

He could not see where the others were. He looked behind him. He saw Liang. He saw Taizu still ahorse, coming through the press.

To the corner, then, into the flare of fire on riverside, the roll of smoke from burning boats, fire outlining the timbers of the bridge as riders poured off it by the hundreds.

He reined back, pulled his horse against the screens of a restaurant, wood cracking as the horse edged back. Eidi came up beside him, and Chun. Liang. He saw Waichen across the heads of rushing soldiers, saw Yandai and Nui take off across the riverfront toward the bridge.

"Where's Taizu, dammit?"

As he heard the roll of drums and saw the banners on the bridge, the red and white of Feiyan, the white and black lotus of Hoishi in the glare of fire.

"M'lord!" Chun cried, spurring off. "Stay there!"

"The *hell!*" He kicked his horse and shouldered past Eidi's grab at stopping him, back around the corner into the street, into the press of retreating soldiery.

No sign of her. None of Panji or Wengadi either. He had hope. Wengadi might have gone off down the side street, Taizu with him, if they had gotten pushed aside. Might just have gone with the flow that had become a rout, become a riot, horses skidding on the street, men falling to be ridden down. . . .

"My lord!" Eidi yelled, forcing his way through. "Get back, get back, for the gods' sake we can't lose you!"

He reined about and came back to the shelter of the doorway, held there while the tide rolled past and became the vanguard of Feiyan cavalry, fluttering with the red and white banners—

Gods, go to ground, girl, get somewhere and get off that horse and hide!

Gods, where is she?

"M'lord Saukendar!" Chun shouted.

Riders came up on them, lotus banners of Hoishi, lord Reidi's men—lord Reidi himself, white hair flying in the smoky wind.

"M'lord Saukendar," Reidi said, as men of his climbed out of their saddles and came around him, "we saw your signal from the hills. We rode down through Lungan south-shore with more speed than I would have thought possible— The mercenary units . . . they broke and scattered, m'lord—at the bridge, the barricades were virtually unmanned—"

He heard Reidi's voice, telling him things he would have, under other circumstances, been pleased to hear.

He would be delighted still, if a smallish rider somehow turned up around the corner. He pressed his horse forward to see.

"My lord Saukendar—"

"My wife is missing," he muttered. He pushed past the corner, past the men who interfered with him, and saw a street in which the fighting had gone far down the lanes, leaving its detritus of bodies and spent missiles in shadow and sporadic lantern-light.

"My lord." It was Chun, riding near him to offer a robe that glittered gold and silver in the dim light. "Wear this, so our men make no mistake—"

"Find her, Chun! You and Eidi, get a search up and down this street! She knows your voices."

"Take it. Please, m'lord Saukendar."

Go to cover, go to the east gate—

Hell if she would. Not if she was cut off, on her own—

Get Gitu. That's what she'd do.

But where is he?

The Liang house . . . the headquarters. The gold would be there and not the camp—and he's dead without funds. No troops, no prospects—

And Beijun, in Ghita's hands—Ghita's sole claim to legitimacy—

"M'lord, —"

"I need a handful of men. You stay here and keep

looking! If you find her—" He reined around to the open, where he had his choice of Reidi's attendants, and called back: "—find me at their headquarters!"

It was more than a handful of men that went with him, black and white banners about him, safe-passage through the streets at a wild pace that racketed echoes off the walls and scattered isolated groups of rioters from their path. "It's Hoishi!" people yelled from balconies. "It's the rebels!"

And from the streets: "Down with the Regent!"

Lungan shook the beast from its back. Lungan smashed wine-shop doors and made its own kind of beast, dancing in lantern-light, in the wreckage of neighbors, chaining down rock-littered streets and arming itself with dead men's weapons.

"Drop it, drop it," someone shrieked from above, "it's the rebels!" And a rope stretched across the street fell slack in front of their horses, trampled underfoot as they went through. They turned onto the street that led from the market north. There were dead men and dead horses, arrow-shot; and Shoka took them by the alley, quickly, and drew up there.

It was Reidi's lieutenant who had come with him, at Reidi's quick insistence—Reidi's lieutenant and a squad of Reidi's guard with their unit captain to lead the way and find out the situation, for Reidi himself to follow as he got his main forces organized and came in their wake—a more practical understanding in that old gentleman how to set up a fast response than there was in all of Kegi's books. Two names from Reidi and they were off, no questions, no delay, and no confusion then or now in these men.

"It's the Lieng house," Shoka said, "any of you know it?" No, evidently. "—Outside this alley, half a block north, lane cuts off to the west to a small scullery entry, dead end alley, main street goes past the gate. I don't know what we're going to run into. If it looks good I want a chase behind me and some shots aimed close enough to look convincing. Understand? If it looks like it's too stiff going, get the hell back and get Reidi here. They can't ride out the scullery gate, the court there is only good for a hand-cart or two and there's no way they can gather there in strength enough—too much chance of getting penned up in the lane outside. It'll be the main gate and a run for the north if they try to break out. But I'll try to get that scullery gate open. Tell Reidi that. You can guide him here, with no mistakes. Can't you?"

"Yes, m'lord," the lieutenant said—Reidi's men all in their proper colors, with their individual pennons—

—and himself, in mercenary's motley.

He reined around and kicked his horse hard, startling it into motion, as far as the end of the alley and the turn onto the street before he heard the company thundering after him.

There were bonfires in the street, heaped up debris that threw a garish light onto close walls, and enough dead in the street to warn him.

So he crossed the street as Reidi's men passed him and reined in against the wall of the estate next to Lieng, deaf to the hiss of arrows in the clatter of hooves on cobblestone as Reidi's men charged the main gate down the street and then shied off again, leaving a man and two horses down—

Dammit. While he delayed—

Stiff resistance—no question. They had men enough in there, whether they were saving their own necks or defending their lord.

Low wall, a simple affair for a rich man's garden, defended from the mansion's balconies, from men set on terraces and in the high windows.

If Ghita himself was inside those walls and not well on the road to Cheng'di he had risked getting himself into a trap—the mob around him, the southern lords advancing through the city— The estate could burn, Ghita, the Emperor, everything in one bonfire—

But Ghita had powerful reasons to retreat here in the

chaos—to grab the mercenaries' payroll and gather up
the remaining members of his staff and the core troops
of his personal guard, that trusted number which would
have guarded the headquarters during his processional.

Damn right Ghita dared not desert those troops—or
the money. The hand-picked commanders of the Imperials and money for the mercenaries had put him in
power, money had held him there, that and Gitu's
Angen officers and the elite of Gitu's hire-ons. And if
they had to, if they could hold out long enough, or
break free—there were the large mercenary garrisons
at Anogi and at Cheng'di, garrisons that could come in
on two sides of Lungan. . . .

If there were a Regent alive to rally to, and pay
promised.

Shoka bit dry, stubbled lips and stared at the corner
where the road cut back to the scullery access. Try the
same thing twice?

Gods knew what Taizu would do.

Or whether she had come this way or could ever
have gotten through the ambushes in the streets.

But damned if he could afford the chance she was in
there, if it came to a siege. This was where the killing
would surely be, the Emperor held hostage, if Ghita
was in there, and the odds were more than even that he
was—

Not that the southern lords wanted Beijun back. But
there were the priests, there were the northern lords,
tied by blood to the dynasty and enjoying their preroga-
tives, were the political repercussions against whoever
caused the death of the Emperor. There was a certain
war of succession—more blood, more craziness, while
the barbarian kings sent their mercenaries into the
heart of Chiyaden and grew more and more necessary,
with the army pinned down in border skirmishes against
those kings' enemies—

The damned, self-indulgent fool . . . *Help* me,
Shoka. . . .

He was alone on the street—just himself, the dead,

and the waiting archers, of whatever side. But a new sound echoed through the streets—a distant thunder of cavalry.

Reidi? Or Meijun or Kegi, sweeping in from the east?

North. My gods. The mercenaries have cut around north, back to their headquarters—some captain worth his hire—

Or Gitu. With the gold to pay them here, at the headquarters—

He urged his horse forward, trusting to that distraction, slipped over to the shadowed side of the saddle before the corner and kept low, hoping that if anyone was looking his way, what was visible from above and from across the street was simply a riderless stray.

It got him across the street. He put his feet down and led the horse along the wall, keeping it between him and the outside, himself constantly in its shadow. He tried to remember the other side, where the terraces and the trees were.

No cart to help him over the wall this time. He stopped the horse, climbed up into the saddle and got a knee onto its back.

It moved. He tugged back on the reins, centered his weight, and got it stopped and mostly steady for the moment. Not so high a wall. Not so impossible, if the damned horse would quit edging forward on him.

Stand, dammit!

He looked up, tugged the rein again and figured on a single instant of stability.

He tucked up further in the scantly flexible armor, got his foot braced, damning the shin-guards, and reined the horse to a momentary stop again.

And thrust up on that foot and jumped from a startled, shying horse, for a belly-down landing on the top of the garden wall.

He rolled off, fast, and plummeted. Not the same distance down. He knew that the instant he had gone. Further.

Thump!

Onto a paved terrace, between two potted pines.

He lay still a moment getting his wind back and finding out if his shoulder was broken. Then he got himself up on his hands and knees and stood up quietly, taking his bearings on the house across the paved terrace, the way down to the scullery access.

There were dead men down there, like puddles of shadow.

He crept gingerly down the slope, keeping an eye to the scullery and the sheds there, and edged along the wall to reach for the gate-latch.

It was already unlatched.

The damned little *bitch!*

Chapter Twenty-two

Shoka crept back along the wall, up to the next terrace, familiar territory. Beside the potted pines and up again, but not toward the house itself, with its terraces and its archers. The main court had to lie near the main gate, and in his mind Shoka could see the front gate from the inside, men running for horses and for defensive vantages the moment the watchmen advised them of movement up the street.

The defenders might well, then, choose to vacate the headquarters and break for the north gate with a weight of numbers that might force a passage to the Cheng'di road—with the gold, with the Emperor, with their alliances to foreign kings—every asset that would mean disaster to the Empire.

And a fool of a girl was loose somewhere on the grounds trying to assassinate one of the two men on whom everything depended.

Curse the decision that had left Taizu with his bow and Wengadi and Panji with the other two, and his own short-sightedness that had not even thought about equip-

ping himself to do more than pull a fool out of a
death-trap—

Ill-thought, ill-prepared, ill-done from the start. He
was bruised and exhausted and confounded by the er-
ratic moves of his own allies. His wits were fraying, he
was *tired*, dammit, and people on his own side made
him move again and again and again—there was a limit.
He knew he was beyond it.

How in hell *did she get through the streets?*

How in hell *did she get in here without raising an
alarm? She's too short to do what I did.*

If I knew where she got in I might know where she is.

*No, no need to wonder. Find Ghita, find Gitu, that's
where she is.*

If they haven't found her first.

No bow, none with the dead men back there; so the
work had to be close-in, and that meant mixing in with
the mercenary guard around the house.

Close-in enough to reach Ghita, who knew his face as
well as Beijun did, damn right he knew it; and he had
to beat a fool kid to it.

He kept low as he crossed the terraces, and dropped
off the wall of the highest to a soft slope under the
shade of pines, slipped down a path and around the
meanderings of a hedge. He heard horses, beyond the
shoulder of the house, and where the hedge ended he
saw lanterns, the front gate, and the great courtyard of
the estate, where the gate let in on a paved expanse
large enough for the hundreds of horses that were
gathered there, and up onto the delicate garden-slopes—
everywhere an animal could stand.

Men were running to the gates. Whoever had come in
to join them had arrived at the front with a great deal
of commotion in the street, but no attack. There were
too many horses inside to admit more riders, but the
gates opened a crack and they began to file inside all
the same, riders crowding up into the gardens on this
side of the courtyard.

Staying mounted, most all of them. Preparing for an imminent breakout, then.

Dammit, no sign of Reidi. Ghita's lot were organizing, doubtless moving on the street to clear the buildings nearby of rebel archers who might have made things difficult and given Reidi and his men some help— and the group which had gone back after Reidi had no idea what else had come in. If Reidi came with only his own company—

Where in hell is Feiyan and Hainan? Chewed to rags in the streets, pinned down? Chasing some damn ragtag down the east road? How did they let a whole damn wing loose to come back here?

Dammit to bloody hell, where are they? They should have been chasing up this company's backside.

Kegi. Bloody hell, Kegi's probably haring off to Cheng'di, Ghita's set him a lure and he's probably hot on it. Ghita's damn good. Set up an easy fight and a retreating enemy all the way down the bridge street and out the north gate and the east—

While he retakes Lungan from a sweep up this street and back to our lighter forces at the bridge, take them out, and get across to hold south while the Cheng'di garrison and Anogi come in to catch us three-sided—

Not damn bad, old fox. But you're discounting the people's tolerance for you.

Or gambling foreign threats will make you the lesser of evils.

And that the Emperor will be your safety with the priests and the north.

Horsemen rode close to the hedge, the crowding becoming that thick in the yard. *Concealing what they do have in here, in the case an attack does come.*

Keeping as many men as they can off the street while they get the gold loaded and the records—I'll bet there are records Ghita doesn't let out of his sight—names and lists, blackmail material—or work for his assassins. He wouldn't separate himself from those. He's too good and too careful.

Reidi, for gods' sake, scout it out before you come in.

He stood up. He walked out, a shadow afoot, he trusted, among the shadows of horses and riders, just one more soldier wandering around, possibly one of the first-arrived out designated to keep the perimeters. He slapped a soldier's horse on the rump to let it know he was there, walked past it and on down the slope.

If Reidi came down that street now he would see a comparatively small cavalry force holding the street outside. He might mistake it for the Regent's forces, drawn up to defend the headquarters . . . chase it past the gate and then discover himself attacked from the rear and the front.

No damn *time* to wait. Reidi was due, any time now, depending on how fast he had been able to muster a force and pass necessary orders to other companies.

Right into a trap.

He walked the high part of the slope, trying for a clear view over the backs of the horses, worse now that men were mounting up. No sight of Ghita or Beijun, which might mean that they were not—

But there was a wagon near the terrace at the main house doors. A good sturdy wagon and a double yoke of horses. That was where something had to come—the records, the gold, and likely not far off, the officers and the staff who had to make sure that wagon stayed safe. The elite guard, the Imperials, or the native Angen troops would be watching that, damn sure no random lot of mercenaries who might take it into their heads, considering all that had gone wrong, to pay themselves all at once and the hell with the commander and Chiyaden.

"That's the gold down there," he muttered to another man afoot. "Damn bet it is. Wouldn't y' like t' guard *that?*"

"Ain't a chance," the man said wistfully, and spat. "You come near that, you're dead."

"Where's the commander?"

"Ought to be out. Don't know what they're doin' in there."

"Waitin' for th' rebels. I had a bellyful of waitin'. I lost m' tent, lost ever' damn thing—"

"Me too." Another spit. "Not that it was much."

"Lot of gold down there."

"Don't say it. You can die for thinkin' it."

"I ain't. I ain't thinkin' a thing. If I was thinkin', I wouldn't be here."

He walked on, sauntered down the slope, down among the horses—looked up as the doors opened and light flooded out, with the shadows of Imperial guards and a number of official types coming out onto the terrace.

"Clear it back!" an officer yelled, and Imperials moved down to clear a space around the wagon, and to bring certain horses in close to the steps. Moving fast now. Shoka edged his way closer to the line the Imperials were making, and kept an eye to the porch.

Plan your retreat, master Shoka.

Up the steps, cut a few throats and run like hell down the terraces for the scullery gate—if the leg still has it.

Damn scullery lane's a dead end. Got to make that streetside corner in a hurry.

Where are you, kid? For gods' sakes, where are you?

He looked up to the porch as more men came out, one smallish man in robes being hustled along by others. And one tall, lank one in plain armor, with a gilt-embroidered robe thrown over it, and a helmet fancier than the armor.

None of that mattered. He knew Ghita's face, every nuance of body movements.

"You!" a voice snapped from the height of the steps, and he looked, alarmed, straight into an Imperial's face.

"Get him!" the guard yelled. And Imperials poured off the porch as soldiers scattered—as Shoka drew and took out the first and second to come at him, and charged for the porch, hell with anything but the target, who was retreating behind his guards.

Horses screamed of a sudden and wheels cracked into the terrace steps, splintering wood, then jerking forward. Shoka cleared himself a space about him and staggered back as a horse bolted between him and the guards, horses scrambling every way in mortal terror, over the terraces, breaking down railings, crashing through hedges—

He whirled clear of pursuing guards and reeled under the buffet of a horse's shoulder, dived into the general chaos of bolting and rearing horses and struggling riders and saw the fire burning, saw a fiery trail come through the air and rebound off a horse's rump, to fall and panic others as it burned under their feet.

"Taizu!"

He saw the outer gate opening, saw men running out into the lantern-lit street. Horses escaped that way. From somewhere high in the air came a booming, echoing voice.

"Damn you, Gitu!" it howled, female and huge. *"Damn your cousin too! You pack of thieves, I'll have your eyes for pig-food! I'll roast you in hell and have your bones for a necklace! And anyone with you, I'll lay diseases on him, I'll give him the plague and the pox, I'll curse you with cold beds and cold feet and cold in your bones all your life, till you die and I carry you off to hell for my dinner, every one of you!"*

Men ran in the firelight, crazed as the horses, bolting for the gate, the terraces, the gardens, grabbing onto horses and escaping as they could.

Ghita stared, looking up at the balconies, and Shoka jumped for the porch, vaulted the rail and sliced his way through startled guards and staff, two blows dealt before Ghita realized where he was and backed up to shelter behind clerkly men who wanted no part of it.

"You damn dog!" Shoka yelled, and took his head off while staff ran for the inner halls and guards rushed to defend a dead man.

One, two, and three died, before the quick-thinking

fourth assessed the situation and somersaulted backward over the terrace railing, out of his way.

There was Beijun cowering on the porch. There was his wife up there on the balconies somewhere, and he had no hesitation in that choice.

Even when at the bottom of his gut he wondered if there *were* demons, and if he was rushing up there to confront a sight he would never want to see.

He took the stairs at the corner up and up, one turn and another, while the firelit courtyard and the dark alternately swung past his vision, and he saw the paved area emptying, the wagon burning, riders rushing out the gate, to shouts and curses inside and outside the walls.

He came out on a balcony at the very top of the house, face to face with a white demon shape and an arrow aimed for his heart.

"Taizu!"

The apparition whirled and sent the arrow out through the railings, several stories down into the courtyard.

And looked back to him, white-faced, white-armored, white hair streaming in the wind.

He stared. She said, with a breath: "It's flour."

"You damned *fool*, wife!"

"I figured you'd come here." She drew another arrow from her quiver and studiously let fly at the chaos below.

"How did you get in here?"

"With Ghita's bunch." She picked out another arrow. "I rode in, slipped down in the dark and got the scullery gate open. And got some flour and coals and stuff in the kitchen. Walked right up here." Another shot. "The kettle there's the echoes. I was going to wait till they got the gates open, but I heard a commotion and I thought it might be you. —Is help coming?"

"I damned well hope so! But I've got no guarantee. Come on, come on, dammit!" He lunged after her and grabbed her by the arm, hauled her to the stairs. "Drop the damn bow!"

"It's yours!"

"*Drop* it, dammit!" He hauled her down around the turns, running, hell with the pain in his leg. She followed that order the way she listened to everything, but he let her go, to follow him on her own. The bow banged on the railings and the steps as she struggled to stay with him, shedding flour all the way. "The Emperor's down below. He *was*. I went to save *your* neck! *Drop the damn bow!*"

She still had it when they hit the second floor. Fire was everywhere below, the courtyard deserted, the burning wagon lying wrecked, horseless, overturned against the terrace corner. A pine had caught fire, gone up like a wick. Loose horses still ran the garden and the courtyard, darting this way and that in thunderous panic, ignoring the open gates and the safety of the lantern-lit street.

He rounded the last turn, felt the shaking of the stairs, and in the next instant came face to face with guards coming up.

He yelled. Taizu yelled. They yelled. He took out the first one who stood paralyzed in shock and the hindmost three lit out down the stairs. The second came to life as he stumbled on the corpse. A sword flashed past his head and took the railing out with a downstroke: he followed up in the same direction and the man and his head followed the railing down.

Shoka ran, charged the rest of them, trying to keep the momentum, trying to gain ground—damned if he knew where anything was at the moment, except the terrace and the gate that was escape; and the place where he had parted with Beijun.

The guards ran, skidded around the corner, hit the railings and left them in sole possession of the porch and the burning wagon.

"Beijun!" he yelled into the lighted hall—the way he would call the boy-heir twenty years ago. "Beijun, dammit!"

Forgetting all the years and the titles.

"Beijun!"

"Shoka!" the Emperor cried—came staggering out from beside the door, robes askew, lost in the weight of brocade and gilt.

Like the damn fool horses, hiding in a burning building, with the open gate in front of him.

"Master!" Taizu yelled from behind. He turned, twisted away with the sight of a dozen men rolling across his vision as he hit the boards with his shoulders and came up again in a charge at the men who came at him from the courtyard.

He could not make it, he thought, while the sword was swinging, not so many, not with a trap closed on them. He trusted Taizu to get Beijun off the porch, to follow him to the gate and hope to hell he had not cleared the way only to more of them. He stopped thinking then. He killed, anything, everything in his path.

That was all he could do, the last he could do, with his knee threatening to give, his lungs shooting fire and his shoulders going numb from strain and repeated shocks.

Get to the gate.

Get the way open.

For Taizu and Beijun behind him. . . .

Someone shouted at his back. No stopping. *Her* business. He was engaged on two fronts as it was, desperately extended himself to cripple a man, to finish his partner, to jump clear and swing at the man who was trying to hamstring him. . . .

He spun in that move and in a passing blink saw Beijun running and Taizu running in front of a band of men coming around the corner of the porch.

He spun on around, dodged again and killed his man in a desperate, awkward strike, completely off his balance. He caught it again with a tearing pain in his leg as he turned, as Beijun grabbed him and swung behind him, Taizu lagging back with a trio of enemies pelting off the porch after her.

Going for her back. He ran and yelled, but she was already turning—she caught an attack on her blade, canted parry, but not in balance.

She sprawled—and did that damned stop-thrust, right up under her enemy's armor-skirts—

Shoka got the one behind, with no more grace. And the one after. There were four dead men on the terrace. Her doing. He staggered aside and grabbed Taizu's shoulder as she gained her feet and stood watching the man squirming on the ground.

"Gitu," she said, shaking free of his hand.

And killed what was still trying to live, a simple beheading stroke.

Shoka caught his breath, reached out for her, held her by the arm.

Riders were coming, hooves on cobblestone, shadowy figures filling the gateway and pouring inside. "Beijun," Shoka yelled, shoving Taizu for the garden, toward shadows and the escape of the scullery gate.

She grabbed him by the sleeve, pulling at him to run with her.

But the banners of the invaders were black and white. Reidi's lotus emblem. Shoka let his sword-arm fall, let the fingers relax. It was about the limit he could go, just to stand there, but he walked forward, bowed to his Emperor, bowed to lord Reidi, everything in good form.

Reidi climbed down and made his respectful obeisances. Beijun babbled something about lord Gitu, treason, and the affront to his person. The fire and the shadows swam in Shoka's eyes, and he trusted himself only to little, familiar motions, flicked his sword clean and wiped its hilt and put it in its sheath.

Gods, there was too much blood on him.

And Taizu—white spattered with dark—

A railing crashed in fire on the terrace, startling everyone. A pillar followed. Reidi ordered a detail of men to fetch buckets and axes and prevent it spreading.

Beijun came and thanked him— "They made me go

along with them," Beijun said, "they lied to me— Shoka, believe me—"

He wanted a bath. He wanted to sit down. He wanted to be anywhere else.

He looked around when he could do it without offending the Emperor. Taizu was not where he had left her. He sweated, decided she *was* sitting down, somewhere inconspicuous in the gardens, sparing herself this babble of power-mongering and ephemeral gratitude.

"Excuse me," he finally said, no longer caring whom he offended. "Excuse me, my wife's somewhere around here—"

The roads were scantly trafficked yet. The smell of smoke was still in the air, and a woman trekking the road down to Choedri, even a ragged peasant with flour in her hair, had reason to worry; but Taizu carried her sword to hand, wrapped up in the bundle of rags on her back, just a rag-wrapped hilt where she could get to it in a hurry if she had to.

Not that there was much magistrate's justice to worry about. Just the occasional soldiers.

A band had followed her last night, and she had worried. She worried now, when she looked back and found riders coming up behind her.

But: "M'lady," they said when they came up even with her. "You *are* lady Taizu."

"I'm a peasant," she said sullenly. They were men of Taiyi. Kegi's. She scowled at them. "I'm going home."

They went away, but one of them stayed, riding just out of speaking range. She waited sometimes, and yelled curses at him, and finally he dropped back further.

But another one came toward evening, all in red and gold, riding a red horse and leading a very conspicuous mare.

She kept walking. She kept walking after he caught up to her.

"Taizu," he said.

Hearing his voice was hard. Damned hard. She walked

on, looking at the fields in a kind of sunset glitter, and he stopped.

And got down and walked along beside her. It was Jiro, of course, that he had been riding. And it was her white-legged mare he was leading along with Jiro.

"Going home?" he asked her.

She shrugged and looked his direction, but he glittered so much he hurt her eyes. Jiro, on the other hand, was just Jiro; and when she stopped he nosed up to see if it was really her, and to get his chin scratched. She felt a fool. The whole damn country did what Saukendar wanted. She had seen him—from a distance. All the glitter. All the shouting. He had had her followed all the way from the bridge at Lungan. A lord could do that.

"What in hell do you think you're doing?" he asked her.

Third shrug.

The people wanted a story. That was all. They wanted Saukendar and the demon. Her going away was part of the story. Demons always left, once the fighting was done.

"You hate me?" he asked.

She shook her head.

He started walking again, her direction, Jiro and the mare trailing along behind. "I'd give you your horse, but I don't want to have to chase you down."

"You would, too."

"What in hell's into you? I've had men all over these roads for two days—"

She set her jaw.

"Beijun's appointed Reidi his chief Councillor," he said. "I resigned."

That hardly surprised her. "I wish Beijun'd died," she said. "They'd make you Emperor. That's what they'd do, if they knew anything."

"Hell if they would. I said to Reidi—he said they were going to chop old Baigi up in Yiungei. I said that was a waste, just retire the old thief, put someone else in. So Reidi offered me Yiungei. My old estates. I said no."

She listened. It sounded like a fool. "Don't tell me. Hua."

"They want me on the borders. They want me to set up a treaty with Shin, try to keep the borders stable. That's Reidi's old job. I said I'd much rather stand in for him down in Hoishi. Lord Councillor's Deputy. Lord Warden of the South. Some such title."

She glanced over at him. She had to see the face that went with craziness like that, or whether something like that could really happen. It *was* him, in all that glitter. Same eyes, same mouth. Same conniving scoundrel.

"So I'm going out there," Shoka said. "Keido's Reidi's family home. I wouldn't live there. Just a small grant in the hills down by Mon. Widen the border a little. Two or three mountains. Put a little garrison down by the river, a few good men I have in mind— Mostly it's my reputation Reidi wants down there. *And* my wife's. Clear out the bandits, keep the road open. —Where were you going?"

She frowned at him and bit her lip. Demon. Hell! "Are you going to give me my horse?"

He handed her the mare's reins. "Go easy on us old men. Jiro's too old for a chase."

She snorted, threw her bundle on the mare's back, and tied it down, one side and the other, except she took her sword out and slung it on her shoulder. He got on Jiro. She got on the mare, and fixed him with a long, long stare. "Are you lying to me?"

He shook his head solemnly, innocent as any boy.

"Never," he said.

PRAISE FOR
LOIS McMASTER BUJOLD

What the critics say:

The Warrior's Apprentice: "Now here's a fun romp through the spaceways—not so much a space opera as space ballet.... it has all the 'right stuff.' A lot of thought and thoughtfulness stand behind the all-too-human characters. Enjoy this one, and look forward to the next." —Dean Lambe, *SF Reviews*

"The pace is breathless, the characterization thoughtful and emotionally powerful, and the author's narrative technique and command of language compelling. Highly recommended."
—*Booklist*

Brothers in Arms: " ... she gives it a genuine depth of character, while reveling in the wild turnings of her tale.... Bujold is as audacious as her favorite hero, and as brilliantly (if sneakily) successful." —*Locus*

"Miles Vorkosigan is such a great character that I'll read anything Lois wants to write about him....a book to re-read on cold rainy days." —Robert Coulson, *Comic Buyer's Guide*

Borders of Infinity: "Bujold's series hero Miles Vorkosigan may be a lord by birth and an admiral by rank, but a bone disease that has left him hobbled and in frequent pain has sensitized him to the suffering of outcasts in his very hierarchical era....Playing off Miles's reserve and cleverness, Bujold draws outrageous and outlandish foils to color her high-minded adventures." —*Publishers Weekly*

Falling Free: "In *Falling Free* Lois McMaster Bujold has written her fourth straight superb novel.... How to break down a talent like Bujold's into analyzable components? Best not to try. Best to say: 'Read, or you will be missing something extraordinary.' " —Roland Green, *Chicago Sun-Times*

The Vor Game: "The chronicles of Miles Vorkosigan are far too witty to be literary junk food, but they rouse the kind of craving that makes popcorn magically vanish during a double feature." —Faren Miller, *Locus*

MORE PRAISE FOR
LOIS McMASTER BUJOLD

What the readers say:

"My copy of *Shards of Honor* is falling apart I've reread it so often. . . . I'll read whatever you write. You've certainly proved yourself a grand storyteller."

— Lisa Kolbe, Colorado Springs, CO

"I experience the stories of Miles Vorkosigan as almost viscerally uplifting. . . . But certainly, even the weightiest theme would have less impact than a cinder on snow were it not for a rousing good story, and good story-telling with it. This is the second thing I want to thank you for. . . . I suppose if you boiled down all I've said to its simplest expression, it would be that I immensely enjoy and admire your work. I submit that, as literature, your work raises the overall level of the science fiction genre, and spiritually, your work cannot avoid positively influencing all who read it."

— Glen Stonebraker, Gaithersburg, MD

" 'The Mountains of Mourning' [in *Borders of Infinity*] was one of the best-crafted, and simply best, works I'd ever read. When I finished it, I immediately turned back to the beginning and read it again, and I can't remember the last time I did that."

— Betsy Bizot, Lisle, IL

"I can only hope that you will continue to write, so that I can continue to read (and of course buy) your books, for they make me laugh and cry and think . . . rare indeed."

— Steven Knott, Major, USAF

THE SHIP WHO SANG IS NOT ALONE!

Anne McCaffrey, with Mercedes Lackey, S.M. Stirling, and Jody Lynn Nye, explores the universe she created with her groundbreaking novel, The Ship Who Sang.

THE SHIP WHO SEARCHED
by Anne McCaffrey & Mercedes Lackey

Tia, a bright and spunky seven-year-old accompanying her exo-archaeologist parents on a dig, is afflicted by a paralyzing alien virus. Tia won't be satisfied to glide through life like a ghost in a machine. Like her predecessor Helva, *The Ship Who Sang*, she would rather strap on a spaceship!

THE CITY WHO FOUGHT
by Anne McCaffrey & S.M. Stirling

Simeon was the "brain" running a peaceful space station—but when the invaders arrived, his only hope of protecting his crew and himself was to become *The City Who Fought*.

THE SHIP WHO WON
by Anne McCaffrey & Jody Lynn Nye

"The brainship Carialle and her brawn, Keff, find a habitable planet inhabited by an apparent mix of races and cultures and dominated by an elite of apparent magicians. Appearances are deceiving, however... a brisk, well-told often amusing tale.... Fans of either author, or both, will have fun with this book."
—*Booklist*

When it comes to the best
in science fiction and fantasy,
Baen Books has something for *everyone!*

IF YOU LIKE . . .
YOU SHOULD ALSO TRY . . .

Marion Zimmer Bradley .... Mercedes Lackey,
Holly Lisle

Anne McCaffrey .... Elizabeth Moon,
Mercedes Lackey

Mercedes Lackey .... Holly Lisle, Josepha Sherman,
Ellen Guon, Mark Shepherd

Andre Norton .... Mary Brown,
James H. Schmitz

David Drake .... David Weber, John Ringo,
Eric Flint

Larry Niven .... James P. Hogan,
Charles Sheffield

Robert A. Heinlein ....Jerry Pournelle,
Lois McMaster Bujold

Heinlein's "Juveniles" .... Eric Flint & Dave Freer,
Rats, Bats & Vats

Horatio Hornblower .... David Weber's
"Honor Harrington" series,
David Drake's, "RCN" series

The Lord of the Rings .... Elizabeth Moon,
The Deed of Paksenarrion

IF YOU LIKE ...
YOU SHOULD ALSO TRY ...

Norse Mythology ...... David Drake, *Northworld Trilogy*
Lars Walker

Arthurian Legend .... Steve White's Legacy series
David Drake, *The Dragon Lord*

Computers .... Rick Cook's "Wiz" series
Spider Robinson, *User Friendly*
Tom Cool, *Infectress*
Chris Atack, *Project Maldon*
James P. Hogan, *Realtime Interrupt*
and *Two Faces of Tomorrow*

Science Fact .... Robert L. Forward,
Indistinguishable From Magic
James P. Hogan, *Rockets, Redheads, and Revolution*
and *Minds, Machines, and Evolution*
Charles Sheffield, *Borderlands of Science*

Cats .... Larry Niven's Man-Kzin Wars series

Horses .... Elizabeth Moon's Heris Serrano series
Doranna Durgin

Vampires .... Cox & Weisskopf (eds.), *Tomorrow Sucks*
Wm. Mark Simmons, *One Foot in the Grave*
Nigel Bennett & P.N. Elrod, *Keeper of the King*
P.N. Elrod, *Quincey Morris, Vampire*

Werewolves . Cox & Weisskopf (eds.), *Tomorrow Bites*
Wm. Mark Simmons, *One Foot in the Grave*
Brett Davis, *Hair of the Dog*